PRAISE FOR
MONICA BURNS
AND HER NOVELS OF "CUTTING-EDGE ROMANCE."*

"This sizzling hot historical and its compelling characters will leave you panting for more! Monica Burns writes with sensitivity and panache. Don't miss this one!"
—Sabrina Jeffries, *New York Times* bestselling author

"[Monica Burns's] excellent love scenes and bold romance will have readers clamoring for more." —*Romantic Times*

"A cinematic, compelling, and highly recommended treat!"
—Sylvia Day, national bestselling author

"The love scenes are emotion-filled and wonderfully erotic ... Enough to make your toes curl." —*Two Lips Reviews*

"Elegant prose, believable dialogue, and a suspenseful plot that will hold you spellbound." —*Emma Wildes*

"Historical romance with unending passion."
—*The Romance Studio*

"Wow. Just Wow." —*Fallen Angel Reviews*

"A satisfying read complete with intrigue, mystery, and the kind of potent sensuality that fogs up the mirrors." —*A Romance Review*

"Monica Burns is a new author I must add to my 'required reading' category . . . Everything I look for in a top-notch romance novel."
—*Romance Reader at Heart*

"Blazing passion." *Romance Junkies*

Berkley Sensation titles by Monica Burns

KISMET
ASSASSIN'S HONOR

Assassin's
HONOR

MONICA BURNS

BERKLEY SENSATION, NEW YORK

THE BERKLEY PUBLISHING GROUP
Published by the Penguin Group
Penguin Group (USA) Inc.
375 Hudson Street, New York, New York 10014, USA
Penguin Group (Canada), 90 Eglinton Avenue East, Suite 700, Toronto, Ontario M4P 2Y3, Canada
(a division of Pearson Penguin Canada Inc.)
Penguin Books Ltd., 80 Strand, London WC2R 0RL, England
Penguin Group Ireland, 25 St. Stephen's Green, Dublin 2, Ireland (a division of Penguin Books Ltd.)
Penguin Group (Australia), 250 Camberwell Road, Camberwell, Victoria 3124, Australia
(a division of Pearson Australia Group Pty. Ltd.)
Penguin Books India Pvt. Ltd., 11 Community Centre, Panchsheel Park, New Delhi—110 017, India
Penguin Group (NZ), 67 Apollo Drive, Rosedale, North Shore 0632, New Zealand
(a division of Pearson New Zealand Ltd.)
Penguin Books (South Africa) (Pty.) Ltd., 24 Sturdee Avenue, Rosebank, Johannesburg 2196,
South Africa

Penguin Books Ltd., Registered Offices: 80 Strand, London WC2R 0RL, England

This book is an original publication of The Berkley Publishing Group.

This is a work of fiction. Names, characters, places, and incidents either are the product of the author's imagination or are used fictitiously, and any resemblance to actual persons, living or dead, business establishments, events, or locales is entirely coincidental. The publisher does not have any control over and does not assume any responsibility for author or third-party websites or their content.

PRINTING HISTORY
Berkley Sensation trade paperback edition / June 2010

Library of Congress Cataloging-in-Publication Data

Burns, Monica.
    Assassin's honor / Monica Burns.—Berkley Sensation trade paperback ed.
        p. cm.
    ISBN 978-0-425-23416-7
    1. Women archaeologists—Fiction. 2. Psychokinesis—Fiction. I. Title.
    PS3602.U76645A93 2010
    813'.6—dc22
                                                            2010003365

PRINTED IN THE UNITED STATES OF AMERICA

10 9 8 7 6 5 4 3 2 1

For Greg, my personal assassin who slays the laundry dragons, keeps the troops well fed, ensures my carriage is in pristine shape, and who loves me in spite of all my faults and failings. Thank you for helping me achieve my dream. I love you.

ACKNOWLEDGMENTS

Thanks to the wonderful Emma Wildes for talking me over the humps, lasting gratitude to the delightful Jean Marie Ward for paranormal straight talk that opened my eyes, and a special thanks to Katie Dancy for a wicked eye that always made me strive to raise the bar with my characters and their story. A special thanks to Ida Plassay for trying to teach me Italian and Maria Rosa Contardi for her expertise in Italian and Latin. And finally, a huge thank-you to Gabriella Edwards, my newest Italian BFF. Brainstorming with you isn't just a laugh a minute. It's a joy.

Chapter 1

"OH my God, they were right," Emma gasped.

She shifted her body so the light behind her shone directly on the ancient tomb's wall. Her parents had always said the Sicari weren't a myth. No one had believed them. Not even her.

Guilt bit into her. She should have trusted their instincts, even if they hadn't always trusted her academic knowledge. With a gentle stroke of her brush, she tapped another piece of dried mud off the wall. The tangible icon was evidence the elite guild of assassins had really existed. Her father had always said the Sicari were descendants of Ptolemy's personal guard. And here was the proof her father had been looking for.

Awed, she stared at the partially revealed symbol on the sandstone wall. The hilt of a sword rested against the rim of a chakram while the blade interlocked with the circular handheld weapon. The simplicity of the design didn't minimize the mark's ominous appearance.

Excitement raced through her as she peered at the emblem more closely. Her fingertip lightly brushed across the surface of the chakram portion of the icon. The chakram, when thrown, could slice through a skull when it hit its victim before returning to its owner. She knew several warrior clans in India had used the chakrams against Alexander the Great's troops. Ptolemy had been at the conqueror's side then, and his men could have easily adapted the weapon for their own use.

She'd grown up listening to her dad talk about the Sicari. Labeled assassins by the Praetorian Guard under the Roman Caesars, they were ruthlessly hunted down, arrested, and executed. Her father had never found any explanation for the persecution of the Sicari, but he'd had numerous theories. The most plausible being a power struggle within the Guard itself when Constantine I had been Caesar and abandoned pagan beliefs for those of the Church. Her father had hypothesized that the few Sicari who had escaped the persecution had gone into hiding only to become what they'd been branded simply to survive. He'd even speculated that they still existed.

Carefully, she dusted a fleck of dirt off the wall to reveal a little more of the emblem. For once, she appreciated her unique gift as well as her clumsiness. If she hadn't tripped over her toolbox, her hand might never have touched the spot where the icon was hidden. She could have done without the unexpected static shock, but her vision of a scribe etching a symbol into the wall had been enough incentive to scrape away the top layer of plaster.

While her special talent was generally limited to ancient artifacts, it didn't make the initial contact any less pleasant. Just as unpleasant were the fleeting images she sometimes saw when someone handing her an artifact brushed against her fingers.

With another stroke of her small, delicate brush, more of the mark appeared through the dried mud. The radio attached to her belt hissed softly, and she suddenly remembered Charlie. He'd kill her for not calling him right away with the news of her find. He might be her friend, but he was boss and mentor first. Grabbing the walkie-talkie off her belt, she pressed the talk button.

"Charlie?"

Releasing the button, she waited for a response. After several seconds of nothing but a quiet hum, she tried again. "Charlie, I know you're there, so stop ignoring me. I've got something I want you to see, and it's important."

She might be deep inside the burial chamber of Cleopatra's

ancestor, Ptolemy I, but she knew the radios worked. She'd heard from Charlie over the damn thing just an hour ago. This time after a long pause, she heard static echo out of her radio. Gritting her teeth, she waited for her teacher's easy Southern drawl to warm up the dark, musty chamber she'd been exploring. When he remained silent, she stared at the walkie-talkie and frowned. She hit the talk button one more time.

"Stop fooling around, Charlie. This is *important*," she snapped into the receiver before releasing the communication switch.

A gurgling noise burst out of the radio followed by a few seconds of static before the chamber grew quiet again. She growled in disgust. One of these days, he'd cry wolf once too often with her and *then* where would he be if something really was wrong.

The memory of his heart attack more than a year ago made her frown. It hadn't been severe, but the doctors *had* warned him to take it easy. Advice he'd ignored as usual. The thought of something serious happening to Charlie sent a wave of fear sluicing through her. If he *was* having a heart attack . . . spinning around, she grabbed her flashlight off the cool, stone floor and dived for the narrow opening leading out of the burial chamber.

The tight squeeze had her cursing her wide hips, and not for the first time. Coughing from the dust her movements stirred up, she crawled as fast as she could through the narrow tunnel toward the main chamber where Charlie had been working.

If he was having a heart attack, they were in trouble. There wasn't anyone except a couple of locals at the base camp. Mike and the rest of the team had gone to survey the artisans' cemetery almost a mile away. Not to mention the fact that Sayid, the dig's foreman, had taken the truck back to Abydos this morning to pick up their monthly supplies. He wouldn't be back until late in the evening at the earliest, and until then the camels were their only other form of available transport.

Reaching the main chamber of the tomb, she slid out onto the dusty, stone floor. All the lights were out, except for the dim glow of a bulb at the chamber's main entrance more than half a football field away. What the hell had happened to all the lights they'd strung up two months ago?

Sayid. He'd promised her that damn generator wouldn't break down again. If it weren't for the Magna flashlight she carried, she'd be virtually blind. As it was, she could barely see anything. How many ways could she grill the man's ass? She stumbled a few steps toward the center of the huge stone room while thinking about it.

"Charlie?"

Silence. Sweeping the light across the floor of the massive chamber, she pushed aside her fear. But she had a hard time ignoring the *déjà vu* slithering its way into her head. The whisper of a sound reached her ears and she spun around trying to determine its origin. She saw nothing except muraled walls and several sarcophagi yet to be opened. The quiet seemed even heavier than the ancient pillars looked. She shuddered.

"Goddamn it, Charlie. Answer me."

The cold silence pushed the hairs on her skin upward. No, she wouldn't go there. Everything was fine. People couldn't respond when they were unconscious. That's the only reason why he didn't answer her. The beam of the flashlight swept its way across the wall to the last burial tunnel. It illuminated the elderly man slumped over at the tunnel entrance. Emma leaped forward and raced to his side.

Flashlight clattering to the ground, she gently eased Charlie back until he was lying flat on the floor. Kneeling beside him in the near darkness, her fingers pressed into the meaty flesh at the side of his neck. The wet and sticky feel of his skin beneath her fingertips made her swallow hard.

God, he was sweating so profusely. Not a good sign. When she didn't feel a pulse, Emma reached for his wrist, praying for a miracle. Even a fluttering heartbeat beneath his leathery skin would ease her fear. Nothing. Panic latched on to her as she grabbed her radio and screamed into it. Mike knew CPR. He could—no. Mike was at the cemetery with the rest of the team.

The blaring silence from the two walkie-talkies only emphasized how far away help was.

A clattering of falling rock echoed off in the distance. Fear coiled in her belly as her fingers brushed across the gritty floor and she grabbed the flashlight. The sturdy metal tool cooled her hand as she pointed it in the direction of the noise. Not even a rat staring back at her. She shivered and tried to ignore how the mural on the ancient tomb's wall looked almost menacing in the stark beam. She dragged in a deep breath. This wasn't five years ago. She sagged deeper onto her haunches, her Magna slipping out of her hand to hit the floor with a soft metallic thud. Charlie's heart hadn't been any good. She knew that. But she hated how helpless and lost she felt at the moment. A tear slid down her cheek.

One drop became two until a steady stream of tears soaked her face. She didn't think, she simply reacted as a wave of fury swept over her and she pounded Charlie's chest with her fists.

"Wake up, goddamn you! Wake up."

With every sob, she hit him harder, but he still didn't move. As her crying subsided, her anger gave way to a cold numbness. There were things she needed to do, but she didn't know what. She couldn't even think straight right now. She dragged the back of her hand across her eyes in an attempt to wipe away the remaining tears. The sudden, pungent scent of copper made her wrinkle her nose.

There was something familiar about it. Her stomach started to churn. Oh God. That smell had been on her hands the day her parents were murdered. Their blood had stained her hands when she'd held them, and she'd never forgotten the way the musky metal scent had permeated her skin. Teeth chattering from the icy fear sliding through her, she reached for her light.

For the first time she realized the metal had a sticky feel to it, and she wanted to throw up. Blood was sticky. The beam of her flashlight hit her friend's face, and she screamed. The mark carved into his cheek was the same one they'd found on her parents' faces.

Worse still was the slit across his throat and the blood trailing down his neck. Blood she'd mistaken for perspiration. The flashlight clattered against the stone floor as she frantically rubbed her hands against her khaki dungarees. Even without a light shining directly on it she knew some of Charlie's blood had already dried on her hand. She could feel the flakes of it between her fingers and it terrified her. Instinct made her recoil from his body, and she scurried backward like a crab racing for safety.

Murder.

Someone had murdered Charlie. Killed and marked him the same way they had her parents. She froze. Whoever had killed Charlie might still be in the tomb. Hiding in the dark. Waiting. Waiting for her. Self-preservation took over, and she scrambled back toward her Mag. Clutching the heavy-duty light in a death grip, she lurched to her feet and raced toward the light at the end of the vast chamber.

Her boots hammered against the stone floor as she ran, the sound filling her ears with a thunderous roar. By the time she reached the foot of the steep slope leading up to the tomb's entrance, she was gasping for air. Slipping and sliding, she made her way up the dirt-covered incline into the brilliant sunlight.

Blinded, she tripped over the two steps leading down the hill to the base camp. Tumbling head over foot, she careened down the hill-side with a loud cry of pain and fear. Shouts answered her scream, and when she staggered to her feet, she saw Mike and several other team members running toward her.

The next several hours passed in a blur. She wavered between hysteria and an icy numbness. It wasn't until she entered the Cairo police station that she realized how desperate her situation was. She and Charlie had been the only ones in the tomb. For the police, it was cut-and-dried. Literally. The moment she'd arrived she'd been ushered into a small room, which had a large window overlooking the station's central desk.

The main area of the police headquarters wasn't well lit and she imagined it helped keep the room cooler. The interrogation room she sat in was the exact opposite. Already she could feel the heat from the glaring lightbulbs pushing down on her. Through the window, she watched Mike Granby arguing with a swarthy-skinned police officer. Behind her, Roberta Young, the dig's financial backer and self-declared intern, paced the floor. The tall woman's restless movements only served to shred Emma's nerves that much more.

"Roberta, please," she rasped. "Sit down."

The woman immediately pulled a chair out from the table and sat down next to her. With a gentle pat of Emma's arm, the woman's gaze turned toward the action in the squad room. Somewhere in the back of her mind, it registered that Roberta looked like a fashion plate for the latest in archeological field gear. The woman was a Swedish goddess, tall with flowing blond hair that she pulled back in a ponytail. She was always gorgeous. Even in the field the woman managed to look like she could go straight to a fancy dinner with just a change of clothes.

"How are you holding up, dear?"

"I can't believe he's dead." A tremor rushed through her. "I'd talked to him just an hour or so before I found him. He was alive. I swear it."

"I believe you, Emma. I'm sure you'll be cleared of all charges. It's not like you and Charlie fought all the time."

"What?" She stared at the woman in amazement.

"A couple of interns said they heard you cussing Charlie out last week," Roberta said with a careless shrug. "I'm sure the two of them misconstrued the episode."

"I don't understand . . . when . . . oh God, the police aren't going to believe anything I say."

"Christ, I'm sorry I brought it up." Roberta rubbed her hand in a reassuring manner. But it didn't calm Emma's nerves.

"Why don't they tell me whether they're going to charge me or not."

"They aren't going to charge you. Everyone knows you couldn't have done this," Roberta said in that cultured voice of hers.

The inflections were the result of her boarding school upbringing and immense wealth. And money was something the woman had in spades. She'd inherited the family import business when her parents were killed in some type of freak accident. Emma had never heard the details and had never asked. Roberta wasn't one to put on airs, but when the woman wanted something, she usually got it.

Would Roberta use her wealth and power to help her out? It wasn't as if the two of them were best friends. But if the woman kept her out of jail . . . her stomach lurched at the thought of incarceration. Closing her eyes, Emma leaned forward and buried her face in her hands. She couldn't believe this was happening. The police were going to think she killed Charlie. They'd lock her up.

"For someone who complained that he'd be a better team leader if Charlie weren't around, I'm unimpressed by Mike's leadership skills at the moment," Roberta said with disgust.

Emma raised her head to look at the other woman, who nodded

toward the window. With Charlie dead, Mike was next in line to lead the excavation team. Emma watched him gesture angrily in her direction, but the policeman's less than conciliatory expression didn't change. Frustration evident in his manner, Mike wheeled away from the officer. Seconds later, he burst through the door of the interrogation room, his tall, burly frame filling the cramped space. He squatted down next to her and grabbed her hand.

"Emma, they're refusing to let you go."

"Well, there's a surprise." Roberta's voice dripped with sarcasm.

Mike ignored the woman, but Emma saw his mouth thin with anger. He tugged on her hand to make her look at him. "I need you to listen carefully, sweetheart."

"It's okay, I understand why they don't want to let me go." She slowly nodded her head.

"Damn it, it's not okay." Mike growled. "Look, you're in shock, but I need you to hang on for a little while longer. I'm going to the consulate to get some help, and I'll be back as soon as I can."

She stared at him in silence. It made sense that the police wanted to close the case quickly. She was the prime suspect, no, *only* suspect, in Charlie's murder. Blaming her for Charlie's death simplified their job. The way her parents had been killed didn't help matters either. The reality of all of it seemed distant somehow. Almost as if she was watching it happen to someone else. Mike grabbed her shoulders and shook her.

"*Emma*, listen to me. You're not to say anything until we get you a lawyer."

"I'm not to say anything," she whispered.

Mike's large hand squeezed hers tightly and he gave her a hug before he stood up. "Hang in there, doll. We're gonna get you out of this mess."

"I think I'll tag along with you," Roberta drawled.

"No, someone needs to stay with Emma." Mike glared at the Swedish blonde.

"I have some powerful friends at the consulate, which means I'll get results."

Mike didn't bother to hide his anger, but he didn't argue with the woman. Instead, he jerked his head in agreement. With one last pat on Emma's hand, Roberta stood up and a moment later she was alone. The moment they were gone, a shiver raced through her until goose bumps rose up on her flesh.

God, she felt sick. Bowing her head, she shivered despite the room's hot temperature. Whoever killed Charlie had to have been involved in her parents' deaths. That mark mutilating his cheek had been the same one she'd seen on her parents' faces, a diagonal line with a backward C just above it. Bile rose in her throat again, but she swallowed it along with her fear.

There was nothing she could do at the moment except wait. The minutes ticked by and she tried to occupy her thoughts by watching the activity outside the interview room. Anything to avoid thinking about the moment when she'd found Charlie's body. She glanced down at her watch.

Had it been an hour since Mike and Roberta had left or two? She couldn't remember. The hair at the base of her neck stood on end as she suddenly sensed someone watching her. Her gaze scanned the station's front desk. Seeing nothing unusual, she shifted her gaze to the area behind the main counter.

It took her a moment to see him because he stood in the darkest corner of the office space. The shadows concealed his face, but something about his body language told her he was studying her carefully. Arms folded across his chest, he stood with one shoulder pressed against the wall in a relaxed pose. Despite his casual stance, she was certain a police station wasn't his normal environment, yet there was nothing about his manner that marked him as an outsider either.

Unable to take her eyes off him, she felt a light touch against her cheek. Almost as if someone had brushed the back of their hand across her face. There was something comforting about the sensation. It was a soothing touch that made her think everything would be all right.

She closed her eyes and drew in a quiet breath. Perhaps Charlie's spirit was here trying to reassure her. Another feathery caress touched her cheek and she reached up expecting to feel a warm hand. She sighed with disappointment when she encountered nothing but her own skin.

The door behind her opened and she turned her head. She immediately recognized the policeman entering the room. She'd seen him
when she'd first entered the station. He nodded politely at her.

"Miss Zale, I am Detective Shakir. I will be investigating Dr.
Russwin's murder." The officer took a seat opposite her and laid a
pad of paper on the table. "I have a few questions I'd like to ask you
about your colleague."

"I don't think I should say anything until I have an attorney
present."

"Certainly, but perhaps you could tell me if you've seen this symbol before."

With several swift strokes of his pencil he drew a mark she knew
well. Her palms suddenly damp with sweat, she struggled to hide
her fear as she met the detective's watchful gaze. She swallowed
hard at the memory of Charlie's bloody corpse.

"Yes," she said as her breath caught in her throat. "Someone . . .
it was on Charlie's face."

"Can you tell me what it means?"

"No. I've been trying to find out what it means for the past five
years, but I can't find anything like it."

"So you *have* seen this mark before."

"Yes." She nodded as she stared down at the roughly drawn
symbol. "My parents were mutilated with it, just like Charlie."

"Ah yes, your parents were murdered in the same fashion as Dr.
Russwin, correct?"

"I . . . yes . . . I really don't want to say anything else until my
friends return."

"I quite understand, Miss Zale, but you *would* like to find the
person who killed your friend, wouldn't you?"

"Of course." She bit her lip as she met the man's unreadable gaze.

"As I recall, you were the one to find your parents, correct?"

"No, Kareem found them." A warning shot fired off in her brain,
and she shook her head in protest. "If you don't mind, I'd like to
wait until my lawyer gets here before we continue."

"Certainly." He turned in his seat to look over his shoulder.

Following the direction of his gaze, Emma saw the man in the
shadows move his hand slightly. The almost indiscernible movement

echoed with the air of a man accustomed to power and how to use it. Her heart ricocheted off her chest wall as she watched the silent exchange between the two men.

Her gaze jerked back to the detective as he grunted with disgust. Irritation pulling his mouth downward, the policeman sent her a hard look. Whoever the man in the shadows was, the detective definitely didn't like taking orders from him. And that hand gesture *had* been a command.

"Miss Zale, can you tell me what Dr. Russwin might have been searching for in the tomb?"

For a moment, she just stared at the officer. What kind of question was that? They were excavating the burial site of a Pharaoh dead for more than two thousand years. What did the man *think* Charlie had been looking for? It would take hours for her to explain everything they were hoping to find compared to what they would actually discover.

"I'm sorry. I don't understand what you're asking."

"Was Dr. Russwin looking for something special? Something specific? An artifact or inscription you might not have known about?"

"No, I don't think so." Emma frowned and shook her head. Charlie had always been open with her and the team. Although he did have the habit of keeping a new discovery to himself until he'd confirmed its authenticity.

"What about this?" Detective Shakir tossed a small medallion onto the table.

The metal object had a flat, hollow ring to it as it bounced against the wood surface until it spun to a halt. Dull and darkly colored, it blended in with the dark wood of the tabletop. Startled, she barely glanced at the coin before she looked up at the detective's surly expression. The officer was far from happy, and her gaze immediately swung toward the man in the shadows.

She could almost see him narrow his eyes as he lowered his chin just a bit. He had an air of anticipation about him that she recognized. It was the same kind of excitement she always felt when she and Charlie hovered over a new find. The exhilaration that came when you shared a breakthrough with someone who would appreciate its importance. Whoever he was, this guy wasn't a member of the Cairo police department. What made it equally strange was her sudden conviction that he was trying to help her. Dragging her gaze away from the man in the shadows, she stared down at the coin on the table.

It took her a full minute or so to grasp the magnitude of what she was looking at. When her chest became tight from lack of air, she sucked in a deep breath. A Sicari coin. She jerked her head up to look in the stranger's direction. The anticipation she'd sensed in him had evolved into satisfaction. Almost as if it pleased him immensely that she'd recognized the artifact.

"I take it you've seen this before." Detective Shakir's words made her start and she saw the hard look of accusation in his dark eyes.

"No, I've never seen the coin before." She stared at the artifact in the center of the table for a little longer before lifting her gaze to meet the policeman's dour expression. "But the symbol represents an ancient order of assassins called the Sicari."

"Would the doctor have recognized the coin?"

"Absolutely," she said with a sharp nod. "He and my parents wanted to prove the Sicari Order wasn't a myth. Charlie would have been ecstatic if he'd found something like this."

Without really thinking about it, she stretched out her hand toward the artifact then stopped. She hated that first moment when she touched any type of antiquity. She never knew what to expect.

"It's quite all right to look at it more closely," the detective said.

Still she hesitated, but when his eyes hardened with suspicion, she had no choice but to pick up the ancient currency. The instant she touched the coin, the familiar flash that always accompanied her visions occurred.

It was like watching a badly edited movie on fast-forward. Scenes from the distant past flowed through her head like a raging river. First, she saw the coin's creation and the Roman centurion who carried it as a good luck charm. The surreal vision grew more confusing as it exploded in a bloody composite of crucifixions, persecutions, and assassinations.

Then in a brilliant flash, the vision threw her forward to the last few seconds of Charlie's life. The emotions her friend experienced at the moment of his death barreled through her and she dropped the coin with a gasp. Christ, Charlie had been carrying this artifact when he died.

Trembling, her gaze was inexplicably drawn to the man hidden in the shadows. He was connected to the coin, but she didn't understand how. She saw him stiffen, and in the next moment, the door of the interrogation room flew open and slammed against the wall. Startled, she cried out in fear then found herself enveloped in Mike's bear hug of an embrace. Exhausted and overwhelmed with emotion, she sank into a dark well of silence.

Chapter 2

EMMA came upright in bed with a small scream. Her heartbeat pounded loudly in her ears as her gaze darted from one corner of the dimly lit room to the next. Where the hell was she? She sagged as she remembered—Chicago.

Was it morning? She turned her head to look at the clock. Almost six in the evening. Her heart sank with dismay. Just another nightmare. There'd be more of the same later tonight. Pushing a shaky hand through her tousled hair, she scrambled off the bed.

She bit back tears. God, she felt old. Not much past thirty, she was beginning to feel twice that age. A single teardrop slid down her cheek. With a swipe of her hand, she wiped it away. If Charlie were here, he'd ream her good. *Don't go gettin' that hangdog look, Emma Zale* he used to say. *Life is a gift, enjoy it while you can.* No, he wouldn't want her to grieve for him. But it was hard not to. Even harder not to deal with the resurrected sorrow for her parents that she'd buried deep inside her.

With the force of a machine gun, rain pelted her bedroom window. She winced at the sound and pushed her feet into a pair of sneakers. It had been raining just as hard at the cemetery earlier today. She shivered in the October chill. Grabbing her sweater off the rocking chair, she shrugged into it as she made her way downstairs.

Quiet filled the house, and it unnerved her. She kept waiting for the sound of shovels scraping against sand or Charlie's gruff voice chastising Sayid over a small indiscretion. Some sound to tell her it had all been a horrible nightmare and she really hadn't left Egypt after all.

Thunder rumbled overhead as she entered the study. Another flash of lightning lit up the sky followed by an ominous thunderclap. After so much time spent in the desert, Emma couldn't remember the last time she'd seen so much rain. She crossed the room to stand at the window overlooking the small garden at the back of the house where she'd grown up. One hand pressed against a cool glass pane, Emma stared out at the water-soaked grounds barely visible in the fading gray light.

The memorial service today had been a messy affair. Charlie had to have been laughing his ass off at everyone huddled beneath umbrellas outside the mausoleum. He had despised Western funeral traditions. The bastard had probably made it rain as payback for his siblings refusing to spread his ashes across the Ptolemy dig.

The gloomy weather matched her depression and, deep inside, her fear. The nonstop rain since her return just a few days ago reinforced how tired she was of the foul weather. It had taken almost a month for Mike to settle matters with the authorities and arrange transport of Charlie's remains back to the Windy City. More like an eternity.

If not for two of the locals and their testimony about the stranger dressed in a monk's robe leaving Ptolemy's tomb, she'd probably still be sitting in a grimy jail cell at this very moment. Throughout the three-week investigation, Mike and Roberta had been her saviors. Somehow, Mike had convinced the police to release her into his custody, and between him and Roberta, they'd bullied the Cairo authorities into moving more quickly with their investigation.

While Mike had returned to the excavation site to deal with the representatives from the government's Supreme Council of Antiquities, Roberta had stayed behind to keep her company. The days had passed slowly, but the other woman had kept her entertained with stories of high-society intrigue and folly.

Roberta's wit was every bit as sharp as Emma's friend, Ewan Redmurre. Perhaps that explained why Ewan couldn't stand the woman. As an Oriental Institute board member, Ewan hated it when someone upstaged him. And Roberta had done that and more by buying herself an internship with her financial backing of the Ptolemy dig. It hadn't made Charlie happy either.

Although they'd released her, the Egyptian authorities remained suspicious of her, and the university's Oriental Institute hadn't hesitated to yank her out of the country the first chance they got. After the dean's call this afternoon, she had the distinct impression she wouldn't be working a dig anytime in the near future either. In fact, if Stuart had his way, it might be never. That thought depressed her even more.

She turned and crossed the study's hardwood floor to sink into the large, swivel chair her father had loved so much. The well-worn leather held the distinctive aroma of her dad's pipe tobacco. She closed her eyes and drank in the smell. Amazing how after five years the scent still clung to the leather. Her fingers brushed across the smooth, dark wood of the mahogany desk as she scooted closer.

A small stack of mail sat in the center of the desk, and she sorted through it. The invitation to the opening of the Oriental Institute's latest exhibition made her grimace. Just what she needed—intense scrutiny from her peers and other interested parties. Not showing up wasn't an option either.

Most everyone knew about Jonathan's infidelity, and she refused to let him, or anyone else, think she was afraid to be in the same room with the son of a bitch. Resigned to attending the event, she pulled on the handle of the middle desk drawer in search of a pen. It didn't give way easily.

Exasperated, Emma released a sound of frustration. The drawer had been cantankerous since her parents had left home for the last time. She'd just never taken the time to try and fix it. Now was as good a time as any. She bent over and looked at the drawer slide. In the darkened space, she could see where a wad of paper had been jammed up into the groove, making it difficult to budge the drawer.

With a sigh, she tugged harder. It gave way a small amount, enough for her to grab the drawer with both hands and jerk on it. Her efforts pulled the entire drawer free of its tracks so it scattered its contents out onto the floor.

"Damn it to hell," she muttered.

The only things left in the drawer were a couple of paper clips and some crumbs from God knew what. Wrinkling her nose, she scooted her chair closer to the trashcan and flipped the drawer over to knock out the dirt. The moment she saw the envelope with its crumpled corner, taped to the edge of the tray's bottom she frowned. So that's what had been keeping the tray from sliding open smoothly.

The drawer resting on her knees, Emma carefully peeled the yellowing tape off the wood. She reached for the letter opener on the desk. Why would her father tape a letter to the bottom of the drawer? Maybe a safety-deposit box she didn't know about? The opener lifted the envelope flap with relative ease and she pulled out the folded square of paper.

A Vigenère cipher written in hieroglyphs. Why would her father have written a cipher in hieroglyphics? Puzzled, she studied the paper and blinked. Over the years, she'd solved a lot of difficult ciphers her dad had written for her. This one made her think she should have taken up Latin instead. It would have been easier.

By using hieroglyphics instead of letters, her father had brilliantly combined the two mediums. A computer hacker *might* be able to decipher it with the right database, but by hand—the person decoding the message would need to know cryptology *and* hieroglyphics. She was pretty certain there weren't too many people running around Chicago fitting that description.

Quickly cleaning up the drawer's spilled contents, she shoved the tray back into its slot and picked up the cipher. Why had her dad hidden the coded message? For that matter, why tape it to the bottom of a desk drawer?

As she studied her father's familiar handwriting, a tremor went through her. If only her parents and Charlie were here to help her sort out this whole mess. Maybe she'd have answers to questions she was still asking.

Her gaze fell on the Sicari coin lying next to the stack of mail. She set aside her father's coded message to pick up the medallion. She'd found it in Charlie's personal effects a couple of days ago. How the authorities had missed it when they'd searched through his things, she had no idea. She expelled a noise of disgust. The police had taken greater care with his belongings than hers.

The coin was almost identical to the one Detective Shakir had shown her, except this one was far more weathered. When she'd first found the artifact, she'd been terrified to touch it. But when she'd finally succumbed to the necessity of it, she was relieved the artifact had only shown her images from the distant past, nothing recent.

Emma tilted the coin so the overhead light outlined the profile of Constantine I on its head, before flipping it to study the Sicari icon on the reverse. The writing was indecipherable, but the icon was the same as the one she'd seen on the wall of Ptolemy's tomb. She frowned. The coin she'd touched in Cairo had been found near Charlie's body. She knew that because her vision had shown him holding it when he died. But this one—this artifact had been in his possession long enough for him to leave it with his belongings and return to the dig.

She turned the coin over to study the worn text. *Iter Sicari Domini factis, non verbis aestimatur.* She frowned and released a sigh. The last six years had been spent reading hieroglyphics, and her Latin was really rusty. She'd need to download some translator software to verify a lot of the text. At least she recognized two of the words. *Domini* was Latin for "lord" and *Sicari* meant "assassin." Did *domini* refer to a deity or was it used in a different context here?

A soft creak of wood echoed in the hall. She jerked her head up at the sound and her heart slammed against her chest. Had she forgotten to lock the front door? No, she distinctly remembered turning the dead bolt.

God, when had she become so irrational? She rubbed her forehead with a sense of self-disgust. What on earth made her think the person who'd killed Charlie would come after her? As the memory of her parents' murder flitted through her head once more, she shivered. They'd died the same way Charlie had and with the same mark on their cheeks. It was stupid to think their deaths weren't connected.

The Cairo police obviously thought they were. It was why they'd taken the easy way out and focused on her as a suspect. But what about the mysterious cloaked figure the locals had seen? An unidentified man carrying a sword. Emma could understand why the locals' story had raised eyebrows at police headquarters. It sounded worse than a B-movie plotline. A puff of air blew past her lips as she flipped the coin over to study the opposite side again.

Even as far back as his college days, her father had believed the Sicari assassin order still existed. When he'd first met her mom, he'd been an intern for the Sorbonne in the south of France in Cathars territory. Even then he'd been searching for signs of the Sicari Order.

Her father had been involved with another woman at the time, but the minute he'd seen her mother, there had never been anyone else. Their marriage had been one of deep love and trust. Something Emma never expected to have. Her parents' kind of relationship was far from the norm.

The coin came back into focus, and her thoughts drifted back to the story the locals had told about the stranger at the scene of Charlie's murder. They'd made the man sound like some avenging monk from the Elizabethan era. Had the Sicari ever dressed like that? Maybe the man at the dig . . . she snorted with disgust at the wild notion.

God, that had to be the most ridiculous thing she'd considered yet. She'd found an icon proving the Sicari had existed. She hadn't found one of them alive and living in Chicago. Another squeak of the hall floor whispered its way into the study. Her gaze jerked up to stare at the room's dark doorway. The pitch-black beyond the softly lit office reminded her of Ptolemy's tomb and finding Charlie's body. With the memory came the fear once again.

The chill of it wrapped its tentacles around Emma. Burying the coin and her father's cipher under some papers, she quickly stood up and glanced around. A weapon. She needed a weapon. The Egyptian dagger on the bookshelf caught her eye. She'd given it to her father on his last birthday. It was just for looks, but it had a sharp point. Better that than nothing at all.

Her hand slid around the metal grip as she unsheathed the blade. Looking down at the silver weapon, she winced. Christ, she was losing it. She'd locked the frigging front door. She knew that. It was just the house settling. Houses did it all the time. Particularly old houses like this one. She didn't like the way a voice in the back of her head laughed at her attempt to dismiss the soft noises. Fine. She'd check the locks in the house. When she finished, she could feel like a fool. But at least she'd be a safe fool.

The dagger sleeve didn't make a sound as she set it down on the papers at the desk. With as much stealth as she could manage, she circled the desk and started toward the door. She only got halfway across the room when a man suddenly filled the doorway of the study. Terror kept her immobile, her scream locked in her throat.

Tall and solidly built, he would have been intimidating no matter what the setting. Dressed completely in black, he moved with a raw power reminiscent of a large predator. The effect was so striking she half expected to hear a low-pitched growl fill the room. Black pants hugged long muscular legs, while a thick, black turtleneck sweater and hip-hugging black leather jacket shouted danger. He wore his dark blond hair cropped short, and his strong features resembled the busts she'd seen of early Roman emperors.

Emma swallowed hard. Throughout history, scribes had depicted Lucifer as a beautiful blond angel. Maybe they were accurate. Her fear almost paralyzed her, but her fingers tightening on the dagger reassured her that she could protect herself. She waited for him to rush her, but he simply stood quietly just inside the doorway. Something about the way he watched her sent a chill down her back. He seemed familiar and yet she was certain she'd never seen him before. This was a man one didn't forget.

"Who the hell are you? And what are you doing in my house?" she managed to croak.

"I'm here to collect something that doesn't belong to you." The deep richness of his voice had a soothing, almost hypnotic, quality to it. Her fingers flexed around the dagger's metal grip.

"You didn't answer my question."

"No, I didn't." His evasive answer held a mocking note that irritated her.

"If it's the coin you're looking for, I don't have it anymore," she sneered with more bravado than she felt. "So you'd better get out before the police arrive."

"Never lie unless you can be convincing." Amusement curled his lips in a slight smile. "I'm not convinced."

The mockery in his expression kicked her anger into high gear. Arrogant bastard. Why in the hell hadn't she taken those karate classes her mother tried to push her into years ago? She might have been able to take him. Then again, maybe not.

Just the breadth of his chest and width of his shoulders would have made her think twice about going up against him even with martial skills. He could easily crush her. So why didn't he? His amusement grew more pronounced as he moved deeper into the room. Sweet Jesus, was he wearing a sword on his back? Her heart skipped several beats before it settled back into a frantic rhythm. Taking a quick step back, she raised her meager weapon in a defensive gesture.

"Come any closer and you'll be sorry."

This time the man actually chuckled. He arched his eyebrows at Emma as a strange pressure bit into her skin at the base of her palm. They were the only two people in the room, but she could swear someone had her by the wrist. The unseen hand squeezed tighter until her fingers flexed open and released the dagger.

The pressure vanished as the blade left her hand. But it didn't hit the floor. Instead, it hovered in the air just below her hand before it flew across the room to become embedded in the wall on her right. The blade wobbled back and forth for a moment, until it grew still and remained buried deep in the wood.

"Now then," he murmured. "I want to know where the *Tyet of Isis* is."

Horrified, she simply stared at the dagger sticking out of the wall. What the—he'd done the impossible. No, she knew differently.

Anything was possible. All she had to do was look in the mirror for proof of weird science. But it didn't change the fact she was in trouble. Trouble with a capital T. She didn't know how he'd performed that particular trick, but it made him even more dangerous than she'd realized. Determined not to show any fear, she shook her head as she dragged her gaze back to his.

"The *Tyet of Isis* is a symbol, not a thing."

"Correct," he said as his mouth tilted upward. "A symbol in the form of a knot often used to represent the Egyptian goddess Isis. But I'm looking for an artifact that goes by the same name."

Arrogant bastard. He was laughing at her. "Well, I don't have what you're looking for."

"I see."

He narrowed his gaze to study her for a long moment. She didn't like the way his intense scrutiny seemed to bare her soul to him. It disturbed her. He walked past her to study the artifacts shelved on the wall behind her father's desk. So much for making him think she was a threat. But with his back turned, she'd be stupid not to make a run for it.

Emma leaped toward the door. It slammed closed before she'd gone two steps. Still racing forward, she tugged on the doorknob, desperate to escape. The door didn't budge. Oh God, if he could make knives stick in the walls, close doors, and keep them shut, what else was he capable of? A sinking feeling gnawed at the pit of her stomach. He'd managed to squeeze her wrist without touching her—could he choke her to death, too?

Panic set in. Whirling around, she realized she had nowhere to run. Her back flat against the door, she rebelliously met his gaze as he moved toward her. Large hands braced on either side of her, the man pinned her between himself and the door. She drew a quick hiss of air into her lungs.

Dark blue eyes narrowed as his gaze slowly dropped to her mouth. It lingered there for a breathtaking moment. A slight shudder rippled through her as his gaze slid downward in open appreciation. She didn't know what was worse, his blatant interest in her physical attributes or the pleasure his interest gave her.

God in heaven. Had she totally lost her mind? The man had

broken into her home, practically threatened her with bodily harm. There her thoughts stumbled. Well, he hadn't actually threatened her. All he'd done so far was intimidate her. Emma flinched as he exhaled a harsh breath.

"You really don't know where it is, do you." Not a question, but a resigned statement. "Show me the coin."

"I'm not showing you anything," she snapped. "Except the door."

If she had to die, then she damn well wouldn't make it easy for him. His amusement returned as he leaned into her more. Less than an inch separated their bodies now. She caught a whiff of spice wafting off him as his warm breath caressed her ear. Damn. She was an idiot to even think the guy smelled heavenly.

"Aren't you the least bit curious?" His whisper tickled the side of her neck with heat. She swallowed hard at the way her body reacted to him.

"Curious about what? How you got into my home? Why you're threatening me? Whether you're going to kill me?" At her words, he jerked back from her, his features hard as an ice sculpture.

"If I wanted to kill you, we wouldn't be having this conversation. Now show me the coin."

Something in his voice warned her to do as he said. She sidled past him, noting the small earpiece and wire that disappeared beneath his clothing. Her heart sank. He wasn't alone. He'd brought backup.

Shaking with fear, she leaned over the desk and pushed the papers aside, taking care not to expose the cipher. Her fingers never even came close to the coin before it flew past her into his hand. God, how in the hell did he do that?

Transfixed by his ability, Emma stared at him in awe and terror. She'd heard of telekinesis, but never seen it in action. And unless he was a magician, she couldn't come up with any other explanation. He studied the antiquity for a long moment then sent her a grim look.

"Where did you get this?"

"Charlie Russwin. I'm not sure where he found it," she answered automatically.

"This one is different from the other one," he murmured as he looked at the coin again. "The Sicari emblem isn't as clearly defined."

Floored by his statement, she stared at him with her mouth open for several seconds. How did he know about the other—? Cairo. He was the man she'd seen in the shadows at the police station. She should have realized it sooner. It was why he'd seemed so familiar and yet unrecognizable. Her gaze narrowed as she watched him examine the coin.

"You were at the police station." At the quiet accusation, he slowly raised his head to look at her. His expression revealed nothing, but she thought she saw a glint of admiration in his dark gaze.

"Yes."

His brevity annoyed her.

"That's *all* you have to say?"

"For the moment."

There it was again, that amusement of his. She wanted to punch him. Who was this guy? There weren't many people who knew about the Sicari Order, even among academicians. He extended his hand to return the coin to her. She hesitated. What kind of thief would give it back as if they'd been discussing work?

His amusement deepened as his dark eyes dared her to take it from him. Infuriated by the challenge in his glittering gaze, she snatched the bronze currency from his grasp. The moment she came into solid contact with the coin and his fingers, a strong charge of electricity charged through her. The images came fast and furious. Dark, mysterious, and potent, they held her powerless.

Suddenly, death filled Emma's mind with its foul stench. Dark, torturous, and bloody. The Roman soldier was dying. He laid the coin in the palm of a young man's hand and wrapped the fingers around the coin. The new owner lifted a young boy up onto a horse then gave the child the coin, pointing to the words on its surface.

As if someone had spun her around until she was dizzy, the images collapsed in on one another until a clear picture came into focus. The hooded figure, his cloak flowing out behind him, strode through a massive cathedral. Deadly purpose filled the assassin's stride, the coin in his pocket a family talisman. He vanished in the shifting images until a woman's face flashed before her.

Death had frozen the woman's pain on her face. Then with the speed of a freight train, the vision threw her forward. The stranger stood over a dead man, his sword dark in the moonlight. Blood covered his hands and she wanted to scream at the sight of it. Rage, pain, grief, love, and something much darker flowed through the coin and his fingers and into her mind. The overwhelming power of it made the room spin as she fought to remain upright.

Desperate to break the connection and find sanctuary from the deluge of emotions, she jerked her hand free of his. The Sicari coin fell to the floor, where it bounced several times with a repetitive clang until it went silent.

The man reached for Emma, but she staggered away with a cry that stopped him. Falling to her knees, she bent over to touch the floor and prayed for the nausea to pass. Once in a while, she'd pick up images from another individual when they'd hand her an artifact. Never anything like this. The intensity of the graphic scenes and the emotions she'd felt had been overwhelming.

"Let me help you."

His words struck her as funny. He'd broken into her home, demanded she hand over an object she didn't have, and *now* he wanted to help her? It was his fault she felt so crappy. She choked out a bitter laugh.

"No . . . *thank you*. I think you've done . . . quite enough for the moment."

"You're a telepath." Crouching beside her, he studied her with thoughtful deliberation. Like Lake Michigan during a storm, the deep blue of his eyes echoed with a mysterious, dark danger. And he *was* dangerous. He'd killed before. She'd seen the blood on his hands. It chilled her. No, it was the coin. Everything she'd seen had come from the coin. None of what she'd seen was related to the stranger. Her breathing hitched at the memory of those last images. She had never been a good liar.

"If you mean . . . I can hear what people . . . are thinking. No," Emma muttered as her equilibrium began to right itself. She uncurled from a fetal posture and eased herself up into a sitting position. "When I touch inanimate objects—antiquities, I see images, flashes of past events."

"Does it always make you this ill?"

"No." She pulled in a deep breath. "But then it's unusual for me to see things when I touch someone."

Unusual? This was the first time she'd ever had a physical reaction this strong—this overwhelming—when taking an artifact from someone else. Occasionally, she'd glimpse some small tidbit of a colleague's past when objects had changed hands. But even then, her physical reaction had been little more that a bite of static electricity. Nothing so intense it would make her sick to her stomach. Even then, all she'd ever experienced was an awareness of incidents, not images. And most definitely not images like the ones she'd seen with this man. She shuddered. He must have served as a conductor of sorts.

"But you did see something when I handed you the coin."

The flat, emotionless statement made her heart pound as fear pumped blood through her veins at an accelerated rate.

"Everything was pretty much a blur," she lied as her gaze slid away from his. Strong fingers grasped her chin, and she stiffened, waiting for the electric shock and the visions to happen again. But they didn't. She closed her eyes in a brief prayer of gratitude. He'd simply been a conductor for the coin, which explained why some of what she'd seen had been associated with him.

"I seem to recall advising you not to lie unless you do it well."

A hint of irony touched his lips as he effortlessly pulled her to her feet. Large hands cradled her waist as he steadied her. The touch made her heart skip a beat as a jolt of awareness slid through her veins. Primal and intense, the sensation swept through her like a wave crashing against a rocky coastline. Suddenly realizing she hadn't contradicted him, she swallowed hard.

"No. Really. Everything was jumbled together. Most of it didn't even make sense."

Releasing her, he folded his arms across his chest to study her with a watchful gaze. His features suddenly brought to mind the bust of Ptolemy they'd uncovered at the dig last year. The arrogance and unrelenting expression on his face only emphasized his likeness to the ancient Pharaoh.

"Most of it?" His eyebrow arched with wry skepticism. "What *did* make sense to you?" That hadn't been a question. More like a command. If she obeyed, he might let her live.

Chapter 3

ARES knew he intimidated her. The fear flashing in those wide hazel eyes simply confirmed the knowledge. Yet she remained defiant. He liked that about her. Even that day in the Cairo police station he'd admired her strength and courage.

She'd been even more frightened then. Frightened and vulnerable. It had been that vulnerability that had made him reach out to comfort her when he shouldn't have. But he'd been intrigued by Emma Zale then just as much as he was now. And that wasn't good—especially when she was so easy on the eyes.

Her light brown hair barely touched her shoulders, and there was just a trace of red running through it. The color suited the fire in her. A flash of spirit that still burned in those beautiful eyes. Long, dark eyelashes almost brushed her cheeks as she averted her gaze in an attempt to hide her rebellious expression.

Then there were her curves. She'd lost some weight since that day in the Cairo police station, but she was still full and lush in all the right places. His fingers bit into his biceps. *Christus*, he needed to focus on why he was here, not Emma's softly rounded body.

But it was difficult to ignore the way her cardigan caressed amply rounded breasts or how her jeans hugged her voluptuous hips. A man could get lost in her body if he played his cards right. He grimaced at how easily she could distract him. She tilted her chin up and met his gaze.

"You've killed before," she said softly.

He went rigid. *Merda*. What else had she seen? Tension stretched the muscles in his jaw so tight his whole face ached. God help him, *and her*, if she knew too much. If the Praetorians suspected for one moment—he dismissed the thought. She flinched as he narrowed his gaze at her.

"You seem quite certain of your facts."

"Well, I didn't actually see you kill someone, if that's what you're implying," she snapped. "But I know death when I see it—feel it."

He didn't doubt her. He'd seen the morgue photos of her parents in her case file, and he'd seen Russwin's body in Cairo. He could empathize with her, too. But when it came to denying his past—he couldn't. As a Sicari, he was trained to kill. Blood stained his hands, but he killed only to protect the innocent or administer justice when the legal system failed. A Sicari didn't kill for pleasure. It was against their code of honor. Now Praetorian warriors—those bastards enjoyed torturing their prey. They didn't believe in honor. If they'd ever had any honor at all, it had died out of their bloodline when the Roman Empire fell.

"There are some who find killing a pleasurable occupation," he said coldly. He didn't like admitting it, but the condemnation in her voice stung.

"I'm sorry." She heaved a sigh. "I felt the pain of your loss, and I understand what it's like to want justice for someone you care about."

The muscle in his cheek twitched. *Mater Dei*, the woman had seen a hell of a lot more than he thought. Did she know the Sicari Order had a file on her—on her entire family? He should have left the house the moment he realized she was here.

But he hadn't.

Biting the inside of his cheek, he turned away from her. Leave it to him to trust his librarians' research and not his gut. Sandro and Octavia were going to wish they were still file clerks when he got through with them. Emma Zale had never heard of the *Tyet of Isis* until tonight. He'd bet his life on it.

Fotte. He'd put her at risk by coming here. All it took was one fleeting thought for a Praetorian to realize she knew something— even if it was only a sliver of information. A growl of frustration rumbled out of him. At this point he wasn't left with much in the way of choices. He whirled around to face her. She jumped back, her hands up in a gesture of surrender.

"Look, I don't have what you're looking for. So just go. I promise to forget the whole thing."

"It's not quite that easy," he muttered.

"Of course it is. You just turn and walk out of here." She pointed toward the door. "You *can* still walk, can't you?"

Despite the gravity of the situation, her sarcasm made him laugh. She refused to be bullied in spite of her fear. Eyes wide with surprise, she stared up at him. With another chuckle, he bent his head toward her.

"I like you, Emma Zale." She looked at him in amazement, and he laughed softly. "You're going to need that humor of yours."

"How in the hell do you know my name?"

"The same way I knew where to find you." He shrugged. The less she knew, the safer she was. The more she knew, the harder it would go for her if the Praetorians caught up with her.

"That's not an answer and you know it."

"True, but it's the only one you'll get for the moment."

"What the hell does that mean?"

"It means you'll have to come with me," he said with resignation. Taking her with him was the last thing he wanted to do. Emma Zale meant trouble. And problems he could do without. She'd only complicate matters for him.

"I'm not going anywhere with you." Her mouth tightened in a rebellious pout.

"Unfortunately, you don't have a choice."

"That's what you think," Emma snapped. With a vicious shove, she knocked him off balance and leaped toward the door.

"*Deus damno id*, woman."

He quickly recovered his equilibrium then reached out with his mind to stop her. She stumbled as he forced her to face him. Gritting his teeth, Ares narrowed his eyes at her. It was time Emma Zale realized exactly what she was up against. Slowly, he pulled her toward him.

She fought every step of the way, but he easily overpowered her resistance. His ability had limits dependent on distance as well as his physical and mental exertion, but she didn't know that. And manipulating her wasn't that difficult. With little effort at all, he forced her to cross the room until she stood less than a foot away from him. Jaw clenched in anger, his thoughts sent her stumbling forward until her body pressed into his.

The scent of coconut butter filled his nostrils as his body reacted to hers. The primal response startled him. Arms at his sides, he held her tight against him with nothing more than his thoughts. *Damno*, she felt good.

"Afraid?" he growled, irritated she could affect his senses so easily.

"No," she snapped.

"Not even just a little?"

His anger gave way to something else as he studied the succulent fullness of her mouth. The moment he visualized rubbing his thumb across her plump bottom lip, she gasped. Her hand flew to her mouth, her fingers touching the spot that fascinated him.

"Let me go." Anger made her eyes flash with amber sparks. Definitely feisty.

"I don't see me holding you against your will." He clasped his hands behind his back with a sense of satisfaction. A second later, he pictured her arms sliding up to encircle his neck. Outrage parted her lips in a loud gasp as she reached up to cling to him. He bit back a smile at the sound.

"If you don't let me go, I'm going to scream," she snapped.

"No. I don't think you will."

Lowering his head, he lightly brushed his mouth across hers. Her body went rigid with surprise, but he barely noticed as he unclasped his hands and reached for her waist. Sweet. She tasted sweet with just a tinge of citrus. He wanted more. His hands cupping her face, he deepened the kiss, teasing himself with the warm flavor of her.

Releasing his mental hold on her, he half expected her to pull away. She didn't.

He nibbled at her bottom lip, waiting to see if she'd open herself up to him. When she did, he eagerly explored the heat of her soft mouth. His body hardened in a split second. *Christus*, she was hot against his tongue. Hot, sweet, and delectable. His hands slid down over her shoulders and across her back until he cupped the lush curve of her bottom.

With a tug, Ares removed the breath of air between their bodies, his cock pressing into her soft thigh. Desire sent his hand upward over her hip until his fingers brushed across the fullness of her breast, and his thumb rubbed over a hard nipple. She felt good. Sexy and tempting in the best possible way.

The image of her naked beneath him sent his temperature sky-rocketing. His control slipped further as she shifted her hips against his in a carnal move that left him throbbing with need. The buttery sweet fragrance of her filled his senses, whetting his appetite for more. A moment later, her hand caressed him through his trousers. He groaned with pleasure as he eagerly pressed himself into her palm.

Damno, he wanted her hand around his bare flesh. No, he wanted a hell of a lot more than that. And God knew she was eager and willing. He couldn't remember the last time he'd been laid, and this woman would be a hell of a lot more than just a one-night stand. The sweet softness of her would keep him coming back for more of the same. The jarring thought pierced the emotions raging through him. *Fotte*. What was he doing?

He jerked free of her and shoved his fingers through his hair. He'd only meant to silence her. He'd known she'd be trouble, but this had the makings of a disaster. He shot her a quick glance then looked away. That flushed, just kissed, look of hers only managed to make him hotter and a damned sight more uncomfortable. Furious with his behavior and his lack of discipline for the second time in one evening, he gritted his teeth. The best way to deal with the problem Emma Zale posed was to keep his distance mentally and physically. Still infuriated by his inability to master his attraction to her, he scowled at her.

"Do you wish me to continue my demonstration?"

"Of what? Your ability to control my physical movements or your unwanted attentions?" She returned his glare as she deliberately wiped her hand across her mouth. His eyes narrowed.

"I don't recall you protesting too loudly," he snapped.

Heat crested in her cheeks as Emma clenched her fists. Hell, he was a manipulative bastard, but he was right. She had kissed him back. She'd enjoyed kissing him. Worse than that, she'd caressed the hard thickness of him with the intimacy of a lover. And she'd wanted him. Wanted him in the worst possible way. The hot ache between her thighs told her that.

What had possessed her to get so caught up in a kiss she'd been willing to let him do whatever he wanted with her? She winced with disgust at her thoughts. She was out of her frigging mind. The man had broken into her home, held her hostage—how in the hell could she be attracted to him?

The muted chime of the doorbell suddenly echoed in the study. He jerked his head toward the closed door. She watched him as he evaluated the situation in the same way a predator calculated threats. The doorbell rang again. Without a word, he reached out and grabbed her arm. Dragging her with him, he pulled her into the dark hallway. The blackened corridor made her balk. It had been this dark when she'd found Charlie.

"No," she exclaimed. "I—"

In a heartbeat, he covered her mouth with his large hand and jerked her backward into his chest. The moment his hard, muscular frame pressed into her back, a rush of heat flooded her veins. Nestled against him like this created a pleasurable, intimate warmth she didn't want to enjoy. But she did. She liked it far too much. God, she really had lost her mind.

"Were you expecting someone?" He breathed into her ear. "Just nod yes or no."

She nodded. Earlier at the memorial service, Ewan had said he might come by to check on her. If it was anyone she knew, it would be him. The doorbell chimed again and once more immediately after. Only Ewan rang the bell like that. Impatient and often irritating, it didn't change the fact that he was brilliant when it came to ancient civilizations.

"It's my friend, Ewan," she mumbled into the hand covering her mouth.

The intruder tightened his hold on her, his arm riding up to brush against the underside of her breasts. Her body tingled at the contact. The warmth of his breath caressed her cheek as he pressed his mouth to her ear.

"It's not safe for you here, Emma." He hesitated. She could feel it in the way his hard body relaxed against hers.

He eased his hand away from her mouth and turned her to face him. The indecision in his expression startled her. After everything she'd seen, she knew it was a foreign emotion to him. For the first time she began to think he really was concerned for her welfare. She shook her head slightly.

"Why isn't it safe?"

"I can't tell you that right now. There's no time. You'll just have to trust me."

"Oh right." She sniffed with derision as the doorbell rang again. "Look, if I don't let Ewan in, he's going to call the police."

"Answer it," he rasped with harsh resolve. "But when he's gone, you're coming with me, Emma. Count on it."

"Go to hell," she snapped in a breathy whisper as the doorbell rang again.

He gave her a slight push toward the foyer. Although it was still dark in the hallway, her eyes had adjusted to the small amount of available light. And for some reason his presence made the darkness a little less threatening. That made it official. She was insane. Stumbling forward, she moved down the hall as the doorbell rang for a fourth time.

"Hold your horses! I'm coming," she called out.

As she reached the front door, she looked over her shoulder. She couldn't see her fallen angel hidden in the shadows, and her heart jumped with dismay. With a quick flip of the hall light switch, she illuminated the entire corridor. He'd simply vanished. A shiver trailed down her spine. God, what the hell was going on here? This guy made Houdini look like an amateur. No, not a magician. The stranger was anything *but* that. Her hand slid over her wrist as she recalled his uncanny ability. Turning back to the door, she reached for the doorknob then froze. The dead bolt hadn't been touched. How in the hell had he gotten into the house? The sudden pounding on the opposite side of the door made her jump.

"Emma? Are you quite all right?" Ewan's distinctive English accent echoed through the door, and she heaved a sigh of relief.

Without hesitation she unlocked the door and tugged it open. For once, she welcomed the sight of Ewan's angular features and graying hair. Most of the time, his pompous attitude grated on her, but after the day she'd had, well, even the devil himself would be welcome. She winced inwardly. Definitely the wrong choice of phrase. Lucifer had come and gone already, leaving her more confused than she'd ever been in her life.

Always meticulous in appearance, Ewan Redmurre was a throwback to a fifties-era professor. Any fashionista would have a stroke just looking at him. But Ewan's look fit his personality. Somewhat stuffy, rich in anal-retentive detail, but mostly—brilliant. Tonight, though, the rain had left him drenched and he was obviously displeased about it.

"What the devil took you so long?" he groused as he stepped into the foyer. "I'm soaking wet."

She jumped aside as he shrugged out of his trench coat and proceeded to shake the rain off it onto the entryway's floor. Gritting her teeth at the action, she took the coat out of his hands. Okay, warm fuzzies about Ewan were gone. Didn't the man believe in umbrellas? Not waiting for him to shake the water off his fedora, she lifted it off his head then hung both items on the peg hooks next to the door.

"I was . . . talking with someone . . ."

Remembering the intruder's concern for her safety, she frowned. Her hesitation surprised her. Ewan might be an ass sometimes, but she'd known him since before she could walk. He'd been a friend of her parents since their college days. Like Charlie, he'd been a rock she'd leaned on after her parents' murder five years ago. She'd relied on him again today at Charlie's memorial service. But the stranger's concern had been so compelling . . . and for some crazy reason, she trusted him to keep her safe. No, she'd tell Ewan later when she had a better grasp of the situation.

"Do you want a drink?" she asked.

"Whiskey neat, if you please."

She nodded at his request and passed through the living room into the kitchen. It didn't take long to find the whiskey because the pantry was bare. She made a mental note to go grocery shopping.

"This someone you were talking with wouldn't be that Frost fellow, would it?" Ewan's crisp accent floated into the kitchen like a brisk breeze. "The last thing you need is to be talking to that moronic jackass."

The mention of Jonathan made her flinch, and she didn't know whether to laugh or cry at the older man's comment. She chose to laugh. Jonathan would have been livid to hear himself referred to as a jackass, let alone stupid. Her ex-fiancé believed himself to be urbane and sophisticated, but he was really a liar and a cheat. Whiskey bottle in one hand and two glasses in another, she returned to the living room and arched an eyebrow at her guest.

"I haven't seen Jonathan since the Institute's annual fundraiser last year."

It had been an awkward evening at best since it had been the first time they'd met since the end of their relationship. She finished pouring the whiskey, and the liquor bottle clinked softly against the wood surface of the coffee table as she set it aside. She forced a smile to her lips and offered Ewan a glass of amber-colored liquid. Deliberately, she ignored the frown of concern furrowing his brow. Instead, she plopped down into the plush corner of the couch. Ewan sent her a discerning look.

"I see. At least you're not still carrying a torch for the fellow."

"Nope," she said in a carefree tone. She might not love Jonathan anymore, but the mere mention of his name could still make her stomach churn with nausea and pain. Finding him in bed with his anthropology intern two years ago hadn't been nearly as painful as discovering the real reason for his marriage proposal.

"Your reluctance to discuss this mysterious individual leads me to assume this is an affair of the heart. Have I met the young man?"

"I don't think so."

She could have told him about her visitor, but she really didn't

want Ewan to fuss over her safety. The stranger's dire warning flitted through her head again. He'd been convinced she was in real
danger and equally concerned about her safety.

An oxymoron given the man had accosted her in her own home.
Well, maybe "accosted" wasn't the right word. Hell, he hadn't even
told her whom she needed to be afraid of. On top of that, she didn't
even know his name.

"Have you heard from the Institute about when you can return
to work?" Ewan's words made her shake her head.

"Dr. Stuart wouldn't give me a date. Apparently, there's some
concern that I've become a liability for the university unless I shift
my field of expertise to something more *local*."

"Local?"

"I believe he mentioned the word 'classroom.'" She didn't bother
to hide her disgust.

"Bloody hell! The man is mad to think about putting you in the
classroom."

"Thanks for your vote of confidence regarding my teaching
skills," she said with more than a hint of sarcasm. He waved her
protest aside as he leaned back in the recliner opposite her.

"No, no, my dear. Stuart's a fool not to send you back to Egypt.
Your work in Ptolemy's tomb has been exceptional. Charles found
the damn thing, but you're the one whose work has made the excavation the success that it is. Even Michael Granby admits that, despite
the man's proclivity to tout his own credentials."

Ewan pulled a pipe from his coat pocket with a pouch of tobacco.
With his usual precision, her friend packed the bowl and proceeded
to light it. Emma closed her eyes briefly as the tobacco's aroma
drifted across the room to tease her nose. The same brand her father
had smoked. Her dad had always enjoyed his after-dinner pipe. She
could still see him sitting in his recliner ready to debate his favorite
topic—Ptolemy and the Sicari who'd served him.

The image was so real in her head, she tensed as she waited for
her mother's voice to echo out of the kitchen. But the sound never
materialized. She opened her eyes and smiled at the man across from
her. Ewan Redmurre rarely handed out compliments, and earning his

praise meant she'd done something special—significant. She savored the thought.

She'd worked hard to build her reputation without the use of her unique gift. An ability Jonathan had thought he could exploit to his advantage. She thrust all thought of her ex-fiancé out of her head. Ewan Redmurre had just paid her one of the highest compliments she could ever receive. His approval wasn't to be taken lightly given his degree of influence at the Oriental Institute. A member of the Institute's Board of Directors, his power could easily advance or sidetrack any career.

"Thank you, Ewan."

"You're welcome." He gestured at her with his pipe. "I don't suppose they allowed you to keep your notes, did they?"

The subtle change of subject didn't surprise her. Ewan always kept the best interests of the Institute at the forefront of anything he did. "Actually, they did. That and something else."

"Something else?"

"It was in Charlie's belongings. A coin."

"*Good God*," Ewan exclaimed.

"Well, it's not like I knew it was there," she snapped in a defensive tone. "It's not my fault the authorities didn't find it when they searched through everything."

This last statement held more than a trace of bitterness as she remembered her ordeal in Cairo and the way her things had been recklessly tossed into several large boxes. Ewan sent her a sympathetic look.

"I can't imagine they made it easy for you. I take it they brought up the subject of your parents as well?"

"Yes."

She bobbed her head and glanced away from him. The rawness of the pain still lingered beneath the surface even after five years. Charlie's murder had brought it all back. The memories she'd managed to keep at bay. There hadn't been anything unusual about the dig she and her parents had been excavating. Everything had been quite normal until the night her mother and father failed to show up for dinner. When it grew late, she'd ordered the men to spread out and find the couple. Kareem had been the first one to find her parents. Even now, she could still hear his wailing cry of terror. She crushed the dark memories and turned her head back to Ewan. A look of assessment darkened his brown eyes.

"So where is this coin?"

"Let me go get it," she said as she gulped down the rest of her whiskey and unfolded herself off the couch. "I'll be right back."

Heading down the hall to the study, she half expected her mysterious stranger to materialize out of thin air. She certainly didn't like the disappointment that flared through her when he didn't appear. As she entered the office, she glanced to her left, fully expecting to see the knife still stuck in the wall. But it was gone.

Startled, she came to an abrupt halt. It had been in the wall when Ewan had rung the doorbell. She turned toward the desk. The knife sat on top of the papers covering the desktop. Her stomach lurched with apprehension as she sprinted forward.

Pushing papers first to one side and then to another, she realized the worst had happened. The bastard had let her answer the door while he came back here to take the coin. Furious, she slammed her fists into the desktop.

Chapter 4

THE rain eased slightly as Ares DeLuca stood in the shadows surrounding the Zale house.

The Emma he'd just met bore no likeness to the dry information in her file. She was feisty, vulnerable, and intelligent, with a bite of sarcastic humor. That, and a body designed by Titian.

Id damno. If he didn't get his head back on straight, he'd make an even bigger mess of things. He'd made more mistakes tonight than in the entire time he'd been *Legatus* of the Order's Chicago guild. Mistakes like knowing zip about Emma's special ability.

How in the hell had Sandro and Octavia missed that? Her file mentioned nothing about a psychic trait. He frowned as he studied the dark window of her study. With just one touch, she'd learned far more about him than she needed to know. Knowledge was power, but it was also dangerous if you didn't have all the facts. And Emma was a babe in the woods when it came to knowing anything about the Praetorians. It certainly hadn't helped matters that she'd seen his past as well. The horror in her eyes had reflected his past in all its darkness. It was the first time he'd ever regretted being a Sicari. His jaw clenched at the thought.

Regrets. He wished he'd never kissed the woman. In Cairo, he'd allowed himself to reach out with his thoughts to caress her cheek. She'd seemed so lost, and he'd wanted to comfort her. But kissing her tonight? That had been madness in itself. All his Sicari training had fallen by the wayside the moment her body had pressed into his.

He couldn't remember the last time he'd failed to block out all emotions and focus on the assigned task. He hadn't screwed up this badly since . . . he released a grunt of anger. The past was done. Emma was the priority now. And it took only one Praetorian passing by her in public to pick up on her thoughts.

Once the pride of Ancient Rome, and Caesar's personal guard, the Praetorians had made the Sicari outlaws. From behind the cloak of the Church, they'd denounced the Sicari as assassins with evil powers. They'd rounded up men, women, and children like cattle and burned them at the stake or crucified them.

Those who escaped went into hiding, eventually becoming the assassins the Praetorians had branded them just to survive. Nor was it surprising their enemy had conveniently forgotten to mention anything about their own special powers. Abilities the Church would have viewed as coming from the devil. Telling their superiors in the Church they were telepathic would have made the Praetorians a target for persecution as well.

Fotte. He should have made Sandro and Octavia double-check their information on Emma before he barged into her home. Russwin's notes had made it sound like she had the *Tyet of Isis*, and he'd been more than willing to believe it. He'd gotten his hopes up thinking he was finally going to learn where the *Tyet of Isis* was. He didn't like making mistakes like this. Just one fleeting thought stirring in her head about him, the *Tyet of Isis*—any of it—could mean her death. Clearly the Zales hadn't shared what they knew with Emma. Unless, of course, she was already working with the Praetorians . . .

Tension made his muscles grow taut. He hadn't considered *that* possibility. In the next breath, he dismissed the notion. Her confusion tonight had been genuine. The Order had placed her under surveillance some time ago. If she'd been involved with the Praetorians, there would have been a note in her file. Her parents had been under surveillance for almost five years prior to their deaths, and extensive background checks had turned up nothing on the couple. It had been the same in Emma's case. There hadn't been even the slightest connection to the sworn enemy of the Sicari. And despite what some in the Order believed, working for the Institute didn't make her guilty.

Scowling, he released a harsh breath through his clenched teeth. It had been a mistake to come here tonight. *Merda*. He should have been more patient. More careful. The *Tyet of Isis* had been missing for more than two thousand years. A few more weeks of surveillance on Emma would have been prudent. But he hadn't chosen that path. Instead he'd put her in danger by plowing into her life like a bulldozer.

Once Emma got rid of her visitor, he'd convince her to come with him. He grimaced. More likely he'd have to kidnap her. The Sicari complex on Wacker Drive would have to suffice until he could figure out a way to protect her. He snorted with disgust. Protect her? He was delusional if he really believed Emma would ever be able to live by herself again. The Praetorians would stop at nothing to destroy the Sicari, even if it meant murdering innocent bystanders. He'd dragged her into this centuries-old conflict and he refused to let her become a victim of it.

The light in her study blinked on, and he retreated deeper into the wet shadows. He could see her clearly through the window he'd made his exit from as she looked toward the wall and then the desk where the letter opener lay. When she slammed her fists against the desktop, he released a low growl of self-disgust. Had he expected her to be happy he'd taken the coin?

An older man entered the study a few minutes later. Her visitor. He ignored the twinge of satisfaction the man's age gave him. Turning away from the brightly lit window, he moved with quiet stealth toward the street. He could keep an eye on the house from the car just as easily as he could standing here in the rain.

Early evening had vanished into the darkness of night as he kept to the deeper shadows lining the residential neighborhood's sidewalk. Slick with rain, the street was devoid of traffic as he quickly retraced his steps back to where he'd parked his Durango. Unlike most cars, there were no annoying chimes or interior lights blinking on when he opened the car door. A mechanic he knew had taken care of that problem within an hour of the vehicle's cash purchase. The small precaution helped keep him from being an easy target. With a well-practiced move, he removed his sword from its scabbard and stored the blade in the special holder under his seat.

With a quiet thud, the door closed out the wet weather. He'd parked only a few houses down from Emma's place, and from where he sat, he had an excellent view of her front door. The angry rustle of his sister shifting her position in the seat beside him made him suppress a sigh of pained tolerance.

He rubbed the dampness off the back of his neck, all too aware of his sister's censorious gaze. She'd given him hell for going into Emma's without her. A quick glance in Phaedra's direction revealed her mutinous expression. He returned his attention to the nearby house.

"I don't understand why you insisted on me staying in the car," she snapped.

"And I don't know why you insist on questioning my orders."

His harsh reply silenced any further comments. Sometimes his sister forgot who led their guild, but he had no one but himself to blame. His indulgence of her had started when the Praetorians had left them orphans almost twenty years ago. He frowned.

The Praetorians were responsible for a lot more deaths than just his parents. Their persecution of the Sicari had been happening for almost two millennia. Once his people had held the same social status and power as their enemy. But as the Roman Empire slowly crumbled into dust, things had changed. The Praetorians had donned the cloak of Christianity to do more than oppress the Sicari. They'd sought their genocide. There was no clear rationale for why the Praetorians had set out to destroy his people. Some stories said it involved a woman, other tales attributed the persecution to jealousy and a craving for power. Most Sicari believed it was the *Tyet of Isis* that had started it all. The only problem was, no one knew *what* or *where* the artifact was. It didn't really matter what had started it all. It was a lot easier to start a war than to stop one.

The sound of Phae's fingers drumming relentlessly against the black leather of her jacket pulled him out of his contemplation. The look of frustration on her face made him bite back a small smile. Patience had never been one of Phae's virtues. His sister sent him a sideways glance.

"Did you get it?"

"She doesn't have it."

"Is that what she told you?" Phae snorted with disbelief.

"You doubt me?" He heard the steel in his voice, and out of the corner of his eye he saw her stiffen as she suddenly recognized the error she'd made.

"Forgive me, *il mio signore*," she said with sincere remorse.

Not responding, he kept his attention focused on Emma's house and yard. He understood his sister's frustration. When he'd received Russwin's personal diary from Shakir in Cairo, he'd been certain they'd find the *Tyet of Isis* soon. The dead professor's diary had made *everyone* think the man had either given Emma the artifact or at least told her where it was. But he didn't think Russwin had given her anything, because he was certain she'd never heard of the artifact until tonight. No matter how much she knew, Russwin's murder put Emma at the head of the class as the archeological authority on the Sicari outside of the Order itself.

It had been a gamble in Cairo to have Shakir show Emma the coin the police had found next to Russwin's body. But it had been important to try and gauge what she really knew about the Order. She'd definitely recognized the artifact, but the answers she'd given to Shakir had indicated only a general knowledge of the Sicari, nothing more. If she knew more than she'd said, he couldn't blame her for holding back. He would have done the same in her position.

Although if he were a betting man, he'd wager she'd seen something when she first touched the coin. With that ability of hers, she probably witnessed Russwin's last few moments, maybe even the face of his murderer. Whatever she'd seen, Emma hadn't shared it with Shakir or anyone else. She was smart enough to know her talent would most likely generate more skepticism than serve as a defense.

What puzzled him was the way Emma's parents, and now her mentor, had been murdered. The Praetorians generally tortured their victims before killing them. Instead, the Zales and Russwin had died quickly. The killer's method had been clean, efficient, and merciful. More like a Sicari execution than the usual Praetorian slaughter. But Sicari never mutilated the dead.

If anything, the brand was more in line with Praetorian practices. But the mark on their cheeks was unlike anything he'd ever seen before. It had taken more than an incredibly sharp blade to carve out the symbol. Great skill and precision had been involved in the creation of the disfiguring brand.

"Are we waiting for something?" Phae's voice held a distinct edge to it, although she managed to inject just the right amount of respect. He nodded toward Emma's house.

"When her visitor leaves, I'm going back for her."

"What do you mean you're going back for her?" she exclaimed. "You're taking her back to the complex?"

"I don't have much of a choice."

"Yes, you do." Phae reached out and grabbed his arm. "This woman isn't Clarissa—"

The moment his sister spoke the name, rage whipped through him. He ignored her gasp of surprise as he visualized her hand being yanked off him. Slowly he turned his head to see her arm held motionless in front of her by an unseen force.

"I love you, Phaedra. But I'm *Legatus* first, your brother second." He ground out the words between clenched teeth as he released his mental hold on her. "Don't forget it again."

"*Il mio signore.*" Dark emotion tightened her voice. "You're not responsible—"

"The *Legatus* is responsible for everyone in their guild *and* for those we endanger. Emma Zale didn't know anything about the *Tyet of Isis* until tonight. That *makes* her my responsibility."

The tense silence between them almost tangible, he rested his elbow against the car window and rubbed his chin with his hand. Clarissa. He closed his eyes against the images flashing in his head. Focus. He needed to focus on his task. Emma Zale needed his protection. Failure wasn't an option.

Down the street he heard a dog barking wildly. Immediately he straightened in his seat then turned the ignition key a notch to clear the windshield with one sweep of the wipers. With his field of vision clear, he saw a figure moving along the sidewalk toward Emma's house. Eyes narrowing, he studied the person heading in their direction.

The sight of a large dog emerging from the shadows on a leash made him relax into his seat. It was a miserable night to walk a dog. Beside him, Phae cleared her throat softly.

"I suppose you're going to have Sandro and Octavia's heads for not being more thorough in their investigation of the Zale woman."

He grunted. "They got sloppy. It tells me we're overdue for some training exercises."

"That will give Lysander something to smile about." A tight note of sarcasm filled her words.

A quick glance at Phae's profile showed she was glowering with irritation. His *Primus Pilus* had always set his sister on edge. She made it her mission to provoke the man at every turn. If Lysander found her insults irritating, he never said a word, which simply made Phae all the more determined to find new ways to annoy him. He wouldn't blame his second-in-command for putting Phae through the ringer when it came time to run exercises.

"Worried he might make things difficult for you?"

"He can try," she said with a snort of derision.

The red flash of the cell phone attached to the dash interrupted their conversation. Leaning forward, he pressed the talk button.

"DeLuca."

"We've got a problem." Lysander's voice echoed out of the car's stereo speakers.

"What is it?" He kept his eyes trained on Emma's front door as he waited for his lieutenant to respond.

"Julian's missing." Lysander rarely displayed emotion, but concern ran under the clipped statement. That alone put Ares on edge. He frowned as he gave the conversation his full attention.

"When did he check in last?"

"Right around five thirty. I sent him to the Gary Airport to pick up a shipment of surveillance equipment."

"Did you get a signal from the truck's GPS?"

"Yes." Lysander hesitated. "It's parked in a warehouse district near the airport."

The terse response knotted his muscles taut with tension as he flicked a brief glare at the phone. Something in Lysander's voice told him his lieutenant hadn't shared everything with him.

"There's more?"

Again, Lysander hesitated. "It's parked only a block away from the Oriental Institute's warehouse."

"*Deus damno id*," he snarled. "He went against my direct order. I told him to stay away from that warehouse until you or I had time to assess the activity levels."

"Octavia hacked into the airport's cargo database. The Institute received some large items from Cairo late this afternoon."

Merda. Knowing Julian, he'd seen something and decided to check it out without permission. He was going to skin the fighter alive when he caught up with the man.

"Can you handle it on your own?" He tensed as he debated whether to leave Emma to an unknown fate for even a brief period of time.

"Thaddeus returned from New York just before dinner, so I'll take him and Bastien with me."

"Good, I'm not finished here," he replied. A long silence drifted out of the phone, and he could easily visualize the stoic look on Lysander's scarred face as he debated asking any additional questions.

"And the *Tyet of Isis*?"

"She doesn't have it." Another quiet pause followed his response.

"I see." Even with such a noncommittal reply, Lysander said a great deal. "As soon as I find Julian, I'll be in touch."

His second-in-command didn't wait for an answer and broke the connection. Fingers wrapped tightly around the SUV's steering wheel, he studied Emma's well-lit front porch. *Christus*, when would Julian learn he couldn't go rogue whenever he got the urge. The Order didn't like it when guild members acted in an unrestrained manner. He knew that from personal experience. But it was more than that. Everyone in the guild knew he despised undisciplined behavior. Julian had the potential to be a great *Legatus*, but his renegade behavior was putting more than just his own life in danger. Now others were involved.

Beside him, Phae sat rigid in her seat with her gaze fixed on the wet road. She and Julian were good friends. At times Ares thought the two of them might even wind up married, but Phae always did something to sidestep the issue when Julian pressured her to take their relationship to the next level.

"He'll be fine, Phae," he said with quiet reassurance. "He's fool-hardy, but he's got good instincts."

She bobbed her head in a sharp nod. Although the tension radiating off her eased somewhat, her lips had thinned with anger. Suddenly he felt sorry for Julian. Phae could be merciless when it came to castigating people, and something told him his sister would have a lot to say to her friend the next time she saw him. Returning his gaze to the front of Emma's house, resignation tightened his mouth.

He had a feeling Emma would have a lot to say to him as well. The sudden memory of her soft curves pressed into his body jolted its way through him. He didn't like the way she made him feel. It made him uneasy to discover his senses were under fire. Not even Clarissa had affected him the way Emma did.

Clarissa. Her death might not rest entirely at his feet, but he'd failed to take appropriate precautions where she was concerned. If he had, she might still be alive. The irony of it all was that the man who'd raped Clarissa before slitting her throat hadn't even been a Praetorian. He'd been just another depraved bastard inflicting random pain on society. It hadn't taken much to hunt the son of a bitch down and rid humanity of one more blight.

But then Clarissa's killer really hadn't stood a chance. Ares's connections had made it easy to find her assailant in less than forty-eight hours. One couldn't be an assassin without knowing people on both sides of the law. Not until the night he caught up with Clarissa's murderer had he ever taken pleasure in a kill. The man had died crying for mercy.

At the time, he hadn't given a damn. He'd only taunted the bas-tard, taken his time splaying him open one piece of flesh at a time, just like a Praetorian would. But now—He dragged in a breath of remorse as the man's terrified face flashed through his head.

He'd overstepped the boundaries of the Sicari code of honor. Not only had he failed to ask the man's forgiveness, he'd killed the man out of revenge and he'd enjoyed hurting the man who'd killed Clarissa. That was something a Sicari *never* did. Phae cleared her throat softly.

"So what are you going to tell her about the Order? The guild?"

"As little as possible. She already knows too much as it is."

"Too much?" Although she took care not to openly confront him, he heard the note of censure in his sister's voice. "Why do I have the feeling you're not telling me everything about Emma Zale?"

The accuracy of Phae's observation made him shift uncomfortably in the seat. Avoiding the penetrating gaze of his sister's violet eyes, he continued to watch for any unusual activity on the street. For some unexplained reason he didn't want to reveal Emma's skill. He trusted Phae implicitly, but something held him back. He wanted Emma to trust him, and that meant keeping her secret until she said otherwise. Remembering what was in his coat pocket, he pulled it out and offered it to his sister.

"Tell me what you make of this."

"What is it?" Phae pulled out a small flashlight from her coat pocket to examine the artifact in the light. A soft gasp echoed out of her as she studied the object. "*Dulis Mater Dei*, another Sicari Lord coin. Where did you get this?"

"It was in Russwin's possessions. Emma doesn't know where he got it. I'll have Sandro review the man's diary to see if he notated finding it."

"And she just gave it to you?" The amazement in her voice made him flex his jaw.

"No." He remembered Emma's display of anger when she realized the coin was missing. Regret nipped at him, and he didn't like it. He'd return the damn thing after the guild had time to study it. Phae sent him an inquisitive look, but didn't question him when he turned his head away from her.

He stared out at the neat row of houses lining the street of Emma's neighborhood. Until Russwin's death last month there had only been one known medallion bearing the Sicari Lord's icon on the back of the coin with the Roman Emperor Constantine on the front. The first one was in a vault in the Order's main headquarters in Genova, Italy. Now there were three.

"Do you think the Zale woman knows anything about the coins?" Phae studied the small antiquity more intently in the beam of her flashlight.

"If she does, she wasn't exactly in the mood to share anything with me."

"If I were her, I suppose I wouldn't have been too happy with you either." His sister released a quiet sound of disgust. "Maybe taking her to our place isn't such a bad idea after all."

This last bit she mumbled beneath her breath, but he heard it just the same. Turning his head, he eyed her chagrined expression. In the glow of her penlight, Phae's face flushed with color. When he didn't say anything, she shrugged.

"Okay, I was wrong. Taking her with us is the right thing to do."

Phae turned off her flashlight and handed the coin back to him. Apologies weren't his sister's forte, and he knew how difficult they were for her to make. For him it was enough she'd admitted being wrong. Now, he just needed to convince Emma to come with him to the safe house. He threw his head back against the headrest in a gesture of frustration. If his gut was anything to go by, he'd find it easier to do battle with a Praetorian than persuading Emma Zale to do something she didn't want to do. Phae had been right. He was going to have Sandro and Octavia's heads.

Chapter 5

FURIOUS, Emma uttered a vicious cry of anger and slammed her fist into the desk one more time. The bastard. How could she have been so stupid? If she ever saw him again, she'd read him the riot act. She closed her eyes and bowed her head as she gripped the edge of the desk. God, she was beginning to think she belonged on a psych ward.

What if she'd dreamed up the coin, the stranger, all of it? It wasn't as if her life had been all that calm and serene of late. Charlie's death could have easily traumatized her to the point she'd gone over the edge. Christ, of course she wasn't crazy. At least not yet. But if that blond Lucifer showed up again, she'd—

"Is there anything wrong, my dear?"

Ewan's voice echoed behind her, and she jumped with surprise. As she saw the look of concern on his face, she waved her hand and shook her head.

"I'm fine. Well, at least I think I'm fine," she said in disgust. "The coin is missing. I left it right here on my desk earlier, and now it's gone."

"Perhaps it's buried underneath all these papers."

Ewan stepped forward and started to riffle through the things on her desk. For some reason, his actions annoyed her deeply. Leaning forward, she grasped his wrist and squeezed. The way her fingers gripped Ewan's arm reminded her of the stranger and how easily he'd controlled her. The memory of how he'd manipulated her made her uneasy. She'd been powerless to stop him, and she didn't like feeling helpless.

"It's not on the desk, Ewan." She sighed as she released his arm. With a frown she stared down at the cluttered desk made worse by her friend's haphazard search. Her desk hadn't been immaculate, but the cipher she'd buried under a stack of papers was now in plain view. Ewan made a noise of interest as he spotted the notepaper. Not really understanding why, Emma quickly reached for the coded message and tucked it into her jeans pocket. She looked up to see him arch his brow at her.

"That looked rather interesting."

"It's just a cipher Dad made for me," she murmured with an apologetic glance in his direction. "I found it earlier this evening."

"Ah, yes. I remember him telling me about the puzzles he designed for you."

"It's been a long time since I've had one to decipher, and that makes this one special." Her breath hitched as she accepted the finality of the words.

Ewan lightly touched her shoulder. "It's quite all right, my dear. I understand. As for the coin, it will turn up soon enough."

"I suppose you're right."

Without any protest, she allowed him to guide her out of the study. For once, Ewan was wrong. The medallion wasn't going to turn up unless the stranger came back. He'd been spinning a tale bigger than the Pyramids. Hell, even Charlie, for all his storytelling skills, couldn't top the stranger's believability. And she had believed him—all that BS about her being in danger—it had been nothing more than a scam to get the coin. Well, maybe not all of it. His ability seemed real enough.

"I believe you need another drink." Ewan interrupted her thoughts as he guided her out into the hall and toward the foyer. "In fact, I'm going to leave you to get quite trollied. It will help you get a solid night's sleep. Something I'm certain you haven't gotten in a number of weeks. Am I correct?"

"God, I hate your arrogance sometimes, Ewan." She brushed off his fatherly touch. "Especially when you're right."

She muttered this last bit, which made him chuckle. "I understand it can be difficult to put up with me, my dear Emma, but I have nothing but your best interests at heart."

"I know that, and I'm grateful."

They came to a halt in the foyer and Ewan took his coat off the rack. He shrugged into the garment and turned to face her. With a nod toward the whiskey bottle on the coffee table, he eyed her sternly.

"Then heed my advice. Alcohol is an excellent sedative and my guess is you could stand a good night's sleep given the circles under your eyes."

"Flattery will get you everywhere," she said in disgust.

"Don't be snide," he said. "You need sleep. As for Stuart, I'll talk to him. I might as well use my clout for something. The man's a fool to think you belong in the classroom."

She smiled at the umbrage in her friend's voice as she opened the front door for him. The two men had despised each other for years. "Thank you, Ewan—for everything. It means a lot."

"With your parents gone, and now Charles, I feel the need to mother you a bit." He pressed a light kiss to her brow. "I'll call you Monday after I've talked with Stuart. I'm actually looking forward to verbally castrating the man."

"Why do I have the feeling you're taking Stuart on just because you want to humiliate the man as opposed to keeping me out of the classroom?"

His shoulders rolled in a gesture of scholarly refinement as he settled his trim Fedora on his head. "I confess to a certain amount of perverse anticipation at the thought of eviscerating the man with words. Not even that pretentious Roberta Young would provide me with as much entertainment."

"What is it with you and that woman? Charlie didn't care for her either."

"She's an amateur." Ewan's exaggerated shudder made her bite back a smile as he puffed out a breath of disgust. "Little more than a hobbyist playing at archeology."

"I think you underestimate her, Ewan. She's got a knack for digging. Charlie refused to admit it and Mike is the same way."

"It's the fact that she's not qualified that I object to. No matter how *good* she might be at digging, there are others far more qualified to be on that excavation site. She's there because she bought herself a position on that dig with her obscene wealth, not because she knows what she's doing."

"I still think you're wrong."

"Perhaps, but nothing changes the fact that my tryst with Stuart will be much more cathartic than dealing with Roberta Young. Dueling verbally with Stuart will be like picking the wings off a fly."

"God help Stuart." She chuckled at her friend's acerbic wit.

"Precisely, my dear," he said with a wily grin. "I'll talk to you on Monday."

With one last smile at her, Ewan strode out of the house and down the sidewalk to where he'd parked his car on the street. Her gaze swept over the front lawn then up and down the block as far as she could see. Everything looked normal, and yet she didn't feel normal at all. Every one of her senses seemed wound tight and poised to startle her.

With a nonchalance she didn't really possess, she waved good night to Ewan once more before retreating inside. The front door closed, and she threw the dead bolt into its chamber with a nagging sense of foreboding. Maybe she should consider buying a gun. She shivered as she remembered the sensation of death that had enveloped her when she'd touched the coin in the stranger's hand. No. She didn't want a gun. What she wanted was another good swig of whiskey.

She marched back into the living room and poured herself a strong shot of the liquor. It burned on the way down, but she didn't care. Ewan was right—she needed to get good and drunk. But she needed music to do it by. Drink in hand, she headed toward the CD tower beside the stereo system. In less than a minute, the sultry voice of LeAnn Rimes filled the room. Emma drank the remaining alcohol in her glass then closed her eyes and allowed the music to wash over her like a gentle wave.

As the words of the song floated around her, an image of her dark, mysterious visitor took hold in her head. No, that description didn't exactly match—not with that short, dark blond hair of his. The style gave him that bad boy look. On second thought, his eyes did that. The color of the lake during a bad storm, they'd glinted with a variety of emotions. But it had been the occasional wicked amusement dancing in his eyes that had made her heart flip-flop.

At five-foot-eight, Emma was used to being close to eye level with most of the men she came into contact with, but the stranger had easily topped six feet, forcing her to look up at him whenever he got too close. Too close? She could have absorbed him into her body if he'd been any closer. She could still feel his hard body against hers. And he had a great body. Solid and muscular, he obviously worked out regularly.

Her eyes flew open, and she shook her head in a ridiculous effort to clear her thoughts. Okay so the guy turned her on. There weren't many men she found herself attracted to. Of course, most men she worked with were older. More along the lines of Ewan's age. There weren't too many History Channel babes like Josh Bernstein running around Egypt or the hallways of the Oriental Institute.

For that matter, there weren't too many men her age period out in the desert. At least not any that interested her. But the stranger had piqued her interest. Something that didn't make her happy at all. She hated to admit it, but his kiss had been the hottest thing she'd tasted in a long time. The devil in her shrugged with defiance. Why shouldn't she enjoy the feel of his mouth against hers? There was nothing wrong with a harmless kiss.

Who was she kidding? Harmless? That had to be the understatement of the year. There hadn't been a damn thing harmless about that kiss. She'd been wet with heat the moment his tongue had teased hers. And she couldn't remember the last time she'd kissed a man and wanted more. A whole lot more. No, that kiss hadn't been even remotely safe or sedate. It had held a promise of dangerous passion and pleasure.

God, she needed another belt of whiskey. In less than three seconds, she was filling her glass with another generous portion of
liquor. Not bothering to sip the drink, she simply tossed it back in
one gulp. Fire streamed down her throat, and she coughed violently.
Damn, she needed to remember this stuff was a hell of a lot stronger
than the Stella beer she always drank at the dig.

When her coughing spasm ended, she realized nothing had
changed. The whiskey was doing little to drown out the memory of
being in the stranger's arms or how good she'd felt. No, better than
good. She wouldn't have protested one bit if he'd pushed his advantage. Hell, she'd as much as said she wouldn't object. Caressing him
with the intimacy of a lover had been an open invitation if ever she'd
given one. Her stomach lurched at the memory.

His erection had been hard and full against her palm. The sudden image of him sliding into her tugged a small groan from her
throat. She might be going crazy, but she couldn't think of a more
pleasurable way to go insane. A rush of liquid heat dampened her
panties. How could somebody she didn't know, someone who'd broken into her home and held her against her will, make her feel so
hot and needy? And he'd been right. She had kissed him willingly. It
didn't help matters that she wanted a repeat of that kiss.

She tried to block out everything she remembered, but failed. Even
his scent still filled her senses. The strength of it almost made her
think he'd returned. But with her eyes wide open, she knew better.
He'd smelled clean and woodsy—as if he spent a lot of time outdoors.
But it had been more than that. The raw earthiness of his scent had
aroused a primal response in her. A dangerous sensation that could
easily burn her. But then everything about him screamed danger.

Desperate to change the direction of her thoughts, she reached
into her pocket and pulled out the crumpled piece of paper. Here
was something to occupy her for quite some time. She eyed the
hieroglyphs on the sheet with bittersweet emotion. She missed her
parents, but finding the cipher helped ease her grief somewhat. This
was something tangible that made her feel they weren't gone from
her life completely. She grabbed a pad and pencil off a nearby table,
then kicking off her shoes, she sat cross-legged on the floor in front
of the coffee table.

The bold strokes of her father's handwriting made her pause as she stared down at the paper in front of her. She'd learned her first cipher at the age of eight. Her father had taught her using Julius Caesar's method for hiding messages. It was a special pastime she'd shared with her dad. He would write a hidden message for her, and she had to decipher it. As she grew older, the ciphers became harder.

She trailed her fingertip across the top row of glyphs and frowned. This cipher's complexity surpassed all the others her father had devised for her to solve. Even with her extensive knowledge of hieroglyphics, it wouldn't be easy to solve this particular puzzle. Hell, she wasn't even sure she *could* break it.

"Horus" had always been the key word her dad had used for the ciphers she solved. She studied the ancient script for a few minutes then started translating the text one word at a time. After only five minutes, she realized her father had used a different key word. Not knowing the key word didn't make it impossible to solve, but the difficulty level had gone up at least ten notches.

She rolled the pencil back and forth between her fingers as she stared down at the hieroglyphs. For some odd reason, instinct told her this cipher had been a last resort type of thing for her father. He'd designed it with her in mind, but somehow she didn't think he'd ever thought she'd be deciphering it.

Of course, he wouldn't think it likely. She blinked her eyes and swallowed hard. Dad had always been an optimist. Every time she'd balked at touching a newly found artifact, he would ask her to imagine the worst thing that could happen. When she couldn't think of something terrible, she always knew she'd have to touch the object just to tell him what it told her.

Although he'd never forced her to handle the artifacts he and her mother had found, she'd always feel bad when she refused. Although he always hid it, she could feel his disappointment whenever she objected. Like any other kid, she'd just wanted to please her parents.

Thunder boomed outside and Emma jumped at the sound. The thought of a power outage sent a shiver through her. She was terrified of the dark. Had been ever since the age of seven when she'd been trapped in a tomb for several hours until her father had found her. She scowled at the liquor bottle in front of her. There had been times when she'd prayed really hard that her parents would make some big discovery and they could come home to Chicago for good. But even when they'd found something of merit, they remained in the field. It had been in their blood.

Hers, too, if she really admitted it. When she completed her undergrad degree, she'd suddenly realized her entire track had been geared toward an anthropology degree and then the archeology graduate program. It had not been a pleasant awakening, particularly because of her ability. But the one thing she tried to do was avoid using her special talent. Her parents had always encouraged her to use her gift, but she'd always seen it as a liability.

She hated touching old things—experiencing all the pain and suffering that came with each new artifact she touched. There were times during her childhood that she'd wondered if it wasn't her special talent her parents loved more than her. Deep down she knew it had been unfair to think that. Her parents had loved her very much and she'd had a reasonably happy childhood. But they hadn't hesitated to use her ability when it suited them.

And Charlie. His death had simply brought all the emotions she'd managed to bury deep inside her right back up to the surface. Grief crushed against her chest like a heavy weight. In seconds, sobs wracked her as she leaned over the table and buried her head in her arms. Even five years hadn't blotted out the bitterness of her parents' loss.

The heat of her tears still warmed her skin as she finally lifted her head and reached for her whiskey glass. Obviously, the whiskey was beginning to work its charms. No one would ever accuse her of being a happy drunk. Blue and morose were more her trademarks when she drank too much. Choking back a sob, she took another drink of the amber-colored liquid.

The whiskey went down smooth this time as she dragged the back of her hand across her face to wipe tears off her cheeks. She hated it when she cried. She reached for a tissue and tugged one free of the box as she stared down at the cipher.

What word beside "Horus" would her dad have used for the puzzle? Sicari? Nope, too obvious. Her name or her mom's name.

Again, too blatant. They'd originally chosen Horus as a key word when she was a kid. It had been the first Egyptian god she remembered. Horus and then his rival, Seth. She grew still. Could it be that simple?

Comparing the word to her hastily drawn Vigenère table, she translated the first sentence in less than a minute. She grimaced at the results. This puzzle was growing more bizarre by the minute. Her dad always made the translations of his ciphers educational, and *"trust no one with this secret"* certainly didn't sound like the beginning of a history lesson. Maybe "Seth" wasn't the right key word after all or she'd screwed up the transliterations of the hieroglyphs. Carefully, she examined the first line again. When her translation didn't change, she shrugged. If the second line of the code didn't make sense, then she'd have to start over. The transliteration of the hieroglyphs moved quickly, and when she compared the results to the Vigenère table, she grew rigid with shock.

Any other time, the translation would have meant nothing to her. She would have never recognized the significance of the words staring back at her—*Tyet of Isis*. The pencil slipped out of her numb fingers as she studied her translation. What was the *Tyet of Isis*, and how in the hell had her father known about it?

The sudden howl of a cat outside made her jump to her feet in reaction even as she heard the cat's cry die in an abrupt fashion. In her scramble to stand up she viciously stubbed her toe against the leg of the coffee table.

"Damn it to hell!" She hopped a couple of steps to the left as her toe throbbed. "That'll teach me for taking off my shoes. God that hurts."

Still nursing her injured toe, her sideways movement allowed her to see through the darkened kitchen all the way to the back door. She froze as a flash of lightning lit up the back door stoop. Jesus Christ, what the hell was that? Her heart thundered to a halt before it began to pump with the furor of a freight train at full speed. She blinked her eyes and waited for another flash of lightning. When it came, she screamed as the brief flare of light lit up the hooded figure standing outside the kitchen door.

For a moment, she stood there totally unable to move. Oh God,

Charlie's killer had found her. The description all the workers had given the Cairo police was a damn good match of the person standing at her back door. She looked toward the phone and then the table. The cipher. She didn't know why it popped in her head, she simply reacted. Leaping forward, she grunted in pain as she scooped up the papers containing the puzzle and her translation then fled the living room.

Behind her the sound of the storm outside grew louder. Jesus, he was in the house. Terror propelled her down the hall to the office. The throbbing in her toe made it difficult to run without pain, but she managed to cover the distance quickly. Slamming the study door closed behind her, she turned the skeleton key and pulled it out of the lock. She stared at the lock for a fleeting moment and remembered how easily her other visitor had gotten into the house. Her gaze jerked toward the tall, wooden statue of the Egyptian sun god, Ra, her mother had found in a Cairo bazaar. In seconds, she'd wedged the carved figure under the doorknob to brace the door shut.

Hopefully Ra would live up to his all-powerful reputation and keep the intruder at bay, but she didn't feel like testing that theory. She needed to get out of the house. She flipped the light switch off and plunged herself into darkness. The old terror crept through her and chilled her skin. Shoving the notes she carried into her jeans pocket, she stumbled forward. Hands outstretched, she made her way to the window that overlooked the garden. Lightning flashed again, and her stomach lurched with incredible violence as she thought she saw someone move outside.

She darted to the side of the window and pressed her back into the wall. She squeezed her eyes shut to gather her courage. Had the son of a bitch brought friends? Cautiously, she chanced a quick peek out the window. Below her, the garden was dark, but not as dark as the office. Light from neighboring houses created a dim glow in the backyard. Her gaze searched the grounds for any sign of movement, but found nothing. Still breathing heavily with fear, her breath warmed the glass panes. It surprised her. How could she be freezing and still have enough warm air in her lungs to fog up the window? If she weren't ready to throw up, it might be funny. The hall floor creaked softly. Someone was headed toward the office.

In the dark, she couldn't see the doorknob, but she heard someone testing it. To hell with this, she'd take her chances outside. At least out there one of the neighbors might hear her if she screamed. Not caring how much noise she made, she struggled with the wooden window. It screeched upward slowly, and she heard the sound of wood splintering behind her as someone tried to force his way past the locked door. The solid statue of Ra held fast against the hard pounding from the other side.

Desperate now, she tried to force the window higher, but it wouldn't budge. Behind her, the door hinges protested loudly. Terrified, she slammed the base of her palms up against the top frame of the window. The force of her blow sent her right hand sliding off the wooden frame and straight through the glass. Stunned, she simply stared at her hand sticking through the broken pane, the rain dancing off her fingers.

Trembling, she saw dark rivulets of blood dripping off her hand. Getting drunk obviously had analgesic purposes as well. Suddenly, dizziness combined with her nausea. Even with the liquor deadening her senses, her hand still hurt. On fire would have been a more accurate description, and every drop of rain that hit the cut stung like a bee. She drew in a ragged breath as the office door screeched a protest against the attack coming from the other side.

Struggling to remain conscious, she tried to navigate her hand past a tall shard of glass. When she couldn't, she started to cry. Goddamn it, what was wrong with her? Crying wouldn't save her life. With a sob, she used her free fist to land a quick blow to the middle of the shard. As the glass broke away from the window, she pulled her hand back inside. She swayed on her feet then bent over and slid the upper half of her body through the window's narrow opening.

With a grunt of pain, she slammed her back into the sash to send it crashing upward. In that same instant, she heard the terrible scream of wood ripping away from the door hinges. She couldn't remember exactly how she made it through the window. But in seconds, she found herself lying on the ground. Already soaked from the rain, she scrambled to her feet.

She couldn't see the blood soaking the sleeve of her sweater, but she knew what she was feeling wasn't rain. It was too sticky. The

ugly memory of Charlie's blood coating her fingers rose to the surface. Brutally, she tossed the thought aside. There wasn't time to
dwell on the past if she was going to survive the night. As fast as she
could, she ran toward the back of the garden. A stone bit into the
bottom of her foot. In the back of her mind, she screamed angrily at
herself for removing her shoes. Lightning filled the sky again, and
without thinking, she glanced over her shoulder.

The sight of a figure leaping out of the office window nearly
stopped her heart. Survival mode sent her bolting past the garden
gate into the alley. There were dozens of places in the narrow lane
where she could hide. Better yet, maybe one of her neighbors had
forgotten to lock the entrance to their backyard.

Emma tried the first gate she came to. Locked. Racing onward,
she grabbed the next gate with her good hand and shook the iron
scrolled barrier wildly. It didn't budge. Enough with thinking she'd
find refuge in someone else's garden. She needed to just run. If she
made it to the street, she stood a better chance of someone passing
by who could help her.

Pain lashed at her soles as she charged forward along the road's
gravel surface. She had almost reached the side street when she
stumbled over a small hole. Her foot twisted out from underneath
her, and she pitched forward. Without thinking, her hands stretched
out in front of her in an instinctive reaction to save herself.

Gravel bit into the cut on her hand, and she struggled not to faint
as her stomach heaved with a sickening lurch at the intense pain.
In the back of her mind, a part of her found it odd that she hadn't
screamed. For a moment, she lay there as her body sent wave after
wave of nausea pouring over her. Then the honk of a horn out in the
street pulled her back to her senses. Panic sent her clambering to her
feet, and she tried to run. Her ankle almost gave way beneath her.

Crying in earnest now, Emma dragged in deep breaths of air
as she staggered forward in an attempt to put as much distance
between her and the man chasing her. She'd passed at least three
houses when she heard him behind her. Unable to stop herself, she
looked over her shoulder. Lightning lit up the world around her, and
with a scream, she sank to her knees in defeat.

Thunder drowned out her shout of terror as she watched her

relentless pursuer stride toward her. His dark cloak streaming out behind him, the man epitomized everything her childhood had taught her about the angel of death. Rain glistened on a sword he carried out to the side of him. This was the man the locals had described leaving the scene of Charlie's murder. Oh God, she was going to die just like her parents and Charlie. The man would slit her throat, and she didn't even know why.

Chapter 6

ONE hand rubbing his chin, Ares watched Emma wave goodbye to her friend before disappearing back into the house. Beside him, Phae made a soft sound. His gaze flicking in her direction, he frowned.

"What?"

"I'm sensing something." She leaned forward to study the man as he walked around to the driver's side of the car. With a slight shrug, she shook her head. "No, I guess not."

"You're certain?"

Frowning, he sent her a sharp look. While there were a few Sicari women with telekinetic abilities, most of them had intuitive abilities that covered a wide spectrum. Phae had inherited their mother's healing and sensory abilities, but her healing abilities were unparalleled. Her gift made her a valuable member of his guild. She grimaced as she shook her head.

"No, it was nothing. Sorry. I'm just a bit on edge right now."

He nodded. Whatever had made her nervous was affecting him, too. Something didn't feel right. His gut told him that and his gut was never wrong. Impatiently, he waited for Emma's visitor to start his car and leave. The sooner the old man left, the better. If getting

Emma to safety meant extreme measures, he'd do it. And he sure as hell didn't need some aging Galahad interfering with his plans.

Minutes seemed like hours as the man started his car then disappeared down the length of the street and around the corner. Determined to avoid any surprises, he deliberately waited another twenty minutes, just in case Emma's friend decided to return. When he was ready, he reached out with his thoughts and popped the bulb in the streetlight one car away. An instant later Emma's front porch light winked out, followed by the porch lights of several neighboring houses.

A quiet hiss of air escaped Phae's lips. "What the—you didn't do that, did you?"

"No," he said in a grim voice. The only light he'd extinguished was the streetlamp. From the look on his sister's face, he knew she'd sensed a threat nearby. The question was who?

"It's the same presence I sensed a few minutes ago."

"It can't be a Praetorian." He didn't voice the other possibility. If it was a rogue warrior—no, there hadn't been any reports of a rogue Sicari in the guild's vicinity.

"Whoever it is, they're powerful, and they're close." Phae's voice held a note of worry. "Maybe we should call for backup."

"If this person is that strong, I don't want to wait."

With a quick movement, he exited the SUV and discarded his jacket. Seconds later, his hand grasped the smooth leather grip of his weapon from beneath the driver seat. In a quick movement, he pulled the sword from its sheath. It was the weapon of an assassin. The solid weight of the *Condottiere* blade once used by his great-grandfather provided him with a sense of comfort. The old ways were deeply ingrained in the Sicari. Anyone could take a life with a gun, but it required strength and great skill to do it with a sword. It was the one thing the Praetorians and Sicari had in common, but nothing more.

Beneath his black turtleneck shirt, his skin tightened as the crisp fall air and light rain penetrated the knit fabric. A quick upward glance assured him cloud cover and the lack of outdoor lighting would keep their movements virtually undetected. He gestured toward the right side of Emma's house as Phae joined him from the opposite side of the SUV with a small broadsword in her hand.

"Take the—"

A muted scream pierced the darkness. The distant cry slid through his head like a sword scraping against metal, sharp and pure. Those untrained in the Sicari way would never have heard the sound. Lightning lit up the sky and another clap of thunder drowned out the shriek completely. He didn't finish his command. He simply raced down the street toward Emma's house. Charging through the shadows along the sidewalk, he turned and followed the tall hedge separating Emma's yard from her next-door neighbor.

Small splashes of water from the soaked earth flew up and over his leather boots as he raced around the back corner of the house. Another flash of lightning illuminated the yard. The sight of the broken office window pulled him to a slippery halt. Shards of glass lay scattered on the ground. Broken from the inside. Ice slid down his spine. Had she broken it herself or had someone else? Another shrill cry ripped through the air.

The alley.

At a full sprint, he bolted toward the rear of the garden and charged through the open gate into the alley. Opening all of his senses to everything around him, he waited for the smallest noise or scent that would lead him to Emma. The rain made it difficult to see as he came to a halt and looked in both directions. From where he stood, he saw headlights from a car as it passed by the alley. *Merda*, where the hell was she?

Lightning lit up the narrow lane, and he drew in a harsh breath. Crumpled in a heap on the ground, Emma had her hand raised in a defensive manner. The tall, cloaked figure towering over her caught him off guard for a moment.

Praetorian warriors no longer dressed as their religious order once had. A flash of light from the heavens lit up the silver blade at the man's side. *Mater Dei*. Whether the man was a Praetorian or not, his sword made his intentions clear.

Ares launched himself into a dead run. Adrenaline pumped furiously through his veins. Because of it, he ran faster than he ever thought possible. In seconds, he eliminated the distance between him and Emma's attacker. As if expecting him, the man suddenly turned and swung his sword through the air in a familiar move. Then a solid, yet invisible, push knocked him off balance.

Sicari. The bastard was a Sicari.

The warrior's blade whipped through the air in a series of small arcs. He ducked as the man's sword whispered across the top of his head. Probably taking a few hairs with it. Not that it mattered. He needed a trim anyway. The moment he visualized his foot landing a solid punch to his opponent's stomach, the man grunted.

In little more than a heartbeat, he found himself on the defensive again. His opponent's blade flew downward in a stroke filled with deadly purpose. Only years of training kept the sword from splitting his head open and killing him instantly. As he twisted his body sideways, he visualized knocking his opponent's sword out of the way. The man's mental abilities rebuffed his attempt and the blade bit into his upper arm as an unseen foot planted itself squarely in his ribs.

Growling loudly in pain, he dodged the fighter's second strike. Blood soaked his shirt, and his arm hurt like hell. *Merda*. This guy seemed invincible. Worse, he could already feel his own mental ability beginning to fade. If he didn't do something fast, he'd be dead.

The Sicari fighter's sword whipped effortlessly through the air in yet another skillful sweep. This time the blade headed straight for his jugular. Another move Ares knew well. He could have been fighting himself. Their swords glided off each other in a spray of sparks. An uneasy feeling shot through him.

There was something very different about this man. He couldn't quite put his finger on it. The man fought like a Sicari, but not like any fighter in the Order he'd met over the years. The hooded cloak he wore didn't help matters either. An opponent's eyes always revealed something, but he couldn't see this man's face. That increased the difficulty in battling him.

"Do not interfere in that which you do not understand, DeLuca." The man's voice rang out flat and without emotion.

How in the hell did the bastard know his name? Ignoring the

warning, he centered himself and threw his sword up to block the man's swing. Steel scraped along steel until their blades met at the hilt. Even up close, his opponent's expression remained hidden in the dark folds of his hood.

He threw a large portion of his mental strength into his effort to push the Sicari away from him, and the man retreated a small measure. *Christus*. This guy had abilities that made him look like an untrained Sicari. Suddenly the fighter released one hand from his sword and drove a fist into Ares's injured arm. *Merda*. That was a Praetorian tactic. The pain sent him to his knees. This time a very real and solid foot slammed into his side. Swallowing the bile rising in his throat, he used his ability to roll effortlessly away from the brutal attack then struggled to his feet.

His reaction time had slowed almost to a crawl, and he barely blocked the blade about to split his skull. With a loud grunt, he somersaulted past the man on his good side and almost landed on top of Emma. He didn't look to see whether she was conscious or not. It wouldn't matter if he wound up dead. Gritting his teeth, he forced himself to clear his head of everything but the sword in his hand.

It was time to end this. Determination swept through his body as he sprang to his feet in a battle-ready position. The fighter raised his weapon in a familiar move, and Ares prepared to counter the attack. Then in a flash of movement, the Sicari warrior unexpectedly changed the direction of the sword's arc. Caught off guard, Ares leaped backward just in time. Still, the tip of the other man's blade sliced through his sweater and bit into his chest.

Fotte. Who *was* this bastard?

Leaping to one side, he swung his own sword in retaliation and barely missed the man's shoulder. "Barely" wouldn't keep him alive for much longer. His breaths coming loud and hard, he watched as the man suddenly straightened and then leaped past him.

In response to his opponent's surprise move, Ares whirled around expecting the fighter to come at him from a different angle. But like a magician, the unknown assailant had disappeared into the night. Several seconds passed before he realized the Sicari had given up.

What the—? Sicari never ran. Not to mention the man had been winning. He looked down at his chest. His sweater hung open, exposing the deep cut the Sicari fighter had made. Hell, in just a few more seconds he would have been dead. Why would the warrior run now?

He spun around at a soft sound echoing behind him. As he saw Phae running toward him, he lowered his weapon. Had the bastard heard his sister approaching before him? He grunted. Later. He'd sort it out later.

Reassured that Phae had his back, he handed his sword to her and crouched at Emma's side to examine her for injuries. He lifted her arm and grimaced at the gash at the base of her palm. Now he knew who'd broken the office window. She stirred beneath his touch. Gently, he pushed wet strands of hair off her face.

"Emma. Can you tell me where you're hurt?" Carefully, so as not to cause her further injury, he shifted her onto her back and examined her other arm.

A soft moan echoed out of her as he ran his hands over her right leg and brushed his fingertips over her ankle. *Christus*, with the swelling in her ankle, he'd be surprised if it wasn't broken. Returning his attention back to her face, he lightly patted his hand against her cheek.

"Emma. Answer me," he commanded.

Her forehead wrinkled in a frown of pain as her eyes fluttered open. Panic lingered in her expression as she glanced around with several frantic jerks of her head. As she slowly realized she was safe for the moment, her gaze returned to his face. The recognition dawning in her eyes hardened into a cold stare.

"*You.*"

"I said I'd be back for you, Emma. I'm going to take you someplace where you'll be safe," he said quietly.

"Safe from whom? You or the Obi Wan character who just tried to kill me."

"We would have been here sooner, but we were delayed."

"We?" Her elbow pressed into the gravel as she looked over her shoulder at Phae. Panic flashed across her face. "Oh God, more swords. Who *are* you people?"

She struggled up into a sitting position and shook off his attempt to help her. With her good hand, she wiped rain out of her eyes and pushed her wet hair off her face. A streak of mud marked her cheek and she looked in need of a strong shoulder to cry on. The muscles in his body that didn't ache grew hard with tension. When in the hell had he become the guild's poster boy for knights in shining armor?

"At least you're still capable of asking questions." He baited her as he remembered her earlier sarcasm about his ability to walk out of her office.

"Don't you dare mock me, you thief."

"You'll get it back." He clenched his teeth with irritation. He didn't like the way her acid accusation made him feel. "That damn coin is the least of your worries."

"*Worries?* Anybody ever tell you, you've got a knack for understatements?" She arched her eyebrows.

"Which is why we need to get you to safety," he snapped.

"There *is* no 'we' in this conversation." She blinked as rain ran down her face in rivulets. Lifting her injured hand, she peered at it in the dim light and blanched. "What I need is a hospital because I'm going to need stitches."

"I have every intention of seeing that your injuries are treated."

"I think you need to take care of yourself first before you worry about me." She nodded her head toward his chest. "I'm not the only one in need of sutures."

"Then stop arguing with me, and let's get on with it."

"Look, whatever your name is, I'm grateful you saved my life, or at least I think you did, but I—"

"Ares DeLuca."

"What?" She stared at him as if he'd suddenly sprouted a new head.

"My name. It's Ares DeLuca."

"The god of War?" She snickered with sarcastic disbelief. "You've *got* to be joking."

"Hardly, although my friends find it a constant source of amusement."

...ot laughing," she said sharply as she tried to stand.

...iled miserably and tumbled backward into a muddy puddle. Frustration mixed with pain swept across her face as she burst into tears. He crept forward on his haunches and caught her chin in his hand.

With a tug, she tried to free herself from his grasp, but failed. If possible, her tears fell harder now. *Dulce matris.* He never had been able to handle a woman crying. It always reminded him of Phae and how she'd cried for months after their parents' murders. He winced.

"It'll be all right, Emma," he murmured. "I promise you. It will be all right."

"Just leave me alone," she yelled at him over the thunder rumbling above their heads. "I don't need your sympathy, okay. Just leave me alone."

Her sobs tugged at him in a way he didn't like at all. Damn it to hell. They didn't have time for this. She could protest all she wanted, but she was damn well going with him. They had more than the Praetorians to worry about now. The rogue warrior he'd just fought had changed the rules of the game, and he didn't have a clue as to what might come next.

Scooping her up into his arms, he stood upright. The action made his arm and chest protest viciously. Emma's gasp of outrage didn't surprise him, but he ignored it. Instead, he gritted his teeth against the pain streaking through his body. *Merda*, he couldn't remember the last time he hurt this bad. He was used to walking away with just a few scrapes and bruises. It had been a long time since he'd fought anyone with skills equaling his own.

"*Il mio signore*, you're injured," his sister exclaimed in a loud protest. Springing forward, she touched his hand. A familiar tingle raced up his arm and eased the pain in his upper arm. "Let me help her walk to the car."

"*My lord*? Fancy title for a thief." Another hiccup followed Emma's softly muttered sarcasm. He grimaced. He'd forgotten her résumé listed one of her foreign languages as Italian. He sent her a dark scowl before he looked at his sister.

"I'm fine." He met the concern in Phae's eyes and shook his

head. "Bring the car around to the end of the alley, Phae. And let Doc know he needs to meet us at the apartment. You're not going to be up to healing us both."

"But if the warrior—"

"Do you still sense him?" His sharp rebuke made Phae shake her head. "Then go."

Aggravation flashed across his sister's face before she sprinted away. He followed at a slower pace, his body protesting every step he took.

"Put me down." Although Emma tried to make her words a command, her sniffling marred the effort. He quirked an eyebrow at her.

"No."

"*No?*" Disbelief and indignation echoed in her voice.

"Do you really want to go there?"

"But I—"

"Enough," he growled. "Not another word, Emma. I'm having one hell of a night, so don't piss me off."

He watched her swallow hard as she debated whether to provoke his wrath. After a short deliberation, she nodded her acceptance of his command. At the same time, she murmured something unintelligible beneath her breath. He shot her a warning look, and she released a sigh of disgust. Satisfaction glided through him at her capitulation.

The faint whiff of whiskey drifted beneath his nose, and it created a sudden longing for a shot of bourbon. Liquor would help take the edge off his pain. Every part of him ached. Fire had replaced the numbness in his chest, while his arm throbbed from the added strain of carrying Emma. The slight healing touch Phae had performed on him had already begun to wear off.

Calling on the last of his mental reserves, he shifted Emma's soft frame so the invisible sling his mind formed beneath her legs could ease some of the strain on his shoulder. A small measure of relief pushed through him as a result. Maybe he should have let Phae help Emma get to the Durango. In the back of his head, a small voice laughed.

Without hesitating, he slammed the door on the mocking sound.

He didn't want to contemplate the reason for the laughter. He just wanted to enjoy Emma's warmth melting into him. Wanted to relish the softness of her body pressing into his. All of it distracted him from his pain. And there were other things about her that helped him ignore the dull throbbing in his chest and shoulder. That plump lower lip of hers reminded him of a succulent raspberry. Dark red, just the way he liked his berries—sweet and juicy.

"I'm going mad," she whispered as if speaking to herself.

The soft statement made him ache to ease the fear and loneliness he heard in her voice. A sudden urge to kiss her fear away swept through him. *Christus.* He needed to watch himself around this woman. Letting himself get too close to her meant trouble. And her kind of trouble he didn't need. He grunted with pain as he reached the end of the alley.

"You're not crazy, Emma."

"Of course I'm crazy." Her head sagged down onto his uninjured shoulder. "Nobody fights with swords anymore."

"My body disagrees with you," he said with a touch of amusement.

When she didn't answer, he looked down to see her eyes closed. "Vulnerable" and "sweet" were the first two words that popped into his head. He gritted his teeth at the emotion she aroused in him. Where the hell was Phae?

The sound of a car wheeling sharply around the corner caught his ear. Turning his head, he watched as the Durango stopped dead on a dime in front of him. Phae threw the car into park before she got out to open the rear passenger door for him. As he set Emma down on the seat, her eyes fluttered open.

"My dad knew about your *Tyet of Isis*, you know."

The slurred words made him freeze. Damn, but the woman knew how to mess with his head. He stared down at her pale features illuminated by the streetlight a short distance away. Despite the pain and shock mirrored in her glazed expression, he could still see the feisty woman he'd met earlier. With a nod, he pulled away from her.

"We'll talk about it later."

Shutting the door of the car, he watched as she leaned her head back onto the seat and closed her eyes again. Phae released a soft sound of annoyance.

"I suppose it's a good thing she was drinking. Helps control the pain level."

"I'm going to sit in the back with her."

"Fine."

Her clipped response tugged a frown to his mouth, but he didn't reply. Instead, he circled the car to climb into the backseat. He couldn't remember the last time he'd felt so drained. No, not drained. Worried. Everything in his body clamored for something he couldn't or didn't want to name. It clawed at him and challenged every lucid thought he possessed. He reassured himself that it was just the pain. He'd be fine once Doc had worked his magic and then he'd sleep. Just a few hours' sleep and he'd be back to normal. Soft laughter echoed in the back of his head once more. Something told him normal had ceased to exist.

HALF-DRUNK and exhausted, Emma jerked awake as the SUV streaked along the highway. Eyes closed, Ares sat next to her with his head reclined against his headrest. When he'd set her down in the backseat of the car, the woman with him had gently touched the back of her injured hand.

A small electric shock had raced across her skin, and in seconds, the pain in her hand had lessened. Even her ankle didn't hurt as badly. When he and the woman had argued in the alley, she remembered him mentioning something about healing. Odds were the woman had some strange power, just like Ares. But at the moment, Emma didn't feel like asking questions or placing bets. She'd had more than enough excitement for one night. She just wanted a doctor to stitch up her hand and give her enough Darvocet to keep her unconscious for a week. Slowly, her head drooped again.

Minutes later, she jerked awake, drawing in a sharp breath. Oh God, they were on Lower Wacker Drive. The three-tiered roadway was open in different spots along its two miles of pavement, but they'd entered the subterranean portion. During the day, business traffic kept the area relatively safe. But at this hour of the night it was a whole new ball game, and the cretins cruising the road would have the home field advantage.

With its concrete pillars and walls, the nineteen-twenties structure had a spooky air about it. It reminded her of a dimly lit ancient tomb with the yellow lighting casting a sickly hue on the dingy concrete walls. Throughout the day and into the early evening hours the loading docks servicing the buildings aboveground bustled with activity.

Now, they were closed off to the world, their gray steel doors projecting a sense of stern sentinels. In some ways, they looked like giant guardians, but for some reason she couldn't help but think they were keeping something in rather than out. Any minute now, she expected to see one of those metal doors give way beneath the weight of some dark creature from a childhood nightmare. She uttered a soft sound of disgust.

When in the hell had she suddenly turned into a wuss? She'd lived in the desert with deadly snakes, reluctantly crawled into holes where the earth could easily have caved in on top of her. She'd survived the brutal murders of her parents and her mentor, all the while knowing deep down inside someone might come after her as well. Tonight's events shouldn't have been all that surprising. Although two men fighting with swords had been a bit over the top.

She still wasn't sure she could trust Ares, but then he hadn't given her a choice in the matter. He'd simply picked her up as though she were a discarded rag doll he'd found and decided to keep. He had to be in phenomenal physical condition to carry her as if she were a featherweight—she knew different.

And he'd done it in spite of his injuries. His chest wound had been the only injury she'd seen while in the alley. She hadn't realized until he sat next to her in the car that his arm also had an ugly gash. The wounds weren't life threatening, but they had to hurt like hell. The man had to have the pain tolerance of a bull because he hadn't protested a single time.

Except for his one or two grunts of pain when he'd climbed into the SUV, he'd been stoic about his injuries. She admired his self-control. Compared to him, she'd been a big baby. Still, and it irked her to admit it, his caveman behavior had been more than just a little exciting.

She'd never had a man carry her like that before. It made her feel exceedingly feminine, sexy even—something she rarely felt. Would he be as commanding in the bedroom? Her insides clenched as she remembered the way he'd kissed her earlier. She winced. Lord, the sooner she put some distance between her and this man, the better. She darted a glance in his direction.

With his eyes closed, Emma had the opportunity to study his profile without him scrutinizing her in return. Earlier this evening, she'd labeled him a beautiful, blond Lucifer. Now she realized her mistake.

His features were a little too rugged to qualify him as truly beautiful. But his face fostered the image of strength and power. He had the face of a solider. No, a warrior. He exuded the aura of a battle-weary fighter who knew there were more skirmishes ahead. Okay, now she was really getting fanciful. For all she knew, the man could be a dangerous criminal. She lightly bit down on her lip. That might be going a bit too far. After all, how many felons rescued damsels in distress? But if her vision was anything to go on, he was more than capable of killing, which definitely made him hazardous to one's health.

And why in the world did he fight with a sword? Didn't he know what a gun was? Not that she wanted to encourage him or anything, but sword fighting? That belonged in the distant past, not in present-day Chicago. Then there was the odd way he spoke Italian. If you could call it that. She knew her Latin was rusty, but she'd *never* heard the dead language mixed in with any other Italian dialect before or any other romance linguistics for that matter. It was as if he were speaking an undiscovered language.

Her attention returned to the man beside her. Lines of tension furrowed his forehead, and his sensuous mouth had thinned to a straight line. He might not be complaining, but he'd obviously reached his pain threshold. She could see it in the drawn corners of his mouth. Impulse almost overrode common sense as she started to reach out and soothe the lines of pain from his face. At that precise moment, he stirred as if aware of her gaze.

The idea of having those dark, mysterious blue eyes staring into hers again made her avert her gaze quickly. No doubt about it. She definitely needed to give this guy a wide berth. She shivered as the Durango slowed down and veered off onto one of the service lanes.

The vehicle made a sharp right then halted in front of a loading dock door. Rolling down her window, the woman leaned out and pressed her thumb on a small digital screen attached to a steel pole. A moment later, the garage door rolled up. Emma couldn't help being impressed by the security measure, but it intimidated her as well. Of course, Ares had been doing that since she first met him a few hours ago.

The brightly lit garage made her blink. The weighty feel of Wacker Drive's concrete walls and ceiling gave way to an environment that almost made her believe it was daylight. A small group of vehicles lined one wall, and the woman pulled into a parking space next to a black Bravada. Behind them the garage door rumbled shut.

"If I'm any judge of Phae's abilities, I think you'll be able to limp your way into the elevator," Ares said.

Low and husky, his voice made her pulse rate skip along like a pebble across a still pond. More to the point, the sound might easily melt her to the bone if she let it. Swallowing her trepidation, she turned to meet his compelling gaze. She couldn't read his expression, but he seemed amused. He confirmed it for her.

"Unless, of course, you'd prefer I carry you."

He leaned into her as he spoke, the scent of him raw and all male. The pounding rhythm of her heart increased, and her mouth went dry. God, the man gave new meaning to the word "sexy." She shook her head as she scooted away from him and exited the car. Her movements cautious, she found she could limp her way around the car door, just as Ares had said. What sort of abilities *did* the woman named Phae have?

No one spoke as he and the woman got out of the SUV. Closing the door behind her, Phae sent Emma a censorious look before turning away. Could jealousy be the root cause of the woman's antipathy? Had Ares's attention toward her irritated the woman? Phae obviously didn't want her here. She sighed. The woman didn't seem to understand she wasn't happy about being here either. An emergency room might be a chaotic atmosphere, but it would at least be somewhat normal.

The thought of doctors made her look down at the cut on the palm of her hand and she frowned. The length of the gash seemed smaller than she remembered and the pain had become a quiet throb. Not to mention her ankle didn't hurt anywhere near as badly as when Ares had carried her to the car.

Well, it had been dark and she'd been terrified. She'd probably exaggerated the size of the cut in her mind, and she'd had plenty of time to rest her ankle during the drive, not to mention all the whiskey she'd had. But then Ares had mentioned Phae and healing in the same sentence. Could the woman be an empath? She dismissed the thought. She was having enough trouble coming to grips with the extent of Ares's special talents. The frisson racing up her neck made her realize Ares was behind her.

The awareness cresting through her alarmed her. No man, not even Jonathan, had ever affected her the way Ares did. She couldn't ever remember a time when just the mere presence of a man made her skin go hot and feverish. His hand pressed gently into the small of her back as he urged her to follow Phae.

They walked in silence toward an elevator, where Ares pressed his thumb against another security panel. In less than a minute, the doors opened. Whoever these people were, they'd left nothing to chance when it came to security.

Warm, rich oak panels lined the elevator's interior, and it had the ambiance of a luxury apartment building. Someone they knew had money. Downtown Chicago real estate was expensive and the technology she'd seen didn't come cheap either. She wasn't even going to estimate the cost of the paneling that lined the elevator's walls. The car whirred softly as it moved upward. The digital display above the doors changed as they passed first one level and then another.

"*Il mio signore*, what accommodations shall I arrange for—" Phae's voice broke abruptly as she looked first at Ares and then Emma. "For Ms. Zale? I believe Cleo has a spare room in her apartment."

"We've a spare room she can use." He sent the woman a harsh glance. "She's under my protection."

Phae eyed him with disapproval but she didn't argue with him.

Emma couldn't be certain if the woman didn't protest out of respect or because she feared him. Probably the former. The Italian phrase she'd addressed Ares with was used to address nobility. It constituted more than simple respect. It represented authority and allegiance. The woman sure didn't agree with him, though. That much was clear from the look of disapproval on her haughty features. The elevator stopped with a gentle jolt.

As the paneled door slid open, Ares ushered her into an elegant foyer, which opened into a large, softly lit living room. The foyer's hardwood flooring extended into the living room, where a large Persian rug served to carpet a large portion of the space.

An elderly gentleman came around the corner and stood just at the edge of the foyer. Arching his white eyebrows, he greeted Ares with a look of concern.

"Phae said you're hurt."

"Not too bad." Ares grimaced. "Cleo's on vacation and I need stitches."

"Is there some reason why your sister hasn't already healed your wounds?"

Emma followed the man's gaze to Phae's rebellious expression. His sister? Well that knocked the antipathy born of jealousy theory right out the window. As Emma studied the woman's mutinous expression, it surprised her that Phae didn't say a word. It was easy to see she wanted to, but she held her tongue. Ares seemed to be thinking the same thing because he sent his sister an odd look. She couldn't decide whether it was approval or amusement. Ares looked back at the elderly gentleman.

"Unfortunately, Emma is injured as well."

"Emma?" The man's gaze fully focused on her for the first time. A wary look darkened his features. "You brought an *aliena* here?"

She knew a lot more Italian than Latin, but she knew that *aliena* meant outsider. Great. Someone else who didn't want her here. She might not have wanted to come with Ares in the first place, but this crowd certainly didn't win any prizes in the hospitality category.

"Emma suffered a cut to her hand and injured her ankle while she was trying to escape an assailant." Ares met the older man's eyes with a silencing look. Immediately, the man offered him a slight bow.

"Then I am pleased to offer my humble skills as a physician, *il mio signore.*"

Ares nodded at the man's response then turned to his sister. "Phae, show Emma to her room. Do what you can for her then come see me."

"We'll be in the kitchen," Doc said as he turned and walked away.

A mutinous expression on her face, Phae jerked her head in a direction opposite the way the physician had gone. "This way, Ms. Zale."

She hesitated as she realized she hadn't even thought about her house. With a broken window, the office was going to be a watery mess. And the back door was unlocked, which meant anyone could walk in and take what they wanted. She turned her head to Ares.

"We need to call the police. My house—"

"I'm going to send someone over in a few minutes. They'll take care of the window and make sure it's locked up tight."

"But I—"

"I promise I'll take care of it, Emma. I'll have a repairman there in the morning."

She reluctantly nodded, knowing there was little she could do about it right now. Her skin tingled as Ares touched her shoulder and gently pushed her in the direction of his departing sister. Alarmed by the heat skimming through her at his touch, she tugged free of his grasp and took a quick step back. His arm fell to his side as he studied her with a thoughtful expression on his face.

"You're safe here, Emma."

"Am I? Then why do I feel like a Trojan about to find a Greek horse?" she muttered as she reluctantly followed Phae. His soft laugh trailed after her. She wanted to turn and glare at him, but she knew it would only encourage him. Ares DeLuca had a wicked streak in him.

She'd known it from the first moment she'd laid eyes on him. And the appalling fact was she liked him for it. He excited her. Reaching the door of the room Phae had vanished through, she paused and looked back. Still standing where she'd left him, she saw a half smile curve Ares's mouth. It was the smile of a sinner and it spelled trouble. Maybe more trouble than she could handle.

Chapter 7

FLUSTERED by Ares's wicked smile, she darted through the door in front of her. The understated luxury of the room reinforced her earlier impression of money. Muted colors of rose and ivory decorated the room, complementing the cherrywood of the empress canopy bed Phae sat on. The woman gestured for Emma to sit next to her. When she hesitated, Phae released a soft snort of disgust.

"Stop acting like everyone's going to eat you, and sit down so I can help you."

"Look, let's get a few things straight." Emma snapped as her patience gave way under the woman's contemptuous tone of voice. "One, I didn't ask to come here, so take that up with your brother. Two, I didn't ask for your help. Stitches would be a hell of a lot easier than dealing with your bitchy attitude. Three, you people seem to think I should accept everything I've seen tonight as normal, when it's anything *but* as far as I'm concerned. So do me a favor, cut me some slack, because I really don't feel up to kicking your ass right now."

The last part of her tirade was a bluff, and they both knew it. Limping her way to the bed, Emma glared at Ares's sister as she flopped down next to her on the bed. Phae stared at her for a long moment with a glimmer of respect in her eyes before she agreed with a regal nod.

"With your permission, I must touch you to heal your injuries."

Still angry, Emma didn't say a single word. She simply stretched out her hands and offered them to the woman facing her. For the first time Phae appeared uncomfortable. Overwhelmed, exhausted, and in pain, Emma didn't give a damn how the other woman felt. At the moment she was too interested in attending her own self-pity party. She watched as Ares's sister gently cradled her hand and studied the ugly cut at the base of her palm. Seconds later, Phae grasped Emma's uninjured hand and closed her eyes.

Uncertain what to expect, Emma watched the woman with a mixture of curiosity and even a trace of fear. Could Phae really heal just by touching her? It seemed a bit farfetched. Particularly given the fact that several seconds had passed and her hand still hurt like hell.

Slowly the seconds continued to tick away. Phae murmured something unintelligible as a tingling sensation suddenly zipped across Emma's skin. The warmth pulsed its way deep into her muscles and worked its way through her entire body. She glanced down at the cut on her wrist and frowned. The injury seemed even smaller than when she'd arrived.

Across from her, Phae uttered a small cry of pain. Startled, she looked up from her hand to see an expression of agony fly across the healer's face. The woman's grip on her uninjured hand grew tighter with each passing second. It was almost as if Phae's discomfort was growing as hers lessened.

She looked down and gasped as she saw a cut developing on Phae's palm. As the wound on Phae's hand grew in size, the smaller and less painful her own wound became. Even her ankle didn't hurt anymore, and looking down, she noticed Phae's ankle swelling as if she'd suffered a bad sprain. Quickly glancing back at her hand, she saw her cut had healed completely.

The expression on Phae's face showed she was still in pain, but already the wound on her palm had begun to heal. With a relieved sigh, the woman let go of Emma's hand and slumped forward slightly.

A thick lock of dark hair had slipped out of the knot at the back of her head to trail over her pale cheek. A shudder shook through Ares's sister as she sat upright and met Emma's gaze. Still stunned by the woman's ability, Emma didn't know what to say. Amusement curved Phae's mouth in a smile that mimicked her brother's.

"I think we could both use a good night's sleep." Standing up, Phae headed toward the bedroom door. "You'll find plenty of towels in the bathroom. If I know my brother, your clothes will be here sometime tomorrow morning."

"Thank you," Emma said quietly as she glanced down at her healed hand. "For everything."

"You're welcome." Phae's expression almost passed for friendly as she left the room.

Left to her own devices, Emma stood up and tested her ankle as she examined her hand at close range. She uttered a quiet laugh of amazement. Phae DeLuca had healed her completely. There wasn't even a scar on her hand to show where she'd been cut. Unbelievable.

She raked her fingers through her hair and moved toward the closed drapes. Not bothering to look for the drawstring, she pushed the heavy material aside where the panels met. Sixteen or more stories below, the Chicago River flowed through the city's downtown. A few blocks away the gothic architecture of the Tribune Tower rose up above Michigan Avenue. She couldn't remember the last time she'd been downtown at night.

The drapes fell back into place as she turned away from the window and stared at her surroundings. The elegant décor had the mark of a professional decorator. The perfect guest room, it screamed money. Hell, the whole apartment did. Could she call it a penthouse? It sure reminded her of ones she'd seen in movies. She had so many questions, her head was spinning.

She didn't have the foggiest notion of what to think about everything that had happened tonight. First Ares and his ability to move things, him stealing her coin, finding her father's—With a gasp, she shoved her hands into her back jean pocket. Carefully, she pulled the crumpled paper out of her jeans. The soaked pages clung to each other with tenacity as she sat down at a nearby table and pried them apart with care. The ink from her father's note had smeared a small amount, but she could still read the cipher easily. Her notes, however, hadn't survived quite so well. She'd have to start over, but she remembered enough that her notes would be easy to re-create. She wanted to sit down and start now, but she knew better. To think clearly she needed sleep. She caught a glimpse of herself in a mirror hanging on the wall opposite the table. Hair matted with mud and smudges of dirt on her face told her the first order of business was a shower. After that, bed. She'd figure out what to do in the morning.

ARES grimaced as the needle bit into his skin for another suture. With his side pressed against the rounded edge of the kitchen's brown marble countertop, one of the ceiling lights spotlighted his arm. Doc had seen to his chest wound first, and now the physician was intent on closing his other wound. Arching his white eyebrows, Doc shook his head as he knotted a suture.

"What were you thinking, boy?"

"I haven't been a boy for a long time, Doc," Ares ground out between clenched teeth as the needle slipped through his skin once more. Even with the numbing agent, a swarm of angry wasps had taken up residence in the shoulder. "As for why I brought Emma here, I didn't have a choice."

"But she's working with the Praetorians."

"I don't think so. The Oriental Institute might be one of the biggest backers of the Ptolemy dig, but Charlie Russwin led the expedition. Emma just worked for the man."

"You *must* give credence to the idea, Ares. The Praetorians control the Institute, which means she works for them, whether she realizes it or not." Doc shook his head as he knotted the last suture in Ares's shoulder.

"She doesn't work for them," he said in a firm, cold voice.

"How can you be so sure?" Phae's soft question drifted over his shoulder, and he turned his head to meet his sister's sober gaze.

"Instinct," he growled. "The same instinct that earned me the right to lead this guild my way and without my directives being questioned at every turn."

Phae sat on a bar stool close to him, her expression reflecting sisterly concern. "I'm not questioning your orders. I'm suggesting you might be trying to make amends for the past. Punishing yourself for things you had no control over."

Ignoring her quiet observation, he watched Doc bandage the cut on his shoulder. It didn't matter what his sister believed. Clarissa had been his responsibility, and he'd failed her. He'd left her unprotected and she was dead because of it. The memory of walking into that apartment and finding her body tightened his torso. The involuntary movement exacerbated the cut running horizontal across his chest and he suppressed a grunt of pain. Clarissa had been an *aliena*, too. He'd met her while buying specialty chocolates for Phae's birthday. They'd struck up a conversation, and he hadn't had the common sense to end it right there. Instead, he'd come to care for her. He started as he realized his sister had asked him a question.

"What?"

"I asked how long she's going to be here. She can't remain indefinitely. The guild won't like it. Not to mention what the *Prima Consul* or the Order will have to say."

"I don't give a damn what the guild or the Order likes or doesn't like. Emma's life is in danger. The man I fought in the alley tonight wasn't a Praetorian, he was a *Sicari*."

"A *Sicari*." Phae sent him a skeptical look. "Are you sure?"

"Yes. And he would have killed me tonight if you hadn't shown up when you did."

"That I seriously doubt." His sister snorted her disbelief.

Shaking his head, he recalled the man's fist driving into his injured shoulder. It had been a Praetorian move, but everything else about the warrior's skills reflected *Sicari* training. And he still couldn't figure out what was so familiar about the fighter. Whoever the man was, he'd been the better fighter.

If Phae hadn't arrived when she had, he wouldn't be sitting here right now with a body that hurt like fire and damnation. The real question he wanted answered was what had prompted the man to target Emma. And why would the warrior warn him off?

He didn't like it when he had more questions than answers. Especially when his people were at risk. The chime of the elevator made his muscles tense. Seconds later, Lysander entered the large gourmet kitchen. Tall and muscular, he always turned women's heads with his handsome profile until they saw the rest of him. Where one side of his face could have belonged to a cover model, the other was brutally scarred. The black patch he wore over his missing eye further enhanced his menacing appearance.

Phae jumped to her feet the moment his *Primus Pilus* entered the kitchen. A grim resignation slid over him as he studied his friend's expression. Just the way the scarred man avoided looking at Phae told him the news wasn't good.

"Where is he?" she snapped. The tension in her was almost tangible, and something flickered in Lysander's green eye but his expression remained impassive.

"He's dead."

Phae didn't make a sound at the flatly spoken words, and Ares quickly shifted his gaze to his sister. It didn't surprise him to see her looking coolly composed. She'd learned over the years to hide her feelings behind anger, sarcasm, or icy silence. The only indication of her grief was her pale features.

"Did he . . ." Phae took a quick breath and swallowed hard. "Did he suffer?"

Again, Lysander hesitated and a muscle twitched beneath his marred flesh. "They skinned him."

"*Merda*." Ares rasped as he briefly glanced at his friend's hideous scars before meeting the man's unreadable gaze. His second-in-command knew firsthand the horror of the Praetorians' torture methods. "We'll need to make preparations."

"Everything's being seen to. I contacted the New York guild and they're sending someone out to Julian's parents' house."

"And the *Rogalis*?" Ares shot a quick glance in Phae's direction, but her expression rivaled Lysander's emotionless countenance.

"Provided his parents can catch a morning flight, the ritual will take place tomorrow night." His *Primus Pilus* cleared his throat softly. "I thought you might like to choose the orator."

"I'll do it." Her voice devoid of emotion, Phae's quiet words made Lysander jerk his head in her direction.

The two fighters stared at each other for a long moment before his second-in-command sent her an abrupt nod and looked away. Surprised by the silent exchange, he narrowed his eyes at the two. They'd never gotten along well, but some unspoken agreement had passed between his sister and the other *Sicari* just now.

A truce perhaps? Probably just until Julian's body joined his spirit. He frowned and pinched the bridge of his nose for a moment. He'd let his sister and Lysander sort out the details of the *Rogalis*. What he needed was sleep. Wearily getting to his feet, he waved off Doc's offering of white pills. He'd sleep well enough without the pain medication. At the kitchen doorway, he stopped at the stainless steel trashcan tucked against the Ground Zero refrigerator.

He wadded up the torn and bloodied turtleneck sweater he'd been wearing and dropped it into the container.

"Lysander, send someone to collect Emma's clothes. I want them here bright and early." He looked back at the three of them. "I'm going to bed. I suggest the rest of you do the same. We've a long day ahead of us tomorrow."

Moving out into the living room, he ignored the low buzz of conversation that started the moment he left the kitchen. Let them talk. He'd done the right thing. It hadn't been possible to save Julian's life tonight, but he'd saved Emma. The comment about her father knowing about the *Tyet of Isis* was enough to tell him that she was a crucial part of the puzzle he'd been piecing together for the last two years. Even if she didn't have any idea where to find the artifact, she knew something.

Although the evidence seemed to point toward Emma's parents being involved with the Praetorians, his instincts said it wasn't true. He'd read their file dozens of times, and the evidence was sketchy at best. Somehow, the idea of David and Katherine Zale working for the Praetorians just didn't make sense. Ewan Redmurre struck him as someone who would look the other way for the right price, but not the Zales. They hadn't been the type of scholars to ignore questions of any kind, and the Praetorians made it difficult not to ask questions. Then there was David Zale's reputation in academia.

His theory that the Sicari Order still existed in modern-day society had earned him ridicule from his colleagues, and it quite possibly had been one of the reasons for the man's murder. By all accounts, even his tenure had been difficult to achieve. Only his unusual archeological contributions to the university had enabled him to cement his position.

Contributions that, in all likelihood, the man had achieved with the help of his daughter. Then there was the murder of the man and his wife. If the Praetorians had killed the couple, then they'd worked hard to make it look like someone else had done the deed. The manner of their death had been quick and clean, and Charles Russwin's death had been just the same.

The Praetorians liked to stretch out their killings. Julian's death was a prime example. And that mark. Caesar and Octavia had been unable to find any symbol like it in the database. The closest thing they'd found to the mark was the Chi-Rho, a sign used during the persecution of Christians under the Caesars. He had nothing else to go on except his instincts, and his gut told him Emma had been an innocent bystander until he blundered into her office.

His jaw clenched as he rolled his head to the left in an effort to ease the tension careening through his shoulders. The move tugged at the stitches in his injured shoulder. He winced. Passing the foyer, he walked down the hall. When he reached Emma's door, he came to a halt.

He should check in on her—reassure her. A mocking laugh sounded in the back of his head. It was easy to ignore the taunting sound. He knocked quietly. When she didn't answer, he knocked again. Still no response. A sliver of concern made him waver. If she'd slipped out of the apartment, he'd have to find her. He turned the knob, half hoping to find the door locked. It opened with a muted click of the latch.

The empty bed caught his attention first and he stiffened, ready to sound the alarm. A second later, the sound of the shower made him relax, but only for a brief moment. Almost instantly, his tension returned as he visualized Emma standing naked under a stream of water. The image twisted his gut with sharp desire. *Christus*, he needed to get the hell out of here before he did something really stupid. She hadn't tried to leave, and he could reassure her in the morning.

As he turned back toward the door, his gaze fell on several crumpled pieces of paper lying on the table near the window. Curiosity got the best of him, and the cream carpet deadened his footsteps as he strode to the table. Several pieces contained blurred writing from where the rain had made the ink run on the page.

Hands braced against the tabletop, he studied the hieroglyphics on the one piece of paper that had survived with minimal damage. Puzzled, he shook his head. The markings didn't make any sense. One glyph described the moon, and in the next word the text moved on to a field in need of sowing. There wasn't any rhyme or reason to the writing. Pulling one of the damaged pages closer, he frowned as he tried to make out the words streaked with rivulets of ink. A moment later, he grew rigid when he was able to make out the remainder of a single word. *Tyet.*

"What are you doing in here?" Emma's sharp tone made him jerk upright.

Framed in the bathroom doorway, she wore one of the bulky white robes they always kept on hand for impromptu guests. He'd never realized how tempting they could make a woman look. And she looked delicious, if the belt around her waist suddenly— Damnation. He quickly suppressed the dangerous urge to reach out and touch her by any means.

"I knocked." He nodded toward the door with an abrupt jerk of his head. "When you didn't answer, I thought you might be in trouble."

"In trouble?" she scoffed, arching her eyebrows at him. "Don't you mean you thought I'd flown the coop?"

"The thought crossed my mind." He rested his hands on his hips and shrugged.

Tension vibrated off her. He could see it in the way she held herself stiff and straight. It wouldn't take much to startle her. Kittens weren't even this skittish. She jerked her head in the direction of his chest.

"I'm sorry you got hurt." Her gaze focused on his chest only to drift downward before sweeping back up to his face. It was like a hot wind blowing across his skin. Color flushed high in her cheeks as their eyes met. Once more, the urge to touch her slid through him, but he crushed the desire before he could act on it

"Tell me where the *Tyet of Isis* is."

"I've already told you I don't know. I thought it was just a symbol and nothing more."

"You said your father knew about it, and these notes tell me you're lying." He swept his hand across the table before picking up one sheet. "Especially when the reference to *Tyet* on this one page is written in a feminine hand."

"I'm not lying to you. I was just as surprised to see it as you," she snapped. Trained to read body language, he studied her for a moment. Although her stance reflected anger, it did not indicate guilt.

"This other note." He gestured toward the note covered with hieroglyphics. "It's some type of code. Where did you get it?"

She heaved a sigh as if realizing he wasn't about to leave without an explanation. "It's a cipher my father devised. I found it this evening in my father's desk."

"Do you know what it says?"

"No . . . I . . . there wasn't time." Her gaze slid away from his the moment she answered.

She didn't verbalize the terror she'd experienced tonight, but the way her arms hugged her waist told him she was remembering her narrow escape from the rogue warrior. He'd hit a raw nerve and the forlorn air about her tugged at his senses. For the second time tonight, he wanted to let her cry on his shoulder. His jaw grew tight at the thought.

"You were in the middle of translating the cipher when he broke into the house," he bit out more harshly than he'd intended.

She paled slightly and nodded her head. Although she tried to shield her fear, he saw it shadow her features for a brief instant. Had the rogue Sicari known about the cipher or had he gone after her for a different reason?

It was no secret Emma's father was the number one expert on the history of the Sicari Order. As his daughter, she would have been privy to her father's knowledge. So why wait five years to come after her—but the rogue warrior hadn't come after her first. He'd only tried to kill her *after* Russwin was dead. The bastard hadn't known she was in the tomb with her friend. Once he'd realized his mistake, the rogue warrior had tried to finish what he'd failed to do the first time.

If there had been Sicari Order artifacts in the ancient Pharaoh's burial chamber, they'd been removed. The Order had sent in two of its own experts to determine if Russwin had found something, but they'd come up empty-handed. If the man *had* made a discovery, it was gone. The only tangible evidence was the symbol Emma had discovered in one of the antechambers. It was the primary reason why the Order thought Emma had found the *Tyet of Isis*.

While he was certain Emma didn't have the artifact, she did have a clue to its whereabouts. And he wasn't letting her go anywhere until she deciphered her father's message. The sooner, the better. He wanted to know what they were dealing with. Then there were the Sicari artifacts in the archives. Octavia had come up empty-handed researching the relics, but maybe Emma's ability would give them more information. He wasn't wild about the idea. Every piece of information he gave her served to endanger her life more. But his researchers were ending up in blind alleys, and he couldn't deny that they could use her help.

"If you're trying to intimidate me with your silence, it won't work." Her voice sliced through his thoughts with that feisty edge he was quickly growing accustomed to. He focused his attention on her, and experienced an unwelcome rush of relief that her color had returned.

"I don't think you're easily intimidated," he said with slight twist of his lips.

"You owe me some answers." The abrupt switch of topic put him on guard as he met her accusatory look. He dipped his head in a sharp nod.

"All right. Ask your questions."

"One, what's the *Tyet of Isis*? Two, what's with the swords? Three, who was the son of a bitch trying to kill me and why?"

"You're not going to like my answers." He blew out a breath of air. He needed to gain her trust, and this sure as hell wasn't the way to go about it.

"Try me." Her belligerent response made the muscle in his cheek twitch.

"The only thing we know about the *Tyet of Isis* is that it dates back to the time of Alexander the Great. Our sources thought you'd found it at Ptolemy's tomb, which is why I was at your house this evening."

"Your *sources* got it wrong."

"Not exactly. You did find the coin, or at least the one Russwin found." He frowned. He'd really like to know where the professor had found the Sicari Lord coin.

"Okay, I'll accept that for the moment." She narrowed her eyes at him. "What about the swords?"

He ran his hand across the top of his head and downward to cup the back of his neck. With a frown he shook his head. "There's not an easy answer for that one."

"Try this one. Why not use a gun?"

She folded her arms across her chest. The action parted her robe slightly, giving him a glimpse of the soft valley between her breasts. His cock stirred in his leather pants. He quickly curbed the lust pushing its way through his lower body to focus on her question.

"Tradition, for the most part." He shrugged. "But a sword requires a lot more skill and strength compared to a firearm. A sword is also a lot less noisy."

"Right—like steel clanging against steel won't bring out the crowds." Her sarcasm made him laugh softly.

"True, but still not as quickly as a gun going off." He sent her a mischievous smile. "Besides, I've been told that women find men who carry swords quite romantic."

"Aren't you funny." She sneered. "And what happens when you come up against some asshole who pulls a gun on you?"

Her sarcastic question set him on edge as he remembered the target he'd killed almost a year ago. The man had managed to get off one shot before dying. It wasn't a pleasant memory because he'd almost gotten Phae killed.

"It means I got sloppy," he said coldly. She flinched and regret stirred inside him. "I meant what I said, Emma. You're safe here. No one will hurt you, including me."

He watched her swallow hard as she looked away from him. "And the man who tried to kill me?"

"I don't know who he is." He grimaced as she shot him a look of disbelief. "I wish I did, Emma. At least I'd know what we're up against."

"What's that supposed to mean?"

"It's complicated." He inhaled a deep breath then blew it out in frustration.

"Complicated?" She snagged one hand in her damp hair. "Remember I said you had a knack for understatements? We're way beyond that now."

The note of hysteria in her voice made him take a step forward, but she raised her hands in a gesture that said not to touch her. Damnation, she was dancing on a wire and he didn't know how to keep her from falling.

"I know you're scared, Emma." He did his best to keep his voice low and soothing. "And I know there's a lot you're trying to take in at the moment, but you've got to trust me."

"Why?" Her gaze met his and her bleak expression made his heart ache. He didn't like the sensation.

"Because I know what it's like to lose someone you love. I know how helpless it makes you feel," he rasped as a chill swept over him. "My parents were murdered when I was twelve. I watched my mother die knowing there wasn't a damn thing I could do about it."

The memory slid a cold knife through him. He'd known from the moment his mother had shoved him and Phae into the Priest's Closet it would be the last time he'd see her alive. The way she'd ordered him to look after his sister, the gentle way she'd touched his cheek and kissed Phae had been her way of saying goodbye. Then she'd sealed them in the secret room.

Moments later the Praetorians stormed the house. He never saw his father fall, but it was the only explanation for the Praetorian that burst into his parents' bedroom. Through a small eyehole he'd seen his mother endure blow after blow from the enemy's blade.

Her screams had terrified Phae, and he'd been forced to clamp his hand over his sister's mouth to trap her cries of fear. All the while he'd watched the Praetorian slice away at his mother until her head rolled off her shoulders. Ice sluiced through him as the memories took him back to a place he seldom dared to enter. The warmth of a light touch jerked him out of the past.

"I'm sorry." Emma's face was gentle with understanding, and he swallowed the knot of pain in his throat.

"It was a long time ago," he said brusquely as he shook off her hand. "My point was to make you understand you can trust me."

"Point taken," she responded in a soft voice.

He offered her a sharp bob of his head and turned back to the table. The moment he reached for the cipher, she was at his side. In a quick movement, she pulled the note out of his hand.

"My father left it for me to translate. No one else."

Instinct made his hand catch her wrist and hold her in place. Tangible and electric, her silky skin singed his fingers. A freight train slamming into him couldn't have shocked him more. Frozen and unable to move, his gaze drifted downward to where her robe gaped open and revealed the side of one round, firm breast. His mouth went dry.

Merda. He needed to get out of here before he did something he'd regret. But he didn't move. Instead, he breathed in the essence of her. The soft scent of vanilla filled his senses as he imagined his fingers stroking her. A second later he heard her draw in a quick breath in a soft hiss. The sound didn't signal her protest. His eyes met hers, and the moment the tip of her tongue flicked out to wet her lips, he knew he was lost. He tried to swallow, but couldn't. He couldn't do anything except picture her robe opening so he could see more of her.

Her gasp was more of a sigh as the white terry cloth garment parted of its own accord and exposed her fully. The curves he'd touched earlier hadn't lied to him. She was ripe and lush. He knew he'd regret this in the end, but at the moment all he wanted to do was touch her, and not just with his mind. With a quick tug, he pulled her into his arms and captured her mouth in a hard kiss.

Tart. She tasted fresh and crisp. The flavor of her slid across his tongue as he probed the inner warmth of her mouth. Like the last time, she didn't pull away. Instead, her arms slid around his waist so her hands could explore his back. Nails scraped lightly over his skin as the heat of her pressed into him. He was rock hard in a split second.

Mater Dei, he needed to regain control. Let her go.

His brain knew what to do, but his body ignored the commands.

Beneath his thumbs, her nipples budded into stiff peaks when he gently brushed across the tips. The caress made her breathe a sigh of pleasure into his mouth, and she thrust her hips forward until she was nestled intimately against his hard erection. He growled at the pleasurable pressure. Hot and silky, her mouth melded with his in a heated dance of enticing need.

It had been a long time since he'd been with a woman, and even then it hadn't felt this good. Another sigh whispered out of her, and he could smell the sensual bite of her desire. The soft murmur of voices slowly thrummed its way through his senses. It reminded him of a buzzing insect and he tried to block the sound from his head. The voices came closer and he groaned with frustration as he lifted his head.

The moment he broke off the kiss, his body objected with a vehement tug on his cock. Emma protested softly, but grew still when he rested his fingers against her lips. The moment she heard the voices, her eyes widened and her cheeks grew pink with embarrassment. Flustered, she adjusted her robe and averted her face from his. The muted conversation outside the bedroom door continued down the hall and he allowed himself to breathe again.

Emma took a quick step away from him as if he might burn her. The way she sidestepped made him wince. He'd asked her to trust him, and yet he couldn't keep his hands off her. She tucked a lock of hair behind her ear and bent to retrieve the cipher from where it had landed on the floor when they'd kissed. Without looking at him, she laid the note on the table.

He was reminded of how vulnerable she'd looked earlier. He flexed his hand into a tight fist. *Merda*, he was a bastard. She was under his protection, and he'd been acting like he could do whatever he wanted with her. If Rinaldo *Souter* were here, the old man would have dropped him to the floor in the blink of an eye just for his lack of control. Never mind the other disciplines he'd broken tonight. The thought made the awkwardness of the moment all the more uncomfortable. He cleared his throat.

"I'm not going to lie to you, Emma. I want to know what's in this cipher." He pointed to the paper on the table. "It might be the key to finding the *Tyet of Isis.*"

"So just like that I'm supposed to hand over my father's message to you? Whatever's in this message was meant for me," she snapped.

"And if it's the location of the artifact?"

"Then I'll find it."

"Do you really think the visitor you had tonight is going to let you live long enough to find it?" he rasped.

His words made her grow pale, and he didn't like the regret coiling through him as he watched the conflicted emotions flashing across her face. She closed her eyes and the tremor flying through her said she was beginning to grasp the reality of her situation.

"Trust me, Emma. We can help each other. I don't know what the *Tyet of Isis* is, but I have the resources to help us find it."

With a sigh of surrender, she looked at him. "All right. You win."

"No, Emma. We *both* win." *Deus*, that vulnerability of hers was back. He fought not to reach for her. "How long will it take you to translate the cipher?"

"I don't . . . know," she stammered. She avoided his gaze and pressed her hand to her cheek. "I'm not even sure I can."

This time the self-doubt in her voice made him take a small step toward her before he halted in his tracks. He needed to remember that the best way to keep from touching her was to keep his distance. In the back of his head, a small voice chuckled with glee. Discipline allowed him to ignore the sound.

"I don't believe that," he said quietly.

Her head jerked up and she met his gaze warily. "Why?"

"Because you're stubborn." Her distrust waned as she sent him a skeptical look. "You don't give up easily."

"No. I never have known when to call it quits," she said in a wry tone as she stared down at the coded sheet of paper.

"Sleep on it. You've been through a lot tonight."

Her only response was a slow nod of her head. Not willing to push her any further, he turned and walked toward the bedroom door.

"Ares, I . . . I'm going to need my purse with my bank card and ID. And some clothes until I go home." There it was again, that forlorn, lost look of vulnerability of hers. He swallowed hard.

"I've already taken care of it. Your things will be here in the morning." When she nodded again, he bolted for the door.

"Ares." His hand on the doorknob, he turned his head to look at her. She bit her lip for a second before meeting his gaze. "I don't think I said thank you. That is, thank you for saving my life tonight."

"You're welcome." His grip would have crushed the doorknob if it had been made of something less than metal. If he didn't get the hell out of here, he'd be more than sorry. He jerked his head toward the bed. "Now get some sleep."

He didn't wait for her answer, but tugged open the door and escaped out into the hall. The moment he heard the doorknob click into place, he released a breath of relief. The sensation didn't last. One hand rubbing the back of his neck, he headed toward his bedroom. Tomorrow he had a lot of explaining to do. If he didn't, that stubborn nature of hers would have her fleeing his protection the minute opportunity presented itself. The worst part was not knowing what her reaction was going to be. He suppressed a groan of disgust. There was one thing he knew for sure. He had a serious problem on his hands, and her name was Emma Zale.

Chapter 8

STOMACH growling, Emma rolled over in bed and stared at the clock. Six o'clock. Daylight edged the sides of the heavy drapes as she pushed herself up into a sitting position. Twelve hours ago, she'd been at home mourning Charlie. It seemed longer than that.

Now she was in a downtown fortress with a group of people who had abilities much more powerful than her own. Powerful and dangerous. Sinfully so. For the first time in weeks, her sleep had been free of nightmares, but not dreams. Those she'd had in spades. Vivid, erotic fantasies about a man she barely knew. She shuddered as she remembered what she'd been dreaming of just before waking. Ares. Images of him sliding into her, filling her until she screamed out his name as she climaxed. She drew in a sharp breath at the thought.

Scooting her way out of bed, she crossed the lush carpet to the bathroom. She didn't know what had prompted her erotic fantasies—well, she did—but she *knew* it was best to avoid that kind of temptation. But she couldn't help thinking how pleasurable it would be. She winced. That was definitely not a path she wanted to tread. She shut off the water faucet and stared at herself in the mirror. God, she'd never realized how good a night free of nightmares could make one look. The dark shadows under her eyes had eased to pale imitations, and she no longer looked exhausted. Maybe her fantasies had been good for her.

Her stomach diverted her attention as it growled again. Food. She needed to find something to eat. The last thing she remembered eating was a sandwich at the church-sponsored luncheon after everyone had returned from the cemetery. Determined to find something to satisfy her hunger, she reached for her robe and headed toward the door. As she pushed her arms into the plush sleeves of the robe, the memory of how Ares had magically parted it with nothing but his thoughts made her skin flush with heat.

The man could have charmed his way right into her bed last night if he'd wanted. The only reason he hadn't was because of people walking down the hall. Given the abrupt way he'd left the room, she couldn't tell whether he was more worried about someone interrupting them or someone finding them together. It didn't matter. She'd been relieved he'd left her alone.

Liar. Frustrated, she made a sharp noise of disgust and shoved a hand through her tousled hair. The man had been a key figure in the dreams she remembered. Hell, his face was the first image that had slipped through her head when she'd woken up a few minutes ago. Frustration made her jerk the door open, and she stepped out into the darkened hallway.

The lack of light made her hesitate. She wasn't crazy about the idea of walking around a dark penthouse where the occupants carried swords as casually as one might a pair of sunglasses. Yet, even in the near darkness of the hall, she felt safe.

It wasn't so much a feeling as it was a knowing. The sensation wasn't just odd, it confirmed her insanity. She shook her head in disgust. Somewhere between the moment Ares had stepped into her office last night and this very minute, she'd lost her mind. Her stomach twisted painfully. Well, even insane people needed to eat. There had to be a kitchen around here someplace.

Cautiously, she made her way down the hall toward the foyer and the elevator doors. Beneath her bare feet, the entryway's hardwood floor was smooth and warm. Overhead a recessed light illuminated the floor, while casting soft shadows on the glossy wood-paneled elevator doors. She stared at the elevator and the buttons on the wall panel for a long moment.

The urge to leave wasn't as strong now as it had been last night. Was that because she felt safe here? With a glance down at her night robe, she grimaced. Even if she did want to leave, it wasn't like she'd get far dressed in nothing but underwear and a robe. She turned away from the elevator and moved into the living room. Beige and chocolate colors warmed the entire living space, and it had an understated elegance that only a great deal of money could buy, just like her bedroom.

Whatever Ares and his friends did for a living, they were making a nice paycheck. She sucked in a quick breath. Christ, were they drug dealers? In the next heartbeat, she relaxed. No. Ares and the others gave her the impression they preferred to stay *way* below the radar. And a drug dealer using telekinesis wouldn't go unnoticed for more than a day or two, even in Cook County. While the unique mix of Italian and Latin they used could make one think crime syndicate, those swords just didn't fit. Truthfully, she didn't *want* to know how they earned their living.

As her gaze swept across the living room and into the large, open dining area, she noted the built-in wine racks and china cabinetry discreetly concealing a kitchen. Her stomach rumbled its demand, and she obeyed its summons and entered the room. Her first impression was that she'd been transported to a warm, open and inviting kitchen in a lush Tuscan villa.

Golden brown marble served as counters for the room, and the same stone covered the top of the large island in the center of the kitchen. Tile patterned with grapes and vines wound its way around the room between the countertop and the bottom of the cabinets. The huge gas stove looked like something only professionals might use, and the big steel refrigerator was something out of a gourmet chef's cooking show. The large island in the middle of the room had a wet bar and overhead copper pans hung from one of those hook racks. She wasn't a cook by any means, but even she had to admit that it would be fun to whip up a meal here.

"Hungry?"

Ares's deep voice made her jump and she whirled around to face him. Oh God, it wasn't her imagination on overload. He was just as she remembered him. Her stomach lurched as her gaze took in his appearance. She was in serious trouble, because this guy was definitely the sexiest man she'd ever seen. He'd discarded his black SWAT-like apparel for a T-shirt and boxer shorts that gave him a wickedly scruffy look.

Well-toned muscles in his arms reminded her how strong those arms could be. The way the T-shirt clung to his chest reminded her how sculpted he was underneath, bandage and all, and she found herself craving another look at his bare chest. She swallowed hard as she briefly looked down at his sinewy legs and strong feet. Despite the dangerous edge to him, there was a sleepy look about him that boldly announced he'd just gotten out of bed.

The image of him in bed made her body grow hot. She had no doubt he could easily tempt a woman into sin, and for once she was ready to be tempted. Was she hungry? Yes, but in this case, she wasn't sure if she'd be the guest or the dessert. The thought made her draw in a quick breath, and his gaze narrowed at her. She quickly gathered her wits and nodded her head.

"Hungry?" She dragged in a breath. "Yes. I haven't eaten since late yesterday afternoon."

"*Christus*," he exclaimed with a scowl. His large hands grabbed her by the shoulders so he could guide her to one of the stools tucked under the island's countertop. The heat of his touch was short-lived. "Sit down. I'll fix you something. French toast sound good?"

"Yes, thank you," she said in a voice she managed to keep relatively neutral. The thought of French toast made her stomach rumble loudly.

A wicked grin tilted his mouth as he moved toward the large refrigerator. In less than a minute, he'd pulled out a bowl and cracked several eggs into it. His touch light, he whisked the eggs together then added milk and sugar to the mixture. She watched him turn and pull out two bottles from the cabinet. Without measuring, he poured a small stream of vanilla into the eggs then followed it with several drops of the other liquid.

"What's that?" She leaned forward, trying to read the yellow label on the small container. With a wag of his finger, he put the two bottles back in the cupboard. When he faced her again, he grinned.

"Secret ingredient."

"In other words, you're not going to tell me."

"Correct." Mischief gleamed in his dark blue eyes as he whipped the egg mixture some more.

"Fine. Don't tell me." She sniffed with amused exasperation.

He just chuckled at her comment. As she watched him work, a comforting sensation engulfed her. The tension from last night had ebbed away, but she wasn't sure what was responsible for her relaxed state. Perhaps it was the warmth of the kitchen's décor and its sunny Tuscan charm, but she knew better. For some odd reason, being here with him was why she felt safe.

The man might be dangerously devastating to her senses, but something deep inside her said he wouldn't let anything happen to her. The grill sizzled as he dropped butter onto a flat, square skillet. Dipping a slice of bread into the egg mixture, he let it soak for a good fifteen seconds before he placed it on the griddle.

"Why don't you get us something to eat on," he said as he continued to load the grill pan with soaked bread. "Plates and glasses are in the cabinet behind you. Silverware in the drawer below."

Plates and glasses on the counter, she pulled silverware out of the drawer and proceeded to set a place for them both. "Napkins?"

"Pantry—far end of the counter. Syrup's in there, too."

He threw her a quick glance over his shoulder and bobbed his head toward a large double door cabinet as he flipped a piece of toast. With their place settings complete, she pulled out another plate for him to use as a serving dish. She set the plate on the counter next to the stove.

"For the toast," she murmured.

The smile he flashed her sent her heart slamming into her chest. God, she was crazy to be anywhere near this guy. He was dangerous to every sensible thought she'd ever possessed. Swallowing hard, she stepped away from him.

"What do you want to drink?" she asked as she tried to breathe properly.

"I think there's some OJ in the frig." His gaze flitted over her briefly before he slipped a hot piece of toast onto the plate she'd set on the counter for him. "You okay?"

"Sure. Just hungry."

"Good, because it's ready."

By the time she'd returned to the kitchen island with the orange juice, he'd already dished out three pieces of toast on both their plates. He pulled out a stool for her at the corner of the island, and waited for her to take a seat before he sat down catty-corner from her. As she poured herself a glass of juice, he added butter and syrup to his toast. She followed his example and took a bite. It tasted delicious, but the flavor was richer, smoother than any other French toast she'd had before.

Elbows on the countertop, he watched her reaction over his folded hands. Her gaze met his and he arched his eyebrows. "Well?"

"It's delicious, but I can't tell what the secret ingredient is."

"Most people can't."

Exasperated by his cryptic remark, she watched him pick up his fork and start to eat his breakfast. All right. Two could play at that game. She popped another syrup-covered bite of toast into her mouth. God, it really was good. Whatever the secret ingredient was, she'd tasted it before, she knew it. But the flavor was so subtle she couldn't place it. She took a sip of her orange juice and found herself meeting his amused gaze over the glass rim.

"What?" she asked as her glass tapped lightly against the marble.

"You really are obstinate as a mule," he said with a quiet laugh. "You want to know what the secret ingredient is, but you're not willing to ask me."

"I'll figure it out eventually."

She popped another bite of toast into her mouth, the flavor melting over her tongue. The minute the man left the room, she was going to be checking out the bottles in that damn cabinet.

"Tell me when you do." His mouth twitched with amusement. Damn the man. She glared at him.

"Oh, all right, what is it," she snapped with exasperation.

The cabinet door behind him opened without any visible aid, and the bottle he'd used earlier sailed through the air to land gently on the countertop in front of her. God, the ease with which he did stuff like that amazed her. She picked up the bottle to read the label. Chocolate extract. It explained the decadent flavor teasing her tongue every time she took a bite of the toast he'd prepared. He took another bite of his breakfast as she set the bottle back on the marble top.

"So what else can you cook?" she asked as she took another bite of the breakfast he'd prepared for them.

"Nothing." Wicked laughter gleamed in his eyes as he met her surprised look. "This dish is the extent of my skill in the kitchen."

"You can't be serious." She sniffed with disbelief. "That odd blend of Italian and Latin you speak makes you sound like you came straight from the old country. Not to mention that every Italian I've ever met, knows how to cook."

"Except me." He sent a wicked smile her way. It made her heart skip a beat. "I even went to one of those cooking schools outside of Venice. I flunked. Lysander is our resident expert in the culinary arts. He makes a mean soufflé."

"Lysander?"

"A good friend. Handy in a fight." Ares took a large swig of juice then set the glass back on the island's countertop. "So what do you like to cook?"

"Me?" She waved her hand in denial. "I'm like you. I don't cook either. My mom, she was the chef in the family. She could make magic out of the limited ingredients we always had on hand at the excavation site."

The memory of her mom working over a Coleman stove made her throat close. She took a quick sip of juice to loosen up her throat muscles. The minute she could, she swallowed the tears lodged there.

"It hasn't been easy for you, has it?" His astute observation made her jerk her gaze toward him then look away just as quickly.

Quiet understanding filled his words, and the empathy in his expression made her feel connected to him. They'd both lost loved ones to violence. Of all the people she knew, this stranger was the only one who really understood what she was dealing with and what she'd lost. She hadn't realized it until now, but he'd lost even more than she had. Someone had destroyed his childhood. Had one of the images she'd seen last night when she'd touched the coin in his hand been of his parents? Had they died by someone's sword? She pushed her unfinished meal away from her and looked at him.

"How did your parents die, Ares?"

The minute she asked the question, she regretted it. The sympathetic look on his face disappeared, replaced by an impassive expression. He didn't answer. Instead, he stood up and picked up their dirty dishes. With his back to her, he scraped off the remains of their breakfast into the garbage disposal.

"They were murdered in a manner similar to your parents."

He flipped the disposal switch. *Fotte*. Her parents had died quickly with little pain. His parents hadn't been so lucky. The memory of his mother's screams swept through him. He'd huddled there in that Priest's Closet and had done nothing. Logically he knew there wasn't anything he could have done, but the helpless feeling he'd experienced that night had never left him.

The only reason he and Phae had survived was because the bastards had received orders to leave. The Praetorian who'd butchered his mother hadn't been happy about it because he'd known they were in the house. Their fear had been easy for him to read. If the son of a bitch hadn't been forced to obey his commander's orders, he would have found their hiding spot. Ares crammed the dark memories into a small box in the back of his head. The sooner they got off this topic, the better.

"I didn't ask. Did you sleep well? Find everything you need?" He turned around and leaned against the sink, arms folded across his chest.

"Yes, thank you."

"Good."

Merda, things had gotten stiff and stilted between them. They'd lost that comfortable camaraderie they'd had just a few minutes ago. It had felt natural—right. He wanted to feel that ease of familiarity again. He frowned. He should be putting distance between them not thinking about closing the gap. She must have sensed the strained atmosphere as well because she straightened her back and sent him a direct look.

"Maybe we should just get everything out into the open." The straightforward comment made him narrow his gaze at her.

"Meaning?"

"You came to me looking for this *Tyet of Isis* my father mentions in the cipher he left me. It seems to be a clue to the artifact's whereabouts. I don't know what this thing is, but my guess is my parents and even Charlie died because of it. So, I'd like to find some answers."

"Not everything is black and white, Emma," he said. "What if you don't find any answers?"

"At this point in the game, I really don't have a choice." She gave a reluctant shrug of her shoulders. "Someone tried to kill me last night, and the Institute's sidelined me for God knows how long, which means I can't go back to the dig to try and figure out what's going on."

Her words only strengthened his belief that she wasn't working for the Praetorians. If the Oriental Institute wasn't going to let her go back, then that meant someone was worried she might start asking more questions than they wanted to answer. And the only people who wouldn't want her to find something would be the Praetorians. Suddenly, last night made sense.

Someone had sent an assassin to eliminate any possibility of Emma continuing her parents' and Russwin's work. Whoever it was thought she was close to unlocking secrets they either didn't want revealed or wanted to find themselves. And until he knew who was really pulling the strings at the Institute, she wasn't safe.

They'd only been able to narrow their search down to five or six possible suspects, and four of them were too damn close to Emma. It was one of the reasons why the Order wasn't going to be happy that he'd brought her into the guild's stronghold.

"They've actually said you can't go back?" he asked.

"I'm a liability," she said bitterly. "Ewan is going to try and reverse Stuart's decision. His position on the university's Board of Trustees is a powerful one, but I doubt it'll change the Institute's position. I think things in Cairo are tenuous when it comes to their digs, and they aren't likely to jeopardize their position for just one person. I don't suppose I blame them."

"Your friend Ewan—have you known him long?" he asked.

"Since I was a baby. He, Charlie, and my parents had been friends since their college days. When my parents died, he and Charlie were pretty much my only support system. Ewan has been there for me since I got off the plane from Cairo."

"Is there a reason why he didn't go to Egypt while you were dealing with the authorities?"

"What are you driving at?" she asked with a frown.

"Nothing really." He shrugged. "I'm just trying to figure out who might have something to gain if you were dead."

"Well, it wouldn't be Ewan. He's already got so many laurels he doesn't need any new ones to add to his reputation. In fact, he never did like getting down in the dirt. He prefers faculty politics and social events to field work."

"Okay, then who else might benefit if you were suddenly out of the picture?"

"Nobody."

"What about your expedition's new team leader?"

"Mike Granby?" She shook her head. "I don't know how he'd benefit if something happened to me. With Charlie gone, he's the team leader with or without me in the picture."

"So who else is there that stands to gain if something happens to you?"

"That's just it. There isn't anyone." She rubbed her fingers over her forehead in a weary gesture. "I've racked my brains for the past five years trying to understand why someone would kill my parents. It makes no more sense to me than last night does."

"Let's look at it from a different angle. What was it specifically your parents, Russwin, and you were all hoping to find in your expeditions?"

"My parents and Charlie were trying to prove the Sicari existed."

"And you?"

"I was there to excavate Ptolemy's tomb. I didn't really believe the Sicari existed until I stumbled onto that icon the day . . . the day Charlie was murdered."

"Then that means one of two things. Either you have an item someone wants *or* you're close to discovering something someone wants left buried."

"But I didn't bring anything back from the . . ." She suddenly glared at him. "Wait, there's the coin you took from my office."

"I said you'll get it back, and I keep my promises." He frowned at her as she rolled her eyes slightly. "Is there anything else? Something your parents might have found, Russwin, anything at all that might be of value to someone?"

"No, nothing. Maybe whoever it is thinks I have something I don't. After all, you were convinced I had the *Tyet of Isis*." She arched her eyebrows at him.

"Touché," he said with a smile. "So if I think that, who else might know about the artifact?"

"I don't know," she exclaimed with frustration. "Archeologists network like anyone else, and last night was the first I'd even *heard* of an artifact called the *Tyet of Isis*, not even as a myth. That sort of thing would be a topic for discussion. And for my dad to just pull it out of thin air and plop it into that cipher of his—well, it makes me wonder if I've been wasting my time working toward my doctorate."

The sigh of disgust she heaved told him how much she loved her job. Regret lashed its way through him as he knew what the future held for her. He gritted his teeth against the feelings her disappointment aroused in him.

"Would you miss it if you couldn't go back?"

"Yes, as much as I wish otherwise, I'd miss it."

"That sounds like you hate it as much as you love it."

"I suppose you're right," she said with a wistful smile. "I didn't plan on being an archeologist. It just sort of happened. I tried to find a different career when I went to college, but everything kept coming right back to anthropology. And when it came time to settle on a specific track, archeology was what I knew. I didn't realize until then that it was in my blood."

"I imagine your ability has been helpful in your work."

"I make it a point *not* to use my ability in my work. I've built my reputation on my research and fieldwork." Fury blazed in her eyes as she sprang to her feet, the stool she'd been seated on clattering to the floor. "I don't deny using it, but it's a last resort method."

"It wasn't my intent to insult you, Emma." He kept his response soft and gentle as he met her angry gaze.

She'd been through a lot, and he had a feeling her reaction probably would have been less vehement if not for the pressure she was under. Beneath his steady gaze, he watched her struggle to rein in her anger. For a brief moment, he thought he caught a glimpse of deep pain flash across her features before she turned away to set the stool back on its feet. When she faced him again, her outrage was under control.

"My ability is a hindrance to my career," she said quietly. "Can you imagine what a freak show I'd be if it were common knowledge I can read ancient artifacts? I'd *never* be taken seriously by academia. You, of all people, should understand that."

The subtle reference to his telekinesis made him tip his head in a slight nod of agreement. Persecution had taught the Sicari to hide their talents in order to survive.

"No one here is going to think you odd because you have a special gift."

"Maybe not, but they're far from happy to see me."

He winced. She was right. The Sicari wouldn't find her ability strange, but the fact that she was an *aliena* wasn't sitting well with most of the people who knew she was here. When others found out, it wouldn't get any better. But here in the guild his word was law. A protest against Emma was a protest against his authority. The first Sicari who stepped out of line where she was concerned would answer directly to him.

"I know Phae and the Doc were less than cordial last night, but you need to understand that we rarely bring in strangers to our home."

"Then maybe I should leave. Go to the police."

"Now *that's* crazy, and you know it. Exactly what would you tell them? That someone with a sword chased you out of your house and tried to kill you?" Tension ricocheted through him at the possibility she might try to leave. He shook his head and took a step toward her. "You're smarter than that, Emma. You saw how they reacted to your story in Cairo. Do you really think it will be any different here?"

She sent him a look of frustration as she shook her head. The relief barreling through him was like an electric shock. *Merda*, this woman was getting under his skin far too easily. He dismissed the notion. All he wanted was to ensure she stayed alive. His inner voice laughed.

"You're safe here, Emma. I promise I won't let anything happen to you."

"God, you make it all sound so simple."

"It is simple, Emma."

"No. It's insane. I don't even know you."

"What have I done that makes you think you can't trust me?"

"Nothing, and that's the irony of it. For some bizarre reason I *do* trust you, even though you play with swords and can move objects just by thinking about it."

"I don't play with swords," he said as he offered her a half smile.

"No, you *don't*, and that's what scares me," she said as she met his gaze with a wide-eyed look.

There was a hint of disbelief and horror in her eyes. Clearly whatever she'd seen in her vision last night hadn't helped his cause any. His jaw tightened as he considered the possible images she might have seen. Events that in all likelihood would be difficult to explain without telling her everything. And he wasn't prepared to do that right now. It had to be done in stages. She was jumpy enough already.

"Are you afraid of me because of what you saw last night when I gave you the coin back?" His question made her flinch.

"I never know what to expect when I touch an artifact, and last night . . . well, I'd already touched that coin before." She frowned and bit down on her lip. "So I was pretty surprised to see anything at all."

"So once you read an object, it doesn't show you anything else?"

"Not usually; sometimes I get additional information, but not like last night."

"It seemed to hit you pretty hard." His comment made her close her eyes for a second as a pained expression flitted across her face.

"Touching an artifact is emotionally draining because the images are pretty graphic. Last night was brutal even on my gruesome scale." She glanced away from him. "You've killed more than once, and I know you're not a cop and you're not in the military, which doesn't leave much of anything else except the criminal element."

Her observation made him go rigid. Whatever she'd seen had been enough to make her think twice about trusting him. But he wasn't one of the bad guys. All he did was protect the innocent when the justice system failed to defend the people it served. If that meant ridding society of vicious killers, drug lords who killed at the drop of a hat, sexual predators, or any other kind of scum the justice system refused to convict then his conscience was clear. When the Praetorians had made them outlaws, they'd taken money for their assassin skills. It had been good money, and throughout the centuries it had also been invested well. Just as the Church had accumulated immense wealth so had the Sicari.

"Now you're the one doing the insulting," he said grimly. "Whatever you saw me do was done for one reason and one reason only. Protecting the innocent."

"In other words, you're a vigilante." There it was again, that dark note of condemnation in her voice. It rankled.

"No." He shook his head with a grunt of anger. "A vigilante takes justice into their own hands. I only step in when a hard-core felon manipulates and beats the system designed to keep them in check. Sometimes I get paid for what I do, but most of the time I do it because I'm all that stands between the monsters and their next victims. Monsters like the ones who killed your parents and mine."

She flinched and paled beneath his hard stare. The breath of air he drew in between clenched teeth was a sharp hiss. *Fotte*. He hadn't meant it to sound so harsh, but the idea of her thinking he was some renegade outlaw bothered him more than he cared to admit.

He didn't enjoy his job, but he knew it made a difference in the lives of innocent people he didn't know. And for that, he wouldn't apologize. It was a burden he carried even if it meant saving only a few people from the worst of mankind. With a growl of disgust, he moved to clean up the breakfast dishes.

The dishwasher door bounced as he flung it open and yanked out the bottom rack. He didn't know if he was more furious with her or himself. She wasn't a Sicari. Things worked differently in her world.

The mixing bowl he'd used earlier came into his line of sight, and he looked up to see Emma offering it to him.

Regret tilted her sweet mouth downward as she met his gaze. The way she was looking at him made him want to hold her close and tell her everything was going to be all right. He took the ceramic dish from her, set it inside the dishwasher, then closed the door.

"You asked me if I was afraid of you," she said softly. "I'm not. And *that's* what really scares the hell out of me, because what I saw makes me think I should be."

The confusion in her eyes made him heave a sigh. "I know I keep saying that there's a lot for you to take in, but it's the truth. I don't know what you saw, but I'm sure it's not the whole picture."

"I know that. I'm sorry." She forced a wry smile to that delicious mouth of hers. "The truth of the matter is, I feel like I've been drop-kicked down a rabbit hole and I'm still falling."

"Then I'll catch you."

The minute the words were out of his mouth, he suppressed a groan. What the hell was he saying? He drew in a deep breath and the scent of her tantalized his nostrils. It was a sweet, delicious smell that sent his pulse rate skyrocketing. He swallowed hard at the way her lips parted in a small circle of surprise. It made him want to kiss her again. *Christus.* There wasn't a word that could define how far gone he was at the moment. A blush crept its way up over her cheeks as she shook her head.

"Why do I think that white knight routine of yours gets you into a lot of trouble?" The light note of teasing in her voice did little to alleviate the desire spinning through his blood. He clamped down on the emotion and shrugged.

"Nothing I can't handle." When it came to her, that was a bald-faced lie and he knew it.

"Well, I'm grateful you came to my rescue," Emma said as she reached out to squeeze his hand with a smile. "*And* I appreciated the French toast."

"You're welcome," he forced out in a strained voice. He hadn't felt this awkward since what? A few minutes ago? He needed to get the hell away from her or he was going to wind up doing something really stupid.

"Right," she said with a hint of embarrassment. She gestured with her hand in the direction of the exit. "I think I'll head back to my room. I want to get started on that cipher."

As he watched her leave, it took every last bit of willpower he had not to use his ability to draw her back to him. The minute she disappeared around the corner, he turned around and gripped the counter edging the sink. He'd never been so grateful for boxer shorts in his entire life. At least they covered the beginnings of his erection. *Fotte*, what had he gotten himself into?

The sound of someone clearing his throat behind him made Ares turn his head. Lysander stood at the end of the island with his arms folded, watching him. His *Primus Pilus* bent his head to avert his one-eyed gaze.

"Do you want me to see to Ms. Zale's safety?"

Lysander was right to ask the question, but Ares didn't want to discuss the matter. That thought alone said he needed to rethink his position where Emma was concerned. He immediately discarded the idea. With a shake of his head, he turned to face his friend and second-in-command.

"No. I'll do it. She's my responsibility." As he spoke, Lysander raised his head and there was just a hint of assessment in his eye.

"Phaedra's concerned that you might be trying to make amends for the past."

"My sister has always worried obsessively when it comes to me."

"Perhaps she's right this time." Lysander's voice held the slightest note of curiosity, and he arched his eyebrow.

"*Christus*, this isn't about me trying to conquer my demons. Whoever I fought last night had made plans to be at Emma's long before I showed up. The bastard was a Sicari dressed in the robes of the ancient Praetorian order."

"A monk's garment." Lysander's expression hardened. "Like the monk sightings at the murders of Russwin and Miss Zale's parents."

"Exactly. I think someone came back to finish the job he didn't complete at Ptolemy's tomb, which means someone thinks she's a threat."

"Then she can't go back." His friend completed his thought for him.

Lysander was right. Emma couldn't go back, not if she wanted to live. The bastard he fought last night was certain to find her again if they didn't keep her safe. And the man was a skilled Sicari assassin. He'd trained in the Sicari way of combat. Lysander's look of concern made Ares's body grow tight with tension. When his *Primus Pilus* seemed worried, things were generally as bad as he thought.

"It's unlikely he'll breach our security, but inform the others to stay on their toes. We've gotten sloppy lately, and I think you need to put everyone through some exercises."

Lysander nodded and turned to leave then paused. His profile was a twisted mass of scarred muscle for a moment before he sent Ares a direct look.

"Despite Phaedra's concerns or how other guild members might feel, you made the right decision last night to bring Miss Zale here. She needs protection, and it's what we do. We defend those who cannot defend themselves."

His friend and second-in-command didn't wait for an answer. He simply turned and left the kitchen. Lysander was right. Emma needed their help, and if anyone tried to get to her, they'd have to go through him first.

Chapter 9

EMMA shoved a hand through her hair before resting her head on her palm. The longer she stared at her father's handwriting, the less sense it made. She released a noise of frustration. What the hell had he been thinking when he'd coded this damn cipher?

The pencil she held tapped a repetitive rhythm against the table as she studied the encrypted hieroglyphs. She hadn't gotten any further than the original lines she'd decoded. At this rate, she might have the note deciphered by Christmas. Any other time it would be a relatively simple cipher to solve, but her father had changed the code word after the first four lines. Although the puzzle seemed like it was a complete Vigenère cipher, it wasn't. It was as if her father had nestled a new cipher inside the larger one. Tossing the pencil down in disgust, she stood up and paced the floor of her bedroom. She just wasn't able to focus.

No. That wasn't the right word. She was focused all right, just on the wrong thing. Ares DeLuca. She couldn't get him out of her head. It had startled her to find him in her room yesterday evening, but oddly enough, his presence had made her feel safe. She didn't know why, but she trusted him in spite of his evasiveness. Last night when he'd carried her to the car, it had reminded her of fairy tales about knights in shining armor. Even though she'd enjoyed the sensation, she'd immediately discounted the shining armor analogy.

Jonathan's betrayal had ensured the death of that dream. Once upon a time, she'd viewed her ex-fiancé in such an idealistic manner, but his armor had tarnished slowly over time. Funny how the first time she'd met Jonathan, he'd been carrying a sword, too. As the Institute's new golden-haired boy, he'd been tasked with developing an exhibit of ancient Egyptian swords. Ewan had never liked him. Probably because Jonathan's thesis on the religious rituals of the Middle Kingdom's Thirteenth Dynasty had contradicted Ewan's theories. But even Charlie had been less than enthused about her relationship with Jonathan. While sympathetic at the breakup, her mentor had emphatically stated that he'd put up with the man only because of her.

She stopped in front of the fruit tray a woman had delivered a few hours ago. A cluster of grapes was all that was left. The red fruit broke easily off the stem and she popped two of them into her mouth and resumed her pacing.

Focus. She needed to focus. Thinking about her ex wasn't helping her get the damn cipher translated. Then again, maybe the memory of Jonathan was a warning. A reminder that Ares probably had tarnished armor himself.

Jonathan had seduced her to get what he wanted. Why should Ares be any different? The man hadn't hidden his attraction to her. Point of fact, he'd kissed her twice in less than a few hours. And each time the temperature between them continued to rise. That's how things had started out with Jonathan. The biggest difference was that Ares was up front about what he wanted from her. He wanted the cipher translated.

She wasn't totally without blame herself. She'd certainly not been able to hide her own attraction for the man. In all likelihood, Ares was playing off that fact. Although she'd never been one for having sex simply for the physical gratification, the man did make the possibility enormously attractive. The train of thought made her puff out a harsh breath of disgust as she halted her pacing.

All she was doing now was spinning her wheels. Primarily because she was preoccupied with the attractions of her host. She heaved a sigh of disgust. What she needed was air. That is, if she could convince Ares to let her go outside. But she needed to find him first. Something she was reluctant to do. The prospect of being alone in the apartment with Ares was alarming for all the *wrong* reasons.

Particularly when the only people she'd seen this morning were the woman who'd brought the tray, and a younger man who'd delivered her purse and a suitcase filled with a selection of her clothes. Neither of her visitors had said more than a few words to her.

But the expressions on their faces had indicated they were just as unhappy with her presence as Phae and the doctor had been last night. It was another reason why she hadn't ventured out of her room since breakfast with Ares. Icebergs had warmer welcoming committees, but she was more worried about the thawing effect Ares would have on her.

If she hadn't been such a pushover last night, she would have insisted on going to a hotel. She frowned. The truth was, she hadn't put up too much of a fight where Ares was concerned from the moment he'd appeared in her study doorway. And as much as it pained her to admit it, that whole caveman thing had been a turn-on. Okay, maybe the caveman label was overkill, but he'd certainly been the one in charge. And she *had* enjoyed it. The realization didn't sit well with her.

But it was difficult to forget the way he'd scooped her up into his arms like a knight of old. It had been sexy and romantic. Her skin grew hot at the memory. Lord, she was in trouble. Since six o'clock yesterday evening, she'd landed in a world where fantasy and reality collided. The whole thing was so surreal. She hadn't even called the police about her attack. Maybe she should.

Of course, she wasn't sure how to describe her intruder. A guy wearing a hooded cloak off a Halloween costume rack and carrying a sword. Yeah, that would go over really well with a hardened Chicago street cop. They'd have her bound, gagged, and on her way to Jackson Park's psych ward in a heartbeat. Even her next-door-neighbor's kid would have a tough time believing her story. And Shannon had a *really* vivid imagination. If she didn't think it possible to convince Shannon, she wouldn't stand a chance in hell when it came to Chicago's checkered hats.

The real problem was going to come two days from now. When Ewan said he'd talk to her on Monday, that meant he'd be trying to track her down shortly after his morning meeting with Dean Stuart. Ewan would call the cops the minute she didn't answer the door. Or would he?

She grimaced. Not once had she ever questioned Ewan's friendship or loyalty. But her conversation with Ares this morning had been enough to make her doubt a man who'd been one of her parents' closest friends. She just couldn't believe that Ewan was in any way responsible for what happened to her parents, Charlie, or the attack on her last night.

Even Mike hadn't escaped Ares's probing questions. She'd known the man for at least eight years. He'd interned with her parents before their deaths. It wasn't possible he could be involved, could he? He *had* been present when both murders had happened, and at the time she hadn't thought about it, but why had he been at camp the day Charlie was murdered?

He and the others were supposed to have been at the artisans' cemetery. Roberta had said they came back for some equipment Mike had forgotten. It was a reasonable explanation, but timing wise, it didn't look good. Then there was Roberta Young. If there were anyone she had reason to be suspicious of, it was Roberta. She hardly knew the woman, and she'd just shown up at the Institute one day and the next thing she knew she was on the team Charlie had assembled for the Ptolemy dig.

The more she thought about it, there was no one she knew who wasn't above suspicion. The only person she did trust was Ares. And if there was anything more insane than that, she couldn't imagine what it might be. Frustration made her release a sigh of disgust. God, she needed to get out of here. She wanted to go someplace where she could get not only fresh air, but a good dose of reality as well.

At least her reality. Maybe a hot dog down at the pier, the wind blowing hard off Lake Michigan, car horns blowing, people talking, anything to help ground her. The sooner she cleared her head, the better. She crossed the floor to her suitcase and pulled out a heavy sweater. October wasn't always chilly, but down near the water, it could be quite brisk. Especially when she was accustomed to Egypt's hot weather. She pulled the soft knit cardigan over her shoulders and left her room.

She didn't hear any voices or meet anyone as she moved down the hall toward the living room. Just as she would on a dig, she studied the open space with a critical eye. Studying Ares's environment would give her more insight into him and this surreal world he lived in. Last night, drapes had hidden the floor-to-ceiling windows that ran the length of the living room and the adjacent dining area.

Now, the curtains were pulled back to let sunlight stream into the large space. The windows looked out over the lakefront part of the city. In the near distance, she saw part of Lake Shore Drive, the pier, and beyond that, Lake Michigan stretched out to the horizon.

As she moved deeper into the living room, she saw a staircase in the far corner leading to a second level. Curiosity getting the better of her, she climbed the stairwell to the balcony that wrapped itself around the living area below. The first door she came to was partially open, and she gently pushed against the wood barrier.

Ares's office. Even from the doorway, she could tell it was his domain. It wasn't just the dark cherry paneling or the large desk situated near the window that shouted male dominion. It was the scent of him. His spicy cologne clung to the air declaring this was his sanctuary. The windows from the living room continued their run along the wall, but while the drapes were open downstairs, here panels of sheer curtains blocked some of the brightness.

She stepped deeper into the room, eager to learn more about this enigmatic man who intimidated and enthralled her in one breath. Bookcases lined two walls of the room, their crown molding marked with detailed scrollwork. The pattern struck her as familiar, but she gave it only a brief glance before gliding her fingers over the spines of the shelved books. Texts on the Roman Empire, Egypt, and Greece filled the shelves, along with classics by Dickens, Twain, and others. Several books looked old enough to be first editions.

In between the two bookcases, a filler panel held a sword mounted on a wood plaque with a faint circular pattern etched into the polished wood. Opposite the bookshelves she saw an end table loaded with a stack of books next to a large recliner. He liked to read with his feet up. She bit back a smile. Somehow it was difficult to picture Ares as a man lounging in a recliner.

The framed photographs on the credenza prompted her to venture behind the desk. They were the type of pictures most people liked to display. She picked up a photo of a young boy with his family. From the blond hair and the mischievous grin on the boy's face, she was certain it was Ares with his sister and parents. Another picture with him and Phae was more recent. The last photo was of Ares with an older man in martial arts apparel.

Setting the photographs back in place, she glanced over at the wall and a large diploma. She moved closer to read the document and her eyes widened. Newcastle University. Great Britain's premier school for Roman and Byzantine archeology studies. No wonder he recognized the Sicari icon last night. That was odd. With a frown, she leaned forward and ran her fingertip over the raised pattern carved into the diploma's wood frame. For a moment, she wasn't really sure what she was looking at.

A second later, she sucked in a sharp breath—a sword intertwined with a chakram. Her stomach lurched. With a jerk, she turned her head toward the sword on the wall. A chakram. The circular impression behind the sword was a chakram. Her gaze flew up to the crown molding on the bookcases. The Sicari icon lay on its side in a repetitive pattern along the decorative wood facing.

Telekinesis. Swords. Sicari icons.

What the hell was going on here? She stumbled backward away from the diploma and hit her leg on the desk. A grunt of pain escaped her lips as the pointed corner of the furniture dug into her flesh. Her attempt to regain her balance caused her to knock over a stack of files, which she quickly put to rights. She was about to turn away when a file in the middle of the desk blotter caught her eye. Tilting her head slightly, she read the name on the file tab again.

Puzzled, she picked up the brown tabbed folder labeled MICHAEL GRANBY. The first page was a listing of her friend's general bio and work history. She flipped the page to study the next sheet of information. A chill swept across her skin as she scanned the document. It was a detailed summary of Mike's activities over the past year. The sheet listed a number of names and places she recognized, including Ewan's name, hers, and even Roberta's.

What the hell was Ares doing with a file on Mike? Dropping the folder back onto the desk, she saw Ewan's name on a folder. She quickly picked up the file folder and flipped through it. The information inside was dated back more than five years before her parents' death. The icy sensation covering her skin made her shiver as she sifted through the files beneath Mike and Ewan's. She recognized names of other Institute staff on most of the files. Her hands shaking, she reached for the largest file on the desk.

She opened her own folder, her heart pounding frantically in her chest. The thick stack of detailed pages in the file horrified her. It documented whom she'd interacted with, where she'd gone, dates, times—the last six or seven years of her life spread out over forty or more pages. Even minor observations about her relationship with Jonathan.

"I see you've found your file."

The quiet words made her jump, and she jerked her head up to see Ares watching her with a guarded expression. The T-shirt and boxer shorts from this morning were gone. In their place was an expensive-looking navy blue business suit. He looked liked he'd just stepped off a fashion runway. Infuriated that she'd even noticed how good he looked in a suit, she used all her strength to fling her dossier at him. He didn't flinch. Instead, he flicked his wrist and the folder stopped in midair before floating neatly down to the desk. Anger had conquered her fear for the moment, and her humiliation fueled her outrage.

"Who the hell do you think you are?" she said between clenched teeth and braced her hands on the desktop in an effort to stop them from shaking so badly.

"I know you're upset, but if you'll give me a chance, I can explain everything." Ares's voice was calm and soothing, but she didn't want to be soothed.

"Explain what? That you like to spy on people? That you've got an obsession with an ancient group of assassins?" She nodded her head at him as surprise flashed across his face and waved her hand at the bookcases and the diploma. "Oh yeah, I saw the Sicari icon splattered all over the place. You like to break into people's houses and steal their possessions. What am I leaving out?"

"You forgot saving your life." His tersely spoken sentence infuriated her more.

"Don't you *dare* try to weasel your way out of this by playing the 'rescue the damsel in distress' card."

"I'm not trying to weasel my way out of anything," he growled. "What I *am* trying to do is explain."

"You can't possibly begin to explain spying on me."

"It was necessary."

"Necessary? The only time something like *this*"—with a sound of disgust, she pointed to the file he'd returned to the desk—"is necessary is in criminal cases. *I'm* not a criminal."

"I won't apologize for protecting my people, Emma." His penetrating gaze locked with hers. "Especially not when I lose a good man like the one I did last night."

"What's that supposed to mean?" she snapped.

"Exactly what I said. One of my men died last night."

The quiet words stunned her and she stared at him, not sure what to believe or even think. He made it sound as if he was the leader of a group of warriors. Her heart skipped a beat at the thought. Oh no, she was so not going there. She refused to even contemplate what something deep inside her said was coming. Ares folded his arms across his chest and drew in a deep breath.

"How much do you know about the Sicari, Emma?"

She eyed him with suspicion, trying to reignite the anger that had evaporated like a morning mist. "Why don't you tell *me* since you've been spying on me for so long?"

"Do you know as much as your father?" he asked quietly. The question caught her off guard and she shook her head.

"Don't you dare bring my father into this." She glared at him, all too aware she was suddenly on the verge of tears. Damn him.

"So you don't know that much then." There was just a hint of provocation in his eyes as he met her gaze.

"All I know are the basics. My knowledge of the Sicari is superficial compared to what my father knew. Even Charlie could run circles around me on the subject. I chose to specialize in other areas, because"—her voice broke slightly—"because I thought my parents were chasing a myth."

"You surprise me, Emma. You make it sound like you know nothing at all about the Sicari."

He sent her a piercing look. Even in a business suit he still had that predator air about him. And like a predator, he was toying with her. She flung her hands up in the air in a sarcastic gesture.

"Okay. Fine. I'll play this little game of yours. The Sicari were part of Ptolemy's personal guard. Later they were part of Rome's Praetorian Guard, which served as the personal bodyguard of the Caesars. Sometime during Constantine's rule, a power struggle split the Guard in two. The result was the persecution of the Sicari and their families. The ones who escaped became assassins to survive, thus their Latin name. Satisfied?"

The brief history lesson finished, she sent him a contemptuous look. What did he expect? She had not been lying when she said she didn't have the knowledge her father had. The only reason people considered her an expert on the Sicari was because she was David Zale's daughter.

Despite thoughts to the contrary, she knew very little about the Sicari. It had never been her field of expertise. Not even the childhood stories she vaguely remembered her father telling her were of much help. Stories weren't the same as detailed research and study. Hell, she'd be lucky if she even could remember some of those tall tales. Although now she was beginning to wonder if they were all that tall.

The calculating look on his face made her clench her teeth with anger. None of this had anything to do with why he'd been spying on her. It was simply a way to distract her. With a frustrated shake of her head, she blew out a harsh sigh. The sound made his eyes narrow, but she refused to be cowered and she glared at him with defiance. He frowned.

"When did your father tell you the Sicari Order was abandoned?" His question was straightforward, but the dark note in his voice made the hair on her arms stand on end. Worse, the grim look on his features made her pulse flutter with fear. She shook her head, knowing in her heart what he was trying to tell her.

"This is ridiculous. You spy on me, and then you try to dodge the issue by—"

"*Answer* me. When did your father believe the Order died out?" The harsh words sent dread creeping along every nerve ending under her skin.

"He thought they were still in existence," she snapped fiercely. "And don't you dare try to tell me the Order still exists and how you're some kind of immortal."

"I'm not immortal." There was just a glimmer of wry amusement in his deep blue gaze.

"But you *are* saying you're a Sicari." She glared at him. The bastard. He really thought she was going to believe him. *Didn't she?* She ignored the whisper in the back of her head as she met his gaze.

"Yes."

The simplicity of his quiet response did more to rattle her than anything else he could have said. A shudder ripped through her and she clutched the edge of the desk in an effort to steady herself. She didn't know whether to feel elated or terrified.

The Sicari earned their living by assassination, and Ares clearly had a great deal of money. What *did* one get for offing somebody these days? She swallowed hard as she struggled to grasp the magnitude of what he was really saying with that simple yes of his. The files, his Italian patrician looks, the swords, the hybrid mix of Latin and Italian speech, his extraordinary powers.

All of it added up and yet she didn't want to believe it. It tossed her normal, sedate world topsy-turvy. Oh God, had he been responsible for her parents' death? Charlie's? She shuddered. The coin hadn't shown her anything about her parents. But that didn't mean he wasn't involved.

"I can't do this." With a shake of her head, she waved her hand at the files and the room. "I don't *want* to do this. I just want to go home."

"Don't be a fool," he snapped. "You'd be dead in less than a week if you go home."

"You don't know that." She slammed her fist against the desktop.

Anger replaced his calm demeanor until his mouth thinned to a harsh, unforgiving line. Trepidation made her stiffen the instant he walked toward the desk, a restrained fury hardening his features. With a vicious gesture, he pulled a file out of the in-box on the corner of the desk. An instant later, he tossed a black-and-white photo down in front of her.

"I *do* know what I'm talking about, Emma. If I let you go home, you'll most likely end up like this poor bastard. Praetorians don't discriminate based on gender."

Her eyes left his face as she looked down at the picture he'd thrown onto the desk. At first she wasn't sure what she was looking at. It looked like one of those medical figures with the skin missing to reveal nothing but the muscle beneath. Then the reality of it sank in, and she sucked in a sharp breath of horror.

"Oh my God."

"God had nothing to do with it," Ares said with a hard bitterness that sent an icy chill skittering over her skin. "Praetorians did. They skinned him *alive*."

The thought of such barbaric cruelty sent bile rising up in her throat. Her fingers pressed against her mouth, she turned away from the horrible picture. Closing her eyes, she struggled to push the image from her head. It was impossible to imagine the pain that man must have suffered. She shuddered.

Ares made a soft sound she couldn't decipher and she looked at him. Indecision flickered in his dark eyes, just as it had last night. The dark scowl reflected on his rugged features amplified his distaste for the emotion. Without saying anything, he moved toward the window and pulled the sheer curtains aside to stare out at the view. His entire posture reminded her of a taut wire ready to snap, and she knew she was the reason for his tension.

"The surveillance was, and still is, necessary." He sent her a quick look over his shoulder then turned his attention back to the lakefront. "There's a Praetorian working inside the Oriental Institute, but we've not been able to figure out who it is."

"And if you knew?" The moment she asked the question, she regretted doing so. He flashed her a frown of disbelief, and she rushed to clarify her question. "Surely the police could help you. We do have a justice system in this country."

"The Praetorians aren't without their own special gift. They can read thoughts and sense emotions. Their ability to avoid detection is as good as ours, if not better." He arched his eyebrow at her. "So what would you do?"

She looked away from him. It wasn't a question she could answer, because if she were ever to find her parents' killer, she knew what she'd want to do. The same thing Ares wanted. Remembering her friends, she tried to make a case for their innocence.

"Well, you're watching the wrong people. My friends and colleagues aren't connected with the barbarians who . . . who killed your friend."

"Are you so sure?" The sheer curtains fell back into place as he turned to look at her.

"Yes," she said firmly.

He gave her a slight nod as if to say he planned on testing her conviction. When he passed her, she caught the familiar scent of spice wafting off him. It immediately set her senses on fire, and she fought to douse it quickly. She watched him reach for Mike's dossier, the crisp white cuff of his shirt emphasizing his strong hand and long fingers. As he laid the file on the desk and opened it up, she was grateful to see that the terrible photo had disappeared. Stepping back, he pointed toward the open file.

"Tell me what you see."

"What am I looking at?" she asked with confusion.

"I can give you the information, but I prefer you come to your own conclusions."

Accepting the unbiased nature of his rationale, she studied the page detailing Mike's activities over the past six years. The first thing she noticed was the number of times he'd gone back and forth between Chicago and Cairo. That in itself wasn't such an unusual thing for a team leader, but the dates were what caught her eye. It was the familiarity of the dates themselves. She frowned. Just before Charlie and her parents' murders, Mike had traveled to the States for a two-day stay before returning to the dig. When people went back to the States, it was for weeks at a time, not days. She looked up at Ares with some of her old anger.

"What are you implying? That Mike killed my parents and Charlie?"

"I'm not implying anything, but I don't believe in coincidences. Look at the dates, Emma. The man came back to the Institute for a couple of days before each murder. Now if he's not involved, then he probably knows who is."

"No." She shook her head in denial. "Not Mike. I know him. He got me out of Cairo."

"Did he?" Ares folded his arms and studied her intently. He looked like he belonged in a boardroom discussing financial mergers.

"What's that supposed to mean?"

"I'm the one who got Shakir to drop the charges. Granby didn't do anything except put on a show with the police and the consulate."

"I don't believe you," she exclaimed. "Mike was the one who got them to release me into his custody."

"No," he said sharply, his expression grim. "Shakir is on my payroll. I made him set you free. I'm the one who convinced him the locals were telling the truth. Even Roberta Young did more than Granby. She tried to buy your freedom, but Shakir is my man and he can't be bought. My price is always going to be higher."

His last statement sent a shiver down her spine. She was certain she didn't want to know what that price would be. Her heart crashed into her ribs.

"But Mike—"

"Trust me, Granby did nothing except make a lot of noise."

"*Trust you?* I've known you for less than twenty-four hours and I've known Mike for almost eight years. I remember when he first joined my parents' dig outside Luxor."

"If you don't want to trust me, then trust your eyes."

The quiet command directed her to look at the file again, and she stared at the dates. It didn't matter whether Mike was guilty or innocent. Ares had sown the seed of doubt as to her friend's innocence. She closed her eyes. What if it was true? Then it meant she'd spent the past five years working and laughing with the man who'd murdered her parents. Murdered Charlie. Oh God. It couldn't be true.

"He can't be guilty. He just can't," she whispered with horror. "I'd know. I'd know if I was working with the person who killed my parents."

"*Christus*. Don't do this, Emma. No one could know something like that. No one." He stretched out his hand to her, but she brushed it aside.

"I'm all right."

She forced herself to straighten upright. Ever since Charlie's death, she'd been walking a tightrope. With each passing hour, there was some new revelation that enveloped her. Some of which threatened her sense of reality. Reality? What was reality when you could read the past of any artifact people unearthed?

"I shouldn't have pushed you so hard." The regret in his voice touched her and she turned to look at him. "My librarians are more concerned about others in the Institute, but I don't like Granby. Circumstantial evidence or not, the man didn't do you any favors in Cairo, and I don't trust him."

There was a deep concern in his voice, and for some strange reason it made her willing to forgive him for having her watched. She probably would have done the same thing if she'd been in his shoes. She forced a smile.

"It's okay. The more facts I have, the better. I just hope your facts are wrong."

"And if they're not." He folded his arms across his chest.

"Then he's someone to avoid until the police pick him up."

"So you understand why you can't go home."

"Well, I can't just up and disappear. Ewan will cause a riot when he finds I'm missing."

"Emma, the life you had up until yesterday evening is over."

"What the hell is that supposed to mean?" Perplexed, she sent him a questioning look. "I can't just walk away from everything."

"I'm afraid you'll have to," Ares said grimly. "You can't ever go back. Emma Zale died last night."

Chapter 10

ARES'S insides twisted with guilt as he watched Emma's face. Disbelief, horror, and anger flashed across her lovely features in rapid succession. *Merda.* He had all the tact of a bear stumbling around a bee hive. He'd known from the start that if he brought Emma home with him, she'd have to have a new identity and her past life would have to be wiped out of existence. It was the only way to keep her out of Praetorian hands. Even then she'd still be at risk until she had training to make it difficult for her thoughts to be read.

He'd just thought he'd have more time to get her acclimated to the idea. He didn't even have the heart to tell her the worst of it. Her days on archeological digs were over unless she chose to work with the Order. Even then, her access would be limited to avoid running into someone she knew. The archeology field was a small one.

"Let me get this straight," she said in a fierce tone. "You're trying to tell me that you're not going to let me go home."

"It's too dangerous." He folded his arms and pressed into the wound across his chest. The action lit up his nerve endings like a wildfire blazing across his skin. The pain was part of his penance for what he was doing to her. "You'd never be safe. We'll give you a new identity and everything that goes with it."

"Oh, is that right." Her voice sarcastic, she arched her eyebrows. "What are you guys, the CIA?"

"No, but the Order has been hiding and protecting people for the last two thousand years. It's how we've survived."

"Well, I happen to like me—Emma Zale—archeologist, and I don't want to disappear off the face of the earth. So you can just forget the witness protection program. I refuse."

"You don't have a choice in the matter." He tightened his jaw. "You'll be in a car accident tonight, and you'll be killed. Police will identify your badly burned body from documents thrown from the car. A distant cousin will come forward to settle your estate. Everything that belongs to you will be stored until we find another home for you."

"You're going to *kill* someone to make it look like I'm dead?"

The horror in her voice exacerbated the guilt eating away at him. *Merda*, he was handling this badly. No, it was more than that. He hadn't done anything right where she was concerned since he first laid eyes on her. He'd interfered in Cairo when he shouldn't have, and he hadn't left her house last night the minute he realized she was in the office. *Christus.*

"We did *not* kill someone to take your place." He gritted his teeth at the notion she thought him capable of killing an innocent. But then what the hell was she supposed to think? She knew what the Sicari were. What he was. An assassin. It didn't matter that the Sicari only served up justice for the innocent. "We found a Jane Doe in the city morgue who'll receive identification documents with your information on them. Our contacts in the police department will do the rest."

"You can't do this." Her voice held a note of hysteria.

"Would you rather I leave you to the Praetorians?" he asked in a harshly cruel tone. "You've already seen what they do to their victims."

She flinched at his words, but he didn't soften his expression. He needed her to understand there was no going back unless she had a death wish. Her mouth set in a stubborn line, she shook her head.

"There has to be another way. The next thing you'll be telling me is that I can't practice archeology." She blanched as she stared up at him. He was certain his expression was neutral, but she was processing things a lot faster than he expected. She blinked away tears. "Oh God, you're going to take that away from me, too."

"No one's taking anything from you, Emma." He bit the inside of his cheek at the lie. "We're giving you the chance to live."

"No, you're trying to fix your mistake," she said with caustic vehemence.

With a violent sweep of her hand, she knocked several of the files off the desk then shoved her way past him and headed toward the office door. Behind her anger, he could sense her fear, and it twisted something deep inside him he didn't want to feel. She was right. He'd made a mistake. But the truth was it had been a mistake in her favor. She'd be dead if he hadn't gone back for her. And he wasn't sorry for that. In three lengthy strides, he caught up with her. His hand pressing into her shoulder, he forced her to a halt and made her face him. Despite her furious expression, fear haunted her hazel eyes, and it chilled him as she glared at him.

"Well, here's a surprise. No special powers to hold me hostage," she said with a sneer. Her pointed look at his hand on her arm made him grimace.

"*Damno id*, Emma, you're not a hostage."

"Then why do I feel like one," she snapped with just an edge of fear.

The heartfelt emotion in her voice tightened his gut. The fact that she wasn't hysterical showed how strong she was. Only someone with incredible reserves of personal strength could have survived everything she had in the past five years without falling apart. She'd shown a courage that rivaled the Sicari fighters he led. And to adapt as quickly as she had to the reality of her current situation only made him like her more. The need to ease her fear surged through him, and he caressed her cheek with his hand.

"You're afraid because you're not in control of events happening around you. It's understandable." When she averted her gaze, he caught her chin and forced her to look at him. "And while I might have made a mistake entering your house last night, I'd do it again if it meant keeping you safe."

"I know that." She closed her eyes at his words and nodded. "And I'm not ungrateful. Really, I'm not. I'm just confused and overwhelmed by it all."

"And all this time I was thinking it was my boyish charm that had you off-balance," he said with a soft laugh, hoping some levity would ease her tension.

Her eyes flew open as she looked up at him with surprise. Satisfaction curled through him at the look of annoyance darkening her hazel eyes. At least she'd lost that woebegone look. That particular look had been making it almost impossible to keep his hands off her. Every time it darkened her features, he wanted to pull her into his arms and hold her until she felt safe. And that was a dangerous path to follow.

"I'd hardly consider your charm boyish," she said in a breathless voice.

He liked the low, husky sound of her voice. With a light touch, he trailed his fingers down the side of her face and across her shoulder. When she shivered beneath his touch, he fought against the urge to pull her into his arms.

"Hmm, now you've aroused my curiosity. How *would* you describe my ability to beguile the female sex?" He leaned into her and smiled as she bent backward slightly without retreating.

"I've not given it any thought at all."

"Haven't we already discussed your inability to lie well?" he murmured as he gave way to temptation and slipped his arm around her waist to pull her close. *Deus*, she was the perfect fit for him. His cock sprang to life while an air raid siren blared out a warning in the back of his head. She trembled against him, but didn't try to escape his embrace.

"I'm not lying." Her breath warmed his skin as he bent his head toward her.

"No? Then I suppose you're going to tell me you've not thought about me kissing you either." His body responded immediately as her tongue flicked out to wet her lips. It pulled a growl from him and she trembled at the sound.

"No . . . I mean yes . . . damn it." She frowned up at him. "God, this is what I mean about being confused. You make all of this feel normal."

"This? You mean my world . . ." He raised one hand to press his fingers against the rapid pulse at the side of her neck. "Or the fact that we're attracted to one another?"

"I'm not attra—"

He didn't let her finish the denial and captured her lips beneath his. It wasn't the smartest move he'd ever made, but at the moment, he didn't care. His body was making demands, and he wanted to tame the beast before he locked it up again.

Besides, he refused to let her get away with lying to herself. He slipped his tongue past her parted lips and delved into the heat of her mouth. An instant later, her arms slid around his neck. All without prompting. Triumph barreled through him. Her actions said something a hell of a lot different than her words had.

She responded to him with a heat that threatened to unhinge him. The way her tongue danced with his was a sensuous invitation for much more than a simple kiss. But then this wasn't any ordinary caress either. The heat of it made him long for another part of her that would be equally warm and moist.

Merda, there were too many clothes between them. His mouth still heating hers, he shrugged out of his suit coat. He threw it in the direction of the recliner, uncaring of where it landed. The warmth of her penetrated his dress shirt as he slid her sweater off her arms. She didn't protest and the sweater fell to the floor.

He breathed in her scent. Warm, soft, and fragrant like vanilla. She smelled good enough to eat. His mouth nipped and nibbled its way along her jaw and then sought the small dimple in the curve of her neck. Her hands caressed his shoulders then continued their exploration down to his waist. With a gentle tug, she pulled his shirt out of his pants so she could touch him.

The minute her fingers brushed across his skin, it was as if he'd been shocked. He drew in a sharp hiss of air. If she had this effect on him just touching his waist, how the hell was he going to react the minute she held him in her hand? The sound of a door shutting somewhere in the apartment made her stiffen and she drew back with a gasp.

"I . . . we . . . someone might—"

"No one is going to come in here," he murmured as he envisioned

the office door closing. The soft thud of the door and the lock falling into place signaled their privacy. He brushed his mouth across
her ear. "As I was saying, you don't lie very well. I think you're very
attracted to me."

His hand slid up under her shirt to cup a full breast as he drew
back slightly to look at her. Desire sparkled in her hazel eyes, and
with an unintelligible sound, she tugged his head downward and
kissed him with an eagerness that sent his blood roaring through
his veins.

The woman was driving him beyond coherent thought, and he
wasn't about to resist it. Because it felt good. Really good. Her tongue
teased and tantalized the inside of his mouth until she slowly withdrew to trail her lips across his jaw and then downward to the base of
his throat. As she undid his tie and shirt, his hands explored the softly
rounded curve of her buttocks. Her fingertips were like a branding
iron on his skin. Hot. Fiery. They singed his skin as she pushed his
dress shirt aside to expose his chest. She drew back, her hands lightly
tracing the bandage that protected his sutures. Her gaze flew to his
face, an expression of regret and sorrow on her face.

"I'm sorry you were injured because of me. Does it hurt?"

"Not nearly as bad as another part of me is hurting," he rasped.

The pink color rising in her cheeks made her look maddeningly
adorable, and he groaned with the need to explore every part of
her. He was ready to take her here. Right now. A low purring sound
escaped her as he picked her up and carried her back to the desk. He
set her down on the desktop, not even bothering to clear a space.

Barely able to think beyond the thought of burying his cock
inside her, his hand pressed against the apex of her thighs. The heat
radiating through her jeans made him think she would melt the minute he touched her velvety folds. He kissed her again, his body rock
hard and aching for release.

Devour her. That's what he wanted to do. He wanted to devour
every inch of her until she was a part of him, always there, that
fresh buttery scent of her filling his nostrils to the exclusion of all
else. His hand captured the nape of her neck and he kissed her deep
and hard.

The scent of her, the taste, the feel, the tiny mewls of pleasure.

All of it added up to a package of hot heat and sensual delight that he wanted days—weeks—to experience. Suddenly, she shoved away from him in a frantic move. Her fingers pressed against his mouth and her eyes were wide with alarm. Suddenly, the sound he'd been ignoring for more than a minute forced its way into his consciousness. It came again. An imperious knock on the office door.

"*Fotte*," he muttered. Quickly withdrawing from her, he buttoned his shirt, while Emma adjusted her own clothing. The knock came again.

"Ares? Are you all right?" Phae's voice echoed through the office's solid oak door.

"I'm busy. What do you want?" His bellow made Emma flinch, and he reached out to touch her cheek before tucking his shirt back into his pants.

"Why on earth do you have the door locked?"

He growled with anger. *Christus*, his sister had some foul timing. Actually, make that perfect timing. He'd been on the brink of losing every bit of his self-control. With a flick of his hand, Emma's sweater left the floor and swept through the air to land in her lap. His suit coat hadn't made it much farther than her sweater. Filled with self-recrimination, he stretched out his hand to summon the garment to him. Two seconds later, he shrugged into it.

Emma hopped off the desk and straightened her clothes. Satisfied they both looked presentable, he visualized unlocking and opening the door in his mind then picked up one of the files off his desk. His back to the door, he glanced at Emma. She looked painfully embarrassed. He'd done that to her. *Merda*, he was a bastard.

"It's about time you opened . . ." Phae's voice died off as she entered the room. Schooling his features into an unreadable mask, he turned to face his sister, who was staring at the two of them with misgiving.

"Emma and I were talking about her future." He deliberately dropped the file onto his desk in an effort to emphasize his words and give them *some* credibility. "What did you want?"

"I wanted to know if you were going to ride with Magnus and me or go with Lysander."

Dressed in the standard black garb Sicari fighters wore when on assignment, Phae looked pale, but composed. For the moment anyway. But would she be strong enough to carry out her duties as orator at Julian's *Rogalis*? It was a hard enough task when you were only good friends with the deceased, let alone when it was someone you cared about deeply.

"We'll ride with Lysander."

"We?" His sister frowned, but the moment she met his hard gaze, she responded with a listless nod.

The way she looked reminded him of the months following their parents' deaths. Lost. It wasn't a side of herself that his sister revealed to many. He took a step toward her and she raised her hand as if knowing he was worried about her.

"I'll be fine. I'll see you at the estate."

Phae turned away before he could say another word. As his sister left the office, he turned his head to look at Emma. She must have known Phae was hurting because the sympathy etched on her features warmed his heart. His sister was the only family he had left, and he liked Emma all the more for her compassion. The moment Phae was no longer in sight, her expression became distant and reserved.

"I take it I'm supposed go someplace with you?" she said quietly. He nodded.

"Julian's funeral is being held at the Order's estate up near White Cloud, Michigan. It's a long drive so we'll spend the night. The estate is adjacent to the Manistee National Forest, and I thought you might enjoy some fresh air tomorrow morning."

A lie. The fresh air thought had only just occurred to him. The way she bit down on her lip indicated she was torn about his suggestion. Although the complex was relatively inaccessible without the appropriate security clearance, he'd feel a hell of a lot better if he didn't have to leave her behind. Her silence set him on edge, and he took a step toward her. She didn't retreat, but her expression grew wary.

"I need you to trust me, Emma." He met her gaze with his steady one. "Trust me to keep you safe."

"And does that include trusting you *not* to charm your way into my bed?"

The wry note in her voice emphasized exactly how little he'd done to make her feel she could trust him. He knew better than to act as impulsively as he had with her over the past twenty-four hours. Still, she hadn't exactly been unwilling just now. No less willing than she had been last night.

"I'm asking you to trust me with your life, Emma. And I won't apologize for being attracted to you. We both know it's mutual." He watched as her cheeks flooded with color.

"And if I stay here?" The resignation in her voice said she wouldn't like his answer.

"For your own safety, you'll not be able to leave the building."

She shook her head, clearly not convinced. "I just don't think it's a good idea for me to intrude. Particularly when I've not received the warmest of welcomes."

"The guild is a tight-knit group, and Julian was well liked," he said. "His slaying has everyone on edge. But I can protect you better if you're with me."

Tension slashed through him as she considered his words with a frown of contemplation. He could almost see her weighing the pros and cons of her decision. He'd deliberately chosen to let her make up her own mind. She had a stubborn streak, and she would have balked at any command he issued. Things would go a lot easier if he let her think the decision was hers to make, even though he had no intention of leaving her behind. It was easy to see she was on the brink of a decision, and he offered up the only other point he could think of that might convince her to go with him.

"The Order has a substantial archive of Sicari artifacts and other materials in the research library at the estate. I can get you access to any of it."

Her expression told him that upping the ante was holding considerable sway over her decision. The indecision on her face made him want to arbitrarily decide for her, but he held back. He needed to give her some breathing room given everything he'd laid at her feet in the last hour.

"All right. I'll go."

"Good. Lysander will be here shortly. I'll have him come by your room to collect your overnight bag." He tightened his jaw in order not to display his relief.

With a nod, she took a few steps toward the door then stopped

to turn and look at him. Hesitating, she bit down on her lip as if trying to find the words for whatever she wanted to say.

"I don't have a dress to wear. The one I wore to Charlie's funeral
wasn't in my suitcase." She glanced down at the jeans, dark red
shirt, and black sweater she was wearing. The action tugged his
gaze away from her face to slide over her full figure. Lust slammed
into him with the force of a sledgehammer. *Fotte*. It was like being a
teenager again where this woman was concerned. All he could think
about was her in his bed. Naked and willing. He cleared his throat
and turned away from her.

"The *Rogalis* is held outside, so what you're wearing will be
fine," he said without looking at her.

"*Rogalis?*"

"It's a Sicari funeral ritual." He shot her a glance over his shoulder. Mistake. His lust hadn't burned out. He swallowed the emotion
and turned back to the desk. "I need to change clothes myself, but I
have a call to make first."

She released a soft sound that tugged at him, but he didn't turn
around as he heard her footsteps carry her out of the office. The
moment she was gone, Ares braced himself on the edge of the desk
to stare down at the files on his desk. He knew Emma wouldn't be
able to resist exploring. It's what she did for a living. He'd deliberately left the information out in the open with the clear expectation
that she would find it if she entered his office.

He shoved his shoulders upward then rolled his head in a circular motion to ease the tension holding his neck muscles taut. Then
there was the obvious pain he'd caused her and his reaction to the
fact. It seemed impossible to keep his distance from her both emotionally and physically. And *Christus*, he wanted her. Just looking
at her made him hot. Hot with a need he hadn't even experienced
with Clarissa.

The thought sobered him. He pushed the dark memories aside.
He had no interest in rehashing the past. The only thing he had to
do was remember his training. Anger sank its teeth into him. He
had an obligation to keep Emma safe. And in the past twenty-four
hours he'd forgotten every bit of training he'd acquired since Clarissa's death.

He was supposed to be protecting the woman, not succumbing to base desires. All he had to do was keep his hands off Emma, and when she gave him the translation of her father's cipher, he could continue his search for the *Tyet of Isis*. What could be simpler? He grimaced. Fighting a half-dozen Praetorians would be less painful. And he wasn't certain whether that analogy applied to convincing Emma to help him or staying away from her. A quiet sound behind him forced him to turn around. Lysander stood a few feet away looking stern as always.

"She knows she can't return?" His lieutenant's quiet question made him jerk his head in the affirmative, and Lysander nodded in return. "Are you still so certain you can trust her?"

"You're beginning to sound like Phae." Ares frowned in irritation at his friend.

"Your sister isn't your *Primus Pilus*," Lysander said without emotion. "I am. It's my job to play devil's advocate."

"I know that." Ares scowled with self-disgust as he waved a hand at his friend. "And I haven't changed my opinion. I trust her."

"And the cipher?"

"She's translating it, but I have no doubt she'll share what the message says. I'll bring the subject up tomorrow. I pushed her harder than I should have today." He winced at the memory of her struggling with the idea that someone she knew might be her parents' killer and, perhaps worst of all, being forced to give up her old life.

"The *Prima Consul* wants to meet her."

"*Merda*." Ares sighed.

As the Order's commander-in-chief, a *Prima Consul* had directed the Sicari for two thousand years. From financial investments to the Order's policy decisions, the *Prima Consul* had the final word. They rarely interfered with guild business, but the current Consul had always had a fondness for archeology and the legend of the *Tyet of Isis*.

She'd been the one to order the Zales watched and their finds monitored. After the couple's murder, her interest had grown. She'd visited the scene of their death, and had given instructions that she was to receive quarterly reports on Emma.

He'd never questioned his orders, but he'd be a liar if it hadn't made him curious. It was unusual behavior for a *Prima Consul*, but then Atia had always been unpredictable. It was why she was good at what she did. Challengers found it difficult to know when to speak up or when to remain silent.

"You sound surprised. The *Prima Consul*'s interest in the *Tyet of Isis* and Miss Zale's connection to the artifact makes the request a logical one." Lysander shrugged. "She specifically asked that Miss Zale be brought to her quarters after Julian's *Rogalis*."

"I'm not surprised." Ares drew in a deep breath, and with a slight roll of his head, he looked at the tall man opposite him. "I simply wanted a little more time to help Emma adjust to everything. And I'll be damned if Atia is going to interfere with the way I run this guild. Emma is my responsibility, *Prima Consul* be damned."

Lysander's mouth tipped upward in a slight smile that emphasized the grotesque scarring on one half of his face. The scarred tissue overlaying his facial muscles made his smile half-angelic and half-demonic.

"Clearly, you have no aspirations when it comes to advancement within the Order."

"I'm content to do what I'm good at, and that's leading this guild," Ares snapped. "I need to change clothes. Take Emma and her bag to the car. I'll meet you there."

He didn't wait for a response before he brushed past his friend and stalked out of the office. The idea that, as *Prima Consul*, Atia might use Emma for her psychometric ability angered him. He winced as he recalled what had happened to her when he'd handed the Sicari coin back to her last night. The memory of her curled up on the floor of that office triggered something inside him. He ignored it.

His thoughts flashed back to Cairo and Emma's hesitation in picking up the Sicari coin Shakir had shown her. At the time he'd thought the same thing the Cairo policeman had thought. She didn't want to leave a fingerprint. He now realized it was because she'd known there was a possibility of seeing Russwin's death.

But her reaction then compared to how she was affected last night were completely different. Had he been a conductor of some sort? It didn't matter. She needed time to adjust, and he wasn't about to throw her to the wolves in the Order, including the *Prima Consul*.

He released a low growl of self-disgust. He was hiding behind a façade as well. At least Atia would be up front about what she wanted.

Bribing Emma with the chance to see Sicari artifacts hadn't been one of his better moments. He could try and convince himself that he'd done it to get her to come to White Cloud willingly, but deep inside he knew the real reason. He'd instinctively known the possibility of seeing the ancient relics would intrigue Emma. And if she touched one of them, she might see something that would bring him closer to finding the *Tyet of Isis*.

"*Fotte*," he uttered the expletive beneath his breath.

She'd said this whole mess was his mistake. It was an accurate statement. The problem was, every time he tried to fix his mistake, he only made matters worse. Maybe he just needed to leave Emma to the care of the Order. His gut clawed at him like a wild animal.

Like hell he would.

Chapter 11

EMMA stood in the immense library of the Sicari Order's estate. The massive room had a ceiling that was easily sixteen feet high, a large fireplace, and furniture that reminded her of a stately and very exclusive country club. The bookshelves lining the walls ran from floor to ceiling and were filled with books that reminded her of ancient texts. There were at least a hundred people in the room, and yet the room could have held twice that number.

It had taken them almost four hours to travel from Chicago to the estate in Michigan. During that time, she'd worked on trying to decode her father's cipher. She could tell Ares was eager to know what it said, but he'd patiently allowed her to work uninterrupted.

Like everything she'd experienced in the past twenty-four hours, the Sicari estate was surreal. In the dwindling twilight of their arrival, she'd seen black fencing complete with spiked prongs jutting outward to prevent anyone from scaling the barrier. They'd gone through one manned gate, and then another gate that seemed to magically roll back when their car drew up in front of it.

The mansion itself was something out of a gothic novel. Dark and mysterious, the limestone building reminded her of an ancient cathedral complete with gargoyles. Even the interior of the building had a medieval appearance with its high ceilings and arched beams. The entire mansion looked like it had found its way to the wilds of Michigan from Europe stone by stone.

The moment she'd crossed the library's threshold, everyone's attention had swung in her direction. She'd faltered slightly, but the light touch of Ares's hand on her elbow gave her the confidence to move forward as if she actually had the right to be here. They'd halted in front of one of the bookcases, where Ares and the man who'd driven them to the secluded property flanked her like her own private guard.

A few moments after arriving, Ares had left her side to pay his respects to the grieving family, leaving the scarred man accompanying them at her side. When Lysander had appeared at her door to escort her to the garage, it had taken every bit of her willpower not to recoil at his shocking appearance. The manner of his disfigurement was so similar to the picture Ares had shown her that she was certain the Praetorians had tortured the man sometime in the past.

The scars gave the warrior a dark, menacing appearance, but Lysander's treatment of her had quickly erased that image. Polite, even sympathetic, he'd joined Ares in standing watch over her. And it couldn't be called anything else. Every time Ares left her side, the disfigured man remained to stand guard. It had been that way since their arrival at the secluded estate on the edge of the Manistee National Forest. The two men provided a buffer from the stares and the occasional hostility she'd seen on the faces of some.

Now as she studied the gathering, she felt completely out of place. Almost everyone present was dressed in solid black pants and knit shirts. It was like being in the midst of a military ops exercise with one exception. The only other place she'd ever seen so many swords was on television or the big screen. Some wore their weapons in scabbards on their back, while others wore them at their side. She even saw several of the circular blades called chakrams hanging from the belts of several men and women.

She wondered how many of them had actually killed someone, then she immediately shut out the thought. It was easier to pretend she was at some sci-fi convention. With a soft sigh, she bowed her head. Perhaps she was dead and this was nothing more than a dream. But if that was the case, why did every one of her nerve endings quiver in response to Ares's presence? She darted a glance in his direction.

Dressed in black like the others, he was a feast for the female eye. Tall, muscular, and powerfully male, he stood with arms folded across his chest, watching the room like a sentinel from the ancient past. The sword he wore on his back only enhanced the edgy danger emanating off him. As if sensing her gaze on him, he looked down at her.

He didn't say anything, but the flash of desire in those lake blue eyes of his made her cheeks burn. With a gulp, she jerked her gaze away from his, and a fire coiled inside her belly as she heard him breathe a sound that could have passed for a low growl. The primal, quiet rumble slid across her skin, making her hair stand on end. It was the sound of a powerful predator eyeing his dessert. Afraid to look Ares in the eye, she turned her attention to Lysander.

The disfigured warrior was dressed like everyone else in standard black with a sword on his back. Like Ares and one or two other fighters, Lysander wore leather bracers on his forearms. She hadn't asked what they signified, but an educated guess told her they represented a rank of some sort. Her gaze drifted across the room to where a group of people had gathered around an older woman seated away from the bereaved family.

Ares had approached the woman immediately after speaking with Julian's family. It had been apparent they were at odds with one another. His stiff posture had radiated defiance and the woman's expression had wavered between amused exasperation and unyielding resolve. Now, as she watched the deference each fighter showed the silver-haired woman, Emma wondered who she was. She supposed she could ask Ares, but thought better of it. Just the sound of his voice sent her heart pounding.

Instead, she turned her attention to the visitors gathered around Julian's grieving parents. Behind them on a table was a picture of a handsome young man. Remembering the photo Ares had shown her earlier, she hoped they hadn't seen their son's mutilated body. She knew how traumatizing it was to see a loved one disfigured.

The sudden, sharp hiss of breath coming from the tall, solidly built fighter beside her captured her attention, and she looked up at Lysander. His disfigurement made it difficult to tell what he was looking at, but the muscles lying beneath the scars were taut with tension. She turned her head and saw Phae hugging Julian's mother.

Dressed in a white toga, Ares's sister nodded as the older woman gently wiped away the tears on Phae's cheeks. Emma looked back at Lysander, who remained rigid with restrained emotion. Did he care for Ares's sister? The sudden way he relaxed made her search the room for Phae, but the other woman had disappeared.

She returned her gaze to Lysander and found herself looking straight into his hard one-eyed stare. The green in his eye darkened as he narrowed his gaze at her. It was a warning, pure and simple. Mind her own business. She forced a weak smile to her mouth before turning away.

Uncomfortable under the fighter's stern expression, she shifted her attention to a group of young men huddled around a bar in the far corner of the room. They'd all been drinking heavily, but seemed capable of holding their liquor. At least she hoped they were. It still made her nervous to see men, weapons, and drink mixed together. It seemed like an accidental slaying waiting to happen. Just as unnerving was the fact that one of them had been studying her the entire evening. And *not* with lust.

"I can get you another napkin if you like," Ares said in a soft voice.

The quiet statement made her look at the shredded napkin she held before she jerked her head up to meet his reassuring gaze. She wadded the napkin into a ball and dropped it into the empty beverage cup she'd set down on the bookcase behind them a little while ago.

"No thank you."

"Relax. No one is going to eat you."

"I'm glad you think so," she said through clenched teeth. "Based on some of the looks I've been getting, I'm giving five to one odds you're wrong."

Before he could respond, the sound of a drum with a slow persistent beat drifted into the room from the covered patio abutting a bank of French doors. Silence immediately engulfed the room as the young man from the bar and a companion quietly ushered the older couple out into the night. The sudden brush of a warm mouth against her ear sent a rush of heat through her.

"Lysander and I have to lead the procession. Follow the children when they go outside then stand behind them."

His knuckles barely grazed her cheek as he and Lysander moved forward to head up two columns of fighters at the open doorway. The touch left her feeling safe and protected. It was a disconcerting sensation. How could this man she'd known not more than a day affect her in ways that no other man had before? Even more unbelievable was the fact that she was finding this world he lived in almost normal. She closed her eyes for a brief moment as she questioned her sanity.

Slowly, the warriors filed out into the darkness to the steady beat of the drum followed by the rest of the guests. When the last guest had disappeared through the French doors, a group of children entered the living room from the main hall. Led by a young woman, they somberly filed through the door, the lit candles they carried flickering as they moved. Remembering Ares's instructions, Emma followed the last child out the door onto the patio.

Small pebbles rustled quietly beneath the feet of the cortège as it wound its way down into the trees surrounding the mansion. If not for the votive candles lining the path, the darkness would have been absolute the moment they entered the forest. After a minute or so the procession emerged into a large glade.

Emma stared at the huge pyre surrounded by a circle of stone blocks, which sat in the middle of the glade. Torches bordered the wooden structure, their flames illuminating the body engulfed in white funereal wrappings on top of the platform. Unbelievable. If someone had told her yesterday she was going to witness an actual Sicari funeral ceremony, she would have thought them insane. Now she was struggling to reassure herself this wasn't insanity.

She closed her eyes in the hope she was just dreaming. The persistent beat of the drum told her differently. She was still in Michigan with an ancient order of assassins. Fighters who had telekinetic powers. She winced and focused her attention on the scene before her. Not even her father could have envisioned this type of ritualistic behavior from the scant findings he'd recorded over his lifetime.

What she was seeing now wasn't written down anywhere. She was certain of it. If it had been, her father would have had a field day talking about this. And *this* she would have remembered. With a slight shake of her head, she studied the procession of fighters.

Ares and Lysander parted ways at the foot of the pyre, each of them leading their column of fighters along either side of the massive death bed. When the procession had formed a large semicircle around the pyre, the drumbeat faded into silence. It was the quiet that tugged at her heart.

The unspoken grief was visible in the stoic expressions of the men and women around the pyre. The emotion vibrated off them until it was almost tangible. Nothing broke the silence for a long moment, until out of the darkness a female voice began singing a haunting melody. The heartfelt grief in the singer's voice made her swallow hard.

The raw pain in the woman's voice was an emotion Emma could identify with far too easily. She blinked back tears at the thought of her parents. Charlie. The young man who'd been tortured to death. The woman's song grew louder as the singer emerged from the trees and walked toward the funeral pyre. The fact that it was Phae didn't surprise her. Ares's sister halted at the head of the wooden funereal structure. When she'd finished her song, she lowered her head and her body folded inward in a clear display of sorrow.

Emma saw Ares watching his sister with a look of concern. He even took a step toward her, but Phae suddenly straightened and started to speak. Over the next ten minutes, Ares's sister shared memories of her friend in a moving eulogy. When she'd finished, she threw back her head and shouted out in Latin the words, 'he lives twice who dies well.' At her raw cry, the fighters around the funeral pyre drew their swords and repeated her shout.

"*Bis vivit qui bene moritur.*" It was a roar of pain, grief, and defiance all in one.

Phae retrieved an unlit torch off the ground and set it on fire with a nearby flame. In a singular move the fighters sheathed their swords and picked up unlit torches off the ground in front of them. Phae lit Ares's torch and then Lysander's before thrusting hers into the head of the funeral pyre. The flame from Phae's torch passed its way down the two lines of Sicari fighters. One by one they thrust their torches into the pyre. In less than a minute, the wooden structure erupted with a roar as the fire engulfed it.

The heat from the flames forced everyone back except for Phae. The expression on her face echoed with more than just sorrow. There was guilt there as well. Lysander took two steps toward her, but she must have seen him move because her head jerked in his direction. Pointing to the fire, she shook her head and said something softly to him.

The Sicari warrior went rigid, his angelic, demonic face a twisted mask of guilt. Without a word, he turned away and retreated to the edge of the circle, his tall frame a shadowy figure against the dense forest surrounding them. Ares frowned with puzzlement and moved toward his sister.

With a violent shove, she threw off his touch of comfort and retreated a short distance to turn and watch the funereal flames shoot high into the air. There was a forlorn look about her that made Emma's heart ache for her, but she understood the other woman's need to be alone in her grief.

As the flames roared high into the sky, four Sicari fighters moved to stand guard at each corner of the pyre. This final act seemed to signal the end of the ritual, and the gathering slowly dispersed. More than ever, Emma felt every bit the *aliena*, and she retreated a small distance into the shadows. As the mourners moved along the path back to the mansion, she remained as still as possible to avoid drawing attention to herself.

Although several people glanced her way, no one spoke to her. For that she was grateful. Her luck didn't hold. The young man who'd been studying her so closely inside the house headed up the path. He'd almost passed her before he seemed to sense her presence. Anger filled the man's stride as he drew his sword and headed toward her. She flinched. Oh God, not again.

"Go back to your Praetorian masters, *aliena*, or I'll kill you myself."

The vicious hostility emanating from the fighter sent Emma's heart plummeting down to her stomach. Out of the corner of her eye, she saw Ares running toward her, while Lysander approached from the opposite direction. Before Ares could reach her, the Sicari angrily thrust his sword arm up into the air with a shout of rage. Fear left her as she resigned herself to the fate she was certain to come. With another loud roar, the young man abruptly whirled around and dropped his sword arm to point his weapon at Ares in a defiant gesture.

"Ares DeLuca, I call *Dux Provocare*."

The moment the fighter's words reverberated through the glade, the entire gathering turned toward the new drama taking place. His expression cold, Ares shook his head.

"If you wish to challenge me, fine. But not here, Maximus. It's an insult to Julian's memory."

"You bring an *aliena* into our guild the same night my brother is murdered by those Praetorian bastards, and you dare to suggest I'm insulting Julian?" Maximus sent her a sharp glare before returning his gaze back to Ares. "Her presence here shows you've lost your edge. It's my right to call *Dux Provocare*. Here and *now* if I so choose."

"As you wish." Ares shrugged and turned his gaze on her. "Stay with Lysander and don't interfere no matter what happens."

"But I—"

"*Fotte.* Now's not the time, Emma. Just stay out of this. I'll explain later."

Chastened by his terse manner, she nodded her agreement. Satisfied, Ares nodded sharply at Maximus then turned and walked away from the younger man. The younger Sicari, an expression of rage on face, charged after him.

In a flash of movement, Ares's sword left its scabbard and the light of the funereal flames danced off his blade. With his back still to Maximus, he swung his sword over his shoulder and stopped the other fighter's weapon with a resounding clash of steel. The blades still locked together, Ares pushed upward while twisting his body around and a second later Maximus went flying backward without Ares even touching him. Emma grabbed Lysander's arm.

"What the hell are they doing?" she asked without taking her eyes off the two men.

"It's called the *Dux Provocare*. The leadership challenge. Maximus is challenging Ares's authority and right to lead the guild. If Ares wins, then all is well." Lysander didn't expand on the explanation, and she sensed he'd omitted something. She looked up at him to see a grim expression on the angelic portion of his face. She shivered, but it wasn't from the chilly night air.

"And if he loses?" She returned her gaze back to the two warriors, and gasped as Ares barely missed a vicious swing of Maximus's blade.

"The winner will be the new leader of the guild." Phae's voice broke slightly as she joined them on the opposite side of Emma. "And unless the winner decides to show mercy, the loser forfeits his life. Maximus is not feeling generous tonight."

The strain in Phae's voice deepened the chill crossing Emma's skin and she dug her fingers deeper into Lysander's arm. Why didn't he do something? The only reason the man had challenged Ares was because of her.

"You have to stop this, Lysander," she whispered as she looked on in horror. "All of this is my fault. I shouldn't have come here tonight."

"We cannot interfere. Maximus would have challenged Ares anyway. He blames Ares for his brother's death. Grief is driving him, not common sense. The man knows he's no match for Ares."

Despite the confidence in the grim-faced warrior's voice, Emma knew he was concerned, almost as much as Phae was. The gathering had closed ranks around the two fighters until the two men fought inside a fairly small circle. As she watched them fight, sparks flew off their steel blades with each vicious blow.

With a smooth swing of his sword, Ares knocked his opponent's weapon aside before flipping his sword and slamming the pommel of his sword's hilt into Maximus's head. The young Sicari staggered backward, shook his head, then charged forward again. His expression one of disgusted disbelief, Ares simply stood there waiting for the other man to reach him.

Her heart in her mouth, Emma clenched her teeth in an effort to keep her screams inside as Maximus swung his sword. In a blinding flash of speed, Ares tucked himself into a ball to roll under and past the blade headed toward his chest. The movement happened so quickly that it looked as though he'd rolled forward on a cushion of air. Emma drew in a sharp breath. His telekinetic abilities. He was using his special gift to his advantage. Now that she thought about it, even some of Maximus's thrusts had gone awry without any physical interference. Somehow, the knowledge reassured her.

Exasperation hardening his features, Ares sprang to his feet in a fluid movement of grace and power then proceeded to elegantly slide the tip of his sword across Maximus's back to draw first blood. The counterattack took all of two seconds, and Ares's opponent whirled around with another cry of anger.

Behind the two fighters, the funeral pyre provided a brilliant illumination of the combat. The fire raged inside its stone circle, and its flames danced yellow, red, and blue streams of light off the swords that crashed loudly in the crisp fall air. Neither man gave ground, yet Ares remained untouched.

A fact for which Emma was grateful. Knowing she was the reason for the duel made it painful to watch. If something happened to Ares, she didn't think she'd be able to forgive herself. Both men were breathing hard now, and small clouds formed where the warmth of their breaths met the fall air. Despite the alcohol Maximus had consumed, the only thing it seemed to have done was slow his movements. But what he lacked in speed, the younger man made up in brawn.

Her heart slammed into her breastbone as Maximus's blade came within an inch of Ares's chest before an invisible force deflected the sword's deadly arc. In retaliation, Ares darted forward and brought his sword down and across Maximus's arm. A roar of anger bellowed out of the injured man, and Ares glared at him.

"End this now, Maximus, and I'll grant you *Indulgentia*."

"And give you free rein to have your Praetorian bitch warm your bed," Maximus said with a sharp shake of his head and smiled nastily at the look of cold fury that crossed Ares's face. "Yes, I've seen the way you look at her. Everyone has. So know this. The minute I'm through with you, I'm going to kill her, too."

The rage in Maximus's voice obliterated the embarrassment his accusation sent crashing through her. The fighter meant every word about killing Ares first and then her. God, she hadn't even slept with the man. And if Maximus had his way, she never would. She almost gave in to the hysterical laughter that followed the fleeting incongruous thought. All that mattered was Ares's survival. In a sudden move, Maximus lunged forward and drew blood as he brought his sword down onto Ares's shoulder.

The grimace of pain on Ares's face tugged a moan from her. The pain he was in had to be excruciating because Maximus had reopened the shoulder wound he had suffered the night before. The blade splayed opened his black knit shirt to reveal a wound that flowed with enough blood to sicken her. She closed her eyes to control the dizziness washing over her. Beside her, Phae released a quiet cry of panic. It made Emma tremble with renewed fear. If the other woman was afraid, then it could only mean Ares was in deep trouble.

The two fighters circled each other on the damp grass. Packed down beneath their weight the grass glistened with blood and a slight condensation from the cool, night air. Maximus charged forward. Ares was prepared for his opponent's move. He threw himself up into the air at almost a horizontal angle to slam his feet into Maximus's chest, bringing the younger man's forward momentum to an abrupt halt. Ares completed his move by twisting his body in midair and landing lightly on his feet with his back to his opponent.

His sword glittered in the firelight as Ares swung it out in front of his body then deftly twisted his wrist so the blade changed direction to meet Maximus's forward lunge. Like an arrow finding its mark, Ares drove the sword backward under his arm and plunged it into the younger man's thigh. The other man howled with pain, and for the first time in her life, Emma took pleasure in another person's agony. She closed her eyes in a brief prayer of gratitude.

Beside her, Lysander grunted with something she could only think was satisfaction, while Phae breathed a sigh of relief. His expression grim, yet determined, Ares withdrew his sword then rose to circle the other man as Maximus straightened upright. Favoring his injured leg, the younger fighter glared at Ares.

The two men were so close to where she was standing, Emma could smell the metallic scent of the blood flowing from their wounds. It sickened her. But it wasn't just the smell she found disturbing. The violence of the fight was barbaric. Maximus swung his sword hard, but Ares easily blocked the attack. Steel met steel, and with a shriek of metal both blades slid downward against each other to lock at the hilt. Maximus's face twisted into an ugly scowl.

"I *will* defeat you."

"We shall see," Ares said in a cold voice as he braced himself against the hilt of his sword and shoved the younger man away from him.

His expression resolute, Ares swung his weapon downward with chilling purpose and sliced into the other man's arm. This time, Maximus's expression revealed resignation as if he realized he was losing. With renewed stamina, Ares advanced on the man with a flurry of strikes and all Maximus could do was block the blows. Relief warmed its way through her. He was going to win. He wouldn't die.

Until this moment, she hadn't realized she was more worried about the possibility of Ares dying than herself. She didn't linger on the thought. Once more Ares attacked, but as he did so, he lost his footing on the slick grass beneath his feet. He quickly recovered with a forward roll to land in a crouch. But even that maneuver didn't save him as he encountered another slick patch of earth. Maximus, sensing a victory, grinned with malice as he stepped forward.

"*No.*" Emma didn't think. She reacted.

In the space of seconds, she was standing between the two men with Maximus clutching his sword in both hands above his head. In that instant, she realized she was probably going to die, but she couldn't just stand by and watch Ares be killed because of her. Swallowing hard, she gathered up as much bravado as she could muster and glared at the man in front of her.

"Well, what are you waiting for? You said you were going to kill me, now's your chance."

The moment her words split through the air, everything in the universe seemed to come to a screeching halt. The old adage *so quiet you could hear a pin drop* came to mind as the only sounds echoing in the small glade were from the funereal fire crackling fiercely and the breeze stirring in the trees. Terrified, she was breathing hard, and her breath crystallized in small puffs of cottony white air. Dead silence was an oxymoron because amazement, anger, and intense disapproval pulsated and rippled through the crowd encircling her, Ares, and Maximus. If possible, the gathering's silent, yet fierce, denouncement of her action made the temperature drop several more degrees. She shivered, but she wasn't sure if it was from fear or the cold. The rage on Maximus's face slowly died as she looked him in the eye.

"Well," she said defiantly. "What are you waiting for?"

"That's enough, Emma," Ares said in an icy voice.

At that moment Maximus brought his sword down with blazing speed, and Emma closed her eyes, fully expecting to die a terrible death. The sword didn't come anywhere near her. Instead, Maximus drove it into the earth, and when he released it, the weapon wobbled back and forth from the force of his blow. Ares pushed her aside with something less than gentleness, and she frowned. Didn't he appreciate her sacrificial act? Ungrateful bastard. Maximus dropped to his knees.

"My life is yours to do with as you will, *il mio signore.*" Contrition filled the Sicari fighter's voice, and Ares roughly grabbed Maximus by the cuff of his neck. With a jerk he dragged the other man to his feet with an angry growl.

"If you *ever* challenge me again, I won't spare you any quarter like I did tonight. We both know the only reason you drew blood was because I didn't want you to lose face in front of your parents and the *Prima Consul*. Now get the hell out of my sight before your parents lose another son."

Thoroughly chastened, Maximus turned and walked away, leaving Emma alone with Ares in the circle. The muscles of his back were hard and rigid with tension beneath his knit shirt. When he slowly turned to face her, the dangerous power rippling through every movement he made sent trepidation skating down her spine. Cold fury had chiseled his features into a stony expression, and another shiver of fear slid across her skin. His anger puzzled her, and she trembled as he slid his hand through her hair to curl around the back of her head in a painful grip.

"You have no idea what you've done, *cara.*"

"I repaid the favor. I just saved your life."

"You did no such thing," he snarled. "I had everything under control. Maximus would have been on the ground with my sword at his neck in a single move. But instead, you interfered in a matter that didn't concern you—in front of my guild and other members of the Order."

She flinched at his fury. For the first time she realized it wasn't her attempt to save his life that enraged him—it was that she'd done it in front of everyone watching. She'd made him look weak.

"I'm sorry."

"Not half as sorry as we're *both* going to be," he growled. Something bad was going to happen. She could see it in his stormy blue gaze as he cleaned the blade of his sword with a cloth he'd pulled out of his pants pocket. Grim-faced, he eyed her coldly. "Hold out your hand, Emma."

"Why?" She eyed him with suspicion.

"You lost the right to ask questions the minute you interfered," he rasped.

She winced as her wrist ached beneath an invisible vise for a brief moment before the pressure was gone. Swallowing hard, she slowly extended her hand. His gaze harsh, she flinched as he forced her hand open wide with his unseen touch. A low murmur erupted from the crowd, but it was a startled cry of protest that made her instinctively turn her head. Phae was watching them with an expression of horror.

In that moment, fire blazed across Emma's palm. With a scream of pain, she jerked her head back toward her hand to see blood flowing from a gash across her palm. Her gaze flew upward to Ares's unreadable features. He'd cut her. He'd used his goddamn sword to slice her palm open.

"You cut me," she choked out. Without thinking, she swung at him but an unseen hand easily deflected her blow. "You son of a bitch. You tell me to trust you, and then you *cut* me?"

"Be quiet and keep your palm open, Emma." It was a command, and his cold, deliberate manner made her obey him despite her anger and pain.

"*Vena vinculum*," he said quietly before he proceeded to slice open his own hand.

Appalled, she backed away from him. It was a pointless effort as a familiar, invisible pressure on her arm jerked her forward until she was within an inch of his hard, tension-filled body. Despite his insane actions, the raw maleness of him still managed to send her heart slamming into her chest. But it was his cold, unflinching gaze that alarmed her. This was a true Sicari assassin. A man capable of killing. Yet for some bizarre reason, she didn't fear for her life. He was furious with her, but there was also a glimmer of solace in his eyes. She trembled as he pressed his wounded hand against her cut tightly, their blood flowing as one.

"Repeat after me." The dark authority in his voice edged its way along her nerve endings. "I accept the blood bond of Ares DeLuca."

Despite her fear and confusion, she rebelled. "Not until you tell me what's going on."

"Say it, Emma, or I'll turn you over to the Order without another thought." The implacable expression on his face made her believe he meant every word. And whatever turning her over to the Order meant, she was certain it wouldn't be good.

"I accept the blood bond of Ares DeLuca. Whatever the hell that means." This last part she muttered beneath her breath.

"It means I just saved your life. *Again*," Ares said sharply as he raised their clasped hands high in the air and shouted, "*Vena vinculum*."

She flinched. Whatever he'd saved her from, his dark scowl said he wasn't happy about it. Definitely bad news for when he got her alone. Worse, the crowd encircling them erupted in low rumblings of dark disapproval. Not a good sign either. She tried to pull free of Ares's grasp, but he tightened his hand around hers to hold her firmly at his side.

Out of the crowd, the regal, silver-haired lady she'd seen earlier walked forward at a stately pace. Her hand went up in a command of silence as she halted in front of them. The crowd obeyed. Her stern gaze fixed on Ares, she studied him for a moment then turned toward Emma.

"Do you accept the blood bond this man has offered you?"

Oh lord, if this was some sort of Sicari marriage ceremony—she

shook her head vehemently. The woman arched her eyebrows at
Ares, and the pressure on Emma's hand grew painfully tight.

"*Answer* her," Ares growled. The harsh command warned her
to respond in the affirmative. As much as she wanted to object, an
internal voice warned her now wasn't the time for rebellion.

"Ye . . . sss." She sent Ares a fiery look, but his chiseled expression said he could care less.

"Very well." The woman nodded her head then looked at Ares
with a questioning look in her eyes. "And you, Ares. Do you accept
the responsibility that comes with this blood bond?"

He nodded sharply. Emma frowned at the sudden gleam of
approval in the woman's eyes. Why did she seem pleased by Ares's
behavior when everyone else was angry? And what the hell kind of
responsibility was she talking about? The woman turned slowly to
survey the crowd.

"The trial shall begin. Who will stand for the transgressor?"

"I will." Ares's voice rang out loud and clear in the night air.

"If you do so, her fate is yours. Are you prepared for the consequences?" The matron's eyebrows arched in an imperialistic
manner.

Emma shook her head. Fate? Whose fate—*hers*. Suddenly, she
realized this blood bonding rite wasn't about marriage at all. It was
about something altogether different, and she didn't like where any
of it was leading.

Chapter 12

HIS shoulder was on fire, *again*. He'd let his guard down on purpose, believing Maximus would know he was simply helping him save face in front of the Order. The Sicari warrior had figured it out *after* Emma had interfered. Anger tugged a low growl from him.

Emma . . . *Christus*, it had been a miracle he'd managed to keep from throttling her. He'd told her not to interfere. Yet she'd thrown herself into the middle of the fight, thinking he needed saving. Deep in the recesses of his mind, a small voice reminded him that she'd willingly put her life on the line simply because she believed him in mortal danger. It took courage to do that. And even something else. Not a thought to explore—particularly right now.

He suppressed a sigh of disgust. It changed nothing. She'd interfered in a *Dux Provocare* and jeopardized her own life by her actions, no matter how well-intentioned her motives. Emma jerked her hand from his with an unintelligible exclamation. The action accentuated the protesting nerve endings in his palm. The blood bond. If she'd listened to him, all of this would have been avoided. She erupted with fury as she glared first at him and then at the *Prima Consul*.

"Damn it, will someone tell me what the hell is going on here?"

"You are on trial, Miss Zale."

Ares studied the *Prima Consul*'s expression as she eyed Emma with that piercing silver gaze of hers. After the murder of his parents, he'd spent a lot of time pinned beneath that assessing look. His godmother hadn't been the *Prima Consul* then, but Atia had still been a formidable woman when she'd taken him and Phae into her own home.

"*Trial*? For what?" Emma exclaimed with disbelief.

"You interfered in a *Dux Provocare*, which is strictly forbidden."

"You can't be serious," Emma snapped. "I didn't interfere. Ares was about to lose his life because of me. I couldn't let that happen."

"An admirable motivation, but ignorance of the Order's law does not excuse your transgression." His godmother turned her sharp gaze on him in a look of clear reproof. "For almost two thousand years, the *Dux Provocare* has ensured loyalty and strengthened the leadership of our Order. Interference cannot go unpunished even for *aliena*."

Fotte. That wasn't altogether true. As *Prima Consul*, Atia had the authority to mitigate the punishment. He'd just not been willing to bet Emma's life on Atia's generosity. Was his godmother angry that he hadn't trusted her with Emma's life or because he'd performed the blood bond? He knew he'd bent the rules tonight. *Merda*, he'd done a lot more than bend the rules. At least the punishment for Emma's crime and his unsanctioned blood bond with her was the same. They wouldn't make him do the gauntlet twice—would they? He drew in a deep breath and tightened his jaw. It wasn't like he'd had much of a choice.

Despite her good intentions, Emma had committed the ultimate sin against the Sicari Order. A seditious act. It had been more than a hundred years since someone had tried to stop a *Dux Provocare*. Then it had been a Praetorian defector attempting to save his Sicari wife. The man had barely survived the penalty handed out for such an offense. Emma wouldn't have stood a prayer without the blood bond, and the Order would never have agreed to let him champion her otherwise.

"What's done is done." He met his godmother's sharp gaze with defiance.

"Agreed," Atia said in a crisp tone. "Yet we still must resolve the issue of this trial."

"Get on with it then," Ares snarled. "As the *Prima Consul*, you have the right to set aside the trial and move directly to the sentencing."

"Ah, so I do," Atia murmured as her mouth thinned with what he knew was more than displeasure. She was worried for him. "But a trial would afford you some respite."

"We both know the delay will be of little use."

His godmother drew in a sharp breath and glared at him. "You always were hardheaded. I know the *Dux Provocare* took its toll on your ability."

"I'll manage."

Normally calm and serene, Atia uttered a sound of fury. The unusual response expressed her fear for him more than anything else she might have done or said. With a sharp movement, his godmother turned to face the Sicari surrounding them.

"The *aliena* has been judged and found guilty. Her blood bond with Ares DeLuca gives her the right to choose him as her champion."

Beside him, Emma made a choked sound of anger. "That's it? No defense? Nothing? That's not justice."

"There's no point. The law is the law," Atia said harshly as she whirled around to eye Emma with an icy look. "Be grateful Ares chose to break our law against blood bonding with *alieni*. Otherwise, it would be *you* running the gauntlet."

Concern darkened her silvery gaze as Atia stared at him for a long moment. The unspoken message in her eyes warned him to take care. His barely perceptible nod seemed to satisfy her. Resignation flashed in her gaze before his godmother turned and walked away without a backward glance. In a flurry of movement, the gathering erupted with activity. Emma jerked her gaze toward him as a large group of Sicari fighters formed two long lines a short distance away.

"Gauntlet?" she asked sharply. "As in running between two lines of men who beat you with clubs?"

"Not exactly." He met her gaze and looked away.

Clubs would be infinitely preferable to swords. At least each warrior only got one shot at him, but it would be more than enough when he had no defenses to speak of at the moment. *Merda*, he should have left her in Chicago. She'd be safe and he'd be on his way back to the Wacker Drive complex. She blew out a low noise of exasperation.

"Damn it, Ares," she hissed. "Either you tell me what the hell is going on here or I'm going to make you sorry you ever met me."

"Emma, at this moment a part of me is already sorry, particularly since this isn't an ordinary gauntlet," he said wryly.

A lie. He was beginning to excel at it where she was concerned. The truth was he wasn't sorry at all. He'd made himself responsible for her safety, and he'd done what was necessary. No, it was more than that. There was something about her that aroused every protective instinct in his body. He could call it responsibility all he wanted, but in the end, he knew it came down to something much more. A door slammed in his head as he locked his thoughts into a dark room. His gaze flickered toward the Sicari fighters. The warriors had formed two lines, facing off with the fighter opposite them. The result was a narrow corridor wide enough for three people to walk through abreast. She turned her head and paled visibly as the warriors drew their swords

"Are you telling me *that's* the gauntlet?" She pointed toward the human-made passageway with an expression of horror.

"Yes." He looked over his shoulder and jerked his head in a silent command for Lysander to join them. When he started to turn away from her, she grabbed his arm to hold him still.

"I never agreed to you doing this in my place."

"You agreed to it the moment you acknowledged the blood bond. It gave me the right to take your punishment."

"Then I take it back," she said vehemently. "It's insane."

Resignation tightened his jaw. Insanity? She was probably right, but it was how the Sicari had survived the Praetorians repeated attempts to wipe them out. Without their laws, there was anarchy and annihilation. He couldn't deny the possibility that he might not survive what was to come, but it was the Sicari way. He glanced at the warriors lined up a few yards away. Nothing would have saved her if he had not made the blood bond. He'd done the right thing no matter what happened.

"You may be right. But I had one of two choices. Let you run the gauntlet or run it for you."

"You can't survive that," she breathed and her hand clutched at his arm in a silent plea.

The shock of her touch raced up his arm. It created an intense need to pull her close. The fear in her hazel eyes made him reach out to brush his fingers across her cheek.

"I agree the odds aren't good," he said with a pragmatic expression and shrugged. He immediately grimaced at the pain lashing its way through his shoulder down into his hand. "But *you* had no odds at all.

Lysander and Phae reached them at almost the same instant. The moment she stopped in front of him, Phae glared at him. "You and your bloody honor. It's these kinds of heroics that get people killed," she said fiercely. "Let me heal your shoulder."

"There's no time." He waved her hand off. "You need to see to Emma's hand."

"Emma will live," Phae snapped. "You know a healer can't go near you the first twenty-four hours after a gauntlet run."

Phae's voice reflected her deep fear that he wouldn't survive. He didn't try to reassure her. Rather pointless when even he wasn't sure of his chances. He nodded abruptly as his sister grabbed his hands and closed her eyes. The pain in his shoulder eased considerably in seconds. As he watched Phae concentrate, he experienced the usual guilt that came with seeing her taking on the physical pain of his injuries.

Her knit sweater grew wet with blood at her shoulder and she groaned softly. He sucked in a sharp breath at the sight of her agony. Beside her, Lysander's features were as stoic as always. His *Primus Pilus* rarely showed any emotion at times like these, but the muscle tic in his friend's face emphasized how serious the situation was. He could have done without the silent reminder.

When Phae released his hands, she swayed slightly. Before Ares could react, Lysander extended his hand to steady her. Phae brushed off his assistance and sent her brother a stark look of fear.

"I couldn't heal it completely. The old wound interfered with the healing process." It was the helpless note in her voice that scraped at him. Phae never liked to admit to fear.

"It will do," he said as he tested the shoulder with a slow movement.

He turned to Lysander. "You know what to do if anything happens to me. I charge you with *all* the responsibility I currently hold."

"Understood." The disfigured warrior gave him an abrupt nod. "Your ability?"

"Nothing a little rest won't cure." His ability was so weak at the moment, he wasn't even sure he could deflect the more deadly blows as he moved down the corridor of Sicari fighters.

"Watch Sybil's men. They weren't happy to see you this evening. I doubt their mood has changed." The warning was the only indication his *Primus Pilus* was concerned for him.

Resignation tightened his jaw as he turned toward the warriors forming the gauntlet. Sybil Castella ran the New York guild. The woman had made it her mission to make his life miserable whenever possible because he'd brushed off her overtures years ago. If Sybil's fighters were angry, it meant his godmother's men would not go easy on him. They wouldn't want their honor questioned. Another point against him. He rolled his shoulders to loosen the tension holding them tight. As he glanced in Emma's direction, his gut tightened at the fear on her pale face.

"This is all my fault," she said with a note of panic in her voice. "I can't let you do this."

"You don't have a choice," he said softly. Best to just walk away.

Ares turned and headed toward the gauntlet. He'd only gone a couple of steps when he stopped. If he didn't survive the night, he damn well wasn't about to die without another kiss. *Fotte*, he wanted a lot more than a kiss, but it was the best he was going to get at the moment. He whirled around to stride back to her and roughly tugged her into his arms.

The taste of her flooded his mouth as his tongue mated with hers. She didn't resist him. Instead, her body melted into his and she responded to his kiss with a fervor that heightened his desire for more. Hot and sweet on his tongue, she stirred a primitive need inside him. Every time he tasted her, he found himself wanting more. His hands slid through her silky hair and he deepened the kiss, his mouth drawing every last bit of response from her he could.

With her arms wrapped around his neck, she burrowed her body into his and a soft sound hitched in her throat. The finality of his kiss terrified her, and her lips clung to his in an effort to keep him from what she knew was certain death. The heat of his tongue dancing with hers sent fire racing through her limbs to make every nerve ending in her body cry out with frantic need. A need to keep him with her. To hold on to him and keep him safe.

How was it possible for her to feel so connected to a man she barely knew? Yet, against the surreal backdrop of everything she'd witnessed in the past twenty-four hours, being in his arms was the most natural thing she'd ever experienced. The pressure of his mouth against hers eased. No, not yet. His hands gripped her arms gently, yet firmly, as he pushed her away from him.

The resignation on his face filled her with fear and she reached out to him. He caught her hand and pressed his mouth to her fingertips. There was a hint of mischief in his dark blue gaze as he offered her a slight smile.

"It's all right," he murmured. "But the next time you think about interfering, Emma, *don't*."

Guilt stabbed through her as he turned and walked away. As the distance grew between them, the gash in her hand throbbed a painful reminder why he was putting his life on the line. She took a step forward and a strong hand held her in place. She didn't have to look up at Lysander to know he was keeping her from going after Ares. The sudden beat of the drum echoed in the glade. Unlike the strong cadence it had played earlier, now the drum resounded a soft, insidious rhythm as Ares came to a halt at the edge of the gauntlet. He withdrew his sword from its scabbard and handed it to the woman he referred to as the *Prima Consul*.

"*Bis vivit qui bene moritur*," Ares said in a strong voice then threw himself forward in a low roll past the first two fighters of the corridor.

Taken by surprise, both fighters swung their swords but missed him as Ares rolled past them. The next two men did not. Emma inhaled a sharp breath as he blocked a blade with his forearm. The weapon drew blood. How much she couldn't tell, but the moonlight illuminated the glistening sleeve.

Behind him, the other fighter's sword seemed to dance off his back in what she prayed was little more than a scratch. Relief swept through her. Just as he had fighting Maximus, his telekinetic ability would help him survive. As Ares continued down the deadly corridor, the fighter on his left swung his weapon downward. In a lightning move, Ares stopped the sword's descent by clapping the blade between his palms.

With a quick twist of his hands, he knocked the sword free of the fighter's grip. As the weapon sailed up into the air, Ares snapped his hand out and reached for the sword's hilt. He wasn't fast enough. Instead, the airborne sword went spinning out of his reach as the Sicari warrior behind Ares smacked the weapon aside. In a seamless move, the fighter continued the smooth arc of her sword downward and sliced into the back of Ares's thigh. Emma moaned as she watched him grimace with pain and limp forward along the gauntlet. There were at least a dozen more fighters he had to pass.

She didn't even want to think about his odds, and her stomach lurched at the reality of his situation. He was suffering because of her. All of this was her fault. He'd warned her not to interfere. Her impulsive behavior had most likely sentenced him to death. The knowledge cut into her with the same physical strength as the blows Ares was enduring right now.

Although he hadn't cried out, she could tell he was in great pain because he barely missed the next pair of blades flying toward his head. He only managed to avoid them by throwing himself into the air in a handless cartwheel that ended with his injured leg crumpling beneath him and a sword plunging into his bicep.

She uttered a small cry of fear and took a step forward. Immediately, Lysander's strong hand gripped her arm. She glanced up at the scarred fighter.

"I'm not going to interfere," she choked out.

"Good," the warrior said in a dark tone. "Because he'll not survive a second run."

"He should be deflecting those blows." A rush of panic slid through her as Ares barely missed a thrust to his chest. "Why isn't he using his ability to protect himself?"

"Our ability drains quickly during a fight. He had little left after fighting Maximus."

"Oh my God," she breathed in horror.

The chill engulfing her deepened as she looked up at the fighter's grim expression. The icy cold penetrated her skin and sank its way into every part of her until even her bones felt brittle. Her gaze focused on Ares, silently willing him to keep moving. He stumbled forward as two swords headed straight for his chest.

Like a limbo dancer, he slid under the blades and then rolled forward like a log down a hill. The points of two swords pierced his arms, and for the first time she heard him utter a noise. Anger. He was angry. That was good. It had to be. If he was angry, it meant he wouldn't give up easily. And she didn't want him to give up. She wanted him to live.

Now more than halfway through the gauntlet, he staggered to his feet, barely dodging two more sword thrusts as he moved forward. Still, the tip of a sword sliced open his cheek. Blood gushed from the wound, and he grunted. Only six fighters left. He stumbled in his attempt to stay in the middle of the corridor, and watching him do so made her heart ache with a physical pain.

One of the Sicari he passed managed to land a kick in his groin and he sank to his knees with a loud whoosh of air leaving his lungs. The fighter on the other side of the corridor thrust her sword into Ares's other thigh. Tears streamed down Emma's face as she watched him crawl forward on his belly. The next four fighters jabbed at him as if he were a pin cushion.

Emma struggled to keep the bile from rising in her throat. One of the warriors laid a vicious kick into Ares's side, actually rolling him onto his back from the force of the blow. To her horror he simply lay there. He didn't move. He just lay still on the ground. No, he had to get up. Oh God, was he dead? No. She could see his chest moving from his ragged breathing. He had to get up. If he didn't, he would die for certain. He only had two more fighters to get past.

"Get up," she said softly. "Get up, Ares. Don't just lie there."

Beside her, Lysander grunted with approval. When she looked up at him, the warrior nodded his approval. "Encouragement is not interference."

She looked back at Ares and his still form in the gauntlet. The last two fighters stood ready to attack. A wave of fury swept over her. He was too damn close to stop now. Not moving would be the death of him.

"Goddamn you, Ares. Get up and *move*." At her loud command, dozens of heads turned in her direction. She ignored them and saw Ares stir. "Move, you bastard, or I'll take a sword to you myself."

With what appeared to be a Herculean effort, Ares rolled onto his stomach and began to crawl forward again. The sweater on his back was in ribbons, blood darkening his skin between the black knit pieces. She didn't know how he was able to move. It was easy to see he was exhausted. The last two fighters stabbed at his back, but they didn't draw any blood as he stretched his hand out to claw at the ground outside the gauntlet. With a sob of relief, Emma raced forward. The moment she drew close, several warriors closed ranks around Ares. Not about to let someone stop her from reaching him, she shoved her way past the fighters into the area where Ares lay still on the ground. The *Prima Consul* was kneeling at his side, and as Emma knelt opposite her, the woman's silvery eyes met hers with a look of condemnation.

"His injuries are severe, but he should survive the night."

The woman's detached observation made Emma stop breathing for a long moment. Guilt sliced through her at the accusatory look on the woman's face. Swallowing hard, she dragged her gaze away from the *Prima Consul*'s harsh expression and leaned over Ares. Her fingers gently brushed through his short, matted hair.

He'd put his own life on the line to save her. Having witnessed the brutality of the gauntlet, she now understood why he'd forced her to accept him as her champion. He'd been right. She never would have survived that horrible corridor of punishment. The shallowness of his breathing deepened the icy fear she'd been living with since he first entered the gauntlet.

"He needs medical attention," she said as she looked at the woman.

"His wounds can be dressed, nothing more. No healer or doctor can touch him for twenty-four hours. Justice must have time to ensure he's a Sicari worth saving."

"Worth saving?" Emma rasped in furious disbelief. "The man put his life on the line for me, and you refuse him medical attention just to see if he's worth saving. If that's your sense of justice, I'll take anarchy any day."

"I'll forgive your disrespectful tone—"

"Right now, I don't give a damn what you forgive. I want him carried into the house, *now*." Emma leaned across Ares until her face was inches from the *Prima Consul*'s face. "I'll take care of him myself. I don't have the *ability* to heal him, but I can at least make him comfortable. Unless, of course, the lot of you has something more barbaric to put him through."

A strong hand grasped her shoulders and gently pulled her away from the *Prima Consul*. Looking up, she saw Lysander towering over her with that stoic expression she vaguely realized was normal for him. He gave her a brief shake of his head.

"Come, we'll take him to the house."

Someone pulled her to her feet, and she trembled as she watched six fighters slide their hands under Ares's head and feet. The men locked arms then gently lifted him from the ground. Ares groaned the minute they moved him, and Emma's breath hitched with remorse. God, if only she'd listened to him. No, if only the past few weeks were nothing more than a nightmare from which she'd wake up.

The Sicari warriors moved slowly in an effort to minimize Ares's pain, and it took them twice as long to reach the house as it had to reach the funeral pyre. Once in the mansion, they carried Ares upstairs to a large bedroom and placed him on the bed. She dismissed the men with a sharp word of gratitude then stopped Lysander from following the men out of the room.

"I need bandages, tape, scissors, aspirin, and any antiseptic you can find."

The scarred fighter studied her for a long moment before he nodded his head and exited the room without a word. Emma turned back to Ares and studied him in silence for a moment. Pale and drawn, he looked worse now than when she'd first reached him. Fear coiled its way through her, but she pushed it aside. She could be afraid later. Right now, she needed to get him undressed and cleaned up.

Hot water. She needed hot water and washcloths. Basic first aid was something everyone on an archeological dig knew. Hospitals weren't always close at hand when someone was injured. She headed toward the bathroom, but paused when she heard a knock at the door. She almost ignored it, but something about the sound told her to answer the summons. Quickly crossing the floor, she tugged the door open and saw Phae standing in the doorway. The worry and fear on the other woman's face inflicted another lash of guilt across Emma's conscience.

"How is he?"

"He's bled a lot, I think, but I've not had a chance to look at his wounds." She stepped back to allow Phae to enter. "He needs your help."

Sorrow twisted the Sicari woman's face into a mask of pain and she took a quick step back from the door. "It's forbidden. It is dishonorable to heal him."

"He's your brother. You can't just let him suffer like this."

Phae shook her head. "You don't understand—"

"You're right. I don't understand how you can walk away from someone you love when they're hurting. If I could do it, I would. But I can't." Emma glared at the dark-haired fighter with fierce determination. Silently willing her to heal her brother.

A strange look crossed Phae's face, and she nodded sharply. She glanced up and down the hallway before slipping into the room. Emma closed the door behind her. With a frown, Phae nodded toward the door.

"No one should come to check on Ares until tomorrow. But

whatever you do, don't let anyone in while I'm here. You've already seen that the Order believes in harsh punishments when rules are broken." Emma nodded as Phae quickly crossed the room to take her brother's hand. "I can't heal him completely or they'll know I helped him. And that means we'll all pay the price."

"Do what you can. I'll make him comfortable when you're done."

Clasping her brother's large hands in hers, the Sicari woman closed her eyes. In less than a minute, blood soaked Phae's shirt and pants as Ares's wounds became hers. Then with a gasp, she released her brother's hands and slid off the bed to collapse on the floor. Blood still trickled out from under her sleeve to drip slowly on the carpet.

The sharp knock on the door made Emma jump, but Phae simply looked at her with that same expression of resignation she'd seen on Ares's face earlier. The Sicari woman dropped her head as Emma turned toward the door.

"Who is it?" she asked quietly, her hand on the doorknob.

"Lysander." The Sicari fighter's deep voice reverberated through the heavy door.

"Let him in. He won't betray us."

From the bedside, Phae jerked her head at Emma in a silent command to open the door. The moment she let the fighter into the room, he handed her a first aid kit. A frown tightened his impassive features as he stared down at her.

"Is he worse than—*merda*." The frown on his face dissolved into one of furious outrage as he quickly crossed the room to kneel at Phae's side. "I should have known you'd try something like this, you little fool."

The emotion the man displayed seemed completely out of character and Emma was glad she wasn't on the receiving end of the man's quiet fury.

"Shut up, you arrogant bastard." Despite her weakened condition, Phae managed to send him a contemptuous glare. "I'll be all right in a few minutes."

Lysander uttered a dark word of Italian and lifted Phae up into his arms. "Perhaps, but if anyone sees you like this, they'll make you pay dearly."

The soft growl was dark with anger, but Phae didn't flinch. Instead she glared up at him. "Put me down, you big oaf. You carrying me is going to look a hell of a lot more suspicious than if I just lean on you as you're walking me to my room."

Lysander ignored the woman in his arms and directed his harsh, one-eyed stare toward Emma. "Check to see if it's clear. Phaedra's bedroom is just a short way down the hall."

Obeying his order without a word, Emma quietly opened the door. The empty corridor stretched off in both directions like a dark Roman archway. She pulled the door open wide.

"It's safe."

Her gaze met Lysander's black scowl, but he didn't say a word as he swept past her and out into the hall. As the Sicari warrior carried Phae out the door, the woman nodded toward her brother.

"Take care of him."

"I will," Emma said. "You did the right thing."

"I see now why my brother is fascinated by you." Phae's soft words whispered around her. "The two of you always do what's right, even if it means breaking the rules."

Emma watched the tall, disfigured Sicari stride quickly down the hall with Ares's sister. A moment later, the two of them disappeared into one of the rooms off the corridor. With a sigh of relief, she closed the door of Ares's room and turned to stare at the man on the bed. Pale and unconscious, he didn't look much different despite Phae's healing touch.

The woman had said she could only help ease his injuries slightly. She also knew that, like her brother, Phae drained her abilities every time she used them. The woman had healed Ares before he'd run the gauntlet. It was more than likely she'd been able to heal only the worst of Ares's injuries this second time.

Emma hurried toward the bathroom for hot water and towels. The sooner she helped Ares get back on his feet, the sooner she could tear him apart again when he was better. He could have saved both of them a lot of pain and trouble if he'd just explained how things worked in this world of his. All of this had been so unnecessary. Her conscience, and the stabbing pain in her hand, reminded her that she was the one at fault. He *had* told her not to interfere. She ignored the self-recrimination.

Emma kept her touch light as she gently wiped the dirt and blood from Ares's face. The gash on his cheek wasn't quite as bad as all the blood had made it look. She tried to examine his chest, but the minute she tried to raise his shirt upward, he groaned in pain.

God, if she'd only known what interfering in the *Dux Provocare* had meant. She never would have done it. No, that wasn't true. She would have interfered. Just the thought of something happening to Ares would have driven her forward no matter what the consequences.

The realization alarmed her. She didn't even know the man. Why would she feel such panic at the thought of him dying? Unwilling to examine the thought further, she reached for his black leather boots and removed them, along with his socks. She shifted her attention upward and unlatched his belt then unzipped his pants.

Black leather warmed her fingers as she gently tugged the snug-fitting trousers downward. The intimate act made her tremble, and she puffed out a breath of irritation. The man was injured. She didn't have any other choice *but* to undress him. Aggravated by her hesitation, she tugged the soft leather down to mid-thigh and stopped.

Unable to breathe, she simply stared. It was impossible *not* to look at him. He'd gone commando tonight, and what she saw sent heat crashing straight through her until her sex ached. He was beautiful. Nestled against dark curls, his relaxed staff aroused every wicked thought she'd ever had about a man. The sudden image of caressing him with her mouth made her even hotter. He'd grow thick and hard as she sucked on him.

She dragged in a sharp breath at the imagery. God, she was more insane than him or the rest of the Sicari. She bit down on her lip at the sensations ripping through her. Her reaction to him was natural. She could appreciate the beauty of a male body. She just needed to remember she was his nurse. The best thing to do was cover him up. If someone came in and caught her staring at Ares's naked body—heat flooded her cheeks.

With a swift movement, she reached out to grab one of the bath towels she'd found in the bathroom. Her fingers wrapped around the soft fleece, and with a sharp snap of her wrist, the towel became a loincloth. There. Much better. At least, she wouldn't be embarrassed if someone like that woman called the *Prima Consul* actually did check up on Ares. Just because Phae had said no one would come until tomorrow didn't mean it wasn't possible.

She returned her focus to removing the black leather pants off Ares's long legs. The moment the gashes on his thighs were fully revealed, she winced. Even with Phae's healing touch, they were still brutal to look at. Last night she'd marveled at his mastery of pain. Tonight he was all the more impressive at his ability to have run the gauntlet. She dipped her head to examine his wounds more closely.

As gently as she could, she cleaned his wounds, removing the dried blood from both legs. The muscles in his legs were whipcord lean, and while his wounds were long cuts, they weren't anywhere as deep as she'd expected them to be. They seemed almost superficial in spots.

Was that Phae's healing touch or had he managed to reserve enough of his ability to deflect the worst of the blows? Her hand touched the inside of his thigh as she wiped away another streak of blood. A low, primitive sound caused her to stiffen. Heat washed over her as she raised her head to see Ares watching her with a mixture of pain and something else in his dark blue gaze. He closed his eyes and released a harsh breath.

"*Fotte.* And I thought last night was bad." The dry note in his voice eased her fear, but deepened her guilt.

"I need to clean the rest of your cuts," she murmured. "Do you think you can help me get your shirt off?"

"Why, Ms. Zale, are you propositioning me?" His teasing made her whole body go hot as she met his amused, yet exhausted gaze.

"I don't think you're in any condition to do anything except lie here."

"True," he sighed heavily. "I'll take a rain check then."

An electrical spark of anticipation skimmed its way across her skin. Alarmed by the sensation, she ignored his statement. The minute he pushed himself up onto his elbows, she quickly moved to slide her arm behind his back in the form of support. The instant her arm pressed against his shoulders, he drew in a sharp breath. If he hurt like this, either his sister truly hadn't been able to alleviate most of his injuries or they'd been worse than she thought. Guilt slashed at her as she shifted her touch from his back to cradling his neck.

"Damn, I'm so sorry."

"It comes with the territory, Emma," he said without any bitterness.

His complete lack of rancor simply served to increase her guilt. She grimaced as she helped him ease one arm out of the long-sleeved garment. When his other arm was free, she gently pulled the badly torn shirt over his head. The moment she saw his back, she uttered a soft cry of horror.

Phae had clearly not tried to heal these wounds. More than a dozen gashes covered his back from his waist to his shoulders. The length and depth of the cuts made her marvel at his constitution. She'd be unconscious or sobbing with pain from wounds like this.

"That bad, huh," he grunted.

"No. Not really." She forced herself to sound matter-of-fact.

"Emma, we really need to do something about this lying of yours."

There it was again, that light, teasing note that made her go weak at her knees. Not a good thing, but at least he wasn't kissing her. That would be a disaster. Clothed he was dangerous. Naked he was devastating.

"I need to warm up these washcloths. These cuts need to be cleaned to avoid infection."

She took a step away from the bed and his hand snaked out to capture her wrist. With a tug, he pulled her back to him. She stumbled over her feet and landed on the bed next to him. Seated hip to hip with him, she stared into his blue eyes. The emotion blazing there sent her heart slamming into her chest.

"I think I've discovered a remedy for your lying."

"Remedy?" she breathed.

"A kiss for every lie."

"I . . . I . . . don't be ridiculous. Your injuries—"

"I'm hurt, Emma, not at death's door," he murmured with amusement. "Besides, we both know you want to kiss me."

"N . . ." He arched his eyebrows at her and she clenched her jaw at his arrogant statement. Arrogant because he was right. "You're a devious, manipulative man, Ares DeLuca."

"And you're fighting a losing battle," he murmured as he cupped the back of her neck.

The heat of his fingers against her skin sank through her pores until the warmth threaded its way through every inch of her. She gulped at the sensation and braced her hands just below the sutures on his chest. It was the only part of his anatomy that had remained unscathed from his brushes with death in the past twenty-four hours. Was this what his life was like on a regular basis? If it was, she was amazed he'd managed to survive this long. And even if it wasn't the norm, it still made her fear for his safety. An irrational fear that something terrible would happen to him. Lord. She didn't know the man well enough to feel this overwhelming sense of panic when it came to the thought of him dying. She strained against the large hand at the nape of her neck.

"I think you've seen one battle too many," she snapped, alarmed by the emotions crashing through her. "Too many knocks on the head have made you delusional."

Despite his weakened state, he still managed to pull her close enough to brush his lips across hers. It was a light touch, but hot enough to ignite every nerve ending in her body until a blazing heat pulsed through every inch of her. With a heavy sigh, he released her.

"I think you're right. If I start kissing you, I'm not going to be able to finish what I start. But be forewarned, Emma, the time will come when I will."

The flash of emotion in his dark gaze let loose hundreds of butterflies in her stomach. He was serious. The knowledge sent excitement and fear sliding through her. But the devilish smile on his mouth couldn't hide his exhaustion. She shook her head.

"I'm going to warm up these towels." Without waiting for

a response, she pulled away from him and headed toward the bathroom.

"I'm not going anywhere," he muttered as he gingerly lay down on his side and closed his eyes. As she headed toward the bathroom, she knew he would be sound asleep when she returned.

Chapter 13

ARES slowly blinked sleep out of his eyes and stared up at the ceiling. *Christus.* If he kept this up, he wouldn't see his next birthday. He cautiously tested his flexibility by sitting upright. At least he didn't hurt as badly as he'd expected. In fact, he felt a lot better than he should for someone who'd run the gauntlet. He frowned.

Had Atia allowed a healer to relieve him of pain last night? Not likely. But then everything beyond the gauntlet was fuzzy at best. The one constant had been Emma. He'd heard her, felt her touch, smelled that sweet scent of hers throughout the night. The one thing he *did* remember clearly was her voice ordering him to get up and move.

It had been her voice that had penetrated the haze of pain to make him crawl toward the end of the gauntlet. What was it she'd said? She'd take a sword to him. The smile on his mouth turned to a grimace as he slid out of bed. *Damno,* but he was sore. At least someone had removed his clothes. There wasn't anything worse than ripping leather off a wound that had already clotted and bonded with the material.

The shadowy memory of Emma cleaning his wounds drifted through his consciousness. He frowned as he tried to recall the moment more clearly. He had a vague sensation of having kissed her, but he wasn't even sure that had happened.

He moved toward the bathroom. A warm shower would make him feel human again. One hand splayed against the partially closed door, he frowned slightly at the humid air hitting him in the face. Before his brain could process the fact that something was off, he pushed the door open.

The only thing he could do was stand there. Emma had just gotten out of the shower. Her body glistened with water droplets as she used a towel to dry her wet hair. *Fotte*. He was hard in an instant. This wasn't good. No, it was better than good, which confirmed why it was bad. He stretched his neck and swallowed hard as he stared at her sweet curves.

She was like Botticelli's *Fortuna*. All she needed were angels to dress her. No. He didn't want her dressed. He wanted her to stay just like this until he had spent himself inside her. That pleasurable thought tightened the muscles in his groin. He needed to get the hell out of here before he did something stupid. The blood bond. He needed to remember the blood bond.

Eyes closed, her towel dropped to the floor as she laced her fingers through her damp hair. The action lifted her full breasts, and everything else but the sight of her receded into the background. He was insane not to leave this minute. Even if the blood bond hadn't been an issue, the last thing he needed to do was get involved with her. He closed his eyes briefly. Who was he kidding? He was already involved. Somewhere in the back of his mind, he heard shouts and curses, but he ignored the warnings.

Instead, he used his mind to reach out and cup her, brushing his thumb over one nipple. She immediately stiffened and jerked her head toward the door. Silence hung between them for a long moment before a blush crested over her cheeks.

With a quick movement, she bent to retrieve her towel. In a blink of an eye, he commanded the towel to fly out of her reach. She gasped, but didn't say a word as she slowly straightened and watched him move toward her. All he wanted to do was hold her. Feel her soft, dewy skin against his scarred flesh. Holding her would be enough. He knew it was a lie. When he pulled her into his arms, she shook her head

"You're hurt—"

"I'm fine," he murmured, eagerly welcoming the warmth of her seeping into his aching body.

Just as intoxicating was the scent of her. A fresh citrus aroma filled his nostrils as he dipped his head and brushed his mouth over her damp shoulder. His tongue flicked out to lick a water drop off her skin. It was sweet and warm. He'd never tasted a woman so soft or delectable. She shuddered.

He lifted his head to stare down at her, and he lightly stroked her face. Holding her like this made him realize how easy it would be to lose himself in her. The thought set off another round of alarms in the back of his head. He knew he should listen to the warnings, but something inside wouldn't let him.

"But what if . . ." Her voice trailed away. She averted her gaze and pink flooded her cheeks once more.

Mea Deus, she was beautiful. He captured her hand to kiss her palm, but she winced and jerked her hand away from him. Puzzled, he gently forced her hand faceup. The gash on her palm made him frown.

"Why didn't a healer take care of this?"

"I didn't exactly endear myself to anyone last night," she murmured wryly.

A vague memory of her giving orders as he slipped in and out of consciousness after he'd escaped the gauntlet made him smile. An *alieni* giving any Sicari an order would definitely cause tempers to flare. The memory of how defiantly she'd faced Maximus last night made him kiss the fingertips of her injured hand. She'd been afraid for him. Fearful enough to put her own life in danger simply to save him. He looked down at the cut on her hand.

"Someone should have healed this for you. Atia or Phae should have seen to it."

"I think they were a lot more worried about you than me."

"If there had been a better way to keep you safe, I would have chosen it," he said with regret as he lightly touched the outer edges of her wound. The memory of her cry of pain followed by anger created a knot in his throat.

"I know." She nodded her head, her damp hair slightly tousled from the way she'd towel-dried it. With a light touch, she carefully examined the cut on his cheek then smiled. "You'd better be careful, though—the last I heard, you were up for this year's knight in shining armor award."

Although her tone was light and teasing, something else laced its way through the words. He recognized it, but he wasn't willing to give it a name. All it did was emphasize the fact that he needed to let her go, while he took a cold shower. Yet he didn't let her go. He couldn't.

"I think I disqualified myself a few minutes ago when I didn't retreat back into the bedroom." He searched her face, hoping she'd help him come to his senses by breaking free of his light hold.

"Do you want to leave?" The soft question pulled a groan from him. She was asking him if he wanted to *leave* her? *Deus*, if she knew the power she had over him at this moment, she wouldn't have asked the question.

"No," he rasped. "But I'm thinking it might be the better part of valor to retreat."

She reached out to touch his chest directly below his injured shoulder. The touch made him ache for her. He was right. He needed to get out of here. *Now*. If he stayed, the consequences—in a move that took his breath away, she leaned forward and feathered a trail of kisses across the breadth of his chest. Tenderly, she caressed his skin, just above the cut Doc had sewn up two nights before. *Fotte*, she was making it impossible to retreat.

He swallowed hard as her hand slid down his side then across his abdomen to his rock-hard erection, where she lightly scraped her fingernail along the length of him. The action tugged a low growl from him, and she pulled back to look into his eyes. The invitation in her gaze made his muscles contract tight with need.

With his mind, he stroked her breast, teasing her skin with invisible touches. Her gaze locked with his, she inhaled a sharp breath of pleasure from his mental caress. Taking his time, he lowered his head to nibble at the spot where her pulse throbbed wildly against her peach-colored flesh.

"You taste good, *dolce mia*. Sweet and fresh," he murmured against the side of her throat.

"I want you, Ares."

The quiet declaration made him grow still and he lifted his head to look down at her. If they did this—no, if he did this, she needed to understand what the blood bond meant from this point forward.

"And I want you, *cara*, but I have to explain about last night."

"It's all right. I understand."

She wrapped her hand around him, and the thunderous beat of his heart echoed in his ears. *Deus*, he wanted her. Every inch of him craved her. Needed her in the worst way.

"*Carissima*, I need to . . . *Christus* . . ." He struggled to breathe as her hand slowly stroked him. If she kept that up, he wouldn't have to worry about sealing the blood bond. "The Sicari blood bond—"

"If you want my forgiveness, you have it."

"*Inamorato* . . . you have to . . ." He fought desperately to clear his head, but her touch crowded his mind with pleasure and a desire that was escalating out of control. The warmth of her breath brushed against his earlobe as she nipped at it. "*Dulcis Mater Dei* . . . *cara*, listen to me."

"I'm listening," she murmured as her thumb rubbed over the top of him. "But you're not making a whole lot of sense."

"That's because you're driving me crazy, *carissima* . . ." He shuddered beneath her touch. "I can't think straight when I'm around you."

"I like that mix of Latin and Italian you speak. I find it very sexy."

An alluring smile curved her mouth as she looked up at him. Her hand curled around his neck and she gently tugged his head down to hers. The minute her lips slid across the edge of his jaw and down to the base of his throat, he could feel his last bit of control slipping away.

"*Deus* . . . Emma . . . I need . . ."

Her mouth found his in a whisper-soft kiss that annihilated all rational thought from his head. She tipped her head back slightly and her gaze locked with his. If he hadn't known he was already lost, the desire in her beautiful hazel eyes would simply have confirmed it.

He captured her lips beneath his and teased her mouth open. The taste of her was enough to drive him insane. Crisp and tangy, she filled his mouth with a promise of more pleasure than he'd ever imagined. And ever since the first time he'd set eyes on her, he'd imagined a lot. He just hadn't counted on her getting under his skin this way. His body pressed her back into the wall as he eliminated the space between them. The minute his erection brushed against her sex, he drew in a sharp breath of anticipation. It pulled his body taut with an emotion so powerful, he thought he'd come without even touching her. What kind of a hold did this woman have over him that made his anticipation to possess her so intense?

In a clear expression of her own need, she thrust her hips forward in a silent demand. He answered by sliding his hand over her hip to delve his fingers into her warm, slick folds. A soft mewl sounded in her throat, and he deepened their kiss as he continued to stroke her. She kissed him back with a fervor that sent his pulse skyrocketing.

The woman was heat and sweetness all wrapped up in one soft, feminine body. She wasn't just intoxicating, she took his breath away. Even the way she trembled against him was something to savor. Eager to taste all of her, his mouth caressed her jaw before moving to the side of her neck then downward to a luscious breast. The moment he suckled her, a soft cry parted her lips.

It was a sound of keen pleasure and his cock jumped with the need to please her more. A minute later his hunger increased tenfold as her fingers encircled his erection and she slowly stroked him again. Intense and potent, the desire building inside him had become a sharp craving. No woman had ever made him feel like this one did. With a grunt of discomfort, he ignored the fiery protest his injuries made as he cupped her soft derriere and lifted her until he was positioned to slide into her.

She automatically wrapped her legs around his hips, her heels pressing into the hard flesh of his buttocks. It was an erotic sensation. Head thrown back, he looked into her passion-filled face.

Desire had turned her eyes a shade of emerald green, and if possible, she was even more beautiful than when he'd first entered the bathroom. It set his heart lurching in his chest. He knew from the beginning she'd be trouble. He just hadn't figured on trouble being this heady.

Gently, she explored the contours of his face, avoiding the painful cut on his cheek. Her touch light, she slowly traced the outline of his lips. Immediately, he drew one of her fingers into his mouth, swirling his tongue around it. In his mind, he mimicked the action with her breast. It pulled a cry of surprised pleasure from her as she arched into him.

"For the love of God, Ares," she whimpered between ragged breaths. "I want you. *Now*."

"Like this?" he rasped as he thrust up into the heat of her.

"*Yes*—oh God, yes," she exclaimed in a husky sob.

He closed his eyes the minute her slick heat engulfed him. *Deus*, she felt incredible wrapped around him. She was like the perfect glove, designed for him alone. The way her insides clenched and rippled over him was unbelievable. He'd known it would be good between them, but not like this. Not this intense craving to possess her until he made her forget every man that had come before him.

The sensation shook him with its intensity. *Merda*, she was going to be his downfall. No. She'd already brought him to his knees. He'd fallen the moment he'd touched her. Violently, he crushed the voice that whispered about the repercussions. It was done now. There was no going back.

The wounds on his thighs protested viciously as he thrust into her velvet heat over and over again. But the pleasure drowned out the pain. Aware that his physical strength fell short of its usual level, he created an invisible cradle with his mind to hold her in place as his hand flew out from under her to brace himself against the wall.

The way he held her didn't allow her the ability to match the intensity of his thrusts, but the way her hot, wet sheath milked his cock pushed him into a mind-numbing place he'd never been before. With a low roar, he buried himself deep inside her, his head burrowing into her breasts as he came with a force that blinded him.

A second later, she uttered a similar cry of release and her body clutched at his with a ferocity that reignited the pleasure starting to recede from his body. He held her tight for several long moments until his rebelling muscles won the war against his desire to remain inside her.

Slowly he eased her down onto her feet, where she stood trembling against him. There was little space between them, and he rested his forehead against hers as they both fought to regain control of their breathing. Everything had changed now. The blood bond was only part of it. Somehow she'd breached a wall inside him that hadn't been cracked since the death of his parents. He couldn't describe how it had changed him—no, he refused to. He just knew it scared the hell out of him.

The knowledge hovered on cognizant thought, but he managed to slam it back into the dark compartment it had emerged from. He'd deal with the consequences of everything when he could think straight. Swallowing hard, he cupped the side of her neck with his hand, his thumb pressing into the bottom of her jaw. Gently he forced her head up so he could kiss her long and deep.

He took his time, enjoying the sultry scent of their lovemaking and the warm, sensuous taste of her lips against his. It would be easy to be with her like this all the time. He ignored the protests in the back of his head. When he released her, he splayed his hands on the wall so she was boxed in by his arms. There was a sleepy look about her that indicated how relaxed she was. He smiled.

"That, *dolce mia*," he whispered in a teasing tone, "was worth every bit of the pounding I've taken in the past two days."

She gave a small shake of her head, an expression of remorse sweeping across her face. "I'm so sorry. I shouldn't have interfered, but you were . . . and I couldn't let him . . . I didn't want you to die."

"Hush, *cara*."

He dipped his head to kiss her again. It was the cut on his hand from the blood bond that slowly broke through his consciousness. It slowly registered on his pain scale as a stark reminder of what he'd done. He stiffened, and it only made matters worse when she curved her body into his. It was as if she were a part of him. As if he'd found a missing piece of himself.

No. He was confusing great sex with something else. It was a passing attraction. Feeling anything else was out of the question. But he was lying to himself, and he knew it. He just wasn't going to acknowledge it. Even if he were to acknowledge it, he'd changed everything by making her his. Slowly, he stepped back and drew in a sharp breath as his body reminded him he'd been through hell the night before.

"*Christus.*"

"It serves you right," she muttered huskily. "Getting out of bed and . . . and . . ."

"And making love to the *bella* I found in my bathroom?" He managed to keep his tone light. But he was feeling far from lighthearted.

"You could have died," she said quietly.

"But I didn't."

"No thanks to me. If I hadn't been at the funeral, none of this would have happened." Her voice echoed with regret and frustration. With a twist of her body, she slipped under his arm. "Last night is a vivid reminder that I don't belong here."

He watched her retrieve her towel off the floor where it had landed the moment he'd mentally plucked it out of her hand. The towel cracked loudly as she shook it out and wrapped it around her. He didn't like seeing her vulnerable like this. He closed himself off to the feeling.

"In time you *will* belong, Emma." His gaze met her troubled one. She might not know it, but she already did belong. He just didn't know how to tell her. She shook her head in disagreement.

"I'm not convinced, and I'm not sure I want to be."

The quiet resignation in her voice slashed into him more than he cared to admit. In silence, he watched the bathroom door close behind her. He wanted her to feel as though she were part of his world. Wanted her to be happy. And if she was going to be happy, she had to accept his world for what it was.

Especially now that his body had managed to overrule his head and he'd sealed the blood bond. He released a low growl of anger. The importance he placed on her happiness said she'd reached inside him and touched a part of him that he'd hidden away for a long time. The realization filled him with a mixture of frustration, anger, and another emotion he ignored.

"*Fotte.*"

With a vicious tug, he yanked the shower door open and turned on the water. He'd known better than to let this happen. Never get too close, never get involved. And thin ice on Lake Michigan would be less dangerous to tread than getting involved with Emma Zale. *Merda.* Involved? He could be at the bottom of Lake Michigan and it wouldn't begin to touch the depths of his involvement with the woman.

Di tutti i bastardi stupidi. Stupid. That's what he was. Just one stupid bastard. Not to mention selfish. He'd seen her and just taken her. She hadn't protested. Hell, she'd done some of the seducing herself. It made his mouth go dry just thinking about the way she'd offered herself to him. He groaned. He'd tried to tell her, but not hard enough. *Deus,* where was his control when it came to this woman? First, he'd dragged her into his world. A world she didn't know or understand. Now he'd made her one of them by sealing the blood bond. Steam filled the air as he stepped under the shower spray.

With a grunt of pained surprise, he took a small jump backward and quickly adjusted the temperature before testing the water again. Even though the heat level had dropped from scalding to hot, the water still felt like a knife slicing into his open cuts. He deserved it. Every bit of the pain he experienced he deserved.

Last night he'd known there was a chance of transferring his abilities to Emma. This morning he'd doubled those odds by making love to her. It was why a blood bond with an *alieni* needed the Order's stamp of approval. It had been easy to break the law last night to save her life, but today—today he'd simply leapt off a cliff without thinking.

He could reassure himself all he wanted that he'd tried to explain the blood bond, but the truth was his honor had suffered a severe blow. The most condemning thing was—at the time he hadn't cared. And that scared him worse than anything the Order might do to him if they found out what had just happened.

He slammed his fist into the tile of the shower with a furious blow. He'd made it his responsibility to protect her, and yet every move he made seemed to increase the odds of something happening to her. Getting involved with Emma had to be the biggest mistake he'd made since Clarissa. He dropped his head to let the hot water flow ruthlessly over his scalp, his thoughts racing backward in time.

As hard as he tried, he couldn't block the image of finding the door of her apartment ajar and what lay beyond. Clarissa's body had been on the living room floor, her lifeless eyes staring up at the ceiling. Blood soaked her white camisole where her killer had stabbed her repeatedly before slitting her throat.

Lacerations covered her hands and arms, showing she'd tried to ward off her attacker. From the cuts on her thighs, the bastard had cut her panties off before he raped her. He shuddered and rubbed water out of his eyes. *Christus*, if someone were to do that to Emma—he didn't finish the thought.

With a growl of anger, he slammed his fist into the tile again. No matter how unbelievably mind-numbing the sex had been. No matter how deep she'd gotten under his skin, it didn't excuse his behavior. What the hell was his Sicari training for if not to keep him balanced and in control? But where Emma was concerned, he didn't have any control.

Even his subconscious had betrayed him to the point that he'd lost his perspective on everything around him, except for Emma. But it wasn't just the fact that he'd made love to her without explaining the risks. Losing command of his senses illustrated just how far gone he was where she was concerned.

Worse, he knew exactly how she was going to react when he explained what the intimacy of the blood bond meant. Frustration snarled its way through his body. She was skittish enough about her own ability. Somehow he didn't think she'd be too happy if she gained new ones.

With a growl of self-disgust, he quickly shampooed his hair then lathered his body with soap. The moment the soap sank into the open wounds on his arms, he drew in a sharp hiss of air. *Damno* but that hurt. He gritted his teeth against the burn biting into his injuries. He knew how to control the pain with just a few moments of meditation, but he wasn't about to ease the fiery sting. It was a poor penance to pay for making love to Emma.

Still, it was nothing compared to the way he'd felt last night.

And it surprised him that he didn't hurt worse than he should. He'd endured his share of wounds over the years that had required standard medical attention simply because a healer hadn't reached him soon enough. The end result after treatment was a few days of minor pain from the injuries as they healed. Pain that was a lot like what he was suffering now. Frowning, he turned his head to examine the gash on his bicep.

Even without having seen it last night, he was certain it hadn't been this shallow a cut. A quick examination of the wounds on his thighs told him they weren't nearly as bad as they should have been either. *Merda*.

Atia *had* sent in a healer. Last night he'd had his ass kicked, and the only explanation for why he'd been strong enough to make love to Emma the way he had was because a healer had touched him. His godmother had defied tradition and Sicari law by sending a healer. Even worse, she'd done it in a politic manner. His wounds had been healed just enough to ensure there wasn't permanent damage and guarantee a speedy recovery all without it appearing that a healer had been anywhere near him.

He might break the rules, but he did so with the understanding that he would pay a price of some sort. There wasn't much outside of the *Prima Consul*'s power, but this—this bordered on heresy. It was even worse than his behavior with Emma. And *Deus* knew he would pay a steep price for that transgression. With a vicious snap of his wrist, he slammed the water valve off and stepped out of the shower. A towel whipped off a nearby rack and flew through the air to wrap its way around his waist as he stalked into the bedroom dripping water.

"Besides yourself, who came into this room last night?" he demanded harshly.

In the middle of putting on her cardigan, Emma jerked her head up in surprise at his angry question. Her gaze wary, she frowned and finished sliding into her cardigan.

"Lysander and the men who helped carry you up here."

Irritation gripped him as he looked at the white bandage encircling her hand. Atia had sent a healer for him, but not for her. The urge to throttle his godmother made him glad the woman wasn't present.

"Who else?" The guilt flitting across her face was fleeting, but there was enough to make his stomach suddenly twist into knots. Maybe Atia *wasn't* responsible for his fast recuperation. Emma met his gaze then turned her head away from him.

"If you're thinking about lying to me, Emma, keep in mind that I'm not in a charitable mood at the moment." The cold, clipped words made her jerk her head back toward him again.

"Your sister came to see you." She bit her lip nervously.

"Phae?" He choked out his sister's name with a sense of disbelief. His sister knew better than to be caught within a hundred yards of a fighter that had gone through the gauntlet.

"She was worried about you."

"Did she try to heal me?"

There it was again. Guilt sweeping across her face. Somehow, she'd convinced Phae to do the unthinkable. Once again, she'd interfered with the natural order of things. The woman wasn't just a danger to his sensibilities—she was a threat to the Sicari Order itself.

Atia sending a healer would have been bad enough. As *Prima Consul,* she would have gotten away with it, but she would have taken a lot of heat for her actions. Not to mention jeopardizing their personal relationship by not allowing the judgment to stand. He'd known the risk and had chosen it willingly.

But if anyone found out Phae had taken it upon herself to heal him, they'd call for her head. For a healer to alter the possible outcome of a Sicari's sentence was the act of a heretic. His sister knew better. She would have known he would reject a healer's touch.

Christus, he'd lost complete control of the situation. Emma had been turning everything upside down from the moment she'd arrived. He could excuse her not understanding the Sicari culture. But no matter how foreign and savage she thought the Sicari were, she would obey him, or he wouldn't be able to protect her from the Order. He glared at her.

"*Deus damno id*, I specifically told you not to interfere again."

"I don't call it interference when *she* came to the door and *she* made the decision to heal you."

He shoved his fingers through his cropped hair. First he'd betrayed Emma's trust in him by sealing the blood bond, now his sister had dishonored him. Phae had cheated and made him a part of her heresy. With a deep growl, he used his mental strength to drag Emma across the floor until she was pressed tightly into his chest. The fresh, delectable scent of her teased his nostrils and the memory of dipping his fingers into her hot honey made him hard in an instant.

He was losing his mind. His honor was in shreds and yet he was ready to toss it all aside just to possess her again. Anger. If he held on to it, maybe he could keep from throwing her on the bed and holding her hostage there until he'd sated his need for her. He slipped his hand around the back of her neck and forced her to look at him. The gleam of defiance in her green eyes helped him maintain his wrath.

"This is the last time I'm going to tell you this," he said in a low, tight voice. "If I tell you to stay out of something, *do it*. Do *not* interfere in the way the Sicari conduct their business."

Chapter 14

HE was furious. It was evident in the way his fingers pressed into the nape of her neck and the rigid tension in his hard, muscular body. It struck her as odd that she wasn't afraid of him. But she knew he wouldn't hurt her. She wasn't sure how she knew it, she just did. It was just an internal knowing she couldn't explain.

She also knew he wasn't being fair. How was she supposed to know what to do or not do? It was like playing one of those child-hood games where everyone else knew the rules and she didn't. Only she wasn't a kid anymore, and the rules of this particular game were a lot more treacherous. Deadly.

"You know, it would be nice if you people came with a manual or something." She blew out a breath of anger. "Exactly *how* am I suppose to know what's interference and what's not?"

"Simple. Don't call our actions into question. Phae would never have done what she did without encouragement." His glare was meant to intimidate, but she was too aggravated to even notice.

"Don't be an ass," she scoffed. "Your sister didn't need any encour-agement. She helped you because she loves you. And if she's anything like you, she breaks the rules whenever it suits her purpose."

"It was dishonorable for both of us. She knew better," he snarled.

With a sharp movement, he pushed her aside. One hand massaging the back of his neck in a gesture of angry frustration, he turned and put several feet between them. There was an air of desolation about him that troubled her.

"But no one will know."

"*I'll* know." Beneath the harsh growl, there was a dark note of resignation and guilt.

For the first time, she realized how important his honor was to him. It was an integral part of him. She'd seen it several times since he first entered her life, but until now she'd never understood how inherent it was to him as an individual. He might break the rules, but if he did so, it was because it was the right thing to do, and he paid the price when called for.

Phae knew him well. It was why she'd been so conflicted last night about healing her brother. And by encouraging his sister to help Ares, she'd had a part in his disgrace. His anger was understandable. Her throat tightened with emotion as she stared at the cuts crossing his back.

Watching him make his way down that line of Sicari warriors had been agonizing. Not just because he was running the gauntlet for her, but because something else had wrenched at her heart. An emotion she didn't want to accept because it was ludicrous to even consider given the short amount of time they'd known each other.

Afterward when the *Prima Consul* had said he couldn't receive medical attention, she'd known she couldn't let him die. She was willing to do anything to save him, even if it meant bringing the wrath of the entire Sicari Order down on her head. And she couldn't express regret for something she'd do again without hesitation. She closed the distance between them, her hand lightly touching his shoulder, taking care to avoid his injuries.

"I'm sorry. I didn't understand the importance of it all." She met his gaze as he turned to face her. "But I don't regret interfering. The thought of you dying . . ."

She didn't finish the thought. Losing him would have left her bereft of something she didn't understand yet. Without Ares, there was no one left to turn to. Even Ewan was dead to her because the

Sicari had arranged *her* death. The only person who had any under-standing of her was Ares. If he had died last night, she'd have been completely lost.

She trusted him to keep her safe. And the idea of having to fend for herself in this strange world of his terrified her. His strength made her stronger. She realized that now. A strong hand captured her chin and turned her face up so she was looking into his eyes. Frustration and something else darkened his gaze, but she saw the beginnings of resigned acceptance there as well.

"You seem determined to think the worst when it comes to my early demise."

"Self-preservation," she muttered, unwilling to expose the emo-tions she was feeling. Particularly if he might use them to manipu-late her. "If you die, where does that leave me?"

"Lysander agreed to take on my responsibilities if I didn't sur-vive the gauntlet. He would have looked after you."

"Your responsibilities?" She sucked in a sharp breath and jerked free of his light grasp. "So what happened just now—was *that* part of your responsibilities, too?"

She took two steps back from him as humiliation slashed through her. They'd just shared the most incredible experience and now he was referring to her as one of his responsibilities? God, she was a fool to hope he'd think that passionate interlude was anything more than just sex to him. And the idea that *she* thought it meant some-thing at all made her sick to her stomach. At least Jonathan hadn't used her in the bedroom like that. He'd simply screwed her to get ahead in his career.

"*Merda.* That's not what I meant," he growled. "Last night, I wasn't sure whether I'd live or die. It's why I assigned *all* my respon-sibilities to Lysander before I entered the gauntlet. I trust him with my own life, and I knew he'd protect you as he does me."

Okay, so he obviously cared about her safety. Did that mean that up-against-the-wall moment a little while ago hadn't been *just* sex for him? She swallowed hard and dismissed the question. She didn't want to know. What she really wanted was some sort of guidebook that told her what to do so she could stay out of trouble in this sur-real world of his.

"Fine. So you were just looking out for me. But how do you expect me to stop breaking the rules if you don't tell me what the rules are?" She shook her head in frustration. "I mean, did it ever occur to you that maybe I wouldn't *interfere* so much if you'd explained things to me *before* rather than *after* the fact?"

"Yes, it's occurred to me, but there's not been enough time to explain things, has there." It wasn't a question, more of a chastisement.

"Well, there's time now," she said firmly and held up her bandaged hand. "So I want you to explain how this blood bond thing works."

"How it works?" A strange expression crossed his face as his eyes focused on her hand then shifted to her face.

"Yes. I *know* what it got me—a get-out-of-jail-free card. But what do *you* get out of the bargain?"

"The blood bond is a contract." His roughly carved features turned to granite. Harsh, striking, and unreadable. "In exchange for my protection, you're required to serve me for no more than a year."

"Excuse *me*?" She stared up at his impassive expression in amazement. Even worse was the disquieting sensation that made the hair on the back of her neck stand on end. Something wasn't right here. "Exactly what do you mean by *serve*?"

"It means exactly what I said. You're to serve me until your debt is paid." His voice was flat and even.

There wasn't one iota of innuendo in his voice, but her blood raced like wildfire through her body just the same. Her imagination immediately presented her with several different possibilities of service. None of which were displeasing, but they definitely didn't help matters where this man was concerned. He was dangerous in far too many ways for her sanity. Even with that unreadable expression on his face, he was still the sexiest man she'd ever seen. And standing there with just a towel wrapped around him, cuts and all, made him look all the more sinful.

She struggled to focus on the subject at hand, but realized she was losing. He turned and moved away from her toward the bed. The moment the towel slipped off his solid, muscular hips, her heart slammed into her chest. With a mixture of fascination and pleasure, she simply stared, unable to take her eyes off him.

Out of the corner of her eye, she saw the towel fold itself neatly in the air then settle on the bed. Her gaze focused fully on taut buttocks and the hard sinews of his legs. When he bent to pull on his trousers, she drew in a quick breath at the raw, naked maleness of him. He was beautiful. Scars and all. In seconds, black leather covered his lower extremities, and she released a quiet sigh. The pants were ripped everywhere he'd taken a blow from a sword, but at least he was clothed.

She refused to decide whether it was relief or disappointment she was feeling, although she already knew the answer. The moment he turned to face her, she knew he'd heard her sigh. Heat filled her face, but it was the regret in his eyes that chilled her.

"You still haven't really clarified what I'm supposed to do when it comes to fulfilling my part of the blood bond," she said quickly in an attempt to break the tension hovering in the air between them.

She met his gaze with a steady look. An undefined glint of emotion flickered in his eyes. It made her think he was unsure of something. Her—himself perhaps? Whatever it was, she could tell he didn't like it.

"The service generally depends on the individual and the guild's needs. In your case, you're going to help me find the *Tyet of Isis*."

His hard shoulders rolled in a slight shrug, a grimace tightening his mouth at the motion. His injuries would take some time to heal, and she doubted a doctor would stitch him up at this point unless the cut was really deep. But she could tell Phae had healed him enough so that most of his wounds were superficial.

"There's something else—" An authoritative knock on the door interrupted him. Frustration darkened his face when he commanded the visitor to enter. His features turned into a fierce scowl as the door slowly opened. She turned her head and met the impassive gaze of the *Prima Consul*. The woman arched her eyebrows at Ares.

"I expected you to be a bit more incapacitated," she murmured dryly. "But at least you're *halfway* presentable."

The *Prima Consul* turned her attention to Emma. Beneath the woman's penetrating gaze, it was impossible not to feel like a kid caught with one's hand in the cookie jar. Amusement danced in the woman's gray eyes although her regal expression didn't change.

"You're a woman of strong character, Miss Zale. There are few people with the audacity to try and intimidate me." She threw Ares a glance of rebuke before returning her attention to Emma. "Yet you didn't hesitate to put me in my place when it came to the well-being of my godson."

Her godson. That explained the affection layered beneath the woman's irritation. Emma winced slightly at the woman's words but didn't try to apologize for her actions the night before. She had no regrets.

"I did what was necessary, Ms. . . ."

"Atia Vorenus, but you may call me Atia. Yes, you were quite straightforward about it, weren't you?" The *Prima Consul*'s mouth quirked in a small smile as Emma flushed at the memory. The woman laughed softly. "I find it refreshing. You remind me of some-one I used to know years ago. He was just as straightforward."

There was a wistful note in Atia's voice as she stared at Emma with an odd expression on her face. With a sudden change in demeanor, the *Prima Consul* turned back to Ares. "Have you explained the terms of the blood bond to Miss Zale?"

"Yes," Ares said with sharp nod.

"Cryptic as always." The *Prima Consul* glared at him in exas-peration.

"I answered your question. What else would you like me to say, Atia?"

"*Mater Dei*, but you're a stubborn man. You blood bond with an *aliena* and *without* the Order's approval, yet you treat the entire affair with no more respect than a Praetorian does his mother."

"My actions may have appeared reckless, but they were necessary given the circumstances. Did you expect something less of me?"

"No. I didn't." Atia sighed quietly. "Does Miss Zale at least understand the significance of the bond itself? It's obvious she didn't know enough about our laws last night."

"She understands that in exchange for my protection, she's to help us find the *Tyet of Isis*," Ares bit out.

The dark look he directed at the *Prima Consul* seemed to be a silent warning, but if it was, Atia ignored it. Clearly annoyed, the woman looked at Emma then back to Ares.

"Well, I hope you've done a better job emphasizing that any interference has serious consequences of the kind we saw last night." Atia blew out a harsh breath so fiercely it sounded like an ancient Latin curse. "I'm tired of listening to the Council rant about your lack of respect for our laws. How in heaven's name do you expect to lead the Order—"

"Enough." Ares growled. "We've already discussed this, Atia. I have no intention of becoming the *Prima Consul*. And none of this has any bearing on Emma or her obligation to the Order."

"*Destinatus diabolus*." In a flamboyant gesture of surrender, the woman waved her hands in the air. "*Molto bene*. But we both know this argument is far from over."

Ares frowned darkly, but didn't argue. His expression said this hadn't been their first contentious discussion on the matter nor would it be their last. Atia turned to face Emma and smiled.

"So, *cara*, Ares tells me you have a special gift that will help us learn more about several artifacts we have here at the house. Items that may help lead us to the *Tyet of Isis*."

For a moment, the woman's words left Emma speechless as she stared at the *Prima Consul*. He'd told her. He'd told his godmother that she could read relics. Correction. He'd led the woman to believe she'd be *happy* to read the artifacts for them. Why would he do that when he'd seen how touching antiquities affected her?

Didn't he remember how she'd wound up on the floor of her office from the shock of taking the coin out of his hand. While that incident had been a lot different than her usual flashbacks to the past, he had to have known it wasn't easy for her. Her gaze flew to Ares's unreadable expression.

The *Tyet of Isis*.

The bastard wanted the damned thing so bad he was willing to use any means possible to find it. God, she was an idiot. He was using her. When he'd been trying to convince her to come here with him, he'd casually dangled a carrot in front of her. He'd planned this. He knew the possibility of viewing a private Sicari collection of artifacts would excite her. Once she was here, he'd probably assumed it wouldn't take much at all to get her to read the objects. It didn't help to know he was right. But it didn't change anything.

He'd asked her to trust him, and she had, only to have him betray her. And she had no reason to believe anything else he said either. The memory of his fingers stroking her intimately made her wince painfully. She swallowed the bile rising in her throat as the sting of his deceit swept across her skin. It was as harsh as an icy wind.

Ares's eyes narrowed and she fought to keep her dismay hidden. She jerked her gaze away from him to look at his godmother. The look of curious puzzlement on the woman's face only made Emma feel more of a freak than she usually did.

"I'm not sure what your godson's told you, but I doubt I'll be of much help with your artifacts. My understanding of the Sicari culture is minimal at best. And those who *did* know something have all been *murdered*. So even if I *did* have a special gift"—she sent Ares a blistering look of contempt"—I sure as hell wouldn't admit it because I'd most likely be next on the list, even though I don't know jack."

"*Deus damno id*, Emma. I told you I won't let anything happen to you," Ares said harshly as Atia looked on with displeasure.

"No," Emma said coldly. "Not as long as you have a use for me."

"*Christus*. I'm not—"

"Why do I think you didn't bother to consult Miss Zale about the artifacts, Ares?" The *Prima Consul* heaved a sigh of disgust as she turned her head to Emma. "Miss Zale, forgive my godson. He obviously needs his head examined. I, for one, would be grateful for *any* insight you might offer on the artifacts we have, even if your knowledge is limited. Fresh perspectives are always good. And hopefully this cipher your father left you will prove useful. Have you had any success with it?"

"I decoded a couple more lines last night while Ares slept. As soon as it's done, I'll turn the translation over to you."

"Excellent." The *Prima Consul* studied Ares for a long moment before she sent a hard nod in his direction. "I'll make sure it's Ignacio who validates your recovery this evening. The two of us will see to it that no one challenges your . . . *amazing* recuperative abilities and that the Council grants you *Indulgentia* for blood bonding with an *aliena*."

Ares went rigid, his expression harsh and unyielding as he met Atia's hard stare. The disapproval on the woman's face as she turned toward Emma said the *Prima Consul* was well aware Ares hadn't recovered so easily on his own volition. Heat rose in her cheeks as Atia frowned at her. It was evident the woman believed Emma was somehow responsible for Ares's miraculous recovery. But there was something else in the woman's gaze too. A glimmer of gratitude? A moment later, she released a silent sigh of relief as Atia turned her gaze back to Ares.

While his features revealed nothing, Emma could read the shame and disgrace in his stiff posture and the corded muscles of his arms and neck. She might be angry about his betrayal, but it was impossible not to feel some regret. He hadn't asked her to interfere, and yet she had. Suddenly, Atia made a small noise of what sounded like exasperation as she looked at Emma.

"Why don't we leave my godson to collect his wits *and* his clothing. I'll take you to our research library, where you can examine our artifacts and work undisturbed on your father's cipher."

Atia directed a stern look in Ares's direction as she headed toward the door. Emma sprinted after the woman, only to have Ares immediately block her path. His hand caught her arm in a steely grasp and he bent his head toward her.

"We'll discuss this later, Emma," he murmured with restrained anger. "There's no need for you to fear your gift or the use of it."

"I'm not afraid of it. I just don't like being used for it." She jerked her arm free to stalk after the *Prima Consul*. She paused in the doorway and sent him a wintry look. "And do me a favor—stay away from me."

EMMA raked her trembling fingers through her hair then focused her gaze back on the paper in front of her. No matter how she decoded the damn thing, it still read the same. She brushed her fingertips over her handwriting with a rising sense of frustration. The harsh breath of exasperation she released sounded loud in the quiet of the small research library.

She quickly glanced at the only other occupant in the room, but the stranger was too deep in thought to notice her. Two days ago, when she'd translated the second portion of the cipher and read about her father's fears that the Institute was spying on him, she'd been stunned.

Her first inclination had been to believe it was the Sicari watching him, not someone inside the Institute. After all, Ares had said they'd been watching her parents for some time. It had made sense. But now this? It turned everything upside down.

Trust no one with this secret. I'm certain the Tyet of Isis exists. I've found several clues to its location and hope to find more when we return to Dawwar. I think the Institute is spying on me. My university office has been broken into twice now. As a precaution, I hid something for you in the secret cubbyhole. Trust no one at the Institute. A colleague I knew years ago, Atia Vorenus, may be helpful. You can trust her. I think she's still with the Sorbonne. I love you, Emma. Dad.

What were the odds of there being more than one Atia Vorenus on the planet? Small, but possible. Of course, the first time Atia had brought her to the research library, the woman had casually mentioned that she'd studied at the Sorbonne in Paris. That reduced the odds to virtually nothing. At the time, she'd thought nothing of it. Most major universities had archeology departments and the Sorbonne was no different. But looking back on the conversation, there had been an intensity about the woman's manner that said she was hoping for some recognition on Emma's part. Her father's message had to be referring to the Sicari *Prima Consul*. Or maybe there were two women with the same name. God, she didn't know what to think. She was so confused. Whom could she trust?

She ignored the immediate answer to her question. No. She couldn't trust Ares. He'd used her. The anger welled up inside her again, and she drove her thoughts about him out of her head. She didn't want to think about him at all. God, she was a lousy liar even when she tried to lie to herself. The sound of soft voices intruded on the silence, and she looked over her shoulder to see Atia and Ares standing in the library doorway arguing.

Emma quickly slid her translation under her scratch paper. She wasn't ready just yet to tell anyone she'd solved the cipher. She needed more time to think. Another peek over her shoulder and her gaze locked with Ares's penetrating look. Her heart slammed into her chest as their eyes met.

For the past week, she'd refused to talk with him. Every time he came near her, she'd taken off in a different direction. It was easy to see he wasn't happy about it. Frustration thinned that beautiful mouth of his into a firm line, but there was a determination in his gaze that said he wasn't going to be put off for much longer. With a glare at his godmother, he spun around and disappeared.

The breath she didn't realize she'd been holding slowly eased out of her. With her heart pounding, she turned back to the papers in front of her. Even from a distance, he had the ability to make her knees wobble. Not good. In fact, it was damn irritating that he affected her at all. He'd brought her to this remote estate in Michigan because it suited his purpose. It didn't get any simpler than that. Well, except for those few blissful moments in his bathroom.

Even now, she was still reeling from that brief interlude. It had left her shaken in more ways than she cared to admit. Jonathan had never rocked her world the way Ares had the other morning. For Ares, it had been nothing more than just sex. She knew that. But God only knew what a woman would experience when he actually *made love* to her. A sliver of disappointment slipped under her skin because she wouldn't ever know what it would feel like. The thought made her hand curl up into a tight fist. What a fool she was.

A light touch on her shoulder made her jump. She turned her head to look up at Atia. The woman's face was almost wrinkle-free and her features were classical. Her face resembled some of the paintings Emma had seen in Roman frescos. Dressed in jeans and a bright turquoise shirt, the *Prima Consul* looked young and vibrant. Not a day past forty. But if Atia was the woman her father had known, she would have to be much older.

"You've a talent for frustrating my godson, *cara*." The *Prima Consul* smiled at her with a mischievous glint in her eyes. "If I didn't know better, one might think you of Italian descent yourself."

"It's not my intent to make him feel *anything*. I simply want nothing to do with him."

"You're both stubborn. One of you will have to give way

eventually. The question is who." The older woman laughed and took a seat at the library table opposite Emma, and set a small wooden box on the table in front of her. "I for one would love to see him forced to bend just a little, and I think you're the woman who can achieve that."

"I doubt that. Once I'm free of this blood bond, we'll go our separate ways." She stared down at her palm and the cut that was healing. "Although where I'm going to go is a mystery since I don't have a life any longer."

The bitterness in her voice made Atia frown. "Emma, I know the past two weeks have been quite difficult for you. But if you let me, I'd like to be your friend."

"Why?" she bit out with fierce suspicion. She was learning the hard way that no one ever did anything just to be nice. And she still wasn't sure she could trust this woman, even if she was the Atia in her father's message.

"Because you and I have something in common," Atia said quietly.

The leader of the Sicari hesitated and looked down at the box in front of her. The pensive look on the woman's face made Emma relax slightly. With a small, wistful smile, the *Prima Consul* opened the box and pulled out an object wrapped in white silk. She carefully unfolded the silk to reveal a small stone cross. Even without close examination, it was easy to see the cross was several hundred years old. Emma narrowed her eyes at the woman and shook her head.

"What do you want from me?"

"This cross was given to me by someone I loved very much," Atia said. "And it can tell you quite a bit about me."

"I'm not sure what you mean." Emma looked at the cross then met the other woman's arched look. "How can a cross tell me something about you?"

"Actually, it can tell you a great deal." With a slight movement of her fingers, the artifact rose up from the table by an invisible force then slowly settled back down onto the silk cloth. "As you can see, I have a gift similar to Ares's."

Emma shook her head in amazement. "I thought Sicari women could only heal."

"There are exceptions to everything in nature. Even those who *choose* to enter the Order occasionally inherit abilities," Atia said with a smile before her expression grew serious. "But our healers are our most valuable defense against the Praetorians."

"Like Phae?"

"Phaedra is quite special. Her healing abilities are some of the strongest I've ever seen," Atia said quietly. "But I'm not here to discuss her. I want to discuss the two of us. We both know you see things when you touch artifacts, Emma. My godson is quite thorough in his reports."

The *Prima Consul*'s direct and matter-of-fact manner told Emma the woman wouldn't believe her, even if she did manage to lie well for once in her life. But she wouldn't be tricked into touching one of the Sicari objects Ares had dangled like a carrot in front of her. She shrugged.

"If you're asking me to touch the cross, I'll pass on test-driving this model. Why don't *you* just enlighten me?" Emma arched her eyebrows with distrust.

"*Molto bene*, I understand your reluctance to trust me." Atia nodded with gentle acceptance. A reflective expression swept across the woman's youthful features. "More than thirty-five years ago I was working an excavation in the Cathars territory near *Rennes le Château*. Your Oriental Institute expressed interest in the dig and sent an intern to work with us. Not only was this young man intelligent and charismatic, he knew who the Sicari were."

The *Prima Consul* paused and reached out to touch the silk that cradled the cross. Across from her, Emma felt a chill slide down her back. She knew what was coming. And if she hadn't seen Atia's name in the cipher, the woman's story would have been difficult to swallow. Palms together, her fingertips pressing against her lips, Atia drew in a sharp breath then continued.

"I'd never met anyone quite like him. He was strong, handsome, bright, and witty. He was the *first* non-Sicari I'd met who realized my people had migrated from Rome with the Cathars to escape

Praetorian persecution. He scoured the hills near the excavation site in search of anything that might prove his theory. I was with him when he found this cross in a nearby cave." Atia sighed and stared at the cross with a wistful expression.

"You loved him very much."

"Yes," Atia answered. "I think a part of me always will. He was my first love."

"Did you ever tell him how you felt?" Her question seemed to startle the other woman. Atia immediately shook her head.

"No. I was nothing more than a friend. I wanted to tell him, I just never found the right moment. And when I did, it was too late." Hesitation crossed the *Prima Consul*'s face as her gaze met Emma's across the table. Suddenly aware of how difficult it must be for the woman to share her story, Emma tried to make it easier for the woman.

"Was it because he met my mother on the same dig?"

"He told you about me?" Atia gasped.

"Not exactly." Emma shook her head, her fingers sliding the translation of her father's coded message out from under all the papers. "He told me to find you. Your story just filled in some of the missing puzzle pieces."

Amazement making her eyes widen, Atia stared at her as she took the translation and proceeded to read it. Worry replaced her surprise as she lifted her head. "*Dolcis Mater Dei*, then he *did* find the *Tyet of Isis*. He left it for you in this hiding place he mentioned."

"No, I don't think so. I was with him and Mom at Dawwar . . . before their murder." Her muscles grew taut with the pain that always accompanied the memories. She focused on the days before the murders and shook her head. "I don't think Dad would have been able to hide his excitement if he'd made that kind of a find."

"Then what do you think he left for you?" Atia's puzzled frown held frustration as well.

"I don't know. His notebook, maybe? I haven't seen it since he died, although I've not really looked for it either." She winced as she remembered all the boxes with her parents' belongings in the garage at home. Boxes she'd never gone through.

"His notes on the *Tyet of Isis*?"

"More like a collection of notes and observations about the Sicari—"

"Notes on where to find the *Tyet of Isis?*"

"I suppose." Emma shrugged. "He never let me or anyone else touch it. I tried to convince him to go digital, but he refused."

"Digital files are easily found and accessed. One's life work can easily be stolen. Notebooks can be written in a personal code, something David excelled at," Atia said with an absentminded expression as she pointed to the translation. "Where is this secret cubbyhole your father mentions?"

"In his . . . my office."

"*Christus.*" The *Prima Consul* lightly smacked the tabletop with her palm. "If David did know the location of the *Tyet of Isis* and left that information for you, someone else might find it before we do."

"I don't think anyone's going to find it."

"You don't understand, *piccola mia*. The Praetorians are looking for the *Tyet of Isis*, too. If they think it's in your house, they'll literally tear it apart looking for it. Whatever's in that hiding place, we have to find it first. It's imperative that we find the *Tyet of Isis* before the Praetorians."

"Why? Ares said no one knows what it is."

A dark scowl on her face, Atia stood up to pace the floor. One hand on her hip and the other waving Emma's statement aside, the woman drew in deep breath. "Ares isn't the *Prima Consul*. I know things he doesn't, and the *Tyet of Isis* isn't just an artifact. It's the key. A key that in the hands of the Praetorians has the potential to destroy your world and mine."

"Then there's only one thing we can do," Emma said with a sense of foreboding. "I have to go back for it."

"Impossible," the *Prima Consul* snapped. "Your death was staged over a week ago. Even if we gave you a disguise, going into that house during the day is too risky. Someone might recognize you, which would undo everything Ares and the Order have done to keep you safe."

"All right, then we go in at nighttime. No one sees me, and we're free and clear."

"It's not that simple—" Atia objected with a sigh.

"Are you trying to tell me the great Sicari spy network can't manage to sneak me in and out of my own house in the middle of the night?" Emma rolled her eyes at the woman. "*Puhleeze*. I've seen what you people can do. If I don't go, something might get missed."

"Not if you tell us where the cubbyhole is."

"My father left the message for me. If something's out of place or missing, I'll know it. I'll know if there's someplace else in the house I might have to look. Your people won't. You need me, and to be quite frank, the sooner I make good on this blood bond with Ares, the better."

"Is it the debt you owe Ares you're so eager to dispense with or is it that you wish to run away as fast as you can from him?"

"I pay my debts." Emma kept her voice neutral as she averted her gaze from Atia's perceptive one. "But *I* choose how to pay them."

"Don't judge him too harshly, Emma. Like you, Ares likes to pay his debts. He's under the misguided impression that he owes me. He knows the *Tyet of Isis* is important to me, therefore it's important to him."

"And I'll help you find it. But I'll do it on my own terms, not as Ares decrees."

"As you wish." Atia nodded her head with a look of thoughtful assessment on her face. "Since you're determined to retrieve whatever your father left you, I should direct my *spy network* to make arrangements for you to return home long enough to secure the object."

"Thank you." Emma exhaled a sigh of relief as she stared down at her father's handwriting.

Doing battle with Atia had been far easier than it would have been with Ares. She needed to go home, not just to find what her father had left for her, but she needed to say goodbye. Everything she'd ever loved was gone, and now she was losing the last tangible part of her old life. It might be foolhardy to go back, but she didn't think she'd find a safe haven ever again.

"And the cross?"

She jerked her head up. Atia's expression was dark with emotion as she looked down at the artifact on the table. There was a longing in the woman's face that Emma could identify with. It was similar to the ache she felt for Ares. A desire for something more from him. The thought made her pull in a sharp breath. Hearing it, the *Prima Consul* sent her a questioning look. Striving to hide her revelation from the astute woman, Emma shook her head.

"It's yours. I have no desire to intrude."

"Thank you." Relief lightened Atia's features and she gave a sharp nod of her head. "I'll go make arrangements now for your trip back to Chicago."

The woman's relaxed demeanor made Emma realize how hard it must have been for Atia to consider sharing such a private moment of her life with someone who was virtually a stranger. The *Prima Consul* passed her on the way to the door then stopped.

"You do realize Ares will do everything he can to keep you from returning to Chicago. The blood bond is a pact between the two of you that has a greater meaning than just a debt. If the bond becomes intimate, it can have far-reaching consequences."

She was grateful the woman was behind her. She was certain her expression revealed far more than she'd like. The memory of Ares thrusting into her the other morning until they were both satiated sent her heart skidding along until it crashed into her chest. And she definitely didn't like the idea that the woman might have suspicions about just how intimate her relationship with Ares was.

As much as she loved being in Ares's arms and experiencing the heat of his touch, the idea of someone even suspecting the two of them had been intimate was unwelcome. She'd suffered enough humiliation at Jonathan's hands. She wasn't up for a repeat performance where Ares was concerned. Especially when this time it had meant more to her than she'd expected it to. Not to mention that it had meant nothing to Ares. She rose from her chair and turned to face Atia.

"If you're worried I might weaken the Sicari bloodline, don't be." She sent the woman a haughty look. Atia narrowed her gaze, her expression unreadable.

"I sincerely doubt you'd weaken our bloodline, *cara*. But you might be surprised by how much it could strengthen yours."

God, the woman had the ability to be as cryptic as her godson.

"It's irrelevant. Ares views me as a responsibility. And I can think of better ways to spend my time than dealing with his arrogant, sometimes Neanderthal behavior."

Atia's laugh of amusement startled Emma and she stared at the woman in surprise. The *Prima Consul* smiled. "The man *can* be arrogant, but I know my godson quite well. When he sets his mind to something, he accomplishes it. Where you're concerned, Ares isn't quite sure which way to turn. But something tells me you'll solve that problem for him soon enough."

With that, Atia left the library. As she watched the woman leave, Emma frowned. What had the *Prima Consul* meant about strengthening her bloodline? She glanced around the library and saw the researcher she'd seen earlier shelving books. Quickly winding her way through the tables, she halted next to the young man, who looked up with a smile.

"Yes, *signorina*?"

"I was wondering if you had any books that discussed the Sicari blood bond."

"We have a couple, *signorina*." The researcher nodded his head. "Come, let me show you."

Setting his books down on a nearby table, the young man headed toward one of the sections she'd explored yesterday. He stopped and brushed his fingers across the spines of a row of books on one of the lower shelves. Obviously not finding what he was looking for, he straightened and frowned.

"Is something wrong?"

"I'm not sure, *signora*. There were two books detailing the *vena vinculum* here just the other day. Now they're both gone."

"Has someone else asked about them recently?" A surge of irritation sped through her. Why did she think Ares had taken the books? He'd been vague about the whole damn bond thing from the beginning.

"Actually, Councilman Cato asked if we had any information on them a couple of days ago. I simply pointed him in this direction. I didn't see him take any books, though."

"All right, thank you." Emma sighed with disappointment and a bit of guilt for automatically assuming Ares had taken the books.

"I can let you know when they're returned if you like, *Signorina* Zale."

"That would be great, thanks." She smiled at him and turned away.

The fact that he knew her name didn't surprise her. As the only *alieni* on the estate, she stood out like a sore thumb. With a grimace, she gathered her things and stored them on the shelf Atia had told her to use. She frowned as she glanced around. For all its size, the library suddenly seemed small and confining. The minute Ares talked with Atia, he'd come looking for her. Without thinking twice, she headed for the closest exit. She knew she couldn't avoid the inevitable, but at least she could find some peace in the outdoors until she was forced to face Ares.

Chapter 15

"DOLCIS *Mater Dei*. You *actually agreed* to her demand?" Ares snarled as he leaned across the delicate desk in his godmother's office until his face was only inches from hers.

"Watch your tone with me, Ares DeLuca," the *Prima Consul* snapped.

Her ire was a tangible force as he found himself roughly shoved backward a good two feet. It was a rare occasion when he witnessed Atia's ability, and her telekinetic response to his anger took him by surprise. Nonetheless, it didn't change anything. She'd given the order for the Chicago guild to find whatever it was David Zale had left for his daughter. But it was Atia's agreement to let Emma go with them that outraged him.

"Is it because she's an *alieni*? Is that why you're willing to risk her life?" He ground out the words, barely able to keep his tone civil. "Is the *Tyet of Isis* so important to you that you'll do whatever it takes to find it?"

"*No*. And for you to even suggest such a thing is an insult," Atia said with a freezing look in his direction. "I would sooner throw a lamb to the wolves than put Emma in harm's way."

"Then why let her go?" he asked with restrained wrath.

"Because if I don't, she'll go on her own—without protection. And I don't want to see anything happen to her."

"Then we keep her here until my team has a chance to find whatever it is Zale hid in the house."

"We are not her jailers, Ares." His godmother sighed heavily.

"*Fotte*." He slammed his fist into the wing-backed chair sitting in front of the desk. "I don't want her going. It's too dangerous for *her* and my team."

"My order stands. You're to take Emma back to her home after you've monitored the house over the next week."

"And if I convince her not to go?"

"Do you really think you'll win that argument?" Atia uttered a small sound of disgust as she eyed him with disbelief. He stared her down until she shook her head. "Fine. But only if she's not coerced in any way. It's her decision. Not yours. Is that clear?"

"Yes," he bit out then spun around to leave the office. He'd reached the portal when Atia's voice made him pull up short.

"Ares, if you care for her as much as I think you do, you should let someone else take the lead on this assignment."

Frozen in place by the comment, his jaw flexed with tension as he turned his head to look over his shoulder at the Sicari Order's leader. Her astute gaze made him uneasy. She had that look that said she was testing the water. Well, she could probe all she wanted, but he wasn't about to let her see she'd thrown him a curveball. He kept his expression neutral and narrowed his gaze at her.

"Emma is *my* responsibility, and I'll keep her safe for that reason," he growled quietly as he sent Atia a warning look. "But if anything *does* happen to her, it'll be on your head, and I won't ever let you forget it."

The doorknob twisted beneath his hand as he flung the office door open and stalked out of the room. His stride ate up the hallway on his way down to the research library. It was the last place he'd seen Emma and the best place to start. He still couldn't believe Atia had agreed to Emma's demand.

Just yesterday, he'd received a report of activity around the house. He didn't care what might be there, Emma wasn't going back. It wasn't just because her presence put his team at risk if she went with them. But he refused to let her undo everything he'd done to keep her safe.

Whether she liked it or not, Emma was no longer an *alieni*. It didn't matter if transference of his ability happened or not, the moment he'd claimed her, he'd made her a Sicari. And she was his. His to protect and care for. He released a dark sound of fury. Hell, she hadn't even given him a chance to fully explain the blood bond to her.

For the past week, he'd been rehearsing how to tell her everything. But every time he got near her, she raced away. That was ending today, right here and now. He was tired of trailing after her like a puppy. He was going to make her listen to him and they'd go from there.

The idea that he could *make* Emma do anything sent mocking laughter flying through his head. His anger crushed it in a split second as he stormed into the research library. The empty room simply added frustration to the mix. *Deus damno id*, where the devil was she? Her room? No. He already knew how she much she disliked being cooped up someplace.

"*Fotte*. Doesn't the woman know she's supposed to stay in one place?"

He blew out a harsh breath and moved back into the hall to see one of the researchers walking toward him. Sandro had his head in a book, but the minute he looked up to see Ares, he came to a halt.

"Have you seen Miss Zale?"

"Yes, *il mio signore*, she took the path that leads to the pond."

Ares nodded and brushed past the researcher and made his way down the hall to the back entryway. In minutes, gravel crunched beneath his feet as he walked quickly along the path Sandro had mentioned.

Overhead, the sky was gray, and it looked like it might rain any minute. He lengthened his stride. If she hadn't changed directions and left the path, she'd eventually wind up at the guest cottage. It was the perfect place to have it out with her. His breath clouded the air in front of him. The temperature had dropped. When he crested a hill, he saw the small pond and the cottage situated near its edge.

A low rumble echoed above him as he saw Emma a short distance away from the cabin. He moved more quickly, and in just a few minutes he'd closed the distance between them by more than half. The first raindrop splashed its way across his cheek. The size of it told him a lot more was on its way.

He was only a few feet away from her when he saw her back straighten. It was as if she'd sensed him. Had she acquired a Sicari ability already? The gap between them closed, he stretched out his hand to grasp her elbow just as the rain began to fall harder. She jerked her head around to meet his gaze with a look of defiance. Not a good start. To hell with good starts—he was going to make her listen to him no matter what. Her efforts to free herself were easy to thwart and he glared down at her.

"We need to talk," he bit out in a clipped tone.

"I don't have anything to say to you."

"Maybe not, but I've got a *hell* of a lot to say to you."

In response to her second attempt to break free of his hold, he half carried, half dragged her the last few hundred yards to the cottage. *Merda*, she wasn't going to make this easy for him, was she? The rain fell harder, and despite reaching the small house as quickly as they did, they still got wet.

The cabin's porch gave them immediate relief from the rain, and as they came to a halt in front of the cottage door, Emma shook her head vigorously. The action sent water everywhere, including his face. Why was he so sure she'd done it deliberately? His jaw tightening with irritation, he unlocked the cabin door with a slight wave of his hand.

A second later, the door slammed backward and into the wall. He barely noted the vicious sound it made. Instead, he fixed his gaze on Emma. Grimly, he met her stubborn expression and jerked his head in the direction of the interior.

The silence stretched between them as she glared back at him defiantly. *Christus*, she was a stubborn little mule. He exhaled the soft growl of anger he'd been holding back. The sound made her flinch slightly. Well, at least she was having second thoughts about defying him.

"Get in the house, *now*, Emma." Despite the quiet command, she didn't budge. *Deus*, she was really testing him. "I won't ask again."

Her face mutinous, she released an exasperated noise of disgust as she crossed the threshold and moved deeper into the cabin. The door crashed closed behind them as he strode to the fireplace. Although the cottage wasn't all that cold, a little warmth would eliminate the chill in the air. And considering Emma wasn't all that willing to listen to him, they'd probably be there awhile. He shrugged off his jacket and threw it over the back of a chair facing the fireplace.

The mantle was bare except for a tin matchbox and he pulled a matchstick out of the container. He checked the damper then sank down on his haunches to light the wood lying in the hearth. There were eight guest cottages on the estate, and each cabin was always ready to accommodate unexpected visitors.

The Order owned numerous properties like the estate all around the globe, but the White Cloud property was a popular retreat. It was known for its serene setting and extensive research library. Then there was the fact that it was the residence of the current *Prima Consul*. At this time of year, though, the cottages were generally empty.

The small two-room cabin was rough and sturdy, but it was also isolated. No one would interrupt them. He fanned the fire slightly with a newspaper that had been left in a rack next to the hearth. As he waited for the fire to begin burning steadily, he shifted his position slightly so he could study her without turning his head.

She was beautiful. The defiant tilt of her mouth only emphasized the fiery spark he'd seen in her the first time they'd met. He didn't know how he was going to convince her to have faith in him after he confessed all his sins, but he'd find a way somehow. The idea of letting her go just wasn't something he was willing to contemplate.

His muscles grew taut at the notion and he shoved it aside. The most important thing at this moment was her safety. A point he needed to make clear with her. He needed to make her understand that it wasn't about him controlling her. It was about her safety and that of others.

After he'd made his case about not taking her back to her house, he'd deal with the blood bond. He drew in a deep breath and slowly released it in his effort to control his temper. She was angry enough for the both of them. He tossed the newspaper back into the rack then stood up and turned to face her.

"I can't let you go back, Emma," he said with a quiet patience he didn't feel.

"Why not? I mean we're talking about the *Tyet of Isis*. It's why you brought me here. You wanted me to help you find it, remember?" She sneered.

"*No*. It isn't why I brought you here." Tension rocketed through him at the sound of his harsh tone. *Christus*. His control had lasted all of about thirty seconds. Swallowing his frustration, he shook his head. "The only reason I brought you to the estate was because I wanted to protect you. I didn't trust anyone else to keep you safe."

"Sorry. Don't believe you. It's always been about the *Tyet of Isis*," she said fiercely. "It's why you were at the Cairo police station, it's why you came to my house, it's why you brought me here, and it's why you had sex with me the other morning."

The anger and disappointment on her face sent a jolt of pain through him. Behind those emotions, he could see she was as vulnerable now as she'd been that day in Cairo. The knowledge clawed at his gut, because he was responsible for that look. She really believed he'd used her just to find the *Tyet of Isis*. And he didn't know what to say to change her mind.

It wasn't often he was at a loss for words, and it infuriated him. He didn't know what to say because at some base level she was right. Except the sex. That hadn't been about the artifact at all. Something else had driven him to make love to her that morning, but he just wasn't ready to label it.

"*Fotte*."

The Italian oath blistered out of him as he started pacing. Outside, the heavily falling rain was a muted roar, and the only other sounds were the creaks the wooden floor made as he walked and the crackling fire. How in the hell could he make her understand that all he cared about was protecting her? If he didn't care about her safety, why would he stop her? He came to an abrupt halt and wheeled about to face her.

"If all I cared about was the artifact, do you really think I'd keep you from going?" he snapped. Not the best tone to use with her, but surely she'd see the logic in his question.

"Truthfully?" she asked in a sarcastic tone. "I don't know, and I don't care."

"*Deus damno id.* I care," he roared. He wanted to shake some sense into her.

"Too bad, because this conversation is over. I'm leaving."

Emma took two steps toward the door, but he reached it before her. In one swift move, he lifted her off her feet and cradled her in his arms. The instinctive move underscored how little control he had where she was concerned. Worse, the minute he caught her up in his arms, his senses exploded. Warmth settled into his body everywhere she pressed against him. Vanilla and the soft taste of rain mixed together to create a heady scent that made him hard in an instant. *Dolcis Mater Dei.*

"Put me down," she ordered sharply.

They could both use a cooling-off period. But the only way to accomplish that was to put some space between them. If they were in separate rooms, it would give them a chance to let their anger drop a notch or two so they could discuss things rationally. He bit back a grunt of disgust. If she was mad now, she'd probably go ballistic when he explained the blood bond. Well, he'd have to deal with that when the time came.

"*Both* of us need some time to cool off."

"So why don't you do that in the pond outside, and I'll go back to the mansion." The sweetly spoken words had acid bubbling beneath the surface.

"Maybe I should drop *you* in the pond," he ground out between clenched teeth.

Christus, she always managed to bring out the worst in him. It didn't matter what he said or did, it always came out wrong where she was concerned. He strode toward the bedroom's doorway, ignoring her gasp.

The minute he entered the room, he realized there was only one place for someone to sit down. The bed. The one place he wanted to be with her was the only place to set her down. He ruthlessly crushed the desire threatening to take control of him as he carried her toward the bed.

"All right, you've had your fun," she said breathlessly. "Put me down. *Now.*"

"With pleasure," he growled and dropped her on the bed. Ignoring her cry of surprise, he turned and walked toward the door. When he reached the threshold, he looked back at her. "Come out when you've calmed down and we'll talk."

With that parting remark, the door crashed shut behind him. Stunned, she stared at the beveled squares carved into the back of the heavy oak door. He'd just dropped her on the bed and left.

Left her *alone.*

The disappointment spiraling through her was infuriating. God, what had she expected him to do? Stay here and make love to her? She didn't like the answer that popped into her head. Nor did she like knowing that from the moment he'd lifted her up into his arms, she'd had to work hard to keep her anger flowing hot and steady.

She flopped back onto the bed and closed her eyes. Twisted, that's what she was, twisted. The manipulative bastard wanted to control her every move. He'd brought her to White Cloud not because he thought she'd be safer with him, but because he'd been hoping to convince her to use her ability on the Sicari artifacts and find that damn *Tyet of Isis* of his. It was all he cared about. She was little more than a means to an end as far as he was concerned. A loud voice in the back of her head protested.

He'd been emphatic that her safety was the only reason why he'd brought her to the White Cloud estate. And that argument about his refusal to let her go home had some validity. Why would he stop her from going if all he really cared about was the *Tyet of Isis*? She blew out a harsh breath and slammed her clenched fists into the mattress. She was making allowances for him. It was a dangerous thing to do.

Dangerous because it would be easy to forget she'd been down this road once before. Her ability wasn't something she readily shared, save for a few select people. But life had taught her that where some people were concerned, her ability was more important than her. Jonathan had made that painfully clear by his betrayal.

He'd asked her to marry him simply because having a wife capable of reading an antiquity would help him move up the career ladder. It had been all the more painful a revelation because she'd been the one to tell Jonathan about her gift. She'd wanted to be honest with him when it appeared their relationship had taken a serious turn.

All she'd done was made it easier for him to hurt her. It was unlikely that he would have ever proposed to her if she hadn't given him the perfect reason to do so. The bastard had even tried to tie her father's success to her ability.

While there had been a modicum of truth in her ex-fiancé's words, her father had been a gifted archeologist. Her ability had simply made his work easier to do. She knew her parents had loved her deeply, but Jonathan's words had raised the old feelings of doubt she'd experienced as a kid.

She sat up and swung her feet off the bed to sit there staring at the oak door. He'd said they'd talk after they'd both cooled off, but there wasn't anything to discuss. She should have stayed in the research library and explored more of the historical riches she knew were there. In the library, there would at least be others around to interrupt them.

When the *Prima Consul* had mentioned the blood bond and Ares in the same breath, she'd been alarmed that Atia suspected her relationship with Ares was less than platonic. The idea that her attraction to Ares might be so transparent to the *Prima Consul* frightened her. One minute the man had her aching for his touch then the next she was ready to kill him.

Even more disturbing was the realization that she longed for something more from Ares. Something that she couldn't put into words even if she'd dared. But Atia had managed to read her so easily, which meant he might be able to do the same. And she didn't want to give him that much power over her.

The sound of the rain pulled her to the window and she stared out at the dreary scenery. From here, the mansion only reinforced her impression of a Gothic structure. The massive structure housed more than a hundred Sicari and was a bustling complex. Raindrops rolled down the glass panes in front of her and she sighed. In the past two weeks, there had been, at most, three days of sunshine. The remainder had been gray, damp, and rainy. She missed the sunny heat of Egypt.

"Are you ready to listen to me now?"

The sound of his voice scared the hell out of her. With a small scream, she whirled around to face him. She hadn't even heard the bedroom door open. One shoulder pressed into the doorjamb, he studied her with a wariness that surprised her. It seemed odd to see him wearing something other than the black leather pants she was used to seeing him in.

He'd discarded the standard black quasi-uniform he usually wore for jeans and a navy T-shirt. The sinewy muscles in his arms flexed slightly as he moved, and she watched him shove a hand into his back pocket. The jeans he wore stretched tight over his muscular legs and the memory of undressing him the night of the blood bond sent a wave of heat through her. God, this was insane. The corners of his mouth tilted upward slightly, almost as if he knew the effect he was having on her.

"I'll listen, but I won't change my mind," she said in response to his question.

"Emma, what's it going to take for me to get through to you?" He kept his voice just as quiet as hers, but that inflexible determination to get his way was still there. "It's not safe. Why do you have to be so stubborn about this?"

She studied him for a long moment then turned away and walked over to the bed to sink down onto the mattress. *He* was the stubborn one. How could she make him understand that she had to go home for more than just her father's note? If he was going to rip her free of her last mooring, the least he could do was give her a chance to say goodbye. She closed her eyes against tears of frustration. She shook her head.

"I'm not the enemy here, *carissima*." He crossed the floor to squat in front of her. "All I want to do is protect you."

"I have to go back," she said softly. "I need to find what my father left for me. And I need to say goodbye."

"Goodbye?" A frown wrinkled his forehead as he studied her with an assessing gaze.

"I grew up there. It's my last connection to my parents. I have to say goodbye. You've taken everything else from me—my life, my career, my friends—can't you at least let me say goodbye, even if it's in the dark?"

His eyes closed as she challenged him. The edge of his jaw was hard with tension as he weighed her words for a long moment. When he looked at her again, indecision darkened his eyes. She knew how much he hated the emotion. It was at that moment that she realized she'd won. It seemed like a hollow victory somehow. He drew in a deep breath and nodded.

"All right, Emma. You win." He raised his hand as she started to speak. "But you follow my instructions to the letter. No arguments whatsoever. You do as I say, when I say. Understood?"

"Thank you."

"I need to have my head examined," he muttered darkly as he stood up and paced the floor. "I knew from the beginning you'd be trouble, and I was right."

"What the hell is that supposed to mean?" Indignant, she stood to face him.

"It means I'm crazy for letting you talk me into agreeing to this." He rubbed the back of his neck with his hand, his shoulders hunching up then relaxing in a gesture of exasperation.

"Oh, the head thing I figured out." She placed her hands on her hips as she narrowed her gaze at him. "I'm talking about the trouble part."

He studied her long and hard for a moment. There was something about the intensity of his gaze that stole her breath from her. Something dark and sensual crossed his face, while a storm brewed in his dark, mysterious blue eyes. He slowly closed the distance between them. With only inches between them, she knew she should run like hell, but she didn't. The man mesmerized her. His fingertips lightly stroked her cheek.

"You're trouble of the worst kind, *carissima*. Smart, brave, a good sense of humor, compassionate, beautiful, and incredibly sexy. Life was complicated enough before you came along. I knew getting involved with you would cloud my judgment, but it's too late. I can't stay away from you."

The husky sound of his voice made her heart skip a beat and then another. Naked desire crossed his face and it sent her senses reeling. It threatened to drown her in a sensually wicked heat. No. She couldn't do this. She couldn't just forget the fact that he'd brought her here under false or near false pretenses.

"Stop it, okay," she said in a low voice. "Just stop."

"What do you want me to stop, *dolce mia*? Stop craving you? Stop dreaming about touching you?" His words were a gentle caress on her senses. "I've tried, *carissima*. I've tried hard to forget how you feel against my body. I've tried to forget because I know being with you is the worst thing that could happen to *both* of us. There are things I need to tell you, and yet every time I get near you, I lose my head. You slide into my senses until I can't think straight."

She drew in a deep breath. Oh God, if she were a piece of ice, she'd be completely melted by now. Definitely time to leave. With as much aplomb as possible, she turned away from him and headed toward the door. The sooner she got out of this cottage, the safer she and her heart would be.

"Look, let's just say we had some hot sex and let it go at that. Okay? There's no need to repeat it." She casually tossed the words over her shoulder as she headed for the exit. Almost to the door, she flinched as a hard, sinewy arm snapped down in front of her to block her way out of the bedroom.

"If I want *hot sex* as you call it, I know women who can give me that and they understand it's just that—sex," he ground out in a fierce tone. "*You* are not one of those women, *carissima*."

There was a primal note of possession in his voice, and it made her heart slam into her chest as she absorbed his words. The tension in him was easy to see by the way his hand gripped the doorjamb. It was a beautiful hand, strong and masculine. She slowly ran her gaze over the length of his muscular arm. An arm that had held her close on a number of occasions. And every one of those times, she'd enjoyed it far more than she should have. She turned her head to look up at him. The hunger she saw on his face sent her pulse racing, but she was reluctant to give in to the need slowly spiraling its way through her.

"What are you saying?" she asked in a breathless voice.

"I'm saying you're special, *cara*. It will *never* be just sex with you."

The desire on his face was enough to weaken her legs, but there was something else in his expression that tugged at her heart. The darkness of the emotion said his confession had come at a price to him. She didn't know what that cost was, but she was certain he believed he'd have to pay it. His hand cupped her chin and his thumb rubbed across her bottom lip in a light caress. She trembled at the emotions cresting like a wave inside her. God, what was she getting herself into? He was right—it wasn't just sex between them.

His mouth slid over hers in a teasing kiss. It undid her completely, her knees barely capable of holding her upright. Damn. Double damn. All the man had to do was touch her and she was ready to follow wherever he led. She clutched at his shirt and kissed him back.

The taste of him engulfed her senses with a silent roar that sent heat skimming through her body. The man had far too much power over her, but she didn't know how to counteract the effect he had on her senses. Her mouth parted beneath his as he deepened the kiss, and in a slow, teasing swirl, his tongue mated with hers. It was a dance of slow seduction that obliterated everything but him and his touch. When he lifted his head, she fought to clear the cobwebs from her mind as her gaze met his.

"Do you understand, *mio dolce*?" he asked quietly. "There's a *hell* of a lot more between us than just sex."

The tension in his muscular frame flowed through hers until her body was taut with an emotion she couldn't describe. The cut on her hand tingled, and she remembered Atia's warning about intimacy. The warning had come too late. She was in way over her head with this man. Something about him pulled at her. Kept her off balance. And this blood bond he'd made with her connected them in a way that was as intimate as when he made love to her.

"I do understand, and that's what terrifies me," she whispered. "We barely know each other and yet it feels right to be with you."

"Is that such a bad thing, *carissima*?"

"It is when I'm the only one who feels that way." Her voice cracked as she realized how much she'd revealed with her retort.

"But you're *not* the only one, *mio dolce*."

He lowered his head and kissed her again. Wrapped tight in his arms, she gave herself up to him without hesitation. It was irrational, but this was where she belonged. It felt right. Here, this moment, it was where she was supposed to be. Warm and silky, his kiss silently commanded her to give up all control. It was easy to do. The man had been in control of her from the first moment they'd met. But in yielding to him, she recognized his need for her.

It was in the way he held her, the beat of his heart beneath her palm, and the slight shudder that pulsed through him when she slid her hands underneath his shirt to caress his skin. Eager to touch more of him, she pushed the navy T-shirt up over his chest and he broke their kiss long enough to tug the shirt off him. Desire uncoiled inside her as she clung to him.

The last time he'd held her like this, she had not understood the depth of her need for him. This time she did. She wanted him. But she wanted his heart as well. Her fingers slid along the waistband of his jeans to the metal button. The moment her fingers slipped between denim and skin, he lifted his head.

A stark hunger etched into his rugged features, he captured her hand and carried it to his mouth to kiss her fingertips. His gaze never leaving her face, he backed away toward the bed and slowly began to undress. Transfixed, she watched with fascination as he removed his clothing. Intense pleasure swept through her, filling her with heat when he stood naked before her. The man was a beautiful male specimen of raw sexuality, powerful muscles, and a command-ing presence that sent a thrill racing down her spine.

Her gaze drifted over the length of him, pausing briefly on his erection before moving on to his long, hard legs then back up to the width and breadth of his shoulders. Desire careened through her. She wanted him. She couldn't remember ever wanting a man this badly before. Quickly removing her shoes and socks, she reached for the bottom of her shirt with her gaze still locked with his. An invisible force gently restrained her, pushing her hands back down to her side.

"Let me," he rasped.

The deep growl of his voice sent a white-hot flame streaking through her blood. The sensation coiled its way through her until she ached for a release. Something told her today would hold even more dangerous emotions than she'd experienced the other day. Of its own accord, her top slowly moved its way up over her head and arms until it fluttered to the floor beside her.

A warm pressure caressed the base of her throat just as if it were his hand. The unseen force moved downward to her lacy-edged bra until the invisible caress cupped her breasts. There was something incredibly arousing about him using his mind to caress her. At that instant, a gentle pressure rubbed over her nipples. It tugged a gasp from her. God, this was the most erotic thing she'd ever experienced.

"Do you like what I'm doing to you, *dolce mia*?" His voice possessed a dark, dangerous edge to it, leaving her trembling.

"Yes," she whispered.

Invisible fingertips lightly, almost reverently, explored the tops of her breasts. First one bra strap slipped off her shoulder and then the other. Her breathing was unsteady and erratic as the warmth of his mental touch slid across her back to undo her bra. As the lingerie fell to the floor, his sharp inhalation made her tremble.

"*Mea Deus*," he murmured. The harsh whisper scraped over her skin in a firestorm of sensation. "Do you have any idea how much I want you right now, *carissima*?"

Unadulterated need glittered in his dark blue gaze and it made her sway on her feet and release a soft moan. She took a step toward him, but his invisible strength held her in place. Slowly the pressure slid downward to undo her jeans and slide the denim off her hips. When she stepped out of her jeans, he released a low, primitive sound of desire. It set her heart racing as her need for him accelerated. Heat flowed through her, dampening the wispy lace underwear she wore.

"Ares, please."

In response to her soft plea, his mental touch slid up her thighs to slowly remove the lace panties. A moment later, his invisible caress explored her intimately. She cried out at the pressure he placed on the sensitive spot between her legs. It sent a wild shudder through her, and in seconds, she'd climaxed beneath his unseen strokes. A soft warm glow washed over her and she opened her eyes to see desire still holding him taut. This time he didn't stop her as she moved toward him.

The instant she was in his arms, he crushed her in his embrace, his mouth taking hers in a kiss that drove her body into a frenzied pitch of passion. The strength and power of it consumed her like a fire out of control. Deep inside, she recognized another emotion spiraling upward. She resisted it, knowing all too well what it would do to her heart. Instead, she broke their kiss and lowered her head to press her mouth to the pink scar on his chest.

Beneath her mouth, the rapid beat of his heart crashed against his chest. The tangy taste of him mixed with his spicy male scent and the rasp of his breathing to send her own heart racing with anticipation. She lifted her head and stared into a pair of eyes dark with passion as well as a possessive glint that thrilled her. The unspoken statement said he was claiming her as his. It clutched at her heart. He had said it wasn't just hot sex between them. His expression made her believe it.

"I want you," she said in a husky voice.

She didn't know how they landed on the bed together, and she didn't care. The warm, hard weight of his body on top of hers was exhilarating as his mouth began to worship her body in a way his invisible touch couldn't. With each heated kiss against her skin, he explored her every curve. The farther down her body he went, the tighter her muscles contracted with anticipation and need.

The fevered pitch growing inside her rolled out in a sharp cry as his mouth found her sex. She jerked against the intimate caress, her body responding to his touch the way an instrument would to a master musician. Wave after wave of tremors laced through her, and when he pulled away to kiss her inner thigh, she murmured her protest. No man had ever worshiped her so thoroughly or with such skill. Her eyes fluttered open as he slid his body upward along hers to brace himself above her.

"I want to see your face when you explode over my cock, *carissima*," he said in a hoarse voice that echoed with desire and passion. "I want to know you're feeling the same thing I'm feeling."

With a quick twist of his body, he was on his back taking her with him. Straddled across his hips, she trailed her fingers over the solid length of him, enjoying the look of hunger that swept across his features. Suddenly, pleasing him was paramount.

He'd taken her to a place she'd never been before, and she wanted to do the same for him. She leaned forward and brushed her mouth across his nipple then gently nipped at it. He rewarded her with a low growl. She liked knowing he found pleasure in her touch. Slowly, she inched her way down his body, just as he had hers.

She could tell how much he wanted her. His body betrayed him. Every time her mouth brushed over a small part of him, he shuddered at the touch. Yet he restrained himself from taking control of the moment. She wanted him to lose some of that self-control. The sound of his breathing grew heavier as her mouth explored the hard line of his hip. But as she moved toward the tip of his erection, his breaths became harsh pants of excitement. And when she took him into her mouth a moment later, his sharp cry of pleasure filled her with satisfaction.

Chapter 16

"CHRISTUS," he cried out as the heat of her mouth encircled him. He didn't know how anything could be better than the other morning, but this was. It was beyond incredible. His body shuddered as her tongue laved and caressed his cock with a tender regard that set off a rush of emotion inside him. An emotion that stated unequivocally that where this woman was concerned, he had no willpower, no control at all. She was tearing down walls no woman had ever touched—not even Clarissa.

Her mouth gripped him tighter, and it made him ready to come out of his skin. Enough. He wanted to be inside her. With his mind, he tugged her upward and set her down on top of his erection. Surprise widened her eyes as she looked down at him.

"Don't say a word, *carissima*, that delicious tongue of yours was driving me over the edge," he growled. "And I want *both* of us to be satisfied."

The womanly smile curving her mouth made his heart slam into his chest. He'd been more than right when he'd said she was trouble of the worst kind. She wasn't just trouble—she was undoing every vow he'd made to himself over the years. With his hands curled around her hips, he held her in place as he thrust upward with his body.

A gasp of pleasure parted her lips, and he savored her expression. He wanted to please her. Wanted to make her sob with delight. And *Deus* help him, he needed her more than he'd needed anything else in his life. As she rocked against him, he stretched out his hand to gently push her backward. When she did so, he touched the deepest part of her and he groaned at the pleasurable sensation. It blinded him to everything around them.

Desire and need merged until the only thing he knew was the hot friction of her slick sex. Deep inside a pulse crashed through him and he urged her to move faster. She obeyed and her features glowed with a delight that pulled his sacs up tight with expectation. Suddenly, her body clenched tight around him. It was an exquisite moment of fire, pleasure, and anticipation.

Twice more he thrust up into her, his cock eagerly seeking every small tremor she released. With each passing second, her body tightened around him like a white-hot vise of silk, and her orgasm rippled over him with a ferocity that only intensified his own pleasure. It was the sweetest sensation he'd ever experienced, and with a roar, he spent himself inside her.

When she slumped forward onto his chest, he wrapped his arms around her, content to enjoy the warmth of her on top of him. He knew it was a mistake to feel anything for her, but he did. With every word, every breath, every stroke of her body against his, the essence of her had penetrated the darkest parts of him. She'd touched him so deep inside that he knew he'd never be free of her.

The revelation didn't really surprise him. He'd known all along why he'd found it so easy to ignore the warnings in his head and seal their blood bond the other morning. He'd just refused to admit it. It had been easier to lie to himself, rather than accept the truth. But in denying it, he'd managed to obliterate the honor he prized so highly.

That he was willing to sacrifice everything, just to be with her, illustrated just how blind he was where she was concerned. Deep inside he'd known this might well be the last time she'd ever let him near her, and as much as he hated himself for it, he hadn't had the courage to tell her about the blood bond. He hadn't wanted to risk her rejecting him. Now it was time to pay the piper. He didn't hold out much hope for her ability to forgive him. The light touch of her finger against his mouth brought him out of his contemplation and his eyes met hers. Curiosity glimmered in her hazel-eyed gaze.

"Where were you just now?" She laughed as he quirked his eyebrow at her.

"Right here with you, *dolce mia*."

"No you weren't. You're worried about something. I can tell," she said with a touch of exasperation.

"Perhaps I was thinking how foolhardy it is to let you return to your house."

The lie wasn't that far removed, given his desire to protect her. Especially when what he really wanted to do was to lock her up someplace special so he could always come home to her. The thought sent fear crashing through him. She broke free of his embrace and scooted across the mattress to the opposite side of the bed. The moment she left him, he had to fight the urge to force her back into his arms. The beauty of her back made him want to have someone create a sculpture of her in this very position with her head turned to look at him. But he'd want to see a sleepy slumberous look on her face, not worried frustration. He mentally traced his fingertips down her spine, but the touch didn't change her expression.

"Are you trying to renege on letting me return home?" she asked in a stilted voice.

"I gave you my word," he ground out harshly. A sense of foreboding tightened his insides. And he'd do whatever it took to keep it. But his word wasn't going to mean much to her when he made his confession.

"I'm sorry. You're too honorable to do that." She inhaled a deep breath then got to her feet and padded her way into the bathroom.

The blanket statement hung in the air as she disappeared into the other room. It sliced into him with so much force he thought he might start bleeding. Go back on his word? His word wasn't worth anything. He'd made a mockery of his honor by making love to her today.

Christus, he'd been a fool to think he could control himself when he was near her. The minute that damn vulnerability of hers showed itself, he'd been putty in her hands, and she didn't even know it. From there, things had gone downhill when it came to his self-control.

That blithe comment of hers about hot sex had cut deep. Deeper than he thought possible. It had made him determined to convince her that what they'd shared had meant a lot more to him than just sex. He sat up and rested his arms on his knees. From the moment they'd met, he'd been sliding down a slippery slope.

He just hadn't realized how fast he was falling. If he'd been thinking clearly, he never would have touched her. No, that wasn't altogether true, but he would have stopped short of making love to her the other morning. And he sure as hell wouldn't have compounded the issue by doing it again this afternoon. All he'd done was make matters worse. If he thought she'd hate him before, she'd want him dead now.

The minute she learned the truth about everything, it was going to drive a wedge between them. A wedge he wasn't sure he could remove. He closed his eyes. *Deus.* No matter what he said, she'd think he'd been manipulating her again. The truth was—he had. From the beginning, he had not wanted to part with her, and when the opportunity presented itself, he'd acted. His subconscious decision to seal the blood bond between them wasn't going to make him look good in her eyes. Particularly when it meant something far more binding now than it had the night she'd interfered in the *Dux Provocare.* The minute she understood the full implications of the bond, she'd see his actions as a calculated way to control her.

The knowledge made him close his eyes in resignation. *Fotte.* Was he ever going to regain the precious control he'd nurtured since executing Clarissa's murderer? Was he so far gone where Emma was concerned that he'd lost his ability to think rationally? As for the *desponsatio,* she didn't have to accept the commitment. While part of him wanted her to say yes, the other half of him wanted her to refuse. The Order could give her a new life somewhere else where she'd be safe. Chicago was far too dangerous for her. If she chose to stay with him—chose to stay? He was a fool. She wasn't going to want anything to do with him, which meant it would be that much harder to keep her out of harm's way.

Deus, if something happened to her—he slammed the door closed on the thought. He wouldn't let anything happen to her. He'd keep her safe, even if she did wind up hating him. The idea of her despising him sent a spike of pain lancing through him. With a growl of self-disgust, he sprang from the bed. He tugged on his jeans and turned his head toward the bathroom.

"I'm going to find a snack. Do you want something?"

"I'd love a diet drink if you find one."

Her voice echoed out into the bedroom with a lighthearted laugh. He grimaced. Grateful she couldn't see how her words were affecting him. Instead of responding to her playful tone, he moved into the main living space of the cabin and headed into the small kitchenette. The refrigerator and pantry were well stocked, although he really didn't feel like eating. He just needed something to do until he could find the strength to bare his soul. He pulled out a brick of cheese along with a couple of bottled soft drinks from the refrigerator, while the pantry offered up an unopened sleeve of crackers. He was standing at the kitchen counter when she entered the room. He didn't hear her come in, but his body knew it the moment she did.

When he turned around, it was as if he'd taken another sucker punch to his gut. *Mater Dei*, she had to be the sexiest woman he'd ever seen. She'd chosen to put on his shirt and he was certain she wasn't wearing anything else underneath it. But it was more than a sexual need for her that made him go still. It was the smile curving her lips that held just a hint of shyness that tightened his chest until it hurt to breathe. He'd never be able to stem the hemorrhaging the minute she eviscerated him.

As she moved forward, his body was tighter than a bow pulled taut before it launched an arrow. When she stopped in front of him, she came up on tiptoe and kissed him lightly. The gentle caress warmed his heart as much as it did his body. The moment she wrapped her arms around him and laid her head on his chest, his heart sank. He wrapped his fingers around the edge of the kitchen counter like it was a lifeline. This was going to be harder than anything he'd ever done. He didn't even know how much to tell her.

In the past two weeks, she'd had to adapt to a lot of change. But how much was too much where she was concerned? She was resilient, but everyone had their breaking point. He was stalling for time. She lifted her head and stared up at him, her hazel eyes shimmering with anxiety. He almost groaned. *Deus*, she was thinking he had regrets about making love to her. The only regret he had was not giving her the choice. He swallowed hard.

"We need to talk." He hadn't meant to make his tone so harsh. Especially when it caused her to flinch and step back from him.

"Okay," she said in a hesitant voice. "If it's about what just happened—"

"*Fotte*. No."

He brushed past her and moved into the small living room. The violence of his action made her jump as she turned to watch him pace the floor. The quizzical expression on her face merely exacerbated his guilt. She was going to hate him.

Maybe if he could convince her that what he felt for her went beyond lust, then maybe it would be okay. The problem was how could he explain his feelings when he didn't even understand them himself? All he knew was that he cared for her. Cared about what happened to her. Needed to be near her if only to hear her voice. See her face. Anything beyond that he couldn't admit to. The fear that came with that confession wasn't something he was ready to face.

"Just tell me what's wrong." The exasperation in her voice brought him to a halt. He met her gaze and gave her a sharp nod.

"I tried to explain the other morning, but I . . . things got out of control . . . I lost my head . . . something I do a lot of where you're concerned." He sighed.

"*What* didn't you explain?" She straightened her shoulders and grew stiff. Definitely not a good start. Tension knotted in his stomach at the wary look on her face.

"The blood bond has more than one customary usage by the Order. What happened the other night at Julian's *Rogalis* is one custom."

"And I pay my debt by helping you find the *Tyet of Isis*." She frowned. "I understand that."

"It's a little more complicated than that."

"How complicated?" She shrugged with puzzlement as she narrowed her gaze at him.

"The blood bond is a complex contract. It's used to adopt a child, to protect someone, and more. When a blood bond is sealed between a man and a woman, there are certain obligations—expectations that go with the bond."

"Fine, there's an obligation that comes with it. What am I missing here?"

Confusion clouded her face, and she pushed a loose strand of hair back behind her ear in a gesture of frustration. An enormous need to grab hold of something lunged through him, and he folded his arms across his chest. His fingers dug deep into his biceps in an effort to keep from reaching out for her. The healed wounds on his arms were still tender, but he welcomed the pain. It wasn't the penance he deserved, but he was certain he'd be condemned to hell soon enough.

"The intricacies of the bond make it possible for certain actions to alter the original contract. One of those actions is intimacy. I sealed the bond the first time I made love to you."

"Why do I get the feeling that's a bad thing?" she said with growing irritation. His jaw grew tight.

"The Sicari also use the blood bond as a betrothal ceremony."

The words sounded like a death knell the minute they weighted the air between them. Stunned, she just stared at him, her jaw slack with disbelief. Behind the disbelief, he could see the warning signs of the anger yet to come.

"Betrothal ceremony?" She was clearly struggling to comprehend his words and shook her head. "As in engagement?"

"Yes," he muttered as he ran his hand through his short hair.

"*What?*" The one-word question was sharp as a Sicari blade.

"When I performed the blood bond in front of the Order, it was a simple contract meant to save your life. A way to protect you. When I made love to you, it altered you *and* the original agreement."

The horrified look on her face shredded what little honor he had left. Not even when Phae had made him party to heresy after the gauntlet had he felt so much self-disgust. He turned away from her, unable to bear the look on her face. He'd promised to keep her safe, but the one thing he hadn't planned on was protecting her from himself. He bent his head and closed his eyes.

"Are you telling me that because we had sex, we're married?" Her voice slowly climbed the scale to end on a high-pitched note of anger.

"No," he growled as he whirled around to face her. "You have the right to refuse the *desponsatio* the Order will offer you."

"No?" She glared at him. "Then what the hell does refusing the *desponsatio* mean?"

"*Merda*, it means *yes*. Yes, technically we're married, but if you refuse the *desponsatio*, you have no further obligation to me. It's a contract you have the right to nullify."

"Contract?" Her eyes glittered with fury. "A contract is when both parties agree to the transaction. I didn't agree to marry you."

"But you didn't object when I made love to you either." The words were out of his mouth before he could stop them. He gritted his teeth for adding fuel to the fire.

"I am well aware of my own stupidity. You don't have to remind me, thank you very much," she said with an angry hiss.

Her anger was almost a tangible force pushing against his chest. *Christus*, every time he opened his mouth, he just dug his grave that much deeper. If she was this incensed now, he could only imagine her reaction to the possibility of transference. He winced at the thought of adding to her pain.

"I'm not blaming you. I knew what the consequences were of sealing the blood bond. I take full responsibility for that. I know you're angry—"

"I bypassed angry and jumped right to furious a few seconds ago. I suppose you had this macho idea that I would just meekly submit to your orders."

"It wasn't like that—"

"No, of course it wasn't." She sneered. "You were so overcome with desire for me you forgot what the ramifications of having sex with me were."

He took a step toward her then stopped when she backed away, her hands up in the air in a defensive gesture. He grimaced. "Yes. *No. Damno ut abyssus*. I made love—"

"*No*. We. Had. Sex," she interrupted him with icy rage.

He met her furious glare with a growing frustration. He needed to make her understand that he'd lost his head where she was concerned. It wasn't just sex for him. If that had been the case, he never would have touched her. There was something more between them that he couldn't define. He'd meant it when he said he could have sex with any woman but that she wasn't one of them. With her, the emotions ran too deep for just sex. She was a part of him, and he didn't want to lose her.

"I *made love* to you because it felt right. Special. There wasn't anything except you and me. Nothing else mattered. I know I should have explained things. I tried the morning after the *Dux Provocare*, but Atia interrupted—"

"Oh, and today you just waited to find the right moment to tell me? When would that have been? Before or after you screwed me?"

"*Fotte.*" The oath of frustration and self-loathing roared out of him. "It wasn't like that, Emma. I lose my head when I'm near you. I can't think straight."

"You need a better excuse than that. God, and to think I almost bought into this whole protection bit of yours."

"*Deus damno id*, Emma, I *am* trying to protect you."

"How? By having me service your sexual needs," she bit out as she leaned into him, her forefinger jabbing him in the chest with a fury he knew he deserved. "I should have let that other guy kill you."

Her words cracked into him like a club. *Mater Dei*, couldn't the woman see he was already on the cross where she was concerned? What he'd done was reprehensible, but did she really think he'd offered her his protection just to sleep with her? He was lost as to the how or why, but the one thing he knew with a certainty was that they belonged together. She had every right to be outraged and hurt by what he'd done, but he refused to let her dismiss what had already passed between them. Furious with himself for creating this bed of thorns he was in, he glared at her.

"He wouldn't have killed me, and we both know it would have only delayed the inevitable. You're mine, Emma. You have been since the first time I laid eyes on you."

"Your arrogance is unbelievable. I'm not a piece of property you can do with as you like."

"You're right, you're *not* a piece of property," he said through clenched teeth. "But you belong to me, just as much as I belong to you."

"Just because you tricked me into sleeping with you doesn't mean you own me." Her words were a battering ram to his chest. "I'm getting this goddamn blood bond of yours dissolved the minute I get back to the mansion."

She spun around and headed for the bedroom. Almost through the door, she suddenly grasped the doorframe and came to an abrupt halt. The shudder rippling through her frame made his heart contract with sorrow and remorse. *Merda*, he was a bastard for what he'd done to her. As he closed the gap between them, she whirled to face him, and he was brought to a stop by her outstretched hand holding him at bay. Pale and trembling, she met his gaze with a look that reminded him of someone in shock.

"You said—altered me *and* the agreement. What did you mean by altered me?"

"Emma, I don't—"

"No, I distinctly heard you say *the bond altered you and the original agreement*." She focused her eyes on him with a fierce intensity. "*Tell me* what that means."

"It means you're a Sicari."

"No. There's more to it than that, isn't there?" she snapped.

"Yes." He closed his eyes for a brief moment. "Transference of a Sicari ability is inevitable. The strength and type of ability are dependent on the individual."

"How long? How long before . . . I'm . . . before this happens?" The horror in her question made his gut clench as he stared at her devastated expression.

"Everyone's different. It could be days, weeks . . . at other times it takes a traumatic event to trigger it."

"Oh, fuck." Her hand floundered through the air as she turned to cling to the bedroom doorframe. When he reached out for her, she slapped his hand away. "Don't touch me. Don't you *dare* touch me."

"Emma, please—"

"*No*." She jerked upright and turned to face him. "No more

lies. Save them for some other woman who's a sucker for a smooth talker."

The fury in her voice held a note of contempt and humiliation. Her mortification was so deep he could hear the pain of it echoing in her voice. But there was something else in her expression. Shock. She'd realized she was no longer the Emma Zale she'd once been. She was different, completely changed, and she'd had no choice in the matter.

Fotte. What sort of man was he that he could cause the woman he loved so much pain? The revelation was so sharp it sucked the air out of his lungs in a single breath. What had he done? He had to tell her. She needed to know—understand that his love for her had driven all of his actions. Every sin he'd committed, every touch, look, and word had been because he'd refused to acknowledge his emotions. Denied the reality of what was happening to him.

Most of all, she needed to understand how much of a coward he'd been by refusing to tell her everything—including how much he loved her. Everything he'd done had been because she was a part of him. The second half that made him whole. If he could make her believe that, then there might be hope for him yet. He reached for her, and she swung at him.

Despite his ability to easily dodge the blow, he allowed her the solid punch to his jaw. His head snapped back from the force of her jab as her fury and humiliation coursed through her arm and fist straight into him. It took him a moment to recover, and when he'd straightened upright, the door to the bedroom had already slammed shut. There was a finality to the sound that sliced deep and the sliver of hope left inside him curled up and died.

EMMA pressed her back to the oak door and closed her eyes with a quiet sob. Oh God, what was wrong with her? How could she have been so easily fooled a second time? When he'd said there was something between them, he'd sounded so sincere. And dear lord, the way he'd made love to her—*no*, it had been sex. Nothing more.

Incredible sex, but nothing more than that. No, that wasn't true. It had meant more to her than she wanted to admit. She opened her eyes and stared at the tousled bed. It was a vivid reminder of what she'd shared with Ares such a short time ago. If she dwelled on what they'd shared, she might never recover from the pain and humiliation she was experiencing now.

A shudder quaked through her, and she stumbled toward the bathroom. At the sink, she stared into the mirror. The woman facing her was a stranger. Eyes wide in her face with the pale complexion of someone in shock, her reflection reminded her of the way she'd looked the night she'd lost her parents. Emotionally devastated. But this time, humiliation was the crippling emotion. Not grief. This was even worse than when she'd found Jonathan in bed with his intern. This humiliation was far more painful because her connection to Ares was far stronger than anything she'd ever felt for her ex-fiancé.

She could have easily forgiven the impulse that had controlled both of them the morning after he ran the gauntlet. She certainly hadn't objected. If anything, she'd been just as much a seducer as he had. She'd encouraged him. And she'd been doing that since their first kiss. Blaming him for what happened that morning was unfair. Despite the heat of the moment, she did remember his reluctance. But today? He'd had plenty of opportunity to tell her everything before touching her. The bond had obviously been sealed the morning after he'd run the gauntlet, but he should have said something. He hadn't offered her a choice this time.

It wasn't the idea of being bound to him that horrified her. And while she might not have liked having a Sicari ability, she would have found a way to live with it just as she had her own gift. She might not have been too happy about it in the beginning, but she would have come around. But he hadn't said a word until everything was a *fait accompli*. That was what hurt the most. It cheapened what she'd had the stupidity to think was something special. To not tell her until *after* they'd slept together—for a man who prided himself on honor, he'd shown none toward her. Where had his nobility been this afternoon?

The man had betrayed her for the second time. First, he'd brought her to White Cloud simply to have her look at Sicari artifacts. When she'd discovered his dishonesty, she promised herself she wouldn't fall for his lies again. But today he'd persuaded her that the artifacts hadn't been his reason for bringing her here. He'd convinced her that he'd just wanted to keep her safe. And she'd actually believed him.

She'd believed him.

What a fool she'd been. Cupping her hands beneath the running faucet, she splashed water over her face. The cold of it stung her skin. Sharp and acute, the pain reminded her of the dark emotion in Ares's eyes earlier. He'd said it would never be just sex with her, and in his expression, she'd seen the knowledge that he would have to pay a price for saying that. Was it possible he'd understood that he'd sacrificed his honor today just to be with her? A shudder raced through her.

She was an idiot for hoping to find an excuse for his behavior. Christ, she didn't need to understand his actions. The why didn't matter. He'd played her for the fool, and she wasn't going to hang around and be fooled a third time. Reading those damn artifacts would have to serve as her debt then Atia could break the bond between them and she'd be done with him.

She ignored the protests echoing in the back of her head. Ruthlessly, she shoved them back into a dark corner. No. He'd violated her trust. There was no room for excuses here. Her heart was already close to breaking, and making excuses for him would just push her over the edge.

The admission sent a bolt of terror through her. It was the closest she'd come to acknowledging that her feelings for Ares were stronger than she realized. And if she didn't get out of here, he was going to find out. The sooner she left, the better. She needed time to strengthen her defenses where he was concerned.

With as much speed as possible, she gathered up her discarded clothes and dressed. Her fingers fumbled as she pulled his shirt over her head. The action made her senses reel as she drank in the warm, male scent of him buried in the shirt. A tear splashed onto her hand. She squeezed her eyes shut. No. She would not cry. She wouldn't give him the satisfaction of knowing how deeply he'd hurt her.

It didn't take long to finish dressing. When she was ready, she turned toward the door and froze. Would he let her leave or would he refuse to let her go? She shivered. She'd have her answer in a few seconds. It seemed to take her a lifetime to reach the door, and her hand trembled as she grasped the doorknob. As best she could, she tried to remove any emotion from her face as she opened the door.

Ares was seated in front of the fire, but he leaped to his feet the minute she stepped into the living area. She didn't look directly at him. If she did, she wasn't sure what might happen. Instead, she pinned her sights on the cabin's main door and moved toward it. He was there to block her way in seconds. He didn't touch her. He just stood there in silence.

The anger she'd felt earlier renewed itself. It sent a fiery wave surging through her, leaving a burning heat in its wake. He'd already humiliated her enough. Did he have to make it worse?

"*Get out of my way.*" She heard the coldness in her voice. It was a small consolation to see his impassive expression flinch at her quiet words. He shook his head.

"I'm not letting you leave until we've worked this out," he said quietly.

"There's nothing to work out."

"*Deus damno id*, Emma. How can you expect me to explain things if you won't listen to what I have to say?"

"I think you've said more than enough." She tried to step around him, but he moved to block her way again.

"I made a mistake, Emma."

"Not nearly as big as the one I made. Now let me by."

"No. I need you to understand. I need to tell you how much I—"

"Tell me what? That courtly line about how your intentions were honorable? You have no honor. You say you do because it helps you justify your actions." It surprised her how cool and emotionless her voice was. What little dignity she still possessed resounded in her words. For that, she was grateful.

"I'm not trying to justify anything," he bit out. "I'm trying to tell you I understand why I didn't explain things to you. I didn't want to see the truth."

"The only truth I can see is that you weren't honest with me. You said I was willing to sleep with you the other morning, and you're right. I didn't protest then and I sure as hell didn't protest today." She shuddered at the memory of how easily she'd given in to his caresses just a little while ago. "I could have forgiven you not explaining the blood bond in the heat of the moment the other morning. But today—today you took advantage of me, and now you think you can just explain away your actions. Well, you can't. You just can't and I despise you for it."

Something swept across his face that sent her heart slamming into her chest. For a fleeting moment, raw emotion twisted his features into a mask of intense pain. Then it was gone. In its place was an emotionless expression that made her wonder if she'd imagined the stark agony. Without a word, he returned to his seat at the fireplace and picked up his jacket from the chair. He took a couple of steps toward her and offered her the coat.

"Take it. The temperature's dropped and you'll get soaked."

She stared at it for a moment and shook her head. "No thank you. I don't want anything from you."

Just as she turned away, she saw that same emotion ravage his features once more. She refused to let it stop her. Something inside her said she'd only be humiliated further if she stayed. She simply headed toward the door and out into the rain.

Chapter 17

EMMA opened her bedroom door to look up and down the hall. Ever since returning to Chicago, she'd been looking over her shoulder, expecting to see Ares behind her. It was almost two in the morning, and if Ares had come back tonight, she didn't think he'd be prowling the hallway at this hour. The thought didn't make her any less edgy.

The dimly lit hall was empty and her hunger forced her to venture out into the corridor. At dinner this evening, her appetite had disappeared the minute Lysander had mentioned Ares was returning to the guild's Wacker Drive complex.

When she'd returned to the mansion that terrible afternoon over a week ago, the pain of Ares's betrayal had numbed her to the downpour. Lysander had passed her in the hall on the way to her room. Although he hadn't commented on her drenched state, his manner had been sympathetic. Even his deep voice had echoed with regret when he'd informed her it would be two more days before they could return to Chicago.

At the time, she'd been far from happy about the delay. Now she recognized it for the blessing it was. The size of the White Cloud estate had helped her avoid Ares, giving her time to gather her wits so she wouldn't fall apart when she was finally in the same room with him. Lysander hadn't asked questions, but he seemed to understand that she was hurting. From those brief minutes when she stood soaked in front of the Sicari warrior, he'd taken her under his wing.

No matter where she went, if he was nearby he made it a point to see to her comfort, including her interactions with the Sicari. With just a look, he'd commanded others to accept her. It was a guarded acceptance, but they were polite and one or two of them even friendly. Phaedra had also opened up to her. The woman's dry sense of humor was similar to her brother's, and it made Emma's heart ache the two or three times Phae had teased her.

The quiet of the penthouse suite was unnerving as she walked down the hall toward the kitchen. Any second she expected Ares to emerge from the kitchen or come off the elevator. She grimaced. If anything, he was sleeping soundly in his bed. Why should she worry about seeing him? The man sure as hell wasn't worried about her or where she was. The thought sliced into wounds that had barely begun to heal. Discovering his deceit had left her heart bleeding. Worse, she hated herself for wanting him to come begging for her forgiveness.

He hadn't.

And if he'd confessed his sins to Atia, the *Prima Consul* hadn't said a word to her about it. Was he waiting for her to ask his godmother to annul the blood bond? She should have gone to Atia as soon as she'd returned to the mansion that afternoon, but she hadn't.

Not because she wanted to spare Ares any pain or humiliation. No, Atia had been the reason why she'd chosen to remain silent. Emma didn't have it in her to provoke the older woman's anger and disappointment when the *Prima Consul* learned what Ares had done. The woman loved him like a son, and Emma was certain the knowledge of what he'd done would devastate Atia. Although his honor was in tatters, she'd been sure he'd speak with his godmother about the matter. When he hadn't, it had only made his treachery cut that much deeper.

The recessed lights in the ceiling warmed the golden brown marble of the large island in the kitchen. The glass she retrieved from one of the wall cabinets clinked softly when she set it on the marble. With a gentle tug, she opened the door of the refrigerator and pulled out a jug of orange juice.

Out of the corner of her eye, she saw something move. With a quiet scream of surprise, she spun around to see Ares standing at the end of the island. The jug slipped from her fingers only to hover in the air before it floated upward and landed gently on the countertop.

Her initial thought was how weary he looked. He had more than a hint of five o'clock shadow, and he looked like hell. It was as if he had the weight of the world on his shoulders. Yet, the sword hanging diagonally across his back gave an edge to him that cried out danger. Even that dark gaze of his sent a tingling sensation skating over her skin.

A desire to comfort him wrapped its tendrils around her heart, but she crushed the need with ruthless determination. Uneasy with his silence, she turned and reached for the orange juice. She shuddered as he removed his sword off his back and laid it on the marble counter before he went to the refrigerator.

The tension in the air was thick with unspoken emotion, and she deliberately kept her gaze averted. It didn't stop her body from recognizing exactly where he was behind her. He bent slightly to pull out a longneck bottle of beer from the fridge and his back lightly brushed against hers when he straightened to close the door.

She stiffened as the heat of him filtered its way through her robe to warm her skin. God, how could she respond to him so easily after what he'd done? Even worse was the way her body longed for him the minute he stepped away from her. She poured the orange juice, eager to escape his presence before she did something stupid. Like try to excuse what he'd done.

The cool air of the refrigerator brushed across her face as she set the container of orange juice back on the wire shelf. When she shut the door, she saw Ares leaning against the counter, his legs stretched out in front of him and crossed at the ankles. The nonchalance of his pose belied the tension in him. Something that was clearly evident in the way he gripped his beer bottle.

"Did Lysander tell you we're going to the house tomorrow night?" His voice was a quiet storm in her head. Something was eating him up inside, and she hated to see him like this. God, what the hell was wrong with her. The man had lied to her, and here she was worrying about him.

"Yes," she said. For a brief moment she stared into his eyes then looked away, afraid of what she saw reflected there.

"I understand you studied the artifacts before you left White Cloud."

He took a swig of beer before turning his head toward her in silent expectation. Did he think she was going to tell him about the Sicari warrior who'd owned the medallion or the dagger that had been in the possession of a Roman officer who could have been Lysander's twin? She shook her head.

"Yes, I looked at them."

"You changed your mind." It was a simple statement, but she heard the question in his voice and it puzzled her. It was almost as if he was disappointed she'd read the objects.

"The more I know, the faster I can find the *Tyet of Isis*."

"And the sooner you'll be free of me, is that it?" The sharpness of his tone sliced along her senses. His anger wasn't something she'd expected.

"Yes. I always pay my debts."

A violent oath escaped him, and she jumped at the sound. He stood up straight, and was less than a foot away from her in a fraction of a second. His stance was rigid and unbending as he stared down at her. The stony look on his face was at odds with the flash of emotion in his lake blue eyes. An emotion that unsettled her, but she refused to consider what it meant. He took another swig of beer before focusing his gaze on the bottle's label. If possible, the tension in him had sharpened to a razor-thin edge.

"Why didn't you ask Atia to break the blood bond between us?"

Of all the things she'd expected him to ask, this wasn't one of them. Her mouth dry, she reached for her glass of juice, but his hand snaked out and stopped her. The minute he touched her, she was on fire inside. She froze and stared down at his fingers wrapped firmly around her wrist.

"Why?" He growled the single-word question with unexpected ferocity.

"Because I didn't want to hurt her," she said quietly as she jerked her gaze upward to meet his. "And she *will* be hurt when she learns how you sealed our blood bond without telling me about the consequences. I didn't do it, because I thought *you* would."

The note of censure in her voice made him drop her hand as if he'd touched a hot iron. She watched in silence as he took a long, hard draught of his beer. She debated whether to move past his hard, taut body or skirt the large island to leave the kitchen. The way her body's radar was acting, the best thing to do was to take the long way around. She turned to circle the counter just as his beer bottle hit the counter with a loud crack. Startled, she turned her head and saw him watching her with a tortured expression.

"I would have gone to Atia before now, but if I had, I wouldn't have been here to see that nothing goes wrong tomorrow night." He straightened upright. "When I bring you back here safe and sound, I'll leave for White Cloud. I'll tell her everything, and you'll be free."

Without another word, he picked up his sword and scabbard then left the kitchen. As he disappeared around the corner wall, she clutched at the marble counter to remain standing. She couldn't remember ever feeling so empty. If it weren't for the needles of pain jabbing at every inch of her, she might have thought she was dead. All the anger she'd been holding inside her melted away, leaving her vulnerable to the truth. God help her, but she loved him.

She didn't want to love him, but she did. He was like a poison she couldn't resist taking. Even her wrist hadn't escaped him. It still hummed where his fingers had gripped her. Bent over the counter, she closed her eyes and tried to collect her wits.

He'd had an air of hopelessness about him that tugged at her heart. And he'd actually been angry when she'd emphasized that she would pay her debt to him. Not angry, furious. Was it possible he didn't want to let her go?

No. He would have said something. Tried to convince her to stay. She closed her eyes as she fought back a flood of tears. The thought of breaking their blood bond was agonizing. What the hell was she going to do?

A soft footstep sounded on the floor and she stiffened, waiting for that familiar frisson that always skated across her back when he was near. She didn't feel a thing. Slowly, she lifted her head to see Lysander and that single eye of his watching her carefully. She offered him a wan smile.

"You okay?" he asked quietly.

"I was thirsty." She raised her glass and took a drink, ignoring his question. No doubt, he'd met Ares in the hall. "What are you doing here? Don't you have an apartment in the building?"

"Yes, I have my own place." There was the merest trace of amusement on his otherwise stoic features as his gaze probed her expression. "And now that Ares is back, I can sleep in my own bed."

"You make it sound like you *had* to stay here until he came back."

"It's what a *Primus Pilus* does." The Sicari warrior rolled his wide shoulders in a casual shrug. "I become the guild's *Legatus* when he's not here."

"*Primus Pilus*. What does that mean?"

Curiosity nipped at her, and she pressed one hip into the counter as she watched Lysander get a glass from the cabinet. He shot her a quick glance before getting some milk out of the refrigerator.

"It means First Spear," he said as he set the milk and glass on the island countertop before he went rummaging through a large bread drawer. He emerged triumphant with an unopened bag of chocolate sandwich cookies.

"Isn't that a Roman military rank?"

"Yes." Short and sweet as usual. Did he take lessons from Ares?

With the milk and cookies in front of him, Lysander pulled out one of the padded stools from under the countertop and sat down. He opened the bag of cookies, took several out of the package, then shoved the bag toward her. She pulled one out and bit into it. He darted her a quick look before returning his attention to the cookie in his hand.

"I understand you used your ability on several artifacts at the estate."

The quiet statement made her choke on her cookie, and she quickly reached for her juice. When she'd recovered, she set her glass down then turned to study the warrior's stoic profile. Had Ares told him she could see the past when she touched an antiquity? The thought of another betrayal stung.

"Did Ares tell you that?" she asked stiffly as she tried to rein in her fury.

"No." Lysander turned his head to look at her. "As second-in-command, I have full access to the reports he's required to submit to the *Prima Consul*. And Sandro, one of our librarians, was the one who brought you the artifacts. He told me you'd asked for them."

The knowledge that Ares hadn't betrayed her to Lysander was a relief, and yet his arrangements for her to see antiquities the minute she asked for them was a painful reminder of how he'd manipulated her. Almost as if he could read her mind, Lysander looked at her with that impassive expression of his.

"Ares didn't tell Sandro to give you the objects when you asked for them. Atia did."

The words caught her off guard for a second time, and her throat grew tight with emotion. She didn't want to feel the relief surging through her, but it was there nonetheless. Had he been telling the truth about his reasons for taking her to the White Cloud estate? She shook her head in denial.

"He took me to White Cloud so I could read those artifacts."

"No. He took you there because he didn't feel comfortable leaving you behind in the care of someone else."

"And exactly how much is he paying you to say that?" she said sarcastically.

The warrior's expression didn't change, but there was a distinct and dangerous edge to his stiff posture as he pinned her with his eagle-eyed gaze. She immediately realized her mistake. Over the past two weeks, there was one trait she'd witnessed in the Sicari she'd actually spoken to at length. Honor was important to these proud people, and she'd questioned that virtue in Lysander.

"I'm sorry."

The man grunted his acceptance of her apology before he ate another cookie then followed it with a drink of milk. It was an incongruous picture given his physical size, appearance, and mannerism. It softened him. Made him seem almost like a little boy lost. His face stoic again, he folded his arms and rested them on the countertop.

"You didn't tell Atia what you saw." There was genuine puzzlement in his statement that said he wasn't asking what she'd seen, but he was curious she hadn't shared it with Atia.

"Not yet. I've been afraid to."

"Why?"

She met Lysander's steady gaze and shrugged. "Because if I'd told her what I'd seen, she might have changed her mind and not let me go back to find what my father left for me."

"You make it sound like you saw where the *Tyet of Isis* is."

She hadn't seen the artifact, but the objects she'd touched had left her shaken. The medallion's violent images followed by visions she'd experienced when she'd held the jeweled dagger had left her exhausted. The images from the dagger had been even more disturbing because the dagger's owner had looked so familiar. Aware that Lysander was waiting for her to respond, she shook her head.

"No, I was worried *Atia* might think she doesn't need whatever my father left for me, but I do. I'm betting it's his notebook, and I think it will help me understand my visions."

"And if there isn't a notebook? What then?"

"I plan on telling her everything after I find whatever it is my father left me." She frowned as she met his gaze head-on. Lysander grunted his approval and took another drink of his milk.

"I'm sure Ares has already told you how dangerous it is for you to return to your house."

"Yes, he told me. But it's something I have to do."

"And if something happens to you, who will you tell then?" His quiet question made her go rigid. The thought that Ares might somehow fail at keeping her safe had never occurred to her. Lysander turned his single-eyed gaze on her.

"The Praetorians want the *Tyet of Isis* as badly as we do," he said without emotion although the scarred tissues on his demonic side twitched. "They won't hesitate to torture and kill anyone to get the information they want. Even *alieni*."

The sobering words made her heart plummet as she remembered Ares showing her that terrible picture of what the Praetorians had done to Julian. If something did happen to her, then what she knew would be lost to the Sicari. She should have told Atia what she'd seen. Her gaze met Lysander's and she nodded.

"If I tell you, will you give me your word you won't say anything until after tonight?"

"I'll write up a report and leave it in my desk."

Satisfied with his compromise, she took a sip of her juice before facing the Sicari warrior seated beside her. "The first object I touched was a gold medallion. It was in excellent condition. Almost as if it had been sealed in a time capsule. It dates back to the Roman Emperor Constantine. It was—"

"*Merda*, she let you touch the coin."

"The coin?" she asked in puzzlement as the warrior stood up and moved past the end of the island, where he proceeded to pace back and forth.

"The first Sicari Lord coin the Order ever found." Lysander turned to face her. "It's kept in a vault in the Order's main headquarters in Venice. Only the *Prima Consul* could get that coin out of Italy, let alone the vault."

"Is that a bad thing?" She frowned as she watched him resume his pacing. Lysander's agitation was completely uncharacteristic, and it worried her.

"No." The Sicari warrior shrugged his shoulders. "It's just surprising."

"You don't say," she murmured wryly. He arched his only eyebrow at her, but didn't comment. She suppressed a smile. "Why is the coin so special?"

"Because it's the first piece of evidence we've found that says the *Tyet of Isis* might not be just a bedtime story. The coin was found in the late eighteen hundreds in the belongings of a wealthy merchant in the Languedoc area of France. A document written in Latin was with the coin. It described how the Sicari were hired as mercenaries to protect Cathars fleeing persecution from the Church. The *Prima Consul* at that time bought the medallion and took it back to Venice, where it's been ever since or at least it has been until now."

"But what does the coin have to do with the *Tyet of Isis?*" she asked as Lysander faced her, his hip pressing into the countertop and his arms folded across his chest.

"The Sicari believe the coin belonged to a direct descendent of the first Sicari Lords. A warrior entrusted with the secret of the artifact."

"Aren't all of you direct descendents?"

"We can all lay claim to the bloodline, but Sicari Lords are special," Lysander said with almost a note of reverence in his voice. "No one knows much about them, although it's said their abilities far surpass even the strongest of us."

"In what way?" Emma asked, the image of the monk in her vision filling her head.

"Immense physical strength, extended stamina." Lysander shrugged his shoulders. "The ability to move objects of immense size."

"Enough to create a rock slide?" Excitement slid through her. Maybe she had seen something important.

"Possibly." Lysander sat down on the stool to face her, a gleam of curiosity in his green eye. "Why?"

"Because I think the monk I saw in my vision might have been one of these Sicari Lords of yours."

"Explain." Although his face showed little emotion, the tension in his body showed she had his full attention.

"If the man was a monk, he wasn't like any monk I'm familiar with. He killed a priest, but he didn't do it right away. He said something to the priest, and when the man nodded, he slit the priest's throat."

"Just as a Sicari would do it," Lysander murmured as if mulling over her story.

"I don't understand."

"The Sicari always ask forgiveness before taking a life, and the monk in your vision appears to have done this."

She didn't know how to respond to this new insight into a culture that was still so foreign to her. If her father were here, he'd be in seventh heaven filling in all the blanks of his research. As for herself, she'd be happy just to go back to the life she had before Ares. No, that wasn't true. She was going to be miserable when she left him. The thought made her wince with pain. Beside her, Lysander touched her arm.

"What else did your vision show you?"

"I saw a large group of men, women, and children hurrying down a steep cliff-side path overlooking a sea. The monk was behind them."

"He was chasing them?" Lysander asked.

"No." She shook her head. "Protecting them. He had two or three men with him. They were bodyguards for the group, but the monk was in charge."

"How can you be sure?"

"Because he's the one who stayed behind."

Lysander stiffened beside her. "What do you mean he stayed behind?"

"They were being chased by what looked like Crusaders. His men argued with him, but they eventually followed the others, leaving the monk behind. He must have killed at least five men before one of the knights managed to bring him down. But when he fell, he stretched out his hand, and seconds later a rock slide crashed down on all of them."

"Then perhaps this Sicari Lord was carrying the *Tyet of Isis*."

Excitement brightened his green gaze, and she realized he was just as eager to find the artifact as Ares. As if aware he'd shown more emotion than he cared to, he slowly and methodically sealed up the cookies.

"You know I overheard your conversation with Ares before I came in here don't you?" His abrupt changing of subjects made her stiffen.

"Is there a reason why you're telling me this?" She averted her gaze and stared down at her empty juice glass.

"He's a good man, Emma."

"That's what everyone keeps telling me." She heaved a sigh. "I know he's your friend, but maybe you don't know the man I know."

"No. We both know the same man. Our rules aren't like your world, Emma. It makes a difference in how you should look at things."

"I know that *all* too well."

She opened her palm and looked at the scar there. It was a vivid reminder of how she was tied to Ares. A tie that needed to be broken, but one her heart didn't want to break. She looked up to see Lysander watching her closely.

"If you love him, you won't break the blood bond between you."

The words sucked all the air out of her lungs. He could have hit her and she wouldn't have been any more surprised. When Lysander said he'd overheard her conversation with Ares, he'd meant everything. She drew in a deep breath, frantic to cover anything that might confirm the man's observation.

"What makes you think I love him?" she breathed.

"Because you looked like your heart was breaking when I came in here in a little while ago." Sympathy was reflected in his gaze as he sent her a steady look. "You need to trust him, Emma."

"I did, and he betrayed that trust." Bitterness etched its way through her as she remembered how he'd made love to her knowing what sealing their bond meant. He hadn't given her a choice. A voice in the back of her head asked her what her answer would have been if he *had* allowed her to choose. She knew the answer, but she didn't want to acknowledge it.

"Men make mistakes, Emma. Some of us make bigger ones than others." Lysander stared off into space, his scarred flesh taut with some personal torment. "I've known Ares for a long time. If he broke his trust with you, he's paying the price now. But if you make him break the blood bond between you, he'll pay an even higher price."

"I don't see how." She got up from the counter to put her glass in the dishwasher.

"Honor is everything to a Sicari," Lysander said quietly. "Breaking a blood bond once it's sealed brings absolute disgrace."

The warrior's words made her chest constrict until it was difficult to breathe. She clutched at the sink and shook her head. "I don't know how to stop him."

"Tell him the truth."

"You make it sound so easy," she bit out angrily and she turned to face him. "But it's not, and you know it."

Lysander's expression was a cold façade of stone. Whatever he was feeling was well contained as he slowly rose to his feet. Regret swept through her.

"Lysander. I'm sorry."

He pinned her with that single-eyed gaze of his for barely an instant before he turned and headed out of the kitchen. He paused at the end of the counter, but didn't turn his head.

"You were right, Emma. I did make it sound easy. But it doesn't change anything. You still have a choice to make."

With that final remark, Lysander strode out of the kitchen. Left behind, Emma swallowed hard. What the hell was she going to do?

Chapter 18

ARES waited for the three clicks in his earpiece signaling the perimeter around Emma's house was secure. It would have been a lot easier to do this in the daytime if she hadn't been with them. He glanced at the rearview mirror to study Emma's features cast in the shadows from a nearby streetlight. Just the way she sat stiff and unmoving in the backseat said she was nervous.

Why the hell had he agreed to this? Because the only other option was to trust her safety to someone else. Something he wasn't about to do. She was his. How she felt about him changed nothing. He'd do whatever necessary to protect her. Her safety, her happiness, was all that mattered.

As if aware of him watching her, she turned her head away from the window and looked into the mirror. The moment their gazes locked, that icy expression she reserved just for him swept over her pale features. Her gaze barely registered his presence before she looked away from him as if he wasn't even in the car. *Christus*, if she'd wielded a sword, she couldn't have splayed him open any cleaner. He deserved every bit of her scorn, but a small piece of him died every time she looked through him like that.

Last night when he'd found her in the kitchen, she was the most beautiful sight he'd ever seen. His first instinct had been to pull her into his arms. Instead, he'd forced himself to grab a beer from the frig. Anything to stop himself from touching her. And *Deus*, he'd needed to hold her. No sex, just her warmth against his icy chill. Her gentleness to ease the tumult inside him.

The job he'd finished with Lysander only an hour earlier had left him drained as always. No matter how repulsive the criminal, extracting final justice wasn't an easy thing to do. He didn't enjoy killing, but it was a necessary evil when it came to protecting the innocent. And if the Order's policy for pro bono work hadn't already been in place, he would have done last night's job for free.

His income came from the companies and properties that had been handed down through his family for generations. Over the centuries, the Order's investments had made it possible for the Sicari to become a silent, unpaid arm of legal systems around the globe. The Order performed its services for free as a way of helping others avoid the persecution and fear the Sicari had lived with for more than two thousand years.

They eliminated the worst criminal elements from society when the system failed due to technicalities or where ideology resulted in the persecution of innocents. The toughest jobs were ones like last night. A Sicari was never allowed to take pleasure in an execution, and last night it had been difficult not to make his target die a slow, excruciating death, let alone enjoy the act itself.

The *bastardo* had murdered two cops. Good cops. Men who were *Vigilavi*. Their forebears were people the Sicari had saved from life or death situations over the centuries. The *Vigilavi* had become an integral part of the Order, and their services in law enforcement, academics, medicine, and other areas were invaluable. But most important of all, they were family. And family was sacred.

Controlling his desire not to enjoy the kill had been exhausting, but there had been a deep feeling of satisfaction knowing justice had been served. The gratification had been fleeting and left him empty inside. But then he'd walked into the kitchen and seen Emma. The mere sight of her had made the night easier to bear. All of his despair had ebbed away, leaving only his love for her. He'd known since that day in the cabin that he loved her.

The revelation had hit him hard. It had nearly crushed him when she'd declared her contempt for him. He'd deserved every bit of her scorn, but knowing that hadn't eased his pain. Last night had been the first time he'd seen her since that day at the cottage. He'd deliberately stayed away from her, hoping that time would ease her anger so he could explain things. Make it right between them. He'd been banking everything on the fact that she hadn't spoken with Atia about breaking the blood bond. It had given him hope that maybe she was willing to forgive him. He'd been wrong.

The only reason she'd kept quiet was because she didn't have the heart to let Atia know what a *bastardo* he was. It was the truth. Tomorrow when he told his godmother what he'd done, she was going to be livid. But more than that, the *Prima Consul* was going to feel just as betrayed as Emma had been. Three clicks sounded in his ear and his tension eased slightly. He was still on edge, but the fact that Lysander and Phae had secured the area so quickly said his fears might have been exaggerated. He turned his head to Bastien in the seat next to him.

"We're clear. Bastien, the front perimeter is yours. Lysander will be at the back with Phae and Thaddeus serving as backup. You know the signal if you see trouble coming." He looked into the rearview mirror and willed Emma to meet his gaze. "Emma, you do as I say, when I say, or I'll drag you out of there so fast your head will spin. Understood."

Her answer was a simple nod of the head. It was obvious she didn't like being under his control, but he didn't care. This was his domain. All she had to do was follow directions. He exited the SUV and pulled out his *Condottiere* sheathed in its scabbard. The strap slipped easily over his shoulders to settle snugly against his back. He took comfort in the familiar sensation of the weapon being in easy reach. The car door behind him closed quietly. The sound made him turn his head to see Emma's pale features staring down the street at her old home.

Fear had drawn her mouth tight with tension and the pulse at the side of her neck was beating at a frantic pace. She wore the same black the rest of the team had on, but on her, the dark color emphasized her pale face. He ached to pull her into his arms, but settled for capturing her chin with his fingers.

"You don't have to do this, Emma."

He fully expected her to jerk away from him, but she didn't. Instead, she almost seemed to lean into him as if seeking extra strength. The need to pull her close pulsated through him, and his thumb rubbed against the small indention beneath her mouth.

"Yes, I do." Her body trembled and vibrated against his fingers as she shook her head. "I'll be fine. I was just thinking about the last time I was here."

"I'm not going to let anything happen to you," he whispered. "I swear it."

"I know," she murmured with a small curve of her lips.

The half smile sent a bolt of lightning through him. *Christus*, had she suddenly had a change of heart about him? Had that look she'd given him earlier in the car simply been her fear? Now wasn't the time to consider the possibility. He needed to focus solely on the task at hand.

"Come on, the sooner we get this over with, the better."

She didn't try to tug free of his hand, and if anything, he could have sworn her hand tightened around his. It made his heart expand in his chest. At least she trusted him enough to ensure she didn't get hurt. Or maybe she just needed something to hold on to and he was handy. The thought nagged at him, but he pushed it aside. Focus.

The street was deserted as they moved quickly down the sidewalk. They cut across the front lawn to skirt the side of the house while Bastien took shelter in the shadows of the front lawn. In less than a minute, they were at the back door, where Phae and Thaddeus waited in the shadows. He couldn't see him, but he knew Lysander stood watch in dark shadows along the thick hedge that separated the backyard from the one next door.

Something dark reared its head deep in the back of his mind. It was more a sensation than a thought. A chill slid down his back, and he froze. He peered out into the darkness, the uneasy feeling not going away.

"Lysander. Bastien. Report," he said in a low staccato voice. He ignored Phae's look of concern as he waited for a response.

"All clear," his *Primus Pilus* said with quiet assurance.

"We're clear here." Bastien's voice was strong and confident in his ear, but Ares still hesitated.

"What's wrong?" Phae asked through clenched teeth as Thaddeus obeyed his silent command to fade into the darkness and serve as backup to the other two Sicari warriors on the grounds.

"You don't sense anything?" he replied softly as he met his sister's worried gaze.

"No. Nothing." She shook her head.

He frowned then cleared his mind and allowed his senses to become in tune with his surroundings. While his senses couldn't detect the smallest hint of danger, his gut continued to protest. He dismissed it. He was just on edge because Emma was with them.

"Stay out of sight, but keep a close eye on the door."

Phae nodded and disappeared into the darkness. With a wave of his hand, he unlocked the back door. The soft snap of the dead bolt sliding back echoed in the air, and he turned the knob. Like the last time he'd been here, the well-oiled hinges didn't make a sound as the heavy oak door swung back. He reached for Emma's hand and pulled her through the door behind him.

A thin beam of moonlight drifted through the kitchen window. He'd deliberately waited for a waning moon to ensure they had just enough light to help with visibility while still keeping their outside movements fairly well concealed. Wishing this whole thing were over, he pulled a compact flashlight from his pocket.

His thumb pressed the on-button once for the lowest setting. The last thing he needed was a nosy neighbor calling the police because they'd seen a moving light inside the house. They'd already alerted their police contacts of possible 911 calls, but he preferred to get in and out of there cleanly. Emma's hand still in his, they moved through the dining room and into the living room. A soft grunt echoed in his earpiece and he came to an abrupt halt, causing Emma to crash into him. Instinctively, he reached around to press his free hand into her back in a protective gesture, while she steadied herself by gripping his waist. Even through the leather jacket he wore, her fingers heated up his skin.

"Report," he snapped softly.

"Secure here," Lysander responded.

"Damn stray just pissed on my new boots," Bastien growled.

Phae suppressed her laughter with a snort over the mike while Thaddeus's soft chuckle echoed over the wireless connection.

"I told you not to have them custom-made, you dumb *il figlio di puttana*," Thaddeus snickered. "Guess they're officially broken in now."

Bastien uttered a soft oath in response to his friend's gentle barb. The brief moment of levity eased Ares's tension slightly and he bent his head to the shoulder mike he wore.

"Tighten up, people. I want this over with ASAP."

His hand slid across Emma's soft, rounded hip as he brought his hand forward and released his hold on her. The way she stiffened and didn't release him quickly made his heart jump. Was it possible—no, he wasn't going there. Especially not now.

They moved forward again, and in less than a minute, they stopped outside the doorway of Emma's study. The morning after rescuing Emma, he'd arranged repairs to the doorjamb and window. The last thing he needed was someone coming to the house and finding evidence of a struggle, which might raise questions. He didn't want Emma's cover blown.

Satisfied the room was empty, he stepped aside and allowed Emma to enter the office. Her tension filled the space between them, and it didn't ease as she crossed the threshold. When she didn't move deeper into the office, he reached out and touched her arm. She jumped away from him and he frowned.

"You're safe, Emma. We're all here to make sure nothing happens to you."

She nodded and moved toward the desk, her fingertips running along the wood desktop in a loving fashion. Slowly, she rounded the desk and headed for the bookcase filled with an equal mixture of books and artifacts. She picked up the Egyptian dagger she'd threatened him with just a few days ago, and turned her head to look at him. The sadness in her eyes gutted him.

He had a lot to pay for when it came to her. She returned the object back to the shelf, before moving on to the next item. Inside, his radar was urging her to hurry up, but he didn't say a word. He knew she needed this. He'd been an ass not to realize it sooner.

As a child, he'd left his home without a backward glance. In the space of minutes, his world had shattered the night his parents were murdered. But he'd been eager to escape because the horror of what he'd seen had obliterated all the happy moments the word "home" had once meant. Emma sighed as she put down another object, drawing his attention back to her. He suppressed the desire to cross the room and offer her a comforting embrace. Instead, he cleared his throat and muted his mike.

"All of this is going to be packed up and stored, Emma. When the Order gives you new quarters, it'll be there. Waiting for you. I promise."

"I know." The palm of her hand caressed the bookcase built into the wall. "It's just that you can't pack up the memories that reside in the walls themselves."

The sorrow in her voice intensified the guilt he was feeling. Rationally, he knew she was still alive because of him, but he still felt responsible for her losing everything. There wasn't a thing he could say to her to ease her pain and it left him feeling helpless. The sensation made him feel far worse than the guilt twisting his insides.

Emma, oblivious to his pain, moved to the end of the wall to kneel on the floor. Using the heel of her hand, she hit the two-inch-high baseboard running along the bottom of the shelves. The molding popped away from the bottom of the built-in wall unit to reveal a dark hole. Without being asked, he moved forward and directed the beam of his flashlight into the dark cubbyhole. Her hand trembling, Emma reached into the cubbyhole and pulled out a small, but thick, notebook jam-packed with an odd assortment of papers. Happiness and sorrow flitted across her features as she stared down at the notebook.

"He must have known he was close to finding the *Tyet of Isis* or he'd never have left this here," she whispered as her hand caressed the leather cover.

In his earpiece, he heard a soft, indistinct sound that made him tense. A second later, he heard Bastien utter a curse, which ended before the man could finish it. In an instant, he doused the flashlight and was on his feet, dragging Emma with him.

"We're out of here."

"But—"

"*Now*, Emma." He turned his mike on again as he dragged her toward the office door. "Code One. We're on our way out."

He heard the hushed voices of everyone but Bastien as they confirmed the alert and current status. The fighter's silence was a clear indicator something was seriously wrong. They'd just reached the doorway when a tall figure blocked the way. *Fotte*. Praetorian. In a simultaneous action, Ares drew his sword and gave Emma a hard mental shove back toward the desk and out of reach.

"What do we have here? An Unmentionable and his whore."

The Praetorian had to bend forward slightly to step through the doorway. *Merda*, this son of a bitch was big. Ares didn't respond to the man. Best to keep his thoughts free of anything his opponent could use now or later. Experience had also taught him that when Praetorians didn't get a response to their taunts, it made them angry. Made them sloppy. And he needed to kill this bastard before Emma got hurt. He was at a slight disadvantage, but then so was the Praetorian. The only light in the room was coming from the house next door, which would make it tough to see anything.

"I don't need to see you, Unmentionable. All I have to do is listen to your thoughts," the Praetorian sneered.

Fotte. He was thinking too much and not acting. He closed his thoughts off to everything but his instincts and training. It was the only way he'd be able to bring the bastard down.

"Perhaps I'll just incapacitate you, before I peel some of that soft skin off your whore's face while you watch."

Despite his best effort to shut down his thoughts, the man's words made him grow cold. The sensation didn't last as he heard Emma snort with laughter behind him. It surprised him almost as much as it amazed the Praetorian. But then the bastard didn't know Emma and her indomitable will to live. He knew she had to be terrified and yet she was reacting the same way she had the first night she'd met him.

"Were you born stupid or did you acquire that trait in nursery school?" she said in a contemptuous voice. "He's gonna kick your ass, you stupid son of a bitch."

The confidence in her voice warmed his heart as the dim light of the office revealed the outrage on the Praetorian's face. But the man didn't leap forward to strike as Ares expected him to. A movement in the doorway made his brain shift gears. Two Praetorians. Tight confined space. Emma. His thoughts clattered together like a chain pulling up an anchor.

"Phae, Lysander. We've got company," he bit out. "Get in here now."

He jerked his head at the window, and it flew upward to slam into the top of the frame with a loud crack. Before he had time to bark a command at Emma, the second Praetorian slipped into the room followed by another shadowy figure. *Fotte.* Mike Granby. He should have followed his instincts about the bastard and had him watched 24/7. The minute he stepped into the room, Granby offered him a smiling sneer and jerked his head toward the biggest Praetorian.

"Andrew here brought several friends. So your people have their hands full at the moment." The man turned his head and caught sight of Emma. Eyes widening, he shook his head. "*Emma.* What the hell are you doing here? They said you were dead."

"Mike?"

The horrified disbelief in Emma's voice clawed at Ares as he struggled to keep his thoughts about her closed off. *Christus*, he'd misjudged Granby completely. He hadn't given the man credit for having enough brains to do anything more than carry out orders.

"What are you doing here, Mike?"

"I'm here because you have something I want, Emma."

"I don't have anything of value here," she said with a note of puzzlement in her voice.

Granby snorted his skepticism. "Don't take me for a fool like your parents did, Emma."

"My parents never thought you were a fool." This time he heard the growing awareness in her voice. *Fotte.* She was putting it together. Where the hell was Lysander or Phae?

"I was little more than an errand boy to them and Russwin," Mike sneered with contempt. "So when they got in my way, I eliminated them."

"You bastard," Emma cried out as she leaped forward.

"*Deus damno id*, Emma, keep back."

Ares's reaction was immediate as he restrained her with a single thought. They needed to get out of here now. The longer they stayed, the greater the chance they wouldn't survive. Taking on two Praetorians any other time wouldn't be a problem, but Emma's presence was drawing on reserves he'd need to win. And he didn't have any idea whether Lysander and the others would be coming anytime soon, if at all.

Draining his mental strength further, he used his ability to shove her toward the window without taking his eyes off the two fighters taking up a battle stance in front of him. He was grateful she didn't struggle, but went willingly. Granby frowned as Emma sidled toward the window.

"Give me the notebook, Emma, and I'll see to it that these men won't hurt your friend." At Granby's statement, the Praetorian called Andrew released a low sound of fury.

"You don't command us, heretic."

"No, but I doubt you'd like to explain to the *Monsignor* why my orders weren't followed." Granby's voice was sharp as he glared at the fighter before turning back to Emma. "As I was saying, give me the notebook and the two of you can go free."

"I'm not giving you anything, you murderer," Emma spat out.

"I'm not a murderer," the man protested with a snort. "I'm an independent contractor. Your friend has similar agreements with people outside his own faction. I don't give a rat's ass who does what as long as I get paid. And I won't get paid if I don't bring home that notebook. Now give it to me."

"Go to hell," Emma snapped. "You're not getting anything except jail time."

"Not likely, sweetheart. And if you know what's good for you, you'll turn over the goddamn notebook now or I'll let these two bastards loose on you and your friend."

"I *said* you don't command us, heretic," the Praetorian called Andrew snarled. With a vicious movement, he swung his sword and decapitated Granby in one stroke.

Training told Ares not to look in Emma's direction. But concern for her overrode everything he'd been taught, and he looked over his shoulder. Her skin was pale as moonlight, her features frozen with shocked horror. Fear slashed through him as he watched her sink to her knees in shock.

"*Christus*, Emma. Get up. *Now*. Out the window."

The whisper of an object near his head made him instinctively duck to miss the blade flying toward his head. The Praetorian's sword sliced the air above his head in a hard whoosh. The bastard had a vicious swing. A second later, a large fist slammed into the side of his head. It sent him reeling backward several steps before he was able to recover his balance.

Dolcis Mater Dei. No wonder the son of a bitch had a vicious swing. The asshole had a fist like a sledgehammer. He shook his head slightly, and out of the corner of his eye, he saw the smaller Praetorian step toward Emma. The distraction almost cost him his life as he barely managed to keep the other Praetorian's weapon from splitting him open from shoulder to groin.

With a jerk of his head, Ares mentally forced the Praetorian's sword arm to miss its mark, while the tip of his *Condottiere* scraped across the man's stomach. The man roared with anger as Ares wheeled away from the fighter called Andrew to deliberately put himself in the path of the smaller Praetorian.

In a smoothly executed move, his sword flew upward to meet the downward swing of his smaller opponent before he twisted his body and his weapon arced downward to meet the blade of the larger Praetorian. Moonlight made the three swords flash with light as Ares blocked and attacked one blow after the other. He fought to keep his thoughts clear, but as his sword repelled the smallest Praetorian, he glanced toward Emma. Crouched near the window, she was watching the fight as if in a daze. If he could only get her to jump out the window. She had a better chance of survival outside. He'd barely looked at her, but Andrew laughed. It wasn't a pleasant sound.

"It seems we've found his weakness, Antonio," he said in a cruel voice. "I'll deal with him, little brother. You take care of the bitch."

Merda, he'd shown them how important Emma was to him. He squashed the fear springing to life inside him and anything else that might distract him. He had one purpose and one purpose only. Destroy his enemy. Out of the corner of his eye, he saw a blade falling toward him. He leaped backward, but not quickly enough. The Praetorian's blade made a nice gash across his forearm.

"*Fotte*."

"That's the first of many to come, Unmentionable."

Ares narrowed his focus and dismissed the pain radiating up his arm. Whipping his body around in a half circle, he swung his *Condottiere* in a smooth, vicious arc. A second later, the blade sliced deep into the upper arm of the Praetorian called Antonio before it continued its circular path and met the downward swing of the larger fighter. The roar of pain from Antonio made Ares smile grimly as he traded blows with the giant brute called Andrew. His opponent snarled with anger.

A second later, a fist jammed its way into Ares's side and pushed the air from his lungs. He went down on one knee, and through a blur of pain, he heard the sword flying downward toward the back of his head. Antonio was back in play. Despite his sluggish speed, he managed to throw his sword over his shoulder and block the blade from severing his neck from his body.

He ignored the pain in his side and rolled quickly away from Antonio and toward the bigger Praetorian. In a fluid move, he sprang to his feet and hooked his leg behind the larger fighter's ankles in an attempt to sweep the man's feet out from underneath him. It was a wasted effort. The man simply staggered backward. The move would have put almost anyone else on his back. But this Praetorian was the biggest one he'd ever fought.

"You *will* die, Unmentionable."

The Praetorian's voice was gleeful as he flipped the blade in his hand so he could drag it across Ares's chest. The sting of the blade was little more than scratch, but the Praetorian had drawn blood for a second time. *Damno*, he was getting tired of someone trying to slice him open. He grimaced and jammed the hilt of his sword into the Praetorian's cheek as he whipped his body around the man's side so he was back-to-back with the fighter.

"Not this time, *bastardo*," he muttered, intent on fighting both men at the same time so he could keep them away from Emma and end this thing as quickly as possible.

In front of him, Antonio leaped forward, his sword whistling through the air as he swung it toward Ares's head. His back still against the Praetorian called Andrew, Ares applied the entire weight of his body hard against the man. Andrew pushed back with a snarl, before uttering a cry of surprised rage.

"Antonio, *stop*."

In that split second, Ares ducked and rolled beneath the Praetorian blade swinging toward his head and landed on his haunches two feet away. He was on his feet in seconds. Satisfaction swept through him as the larger Praetorian, without the resistance of Ares's body, staggered backward into the swing of the other Praetorian. The smaller fighter's sword cut deep into the other fighter's back.

"*Lei stupido inganna*," the brute Praetorian cried out as he whirled around to cuff Antonio on the side of his head. "I can take care of myself, little brother. Go after the whore like I told you to."

Off to his left, Ares heard Emma draw in a sharp breath as the two Praetorians split ranks. Ares didn't look at her. Instead, he visualized butting his head into Antonio's face. The man immediately uttered a cry of pain and stumbled in his movement toward Emma, his hand clutching his nose as blood gushed from it. The first Praetorian growled with fury, his sword flying out in a wide arc and heading straight for Ares's neck.

Ares slammed the steel of his sword against the oncoming blade. Sparks flew as the blades scraped against each other in a grueling screech until the two weapons were locked at the hilt. For the first time, Ares got a good look at his opponent's eyes, and the dark hatred boiling in the man's gaze said this fight was now personal. It would make the man harder to defeat.

"I see you understand me, Unmentionable."

"I'm not here to talk, Praetorian. You came here looking for a fight and now you've got one."

With the last of his reserves, Ares sent the man flying backward across the room. As the Praetorian flew across the room and slammed into the wall, he saw the one called Antonio out of the corner of his eye stumble forward. Ares moved on instinct and training alone as his sword flew up to meet the Praetorian's descending blade and block its descent.

The *Condottiere* knocked the weapon aside with a violent thrust. In a flash of speed, he brought his sword out in front of him in a wide arc as he went down on one knee. With a quick flick of his wrist, he swiveled his weapon so the tip of the blade was directed at the man behind him. The *Condottiere* passed swiftly under his arm as he drove the sword deep into the man's thigh.

It was a crippling blow, but as the fighter went down on one knee, he brought his sword up again in an attempt to slice into Ares's sword arm. The move wasn't unexpected, and Ares stopped the blow with an ironclad grip on Antonio's wrist. He bent his opponent's hand backward until it snapped. The man screamed in pain.

Eager to be done with it all, he tugged his blade out of the Praetorian's leg, aware that the other Praetorian was finally staggering to his feet. Ares straightened and looked down at the man half-prostrate on the floor.

"You fought well, Praetorian, but I must now ask your forgiveness," Ares said quietly as he stared into the eyes of the man he was about to kill. "Do you give it?"

"*Don't*, Antonio." From across the room, the other Praetorian howled a protest.

With an imperceptible nod of his head, Antonio grunted and closed his eyes. Ares inhaled a deep breath and executed the man in one swift stroke. The Praetorian was dead before he even hit the floor. His brother, Andrew, roared with pain and anger.

Emma screamed and Ares whirled around, prepared to match swords with his last opponent. To his horror, he saw the Praetorian heading toward Emma. Before Ares could take more than two steps, the Praetorian was on top of her.

She tried to roll out of the fighter's range, but she wasn't fast enough and the man's sword pierced her side. Her scream of pain chilled Ares's blood until it froze his limbs. *Care Deus*, not Emma. Crumpled up at the man's feet, Emma pressed her hand into her side, blood squeezing its way through her fingers. A silent scream of terror parted her mouth as she stared up at the man above her, and Ares lunged forward as the Praetorian, a cruel smile on his face, raised his blade.

"For my brother, Unmentionable." With blazing speed, the man brought his sword downward with deadly intent.

The sword never reached her. An invisible force wrenched the weapon out of the Praetorian's hands and flipped it in the air until the point was aimed directly at the fighter's heart. His mouth agape in amazement, the Praetorian simply stood there as the sword plunged its way into his body.

For a brief second, Ares thought Phae or Lysander had entered the room, but his gut told him differently. *Dulcis Mater Dei*. The blood bond. He'd told her something traumatic could trigger an ability. But he'd never thought her instinct for self-preservation would be the catalyst.

Ares reached Emma just as the Praetorian sank to his knees. With a violent shove, he pushed the man's body away from Emma then knelt at her side. Her moans nearly undid him as he fumbled for the flashlight in his pocket.

"Emma, *inamorato*, I need to look at your wound."

Gently, he pried her fingers from her side. She protested with a sob of agony that sent remorse ripping through him for having hurt her. The sight of the gash near her waist knocked the wind out of him as if he'd suffered the same terrible blow. Blood oozed from the wound at a slow pace, and he immediately checked her pulse. It was racing.

His stomach lurched with dread. Adrenaline could make a heart race, but it could also mean her heart was attempting to accommodate a drop in blood pressure. His gaze shifted back to her wound. The bastard's sword had probably hit an organ. He looked at her face. Her features were taut with pain and her breaths were more moans than intakes of air.

In the moonlight, her features were deathly pale, and her entire body shuddered as her eyes flew open to stare up at him. The shock, horror, and revulsion in her gaze only increased his agony. Her hand reached out to him as her eyes slid shut and her trembling grew more violent. A second later, his heart stopped as the tremors passed, and with a soft sigh, she went limp. *Christus.*

"Emma," he cried out in a guttural tone.

He bent his head and listened to her breathing. It was shallow at best. Seeing her like this was even more painful than what he'd endured in the gauntlet. He'd told her he'd keep her safe and he'd failed. Just as he'd failed his parents and Clarissa. Fear unlike anything he'd ever known ripped through him. What would he do if—no. He refused even to think it. She was going to live.

Phae. Where the hell was Phae? He reached up expecting to find his mike, but it was gone. Lost in his fight with the Praetorians. He touched the side of Emma's neck. Her pulse had increased, which meant she could bleed out if Phae didn't get here soon. *Fotte. Fotte. Fotte.*

"*Phae,*" he shouted with every bit of air in his lungs.

He knew his call might bring more Praetorians, but he didn't care. Without his earpiece, he had no idea if any of his team had survived. And if his sister was dead, then Emma would die. And if Emma died, it didn't matter how many Praetorians showed up because he was going to kill as many of the bastards as he could find from now until the day he died. He gently lifted her head and cradled it in his lap.

"Don't go, Emma. *Per favore il mio amore,* don't go."

He brushed her brown hair off her cheek, terrified by the wheezing sound she made with every breath. The Praetorian might have nicked a lung in addition to everything else the bastard had done by stabbing her. He closed his eyes and threw back his head to release a roar of anger. Somewhere in his dazed state, he heard the sound of running feet.

"Ares, are you all right? I would have been here sooner, but Bastien is dead and Thad—" He was dimly aware of Phae kneeling beside him and Emma. His sister drew in a sharp hiss of air. "*Dulcis Mater Dei.*"

His hand snaked out to grab his sister's arm. "Can you save her?"

"I don't know. There were four Praetorians and in the . . . Thaddeus was bleeding heavily, and . . . I . . ." Phae shook her head and his heart sank. He knew she didn't want to tell him that her ability had already been taxed healing Thaddeus. More footsteps echoed outside the office and Phae glanced over her shoulder as Lysander entered the room.

"We need to go." Despite his calm manner, there was a stark note of urgency in his *Primus Pilus*'s voice.

"Emma's hurt. How much time before the checkered hats get here?"

"Not much. Can you heal her in the car?" Lysander asked quietly.

"*No*. We need to do something *now*." Ares glared up at his *Primus Pilus* then looked back at his sister. Phae's eyes darkened with a look of understanding, but she shook her head.

"I think her spleen's been hit, Ares. This kind of healing will incapacitate me, which means you'll have two people down to worry about if I heal her here." His sister reached out and touched his hand in a gesture of compassion as he shook his head. "I can stem the bleeding for the moment, but we need to get back to the complex for me to ensure she survives. I'll be weak, but at least I'll be able to walk. Lysander can help Thad."

Phae looked up at Lysander, who hesitated before he simply nodded and left the room. Phae watched him go, an intense emotion darkening her features. The minute she turned her head away from the door, her gaze met Ares's. Immediately, her features went blank as she hid whatever it was she was thinking and feeling behind a stoic expression.

It was the first time he'd ever seen his sister close herself off to him. Beside his leg, Emma moaned softly. *Deus*, she was regaining consciousness. He brushed the hair off her forehead. The skin beneath his fingers was warm. In silence, he watched Phae bend over Emma to study the wound. Then with a deep breath, Phae took Emma's hands in hers and closed her eyes. He heard his sister draw in a sharp breath as her face became a mask of pain. Seconds later, she grunted an unintelligible word and jerked away from Emma. Her features almost as pale as Emma's, his sister raised a trembling hand to her headset.

"Lysander, we're ready to go."

Ares stood up and offered his hand to Phae. She looked exhausted, and she swayed slightly as she stood beside him. Concern slipped through him as he steadied her with his hand. He hadn't realized how weak she was, which meant Emma's injury had been worse than either of them realized.

"Let me call Lysander in here to help you."

"Do that and I'll make you regret it, *il mio signore*," she rasped. "You might be *Legatus*, but *I* decide when I need help, not you and certainly not *him*."

"Fine," he snapped. Sometimes Phae didn't know when to give up and ask for help. She thought it would make her look weak. "Get moving. I'll be right behind you with Emma."

Phae gave him an abrupt nod then shuffled to the door. It was clear her efforts to heal Emma had taken their toll. She had that drunken reel she always got after healing a serious wound. If he'd still had his mike, he would have overridden her wishes and called Lysander back into the house to get her.

As his sister staggered out of the office, he crouched beside Emma. She was still pale and unconscious, but her breathing wasn't labored as it had been. Aware he didn't have much time, he started to slide her gently into his arms when he saw the notebook lying near the window. It was still intact, the elastic band around it unbroken.

He stared at it for a long moment. The damn thing was responsible for him almost losing Emma and the death of one of his men. He wanted to shove it back in the hole it had come from and seal it up again. The memory of her holding the notebook with such loving care pulled a dark growl from him.

She'd come here for the damn thing, and if she didn't see it when she woke up, there'd be hell to pay. His breath was a sharp hiss as he grabbed the book and tucked it in the front of his shirt. He'd taken so much from her already he refused to take this from her as well. In the distance, he caught the faint wail of a siren. Carefully, he gathered Emma up into his arms. Moonlight fell across her still features, and his heart thundered in his ears as he considered what she'd have to say to him when she awoke. When she did, the notebook would be there beside her, and maybe, just maybe, she might forgive him all his transgressions.

Chapter 11

VOICES slowly penetrated the haze Emma struggled to break through. She shifted her body and cried out as a sharp twinge lanced its way through her side. God, was that harsh noise her voice? A strong, warm hand engulfed hers. Ares. She sighed with relief. He was all right.

"Hush, *inamorato*, you're safe now."

"Did . . ."

She blinked several times until Ares's rugged features filled her vision. Her mouth was dry, and she winced again from the bruised feeling at her waist. What was it she'd been going to ask? She couldn't seem to form her thoughts very well. Her brain was sluggish and she wasn't sure what were memories and what were nightmares.

It was like waking up after a heavy night of drinking and not being sure if she'd really danced naked under the moon or not. God she was thirsty. As if reading her mind, he put a straw to her lips. She drew in the cool water and swallowed. It tasted good, and she drank steadily for several seconds before he pulled the straw away.

"Easy. Not too quickly, *inamorato*."

"I'm so tired." There was that raspy whisper again.

"You will be for a few hours. Your injury was too severe for Phae to heal you completely. She did what she could, but your body has to do the rest. It's why you're going to feel out of sorts for a day or so."

"I don't . . . Phae?"

"She's fine, *cara*. You're both fine."

Puzzled, she winced again. Injury. Had she fallen? It would explain why her side hurt as if she'd taken a solid kick to her ribs. She closed her eyes, wanting nothing more than to go back to sleep. Instead, she saw flashes of images that grew in number and strength until they were like a tidal wave crashing into her.

The memories flooded through her, reviving those terrifying moments in her father's office. Mike and his head rolling off his shoulders. Ares's sword flashing in the dark as he fought for his life and hers. And then there was the stranger and the sword plunging into her side. The memory tugged a cry of fear from her, and she came upright in the bed. The movement pulled another cry from her, this one of pain. Strong hands grasped her arms as Ares gently tried to force her back down onto the mattress.

"It's all right, Emma. It's all over. You're safe, *dolce mia*."

She shoved him away and buried her face against her knees as she hugged her legs close to her chest. Hot tears wet her face as she prayed for the images to stop. They didn't and a hard sob shuddered through her as the memory of Mike's death lashed through her. She rocked back and forth as the barbaric act replayed itself in her head with horrifying intensity.

Even if he'd been involved in her parents' death, to die such a horrible death like that—it had been so unexpected the moment it happened, she'd been more shocked than horrified. But now, the scene played over and over again in her head like an endless nightmare. The terrible memory crashed into another image like a race-car skidding out of control.

Her mind tried to slam on the brakes, but her careening emotions drove her forward to the memory of Ares fighting both their attackers and his cry of pain when a sword had sliced into his arm. Her heart crashed in her chest as she remembered the way his attacker had taunted him. The rest of it flowed hard and fast through her head until she felt the cold steel of the fighter's sword piercing her side.

She jerked her head up with a sharp gasp as the terrifying sensation scraped away at her senses. She knew there was more, but she couldn't go beyond that moment when the blade had ripped through her side. Wrenching the curtain aside to see beyond that wasn't something she wanted to do because she instinctively knew it would horrify her. Her mouth dry and her face wet, she looked at Ares.

"Could I have some more water, please?"

He immediately grabbed the glass from the bedside table and offered it to her. When she'd finished drinking, he set it aside then turned back to her. He captured her hand in his strong grip and gently squeezed her fingers.

"Talk to me, *cara*. Don't keep it inside. It'll eat away at you until there's nothing left."

"Phae . . . I . . . how bad was it?"

"We almost lost you. If it wasn't for the strength of Phae's ability, you wouldn't be here."

His grim expression only made the darkness inside her expand. The thought of the other woman taking on her pain and wounds filled her with a myriad of emotions—a mixture of gratitude, sorrow, and dismay.

"How is she?"

"Like I said, she's fine. A bit under the weather, but she's accustomed to it. It's a part of who she is."

She nodded her head as she recalled Atia explaining how Phae was a special kind of healer. Despite her cool exterior, Ares's sister had a generous heart. She shuddered as the memory of that steel blade flashing in the moonlight returned to haunt her. The moment the sword had bit into her, she remembered fighting to remain conscious.

The pain had not been what she expected. Instead of a sharp, stinging sensation, there had only been a deep, throbbing ache. But it was a debilitating pain that had left her feeling helpless. The image of the man's gleefully cruel face swept through her head. She sucked in a sharp breath of fear. No. She wasn't going past that moment.

Ares had saved her. She just needed to hear him say it. Everything would be all right then. She could deal with the horrifying
memory of being stabbed, but the other . . . no, that wasn't possible.
She tried to make her voice lighthearted.

"You can't stop playing the knight in shining armor, can you?"
Her words tugged a grim smile to his lips.

"And *you* don't listen," he said with strained humor. "You should
have gone out the window when I told you to."

"It doesn't matter . . ." She hesitated for a long moment, terrified
that she might be in denial. "You killed him. You saved me."

"*Christus*, Emma." He bent his head and groaned softly. "*Carissima*, it wasn't me. *Deus* help me, I wish it *had* been me."

The agonized torture in his voice sent ice slogging through her
veins. Rigid with cold, she shook her head. "But I saw it . . . the
sword . . . I saw it . . ."

"*Dulcis Mater Dei*," Ares breathed softly.

His hand caught hers and pressed it tightly against his cheek.
After a brief moment, he turned his head to kiss her palm in a tender gesture before looking back at her with a bleak expression. She
shook her head. It wasn't possible.

"But you killed him. I saw the sword—you took it from him."
Why didn't he say he was responsible for the man's death?

"No, *inamorato*, I didn't—"

"Then Phae. Lysander." Denial still held her in its grip. The chill
sweeping over her was now bone deep as he shook his head. "Tell
me it was one of them."

"*Deus*, Emma." There was a tortured note in his voice that set
off a cacophony of alarms in her head as he shook his head. "I
can't."

The anguished resignation in his words sent panic streaking
through her as she tugged her hand free of his. Oh God, he was
telling the truth. It hadn't been him. Maybe he was wrong about
Phae and Lysander. She shuddered. No, he wasn't wrong. Slowly, an
insidious knowing snaked its way through her, dragging with it the
horrible images she'd tried to keep buried in the back of her head.

Terror swept through her once more as the cruel features of her
assailant flashed in her head. She'd been so certain Ares would be

able to reach her in time. It had been a fleeting thought as she faced what she truly thought would be her last breath.

The fear had swelled through her until all she could think of was how she could stay alive. What had been a sliver of a thought became a stark image in her mind, and panic had made the image grow sharper in her head. Her mouth was dry as she tried to swallow the knot closing her throat shut. It *had* been her. She'd been the one to wrench the sword out of her attacker's hands and plunge it into his chest.

"Oh God," she cried out as the weight of the truth crashed down on her.

"Emma, listen to me." Ares grabbed her by the shoulders to twist her toward him. "You did what you had to do to survive. It's going to—"

Horror sped through her like a lightning strike, and she shoved him away from her with a sharp cry. In that split second, she registered the fact that she hadn't even touched Ares, and yet he was flying across the room.

She screamed in terror at the same instant his body hit the wall. Her fingers digging into the bedspread she clawed her way to the edge of the bed. She'd killed him. Tears blurred her vision and she wiped them away with her sleeve. Please, God, don't let him be dead. Please. She ignored the pain in her side and swung her legs off the mattress.

Relief sagged through her as she saw Ares slowly sit up. He shook his head as if to shake off the impact of hitting the wall. If this was what it meant to be a Sicari, she didn't want to be one. She wanted to go back to being plain old Emma Zale. She didn't want superhero powers. Her own ability had never been this painful. Never this dangerous. Trembling with emotion, she'd jumped when the bedroom door crashed open and Lysander strode into the room. He looked first at her and then at Ares, who was struggling to his feet.

"*Deus damno id*," Lysander growled as he strode over to Ares to help him stand. "I told you to let me handle this."

"Get out, Lysander," Ares said in a cold voice as he pushed his friend away and crossed the room toward her. "This is between Emma and me."

"*Fotte*. She just—"

"Get out." There was a menacing note in Ares's softly spoken words that made Lysander hold his hands up in the air in silent surrender and leave the room.

When they were alone, Ares's steady gaze locked with hers. "It's all right, *carissima*. We'll work this out together."

"There isn't anything to work out," she said in a tight voice.

"You need help adjusting to your ability, Emma."

"I don't want *your* help. Let Lysander help me." Her sharp words made his features grow hard with cold fury.

"You're *my* responsibility, not Lysander's."

"I don't want to *be* your responsibility," she said with a savage anger born of the knowledge that she meant little more than an obligation to him.

Her next breath was a gasp of horror as Ares's legs sailed out from underneath him and his body slid across the floor. He hit the wall for a second time, his erratic skid knocking over a small table with a lamp on it. A tremor raced through her. She was doing this to him, and she didn't know how to stop it. As he stood up, he caught his palm on one of the pieces of glass scattered around him.

The sharp hiss of air he sucked in made her freeze with shock as several drops of blood hit the floor. Oh God. She had to make him leave. She was in enough pain already, and seeing him suffer only deepened the terrible ache inside her. There had to be something she could do or say to get him to leave. If he stayed, she could hurt him much worse. The knowledge sickened her. She heard the sound of material ripping and her gaze jerked to where his brute strength had helped him rip his shirt at the shoulder seam. He tugged the sleeve off and made a makeshift bandage around his palm.

"Don't you get it? I don't want you here."

"You don't have much choice, *cara*." The harsh arrogance in his voice made her want to strike back, if only to get him out of the room.

"Any more than I had a choice whether or not I wanted a Sicari ability?" Her voice was icy as she glared at him. His mouth thinned into a harsh line.

"You're right, you didn't have much of a choice. But I can't take it back, Emma."

No. He couldn't. There wasn't any going back, ever. She'd taken a life tonight. It didn't matter how evil that person might have been. She'd killed someone. That alone changed her. She wasn't Emma Zale anymore. The realization left her shaken and scared.

"I killed a man tonight," she whispered with repugnance.

"It was self-defense, *inamorato*," he said gently. "You did what anyone would do. You survived."

He took a step toward her and she recoiled, not wanting him to come near her. She'd barely blinked when Ares stumbled backward again, pushed by an invisible force. A force she'd created by her emotional responses. She flinched. If they stayed in this same room together, she knew she would continue to hurt him. This power of hers was uncontrollable, and she was quickly realizing that the intensity of her emotions determined its strength and unpredictable behavior.

"Get out," she said with a sob.

"I'm not going to leave you, Emma." His expression determined, he stepped toward her again. "You can keep pushing me away all you want, but I'm not leaving you."

"I can't control this," she cried. "Just go."

For a third time, Ares landed on the floor and the sight of him sliding away from her brought tears to her eyes. She didn't want this power he'd given her. She didn't want the ability to hurt anyone, especially the man she loved. Exhaustion sent her shoulders rolling forward as she hung her head. Even before he touched her, she could feel him. Her connection to him was almost tangible in its strength. She shuddered as he squatted in front of her and cupped her face in his hands. Any second now she expected him to go flying across the room again, but she was so tired. Drained. Emotionally and mentally.

"You can control this, *carissima*. I'm going to see you through it."

She sent him a bleak look, her heart breaking as she remembered why he was willing to help her. He wanted her to embrace this thing inside her. But all she wanted was to destroy it. She just didn't know how. To live with the idea that she had the power to hurt others—him. Look at what she'd just done to him. No, what he'd done to her. She drew in a painful sob.

"Please, just go away. I don't want you here. I just want you to leave me alone."

"That's just it, *carissima*, I can't."

"Why, because you're responsible for making me this way?" she said bitterly. "For making me into a killer?"

His body whipped backward from her, and for a moment, she thought she was responsible for his sharp movement. He rose to tower over her, the expression on his face closed off, unreadable.

"I'm paying a steep price for what I did, Emma, but if you'll recall, the reason I performed the blood bond was to save your life because you didn't listen to me." His gaze was cold and unforgiving as he stared down at her. "It doesn't excuse what I did. But you didn't protest my sealing the blood bond, did you?"

The brutal truth of his words washed over her, leaving in its wake the understanding that she bore some responsibility for what had happened between them. If she'd listened to him that night at Julian's funeral, none of this would have happened. Everything would be different between them. She shuddered. It didn't matter who was to blame. All that was left was to pick up the pieces of her heart, and try to move on with this new life the two of them had created for her.

"I want you to go now," she said in a quiet voice.

"Emma—"

"I said *go*." Her heart twisted inside her as she met his gaze. Maybe in time she could forgive him, forgive herself, accept what had brought her to all this, but not right now. "I want you to leave."

He narrowed his eyes as if assessing her strength and determination. "*Christus*, why do you have to be so stubborn, Emma. All I want to do is—"

"Help? You've been helping me since we first met, and look where it's gotten me." The bitter resignation in her voice made him flinch. Exhausted, she met his gaze with a tired shake of her head. "Just go away. There isn't anything else to say."

His features were hard and impassive as he stared down at her.

Once more, his deep blue eyes reminded her of Lake Michigan in a storm. But the emotion she saw there was grim and disturbing. While his stoic expression revealed nothing, his gaze reflected a dark emotion she couldn't decipher. He took a quick step toward her, and she recoiled in fear, terrified she might hurt him again. The stone façade he wore cracked, and for a moment, she saw a bleak torment engulf his features.

The fracture quickly repaired itself and the emotion vanished beneath a granite expression. Without another word, he whirled around and left the room, the door snapping quietly closed. A quiet sob broke past her lips as she curled up into a fetal position. Later she would think things through. It was all too fresh—too raw to deal with at the moment.

The memory of Ares flying across the room not once but several times pulled another sob from her. God, what was she going to do now? If she could do that to him, she could do it to someone else. And he was right. She was partly to blame for all of this. She'd interfered when she shouldn't have, forcing him to save her. And looking back on what had happened the morning after their bonding, he had tried to tell her about the consequences, but they'd both been caught up in the heat of passion. A quiet knock on the door made her stiffen. She didn't want to see anyone.

"Go away," she called out in a hoarse voice.

The door opened despite her command, and she turned her head to see Lysander standing just inside the doorway. She rolled away from him and closed her eyes. She was too tired to argue anymore. He cleared his throat.

"You'll have to talk to someone eventually, Emma." Lysander's voice was quiet yet firm. "You're one of us now. You need to learn how to control your ability."

"Not now, Lysander. I'm too tired. Let me lick my wounds first," she whispered.

The Sicari warrior grunted his response and she heard the latch click softly as he closed the door behind him. She knew the *Primus Pilus* was right, but she needed time to absorb it all. Time to reconcile herself to the fact that her first use of her ability had been to kill someone.

Not even after her parents were murdered did she ever think she had it in her to kill someone, let alone find herself forced to do so. Justice was one thing; meting out that justice was altogether different. Somehow, she'd find a way to live with what she'd done. It didn't help knowing that she bore some of the blame for her current predicament. God, she'd been so stubborn.

A tremor of pain lashed through her as she realized she wouldn't have changed a thing that had led to this moment. Despite all the heartache she was experiencing now, she would do it all again. Exhaustion sank deep into her bones and she thought she heard the door open, but she didn't turn her head. Instead, she drifted off into oblivion. But the last thought flitting through her mind was whether she could survive all of this without Ares.

EMMA hit the training mat hard, the air in her lungs whooshing out of her in a rush. For what had to be the one-thousandth time, Cleo Vorenus had dropped her to the mat when Emma had failed to ward off the woman's attack. So far, the woman's attempt to teach her how to use her new ability for defense had resulted primarily in bruises more than anything else.

The Sicari fighter had an easygoing nature, but Cleo pulled no punches when it came to training. It was proving to be a challenge learning how to control the power she'd received through her blood bond with Ares. The thought of him crept out of its hiding place in her head, and a sudden longing lashed through her.

She missed him. No one had mentioned his name around her, and if he was still in the complex, he'd managed to make himself invisible. He'd taken her at her word and gone away. Instead of asking for him, she'd huddled in her room for more than two days before Lysander had ordered her to work with Cleo.

He'd bluntly informed her that her ability wasn't going to go away, and she needed to learn how to control it unless she wanted the whole world to know what she could do. She hadn't protested because she knew he was right. But she also knew how much she'd been hoping Ares would ignore her request to stay away and come order her out of bed.

Several hours after Ares had left her room that terrible night, she'd seen her father's notebook on the nightstand beside her bed. She was certain Ares had left it there deliberately, but she'd been reluctant to consider why. Was it a sign that he cared for her? That he wanted her to know she was more important to him than finding the *Tyet of Isis*. What if it had been his way of saying she still had to fulfill the blood bond? She was afraid to ask. She loved him so much, and the thought of knowing he didn't feel the same way made her stomach churn.

The diary had left a trail of bodies behind it over the past five years, and the latest casualty had been her heart. It was so bruised and battered she'd been uncertain as to whether she had it in her to even open the notebook. It had taken her almost an hour before she found the courage to pick it up. And just as Atia had suspected, her father had written his most critical notes in code.

It had taken her several days to decipher just two pages of text, and when she'd finished, she'd learned her father had pieced together enough evidence to convince him that the *Tyet of Isis* was in Rome. But he'd believed the key to actually finding the artifact was at *Rennes le Château* in France. Although Atia had been elated to learn Emma had deciphered her father's diary, the *Prima Consul* had been less than enthused by Emma's request to travel to France.

In fact, the Sicari leader had emphatically rejected the idea, citing the fact that Emma needed more training and time to adjust to her Sicari ability. But when Emma had pointed out that she was the best person to go, Atia had at least agreed to consider the possibility. Emma was confident the *Prima Consul* would eventually give in. The woman had no other choice really. Aside from Ares, there was no one else more knowledgeable about where to hunt for the artifact.

What would Ares do when he found out she was going to France in search of the *Tyet of Isis*? Maybe he wouldn't care. No, he'd care. But would it be because he had feelings for her or because he cared more about the *Tyet of Isis*? He *had* left the diary with her. He'd not taken it with him like he could have. It was more than possible that he wouldn't even want her around. She made some hard accusations after she'd . . . she'd killed the Praetorian. Blaming him for everything had been unfair.

She was the one who'd interfered in the *Dux Provocare* when he'd told her not to. If she'd listened to him—trusted him—things would be different. Everything he'd done since the first time they'd met had been with her safety in mind. He'd taken her to his home to keep her safe, bonded with her so he could run the gauntlet in her place, and he'd tried to persuade her not to retrieve her father's diary. Then there were the Praetorians he'd fought to protect her, and afterward, he'd been there when she'd woken up. He'd tried to help her through the adjustment of gaining a Sicari ability, and she'd rejected him.

There was no doubt he'd made mistakes, but so had she. He'd asked her to trust him, and she hadn't. And was she really that sorry he'd bonded with her? After all, the man *had* tried to tell her the morning after what it would mean if he made love to her, but then neither one of them had been capable of thinking straight at that point. What if he'd explained and given her the chance to say no? Would she have refused him? A tremor shook through her at the memory of his touch. It wasn't a question she could answer given the fact that she was in love with him now. She missed him more than she thought it possible to miss anyone.

Instead of days, it seemed like weeks since she'd seen him. But he'd done exactly what she'd told him to do. He'd stayed away from her. Even the small hope that he might ignore her request was a ridiculous notion. His honor was so much a part of him that no matter how he felt, he was compelled to honor her request. He'd stayed away, which meant she'd have to go to him if she wanted any answers. But even if she went to him, what would she say? Worse, what would he say? The thought scared the hell out of her.

"*Fotte*. Come on, Emma. You can do better than that." Cleo's sharp rebuke tugged her out of her deep thoughts. She looked up at the other woman, reminded once more as to how Cleo's language was at odds with her beauty. "This isn't a game. If you don't learn how to control your ability, you could wind up hurting an innocent bystander or, worse, getting yourself killed because you couldn't keep a Praetorian off of you."

With a nod, Emma got to her feet again. Five levels below Ares's penthouse, the gym took up one whole floor of the building.

Equipped with state-of-the-art equipment, the facility was a popular venue from what she'd seen while working with Cleo. Wearily she met the other woman's irritated gaze.

She was still frightened by the strength of her new power, which was one of the reasons Cleo had been kicking her ass. She didn't want to hurt the woman. Or anyone for that matter. The thought of repeating what she'd done to Ares terrified her. She could have hurt him badly, maybe even killed him if he'd hit the wall the wrong way. She shuddered as she remembered the man she'd killed. Not one day passed when the horror of that event didn't send cold chills through her. She wondered if she'd ever get to a point where she could live with herself over it.

Cleo stood in the middle of the mat with her hands on her hips, glaring at Emma with disapproval. Although the pretty woman lacked telekinetic abilities, she more than made up for it by being an exceptional swordswoman and well skilled in hand-to-hand combat. Emma found it irritating as hell, because continuously landing on the thick, but hard mat wasn't the most pleasant of experiences.

"Come on, Emma. I don't have all day."

"All right, all right," she grumbled.

At least she was trying, for Christ's sake. She was looking forward to the day when her control over her ability would require only a simple nod and the woman would be eating dust. Emma narrowed her gaze at the woman. She never would have thought it would be this difficult to move things with her mind. Ares had always made it look so easy. But it took great control and focus. Control. That had been missing when she'd sent Ares flying across the room. She met the other woman's gaze, and Cleo glared back at her.

"Stop thinking about lover boy and get your mind on the matter at hand." The Sicari fighter's words made her freeze.

"What the hell is that supposed to mean?" she asked tightly.

"It's obvious you've got Ares on the brain. I don't see you as the type to sleep around, but you sealed the blood bond with the man." Cleo shrugged nonchalantly. "So I figure you're in love with him. Although why you're refusing to go after him, I've *no* idea, because I'm betting he's fantastic in bed."

Emma closed herself off to everything but the image of the

woman lying flat on her back. The sight of Cleo's astonishment as her legs flew out from under her sent a grim satisfaction sailing through Emma. As the woman landed on the mat with a loud thud, Cleo laughed out loud with genuine pleasure.

"Well, now, that's more like it." In a fluid move, the Sicari woman arched her back and flipped her body forward into a crouch before standing upright. "Do you see how easy that was? You just close yourself off to everything but moving the object you want to."

"Are we done here?" Emma said bleakly.

"For today." Cleo grabbed her arm to stop her from walking away. "About Ares—I was just trying to get you to channel your energy. I didn't mean anything by it."

"It's fine, I'll get over it."

Emma shrugged off the woman's hand. It wasn't fine at all. She wasn't about to get over Ares anytime in the near future, if ever. The thought made her chest tighten until it hurt.

"Who are you trying to kid?" Cleo snorted. "You're crazy about the guy. Actually, I think you're well suited for each other. Ares needs a woman who can take him down a peg or two."

"I'm not that woman."

"No? You could have fooled me. *Merda*, half the guild knows you're crazy about the guy."

"Oh God." Emma closed her eyes at the revelation. To think that everyone else knew. She panicked. What if Ares knew? She wasn't sure she was ready for that yet.

"Relax. Families know everything, including where the bodies are hidden. And we're family now. Besides, your secret's safe. Ares hasn't figured it out yet, and there are only a couple of people who have the guts to tell him."

Relief swept over her and she opened her eyes to look at Cleo. The woman undid the twist at the back of her head and allowed her midnight black hair to tumble onto her shoulders. She looked like an Italian cover model. Better suited to being in a photo shoot for a Ferrari ad than standing in a Sicari training gym. In the next second, the fighter gathered her black silk tresses up in a fresh ponytail and knotted it at the back of her head. As she tugged on her hair, Cleo narrowed her gaze at her.

"For what it's worth, I think you've adapted to your new ability a hell of a lot better than any other *alieni* I've worked with."

"Have I?" Emma eyed the woman with skepticism.

"Yes. You're at a level of control that takes most *alieni* at least three or four months of training to achieve," Cleo said with an earnest expression. "Especially when you take into consideration the fact that you discovered your telekinetic abilities for the first time in a life-and-death situation."

The image of that sword plunging into the man's chest made her stomach lurch. She buried the memory as deep as she could. In some ways, Cleo was right. It *had* been easier to adapt to her new ability than accepting what she'd done the first time she'd used her power. The other woman stepped forward and gently touched her shoulder.

"Look, I know it isn't easy dealing with the harsh reality of what happened to you. The first life I took was really hard on me. But it was a necessary task. The *bastardo* had molested and raped a three-year-old. He got off because some asshole at the police station lost critical evidence. Hell, even the confession was thrown out because of the way it was obtained."

"Oh my God." Emma stared at the woman facing her. Cleo's expression had hardened into one of icy rage.

"I found it easier to live with his death on my conscience than letting that monster do it to another kid. And no one paid me to do it. The Sicari haven't killed for money in almost a century. In the past, it's how we survived. But we don't do that anymore, and we sure as hell don't kill for pleasure like the Praetorians do. We kill only to protect those who don't have the ability to protect themselves."

She contemplated the woman's words as she tried to come to terms with her own actions. The images from those brief moments in her father's study were still a blur. The one thing that stood out was the moonlight flashing off the sword and the way it slammed into the man's chest. She closed off the memory. Instinct or not, it changed nothing. She'd still taken a life. And instead of letting Ares help her, she'd shoved him away. Ordered him to keep away from her. It wasn't the first time she told him not to come near her, but this was different. She'd made it clear she blamed him for everything that had happened to her. Worse, she hated herself for refusing to admit that she bore just as much responsibility as he did. She hadn't listened to him, and now she was a Sicari, capable of killing.

"You grew up with this, I didn't," she said angrily. "So forgive me for wishing it had never happened."

"What? The fact that you killed someone hell-bent on killing you?"

"Yes, goddamn it," she exclaimed. "I'm responsible for a man's death."

"But it would have been okay for Ares to kill the *bastardo* instead? Letting him take on that burden instead of you," Cleo snapped.

"*No*. I've seen what it does to him," Emma denied vehemently.

She was lying and she knew it. She'd been hiding from the truth for days now. Over the past week, she'd secretly been wishing it had been Ares who'd killed her attacker. It had been a silent wish to shirk the responsibility of her new ability, and the way she'd used it in her own self-defense. But when it came down to the bare facts, if Ares hadn't sealed the blood bond between them, she'd be dead. She shuddered at the thought.

"And now you've experienced it firsthand." Cleo heaved a sigh. "You did what you did because you wanted to live, Emma. There's not a goddamn thing wrong with that. *Fotte*, we *all* want to live. I mean it's not like the *bastardo* asked you if it was okay for him to kill you, *did he*?"

There was something funny about the way Cleo phrased the brutal fact, and Emma coughed out a small laugh.

"No, he didn't ask my permission."

"There you have it then. He gave you no choice. And at the end of the day, choosing life over death is definitely the way to go in my mind."

Cleo's matter-of-fact tone made Emma smile. "Are you always this blunt?"

"It's my trademark," the Sicari woman said with a grin. "Totally rankles a lot of people, and it drives Lysander crazy. And the fact that I'm usually right infuriates my mother."

"Lysander? Are you and he . . ." Emma stared at the woman in surprise.

"You've got to be kidding." The woman released a laugh. "That man can't see past Phae DeLuca. No, men are too time-consuming for me. I keep a couple of boy toys around, but the blood bond isn't for me."

Emma stared at the woman in amused astonishment. Aside from Roberta Young, she'd never met a woman so confident in herself before. But then maybe being beautiful gave one more confidence than most people. Something deep inside her said that wasn't true, particularly where Cleo was concerned. The woman didn't strike her as shallow, and that meant there were depths to the woman that lay buried beneath the surface.

A serious expression crossed the Sicari woman's face as she looked toward the elevator lobby area of the training room. Following the woman's gaze, Emma turned her head and saw Lysander walking toward them. The tall warrior towered over both of them as he came to a halt.

"Ares went to White Cloud five days ago to speak with Atia. I just received word that she's relieved him of his command of the guild and all his holdings pending a hearing before the full Council tonight."

"*Fotte*," Cleo exclaimed. "Mother wouldn't do that unless she was boiling mad. Ares has always had the ability to bend her to his way of thinking. What the devil did he say to make her that furious?"

"He asked her to break the blood bond," Emma whispered as she swayed slightly.

An enormous pressure built in her chest as if a tight band had wrapped its way around her and was squeezing the air out of her lungs. It was over. He didn't love her. His honor might have kept him from coming to see her, but there were other ways he could have told her he loved her. She had the answer to her question, and it hurt like hell. The *Prima Consul* would grant Ares his wish and their blood bond would be broken. Despair slid through her veins and seeped its way into every cell of her body.

"What are you going to do about it?" Lysander asked with a quiet intensity.

The disfigured fighter sent her a stern look with his green eye.

He knew she was in love with Ares. Hell, according to Cleo, everyone in the guild knew it. The eyebrow on the angelic side of his face arched upward, but she wasn't intimidated in the least. If anything, Lysander's flat statement infuriated her. He wanted her to go running after a man who didn't want her. Didn't love her. Screw him. Screw the whole goddamn thing.

"Do? He's obviously decided to wash his hands of me, I don't see why I have to do anything at all."

"Don't be a fool, Emma."

"I'm not a fool, but you *are* for trying to play Cupid," she snapped. "Ares went to White Cloud because he knew I wasn't willing to hurt Atia by telling her what he'd done. He sealed the blood bond without telling me what the consequences might be, so he can damn well undo it."

"And only a man in love would be willing to pay the price he's about to pay." Something in Lysander's voice made her skin grow cold and clammy. "The minute he confesses to the Council, they'll throw him out of the Order."

"Why? Because he's breaking our blood bond? He told me *I* could do that."

"*You* can, yes," Lysander said with restrained impatience. "But in order for him to break the bond, he has to confess to the Council that he sealed the blood bond without your permission."

She swayed slightly at Lysander's words and their meaning. "And if they throw him out of the Order, what then?"

"It means there isn't a Sicari stronghold that will offer him sanctuary anywhere in the world, and if the Praetorians hear about it—"

"If?" Cleo snapped. "Don't you mean when? Ares has made some enemies over the years. He'll have only one choice at that point. Die at the hands of those bastards or go rogue."

She didn't even want to know what "going rogue" meant. The real significance of it all was in the way he was setting her free. He was going to confess in front of witnesses that he'd acted dishonorably. For any Sicari, that would be difficult, but for Ares, the humiliation would be devastating. It was the ultimate sacrifice. A silent declaration of his love for her.

"How do I stop him?" She met Lysander's one-eyed gaze and

she was certain she saw a flash of relief in the man's green eye. It endeared the man to her all the more because he cared about Ares.

"You'll have to refuse the breaking of the bond and dispute his confession." Lysander hesitated.

"And?" She frowned.

"As Cleo says, Ares has enemies and some are on the Council. If he argues with you in front of the Order's leadership, they might rule against him no matter what you say."

"Then I'll have to *make* him listen to me."

Chapter 20

ARES stood staring out the library window of the White Cloud estate. Leaves, stirred by a late evening breeze, danced low above the ground. The estate had always been one of his favorite places to visit, even before Atia had become *Prima Consul*. Now, it was about to be taken away from him, just like his home. The Order would exile him once he freed Emma from their blood bond.

He'd thought it would bother him more, but it didn't. Releasing Emma was the honorable thing to do, no matter how humiliating the process. There were several Council members who would enjoy seeing him disgraced. He grimaced. They wouldn't make it easy for him either. Someone would probably call for him to be whipped before exiling him. They'd send him out as weak as possible in hopes that a Praetorian would catch his scent and finish him off.

The thought made him draw in a deep breath. Exile was usually a death sentence. No money, although he had an account no one knew about, no place to sleep, and no friends. The Order banished one or two warriors a year. The ones who survived were the ones who went rogue. And he'd see hell before he'd start drinking with the Praetorians. No matter how he finished off his days, he'd take as many Praetorians with him as he could.

His one regret was Phae. They'd looked out for each other since the night their parents were murdered. Exile meant he wasn't going to be there for her, but Lysander would if she'd let him. As for Emma, he was going to find a way to look out for her. He wouldn't ever be able to hold her again, but he was going to keep her safe if only from a distance.

When he'd told Atia earlier in the week what he'd done, his god-mother had been livid. It had surprised him that she hadn't found a sword to teach him a lesson, she was so angry. She'd been deeply disappointed in him, too. But the minute he declared his intent to end the blood bond with Emma, she'd rejected his request outright. She'd ordered him to think on the matter for several days. What she'd really wanted was time to try and change his mind.

But there wasn't anything she could have said to him that would make any difference to his decision. Emma didn't love him. It was as simple as that. And if her happiness meant giving Emma her freedom, then he'd gladly sacrifice himself for her happiness. It was wrong to keep her bound to him when she didn't love him. He'd destroyed his honor since the first time he'd met her, but perhaps this last act would restore his honor to him as far as the two of them were concerned. To hell with everyone else.

The door behind him crashed open and he turned to see Phae standing in the doorway. The fear and anger darkening her face told him a battle was brewing. He didn't speak, but simply waited for her reaction. She hesitated for a moment then hurried across the floor to embrace him. Startled, he just stood there with Phae holding him tight before he slowly hugged her back. When his shoulder grew wet, he pushed her back from him and forced a smile to his lips.

"Tears? From Phaedra DeLuca? Is the sky falling, because my sister hasn't cried since she was a girl."

"*Bastardo*." She wiped at her eyes with her hand.

"Somehow I expected a much more virulent reaction from you."

"Would it do any good?"

"No," he said with a wry smile. "I have to set her free."

"Did you even ask her if it's what she wanted?"

"I didn't have to." He arched his eyebrow at his sister's look of angry disbelief. "You weren't there when she came to, Phae. If you'd seen the way she looked at me, you wouldn't have asked that question."

"You love her, don't you?"

His jaw tightened at the question before he relaxed. In some ways, he felt like a dead man walking. Life as he knew it was about to end. But he'd survive, and if Phae or anyone else knew he loved Emma, then so be it. He'd made peace with his decision. All that was left now was to see it through.

"Yes," he said quietly as he turned away from her and stared out the window.

Phae moved to stand beside him and leaned her head against his shoulder to look out the window with him. They didn't speak, and it reminded him of when they'd first gone to live with Atia at her house in Chicago. Phae had shadowed him like a ghost that first year. She'd hardly left his side. And the tears. At nighttime, he'd often gone to her room to quiet her sobbing. He'd always looked after her. Now he was about to leave her alone.

"You're going to be all right without me, Phae." He smiled as she lifted her head to look at him. "And whenever you're down, you'll have Lysander to torment."

His sister choked out a laugh as she shook her head at him. She never got a chance to reply as Atia's voice echoed behind them.

"It's time."

The abrasive words filled the large room like a gunshot. Phae jerked beside him and they both turned to face the *Prima Consul*. His godmother looked tired. He regretted hurting her. For the past week, they'd argued until they were both hoarse.

Atia's solution had been for Emma to be brought to White Cloud and be told exactly what would happen if he broke the blood bond. He'd immediately rejected the idea. He wanted Emma, but only on her terms. She'd lived with guilt for most of her life, and he'd be damned if he was going to add to her anguish. He crossed the floor and took Atia's hands in his.

"I know you don't understand my reasoning, but this is the right thing to do. I've dragged Emma into too many situations that weren't by choice, and I won't force more on her. She's better off without me."

"No, she's not. She deserves to know how you feel about her." The *Prima Consul* shook her head vehemently as she tightened her grip on his hands. "Why must you always be so stubborn?"

"Because somebody has to see to it that you don't get your way all the time." The wry smile tugging at his mouth hurt. "Let's get this over with."

Without waiting for her answer, he walked out into the hall and down the corridor toward the Council room. As he entered the chamber, he saw that the gallery was nearly full, and all the Council members were seated with only Atia's chair empty. Obviously, people were expecting a show. He tightened his jaw at what was to come. Compared to baring his soul here, exile would be easy.

An image of Emma swept through his head. *Deus*, he'd been missing her since leaving Chicago, but knowing that in minutes he'd be giving her up forever gouged a hole in his chest where his heart used to be. It hurt worse than the beating he'd taken the night he'd gone through the gauntlet. Muscles taut with tension, he walked to the center of the room and faced the two semicircular rows of Council members.

Behind him, more than a hundred Sicari sat in four tiers of seats overlooking the proceedings. Their censorious eyes only amplified his tension. It was no coincidence that the brightest lights in the room shone down on the spot where he stood, while the second spotlighted the seat the *Prima Consul* occupied. The remaining lighting was dim and gave the room the appearance of an inquisition courtroom.

The Council room door opened again and Atia entered followed by Phae. He cast them both a brief glance before returning his gaze to his godmother's empty seat. It took her more than a minute to reach her seat as she consulted with several Council members. *Christus*, did she have to drag out this bloodbath?

When she finally sat down in her seat, she looked at him then glanced toward the door. The expression on her face reflected disappointment and he frowned. He knew that look. Had she planned something? An interruption that wasn't going according to her plan? She cleared her voice.

"Ares DeLuca. You've asked the Council to grant you *desponsatio annullatus* for the blood bond that exists between you and the *aliena*, Emma Zale."

"Yes." The silence was hard and unyielding, but he was certain he heard someone draw in a sharp breath despite the size of the room. Phae.

"Do you make this request of your own free will?"

"Yes." His voice rang out clearer in the air than Atia's had, and he saw her wince.

"You understand the seriousness of this request?"

Her gaze flitted to the main entrance of the room before darting back to him. *Fotte*. She *had* planned something. She was stalling.

"Begging the indulgence of the *Prima Consul* and the Council, but there seems no point in delaying the proceedings with questions as to my understanding of the request or its consequences." He glared at her for a long moment.

"Forgive me, Madame *Consul*, but for once I must agree with *Legatus* DeLuca. Is there a point to dragging out this little drama?"

Cato. His gaze shifted to the Council member's face and the smug expression the man wore. The man had hated him since his teen years when he'd thwarted Cato's attempt to slander Atia and prevent her election to the Council. Ares narrowed his eyes before directing a cold smile at the short, rotund Council member.

"A rare day, indeed, when we agree on anything, Cato. I don't believe I've ever heard you speak with such brief eloquence or minor self-interest."

Again, the audience behind him stirred, only this time with amusement. Unlike the great Roman orator who was his namesake, Cato was best known for long-winded speeches that always served to benefit himself in one way or another. The man's round face went beet red with anger, and Ares sent the Council member an arched look before turning his attention back to Atia. An expression of pride flashed across her pale face.

"Under what grounds do you ask the Council to grant the *desponsatio annullatus*?"

The pain on Atia's face made him hesitate in replying. *Merda*, he hadn't realized how hard it would be on her, and while he couldn't see Phae, he was certain she wasn't faring any better than the *Prima Consul*. First Emma and now them. He swallowed the knot in his throat and nodded.

"The *desponsatio annullatus* should be granted because I sealed the blood bond without telling Emma Zale what the consequences were."

The words twisted their way through his gut as the rustling in the gallery behind him reflected the anger and disgust on the faces of the Council members. For him to admit such a thing was like admitting to a rape, even if the sex sealing the blood bond had been consensual. *Christus*, this was going to be every bit as unpleasant as he'd expected. Voices carried through the Council chamber doors, and seconds later, Lysander burst through the door with Cleo in tow. As the two of them parted ranks, Emma strode into view.

The sight of her ripped at his insides. *Deus*, now that she was here, he wasn't sure he could go through with this thing. She was the most beautiful woman he'd ever seen, and the determined look on her face made his gut lurch. She wasn't here to observe. His gaze flew back to Atia and his heart sank. The satisfaction on the *Prima Consul*'s face said it all. The only reason Emma had come here was because Atia had sent for her. *Fotte*, he didn't want her like this. Desperate to save Emma from doing something foolish, he reached out with his thoughts and gently forced his godmother to look at him.

"The request has been made, Madame *Consul*. You must grant the petition for *desponsatio annullatus*."

"And I *refuse* this *desponsatio . . . annulas . . . anulltus . . .* whatever the hell you want to call it." Emma's voice rang out as she walked toward him. "Like most men, he didn't bother to ask if it's what I wanted."

"What have I told you about interfering in Sicari matters?" he growled as he whirled to face her and brought her to a dead halt with his mind.

"Not to," she said with a shrug. "But when have I ever listened to you?"

He glared at her as he heard snorts of repressed laughter from the gallery. "Get the hell out of here, Emma. Let me make things right."

"*Prima Consul*, what happens if I refuse this *desponsatio* thing?" She arched her eyebrow at Ares as she defiantly pushed against his mental hold.

"Then the bond remains sealed." He heard the note of complacency in Atia's voice.

"Which means he's stuck with me, correct?" Emma said with a note of hard satisfaction.

"Correct." Again that smug note in his godmother's voice.

"*Deus damno id*, Emma. Don't do this."

"Don't do what? Keep you from being thrown out of the Order?" She blew out a harsh breath of anger.

"*Merda*, don't you see it was the only thing I could do?" His heart ached.

"No, I don't. I thought you were just doing what I asked—giving me time to adjust to everything that had happened. I thought you'd at least wait and give me a chance to come to you. Instead, I have to hear from someone else that you're breaking our blood bond. *Walking out on me.* You decided to play the martyr instead of asking me point-blank whether this is what I really want. You took the coward's way out," she snapped, her eyes blazing with anger. Her words made him jerk his head back at the vicious note in her voice. *Mater Dei*, she knew how to hit him where it hurt.

"*Christus*, Emma—"

"*No.* It's your turn to listen to me for a change, and I want the truth. Why are you breaking our blood bond?"

"Because it's the right thing to do."

"That's not why, and you know it. Tell me the truth. For once, just tell me the truth." There was a desperation in her voice that edged its way across his back like a sharp blade.

"Because I love you," he rasped softly.

Eyes brimming with tears, she shuddered, and his heart slammed into his chest at her expression. The emotion he saw on her face ignited a sense of hope inside him that he'd lost more than a week ago. Was it possible she'd come here for some other reason than agreeing to his godmother's request? The sensation of invisible fingertips and warm hands on his face made him jump. *Christus*, she'd learned to control her new ability.

"Say it again," she demanded. "Only this time, make sure everyone in this room hears it."

"I love you, Emma Zale." His declaration echoed through the hall as he arched his eyebrows at her.

"Retract the request," she said with that stubborn look of hers he loved so well.

"Give me a reason to." Confidence began to spread its way through his body and he sent her a small, arrogant smile.

"Let me go and I'll show you."

The minute he released his mental hold on her, she eliminated the distance between them and flung her arms around his neck. "I love you. Does that suffice as reason enough?"

"Yes," he murmured as his mouth slid over hers in a deep kiss. As he raised his head, he met her warm, loving gaze. "I adore you, Emma."

"I know," she said quietly. "I knew it the minute Lysander told me what you were giving up by breaking our blood bond. I just needed to hear you say it."

"I'll never stop saying it, *amore mia*," he whispered as he kissed her again.

"Madame *Consul*, we still have a request on the floor. We should act on it." Cato's plaintive voice rolled out over the soft rumblings of conversation in the room.

Without releasing Emma from his arms, Ares looked up at the *Prima Consul*. The smug smile on her face made him wince before he nodded in her direction. "I withdraw my petition for the *desponsatio annullatus*."

"The petition is withdrawn," Atia proclaimed loudly. "The proceedings—"

"One moment, Madame Consul. There is still the matter of *Legatus* DeLuca's failure to inform the young woman as to the consequences of the blood bond."

Slowly putting Emma away from him, Ares turned to see Cato watching him. The smug expression on the man's face said he was immensely pleased with himself, and Ares knew he wasn't out of the woods yet. Atia, a frown on her face, turned toward the stout Council member.

ASSASSIN'S HONOR   317

"Would my esteemed colleague care to explain the relevance of his statement. As we just heard, Miss Zale stated she has no desire to break the blood bond. In fact, she insisted that my—*Legatus* DeLuca retract his request for the *desponsatio annullatus*."

"Indeed she did, however, the *Legatus* admitted to this Council that he failed to ask her permission in sealing the blood bond. This is a serious crime the Council cannot ignore."

He heard Emma suck in a sharp breath and her hand grabbed his arm as she leaned into him. "Is he saying you can still be punished even if I don't have any objections?"

"Yes," he bit out in a harsh whisper as he turned his head toward her. The fear on her face made him reach out with his thoughts to touch her face in a light stroke. "It'll be all right, *carissima*. Cato is no match for Atia."

The fear in her eyes made him capture her hand and squeeze her fingers with a reassurance he was far from feeling. To have Emma pull him back from the brink of exile, only to find himself hovering on the edge once more made his gut twist with a combination of despair and fear. If Cato had his way, he'd still be thrown out of the Order. The knowledge made him realize how much more difficult it would be to leave Emma behind knowing she loved him.

And despite any protests she might have, she *would* stay behind. It wouldn't be safe to take her with him. He'd be a marked target, and he didn't have the stomach for taking lives for money. Death was preferable to going rogue as far as he was concerned. He turned his attention back to the half circle of Council members. His godmother glanced in his direction, her mouth curling in a manner that said she was looking forward to crossing verbal swords with her opponent.

"I quite agree with you, Cato. However, as per our laws, we must establish that *Legatus* DeLuca is truly guilty."

"Do you deny that the *Legatus* openly confessed to his crime?"

"What I heard was a man confessing to a crime that would end his blood bond with Miss Zale. A bond, I might add, that *Legatus* DeLuca believed Miss Zale wanted to be freed from." Atia looked around at the Council members surrounding her. "Naturally, in order to break the bond, he would need to confess to an act that would ensure the *desponsatio annullatus* be granted. Don't you agree?"

"Are you suggesting the *Legatus* openly lied to this Council?"

"I am." The Cheshire smile on Atia's mouth widened as she watched Cato sputter with anger.

"That's ludicrous. The man confessed he blatantly sealed the bond without explaining the consequences to the young woman."

"But was it an honest confession?" Atia arched her eyebrows and turned toward the Council to ensure they could see her skepticism.

"You're clouding the issue, Madame *Consul*. The man gave a specific reason for why the blood bond between him and Miss Zale should be broken. Why would he do such a thing?"

"For *amore*, my dear Cato. For *amore*." Atia turned back to the Council, her hands spread in a dismissive manner at the charge Cato had made. "As many of you may recall, the *Legatus* bonded with Miss Zale to save her life. Does it not stand to reason his heart would make him even more willing to sacrifice himself one more time if he believed it would make her happy? Wouldn't *you* be willing to do such an honorable thing for your wife, my dear Cato?"

Atia smiled coolly as she turned back to face the angry, red-faced Councilman. If the man hadn't been the *Prima Consul*'s enemy before this, there was no doubt in Ares's mind that Cato would do whatever he could to make things difficult for Atia in the future. The overweight man looked out at the tiered gallery behind Ares and offered a placating smile to someone behind him. The *worm*'s wife, no doubt.

"I would gladly sacrifice myself for my beloved Cecelia, but I am not the one standing before the Council under such serious circumstances."

"Then perhaps we should put it to a vote as to whether or not *Legatus* DeLuca's confession was a lie for the benefit of another individual." Atia didn't give Cato a chance to speak as she turned toward the men and women behind her. "Members of the Council, how say you in the matter of *Legatus* DeLuca? If he is guilty of fabricating a reason for breaking his blood bond with Miss Zale say aye."

A low chorus of ayes filled the room as Atia sent Cato a hard look. It was clear that even if every one of Cato's supporters were to rally to his side, there wouldn't be enough votes to change the outcome. Cato knew it too, and the man glared at the *Prima Consul* with intense dislike. Atia seemed to thrive on the man's hatred as she returned his scowl with a confident smile.

"Those opposed?" Silence met Atia's question and she smiled with triumph.

The tension holding Ares rigid slowly drained out of his body. She'd done it. Atia had managed to create doubt as to whether his confession was true or false. Frustration darkening his face, Cato turned his head to look directly at him. The sudden, malicious smile on the man's face made Ares tense for the next volley of words. *Now what?*

"Since *Legatus* DeLuca has been judged guilty of lying to the Council with such great speed, I believe his fate should be handed out with equal swiftness. I think it best we not leave him wondering as to his fate." Cato arched his eyebrow at Atia who frowned. Clearly she didn't like being backed into a corner.

"Agreed." With a sharp nod she turned toward Ares. "*Legatus* DeLuca. The Council has found you guilty of lying to its members. As *Prima Consul*, it is my duty to decide and render a punishment for your conduct. For your crime, you will be stripped of your title of *Legatus* and reduced to the rank of *Tirones* until such time as the Council sees fit to reinstate you. You will also be fined twenty thousand lira, payable to . . . Councilman Cato, who brought the charges to the attention of the Council."

Tirones. Fotte, she was thoroughly pissed. He'd expected to be demoted to the rank of *Milites*, but a *Tirones* was little more than a recruit. And that last condition—what the hell was she thinking. Forcing him to give that worm money was like cutting off her nose to spite her face. Cato's face was filled with smug satisfaction as he looked at Ares.

The bastard was enjoying himself, and it stung. Beside him, Emma touched his arm, and he mentally stroked her cheek in an effort to reassure her that it was going to be all right. And it would.

He'd find a way to get back in Atia's good graces as well as the Council's. Out of the corner of his eye, he saw Atia moving along the front row of Council members and then down onto the floor of the Assembly Room. When she reached him, she narrowed her gaze at him.

"Your sword, *Legatus*."

The sharp command made him stare at his godmother in surprise. *Christus*, she meant to make this really hurt. It was rare that a Sicari was asked to surrender their sword when demoted, but Atia was obviously intent on making it clear she was unhappy with him. No doubt for not listening to her over the past week and forcing her into a sparring match with Cato to save his ass.

He reached behind him and gripped the hilt of the *Condottiere* on his back that had been passed down from his great-grandfather. The blade whispered softly against the leather as he pulled it out of its sheath. With the sword resting in the palms of his hands, he held it out in front of him. His jaw tightened as he stared at the blade.

The sword was a connection to his father and others in his family. He would miss it. He swallowed hard as he met his godmother's stern look. The *Prima Consul* took the sword then without another word, she turned and walked away from him. Beside him, Emma's tension was almost palpable, and he reached for her hand.

"It's all right, *carissima*. It's just a sword. It can be replaced."

The moment he whispered the words, he knew it was true. He had Emma, and nothing else mattered. Everything he'd done had been worth it because she loved him. The moment Atia reached her seat, she sent Cato a hard stare, and the man shifted uncomfortably in his seat. Turning to face Ares, she laid his sword on the polished wood railing in front of her.

"Ares DeLuca, you've been stripped of rank and possession. Report to *Legatus* Condellaire immediately after your honeymoon. These proceedings are now *closed*."

He barely heard Atia's words as he turned and wrapped Emma in his arms. For a man just stripped of his rank and a sizeable chunk of change, he was feeling pretty good. The sweetness of Emma's mouth brushed against his, and he reveled in the fact that she was here with him. Suddenly, Atia's command sank into his consciousness. Honeymoon. Maybe his godmother wasn't quite that angry after all. And he knew just the place. Emma was going to love exploring *Rennes le Château*.

Chapter 21

"DULCIS *Mater Dei*, have you lost your mind, Emma?" The violence of the exclamation that came from several feet below her made her peer over the ledge she was sitting on.

At that point, Ares was already sliding his body upward along the rock face and her heart slammed into her chest as she realized just how narrow and steep the path she'd climbed was. He was right. She had lost her mind. She grinned. But he'd forgive her the minute she kissed him.

Her gaze returned to the view in front of her. About a mile away from where she sat, the medieval fortress was still an imposing sight, despite its deteriorated state. Bright sunshine highlighted the colorful fall foliage, while the wind rustled through the trees shaking loose a leaf here and there. It was a scene straight out of a tourism book.

For the past two weeks, they'd enjoyed the luxury and security of *Rennes le Château*, one of the Order's smaller properties in southern France. They'd spent most of their time in their room the first week making love, talking, and just holding each other. The second week they'd explored the grounds, had romantic picnics at the foot of a small stream, and enjoyed gorgeous sunsets from the balcony of their suite. Today was the first time they'd been past the gates of the estate.

It was the first time she'd been to the Languedoc region of France, and when she'd seen the two towers from the balcony of their suite, they'd captured her imagination. She was certain she recognized them, but couldn't remember where. The memory had teased her enough to Google their images one morning while Ares was in the shower, but she'd come up with nothing.

It wasn't until she was flipping through her father's notebook one night while Ares slept beside her that she found the image she'd been looking for. Determined to get a closer look, she'd convinced Ares to visit one set of ruins. Rock slid against rock as Ares reached the ledge and sank down beside her, his frustration evident.

"*Christus*, what the hell are you doing up here?" He growled as she leaned forward and kissed him. It didn't totally appease him, but his voice grew husky. "And don't tell me it's for the view either."

"You're right—it's not for the view. Look." She pointed toward the tower on the steep slope a half mile away from them. He obeyed her, but shrugged and shook his head.

"Another tower just like the one up above us."

"Yes, but that one"—she nodded toward the stone fortress opposite them—"belonged to a Sicari."

"How the hell do you know that?"

"Look at the loops."

She turned her head to watch as he peered at the small, narrow openings placed sporadically around the lower half of the tower. Excitement fluttered through her as she watched his puzzlement change to awed amazement.

"They fashioned the loops in the shape of the Sicari symbol," he said in hushed tones.

"I'm rusty on medieval architecture, but I think these towers are late fourteenth century, which proves there were Sicari here in Languedoc then, and earlier if you consider how long it would take to build a tower like that one. So my vision makes sense. A Sicari Lord *did* help bring the Cathars into this region." She nodded at the tower again then grinned. "Tell me I'm brilliant."

"You're brilliant, *amore mia*."

He captured her mouth in a hard kiss. The caress sent fire streaking through her as she reached up to cup his face in the palm of her hand. When he drew back, she murmured a protest. His soft laugh brushed across her face like a warm breeze.

"This isn't exactly the best of spots for lovemaking, *inamorata*."

"I think you're right." She looked around their surroundings before leaning forward to press her mouth against his ear. "But I do know where there's a nice, soft bed we can use."

"Do you?" He chuckled, but she heard the way his breath got trapped in his throat.

He got to his feet and the warmth of his fingers engulfed her hand as he pulled her upright. Remembering her knapsack, she scooped up the canvas bag and furtively checked to ensure the notebook was safe. To date, she'd been careful to keep it out of sight, but eventually she knew she was going to have to tell him she'd brought it with her. And he wouldn't be happy about it. He'd think she was looking for the *Tyet of Isis*, and he'd be right. The problem was he'd been pretty clear that he had no intention of continuing his search for the artifact.

The damn thing had caused him too much heartache, he'd said. If she had needed further proof that he loved her, his determination to give up his quest for the Sicari artifact would have convinced her.

But she knew the *Tyet of Isis* was important, not just to him, but to the Sicari as well. And she was certain that if they found the artifact, then maybe they'd find the person who'd murdered her parents and Charlie and had tried to kill her. Mike Granby might have ordered their deaths, but he hadn't committed the actual act. In truth, she really didn't think Mike had been as powerful as he'd made himself out to be that night.

And she wanted to know who this Monsignor was. Where did he fit in the overall scheme of things. Despite Mike's threat to report the Praetorians to the mysterious man, Mike had been executed so ruthlessly it made her wonder if the Monsignor hadn't ordered the Praetorians to get rid of Mike along with the rest of them. She was fairly sure Ares had already considered the same thing because she'd overheard him discussing the matter with Lysander the morning they'd left for France.

No, somehow, she'd find a way to make Ares understand she wanted to be his partner in locating the *Tyet of Isis*. God knows, she didn't have any other work prospects opening up for her in the near future. She winced. Even though she would never regret giving up her old life for Ares, she would still miss it.

Looking for the *artifact* was a way of compensating for that loss. So she needed to proceed cautiously if she wanted to convince him it had been her idea from the start. And it had been. Originally, Atia had been emphatic in her refusal to let Emma come to France, but all of that had changed when Ares had proposed coming here to *Rennes le Château* for their honeymoon. At that point, the *Prima Consul* had eagerly given her access to the electronic historical archives. Of course, Ares would automatically assume his godmother had planned the whole thing. That required special handling, too. She didn't want him blaming Atia for something Emma herself had instigated.

It took them several minutes to make safe ground with Ares acting the protective knight the entire time they slipped and skidded their way down the steep trail covered with loose rock. When they were on solid footing again, she tucked her arm in his and urged him down the wide footpath that led back to the car. Her head dipped down to rest on his shoulder as they walked.

"Happy?" he asked softly. She didn't raise her head, but pressed her body deeper into his.

"Very much. You?"

"Yes." His quiet response made her heart swell with joy as a warm silence filled the air between them. They were halfway to the SUV they'd left in the meadow when Ares cleared his throat.

"Of course, I think I'd be a lot happier if I had a wife who didn't hide things from me." The matter-of-fact statement made her stop in her tracks. She jerked away from him and looked up to meet the wry assessment in his gaze. Since she wasn't sure what or how much he knew, she shook her head.

"What am I hiding from you?" Her response made him arch his eyebrow as a dubious expression crossed his face.

"For starters, how you got access to the Sicari archives, and second, what you were looking for in the archives at four in the morning."

Busted. She'd been certain he was asleep. Had that damn software tune at start-up jarred him awake? She bit her lip as she averted her gaze from his probing look. Wait a minute. She'd shut down the computer when she finished. He'd spied on her.

"I don't believe it. You were spying on me."

"*Merda*, it isn't hard to spy on someone when they don't shut off a laptop," he snapped. "I lifted the top, and the first thing that came up was the archives log-in screen, and the log-off time said four a.m."

"Damn," she muttered.

"Well?" The single word was a command, not a request.

"You're not going to like it."

"I'm certain of that."

"You know how you tell me not to interfere in Sicari matters?" She watched as his features clouded over with irritation. "I was looking for some information."

"What kind of information?" His dark blue eyes grew stormy as he pinned her with his gaze.

"The *Tyet of Isis*," she burst out before rushing on with her explanation. "I think I might have an idea where it is, and—"

"*Fotte*," he exclaimed with a violence that startled her.

He turned and headed down the hill at a fierce stride without her. Where the hell was he going? As he disappeared around the bend in the trail, she darted after him. Damn the man, it wasn't like she'd plan on doing something without him. She'd had every intention of letting him in on the whole thing, just not quite yet.

"Ares, wait."

She charged after him, her boots pounding against the rocky dirt. As she rounded the bend in the trail, she saw him stride out of the trees into the meadow where they'd parked the Mercedes. By the time she reached the meadowland, he was already at the SUV.

She winced as she saw him slam his fist into the side of the vehicle then pace the ground. *That* didn't bode well for their discussion. Even though she'd forgiven him for sealing their blood bond without her consent, she knew his conscience hadn't totally freed him of his guilt. It was an issue that had danced between them ever since that night in the Council chambers. Knowing his sense of honor, she was certain he would always carry that burden inside him, even if he didn't show it.

But she'd be damned if she'd let the past get in the way of their happiness. They couldn't go back to change any of it, and even if they could, she wasn't sure she'd do anything different, other than listen to him. She understood how hard it was to deal with the guilt. She'd come to grips with her new skill fairly easily, but it was the life she'd taken that was always there in the back of her head.

Although she knew it had been in self-defense, her actions still haunted her. But the one thing she was certain of was that if Ares hadn't sealed the bond between them, she wouldn't be here now. Wouldn't be here to love him and be loved by him. And she wouldn't trade that for anything else in the world.

When she reached the Mercedes, he was still pacing the grass like a caged tiger ready to tear anyone apart who came near. She wanted to say something, but she decided the best thing to do was wait until he was ready to talk. With a grunt of disgust, he jerked the passenger side of the SUV open.

"Get in, *now*." His tone made her heave a sigh, but she did as he ordered.

The door slammed shut, and he stalked around the front of the vehicle and slid into the driver's seat. He sat for a minute, hands clutching the wheel until his knuckles were white from his death grip.

"Ares—"

"Did Atia put you up to this?" he said in an icy tone.

"*No.* I went to her."

He nodded sharply then started the car. Anger weighed down the silence between them, but he didn't do a thing to remedy the situation. He was furious and he didn't want to say something he'd regret. Instead, he just drove. Driving meant he couldn't throttle her.

Merda, where the hell had she gotten the idea that he'd even consider looking for the *Tyet of Isis* again, let alone allowing her to help. The thought of putting her in another situation like the one he had almost a month ago horrified him. The vehicle squealed as he took a curve too fast, and out of the corner of his eye, he saw her clutch at the handle above her window.

"Are you trying to kill us?" she snapped.

More guilt swept through him. *Christus.* Here he was worried about putting her in danger, and he was doing just that. He adjusted the speed of the SUV as they continued toward the entrance of the Sicari estate. It seemed to take the security guards at the front gate forever to check the car. It was standard procedure at every Order property, but at the moment, he wasn't exactly fond of the rules.

He didn't look at her, but he could sense Emma's tension. She was going to be difficult about this. He knew it. And he wasn't sure he bought his wife's assurances that Atia hadn't been involved in getting Emma to look for the *Tyet of Isis.* His godmother had been just a little too conciliatory when she'd accepted his decision not to search for the artifact anymore. He should have known the woman would find a way to pull him back into the net.

When they were free to proceed, he threw the car into gear and breezed through the second checkpoint with only a brief word to the guard. As they squealed to a halt at the front door of the chateau, he cleared his throat then turned toward her, his hand braced on the back of her seat.

"I love you, Emma, but I meant it when I told you I'm done looking for the *Tyet of Isis.*"

"I know that's what you said, but—"

"*Deus damno id*, why do you refuse to listen to me?" He lunged out of the car. She followed suit.

"Do you want to know why I don't listen to you?" she shouted as he walked into the house. She scurried after him. "Because you're a pigheaded Sicari warrior who continues to think he has to prove his love for me by giving up parts of himself, and the *Tyet of Isis* is a part of you."

Fotte, the woman was relentless. He stopped inside the large foyer at the foot of the stairs and turned to face her. "I'm *not* trying to prove anything. Just let it go, *carissima.* I have. There are others who can search for it."

"I can't let it go because I know how important it is to you." She pressed her fingers to his mouth when he started to protest. "No matter how much you deny it."

"And you have the audacity to call me stubborn," he groused. "You aren't going to give up, are you?"

"I love you, Ares, but I want to help you find the *Tyet of Isis*. Searching for the artifact will give me something useful to do."

"Emma . . ." He heard the indecision in his voice, and she pounced.

"Can you look me in the eye and say you don't care if the Praetorians find the *Tyet of Isis* first?" She had him there, and she knew it from the gleam in her eye. "I didn't think so. We can help each other, and we can beat those bastards at their own game."

She stepped forward and pressed her palms against his chest. He immediately caught her hands up in his and clasped them tight against him.

"*Christus*, it's too dangerous, Emma."

"It's always been dangerous. What's so different now?"

"In case you've forgotten, there's a rogue Sicari out there who tried to kill you that first night. We haven't been able to find out anything about the son of a bitch—where he is or where he came from. Not to mention the Praetorians now know you have your father's notebook. Hell, it was probably a risk going off the compound today."

"And if we do nothing, will that stop them from coming after me?" Her logic made him frown and she shook her head. "No, it won't. For the past five years, I've wondered if someone was eventually going to come after me. But I lived with my fear. I didn't hide because of it. I refused to let my fear control me. Don't ask me to surrender to it now."

"I'm not asking you to surrender to anything. I just don't want anything to happen to you," he rasped with a shake of his head. "I almost lost you once before, *amore mia*. I don't think I could go through that again."

A knot swelled in his throat as he remembered a blade flashing in the moonlight as it descended toward Emma. The image flooded him with pain and regret. He'd failed her that night, and he'd do his damnedest not to let it happen again. He leaned into her, his forehead coming to rest against hers. She pulled his hands to her lips and kissed each of his fingers.

"Has it occurred to you," she murmured, "that I'll feel the same fear when you go out on assignment? Don't you think I'll worry about you coming home safe to me?"

"I'm a trained Sicari warrior. I know how to take care of myself."

"As I recall, you needed stitches in your chest and shoulder the night we first met," she snapped. "So your *training* doesn't do a whole lot to reassure me."

"Those were unusual circumstances—" Her incredulous expression made him grimace. "Okay, so maybe it wasn't that unusual."

"You're also forgetting, *il mio signore*, that your wife is quite capable of protecting herself."

A slight smile touched his lips when she referred to him as *my lord*. It indicated a measure of submission on her part, not something she gave easily.

"You're a babe in the woods when it comes to using your ability, *dolce mia*."

He kissed her fingertips and avoided her gaze. It was impossible to miss the deep note of regret in his voice, and he knew she heard it, too. She caressed his cheek as an earnest expression swept over her face.

"I've come to terms with my Sicari ability, Ares. It's a part of me, and I wouldn't change that even if I could, because we belong to each other. But don't shut me out. Don't try to shield me from the dark side of your life. And we both know the *Tyet of Isis* is a part of that darkness."

"You make it sound so simple, *carissima*. The minute I agree to your request, I've placed you in danger." He shook his head.

"For God's sake, don't you see, I'm always going to be in danger. Nothing you do can change that." She shoved her imprisoned hand into his chest in a gesture of frustration. "Let me be your partner. Let me help you find the *Tyet of Isis*."

He stiffened at her words. Why was she hounding him to renew his search for the *Tyet of Isis*, let alone asking to join him in the *fun*? The woman didn't have any idea how dangerous it was. He grimaced as he ran his hand across the top of his head and down to his neck. No, she knew, she just didn't seem to care that it might end her life a lot sooner than she thought. The notion chilled him.

Although he'd found it difficult to forgive himself for sealing their bond without her permission, he'd managed to reconcile his guilt for that transgression. But it hadn't unshackled him from the knowledge that he'd failed to keep her safe. He'd taken her into a dangerous situation and almost gotten her killed. He should have tied her up and threatened her with bodily harm before agreeing to take her into that house. If he renewed the search for the *Tyet of Isis* and let her help, he'd be repeating his mistakes. Her gaze narrowed at him as if she wasn't sure what to say next. Whatever she saw on his face helped her make a decision.

"Atia told me what the artifact was and what it might contain." Her words stunned him, and before he could think clearly, he'd opened his mouth.

"How in the hell would she know what it is?"

"When she gave me access to the archives, she said the artifact's secret, like a lot of other information, had been passed down from one *Prima Consul* to the next. Over time, key pieces of the story have become distorted or lost. But the one thing she's certain of is that the artifact is a small box engraved with carvings of the *Tyet of Isis* symbol."

"And what's in the box that the *Prima Consul* believes is so important?" he bit out.

"She isn't completely sure, but she thinks it has something to do with how the Sicari and the Praetorians got their abilities. If the Praetorians get to it first, then they might be able to use it against the Sicari."

The explanation made sense, but Atia always had an agenda. And he didn't like the fact that his godmother was willing to put Emma at risk to find the artifact. The memory of that night in her father's study slipped into his thoughts again, and he shook his head.

"No. I can't, *inamorato*."

"Can't?" she persisted. "Or won't?"

"Emma, hunting for the *Tyet of Isis* isn't a game. It's not one of your sedate archeological expeditions."

"Of course it's not a game. I almost died the night we found my father's notebook."

Her words made him flinch as he slammed the door on the memories. She was still here—with him. And it was exactly why he couldn't do what she asked. His eyes met her astute gaze as she released a quiet gasp.

"That's it," she exclaimed. "That's why you won't search for the artifact. You're worried you won't be able to save me the next time something happens."

"That's right," he growled.

"Why? Because I got hurt?"

"Yes." Tension made his muscles taut. "I should have been there to keep that bastard from touching you. I didn't keep my promise. I didn't keep you safe."

"But don't you see, *amore mio*? You did keep me safe." She touched his face with her fingertips. "I'm alive because of you."

"I didn't—"

"What would have happened that night if you hadn't sealed the blood bond and transferred the Sicari ability to me?"

Ice slugged its way through his body until his heart rate was painfully slow. He remembered that helpless feeling that had lanced through his gut as he watched the Praetorian send his blade into Emma's side the first time. He'd leaped forward despite knowing he wouldn't be able to save her as that bastard's blade started its second descent.

Powerless to stop the man, he'd known that his life would be over the minute Emma was gone. And then it had happened. Sheer terror had awoken her Sicari ability as a form of self-defense. An ability he'd given her. He met her determined gaze.

"I wouldn't have been able to reach you in time," he said in a cracked voice.

"And if you hadn't sealed our blood bond, I wouldn't have been able to save myself." She pulled his head down and kissed him. "You didn't fail me. You saved me, *amore mio*."

The love and faith she had in him was humbling. One of the shackles chaining him snapped. She'd saved him. Her love had saved him not once, but twice now. Another chain broke as he lowered his head and kissed her. It was a long, deep kiss that silently expressed how much he cherished her. And as his mouth slanted over hers, he knew he'd give way to her request. He'd already taken so much from her that couldn't be returned. Her life, her work. The only thing he had to offer her was his love, but he knew she'd need more than that. She was too intelligent not to need something else in her life. He raised his head and met her sultry gaze.

"If I were to agree to what you asked—"

"Oh thank you, *cuore mio*." She tugged his head back down to her and proceeded to rain kisses on his face.

"*Deus damno id*, Emma, I didn't say I would."

"But you're going to, aren't you?" She looked up at him with a sense of satisfaction. "I can see it in your eyes."

"The only way I'll agree to this, Emma, is that I have your word you don't take any unnecessary risks," he said sternly.

"There are no risks, *amore mio*, only opportunities," she said with a mischievous smile then laughed at his groan.

"Why do I think this is one of the biggest mistakes I've ever made?"

"Are you sure falling in love with me wasn't the biggest?" She smiled up at him knowing she would never tire of hearing him say he loved her.

"That wasn't a mistake, *carissima*. Falling in love with you is the one thing I've done right where you're concerned."

Ares tilted her head and kissed her long and deep. It was a caress filled with love, and her heart expanded with joy. Here in his arms she'd found a love to last a lifetime. A familiar, lazy heat slid through her limbs, and she eagerly parted her lips to let him explore the warmth of her mouth. The moment his tongue danced with hers, she caught the faint taste of cinnamon from the baked apples they'd had at lunch. It only increased the warmth of his fiery caress.

Hard hands grasped her waist, and he tugged her close. It was a possessive embrace that said she was his. His to love and protect. When his mouth slid off hers to feather its way to her ear, she trembled. But when he nibbled at her earlobe, she was ready to melt because she recognized the intimate touch of his mind as he caressed her lightly all over her body.

She released a small moan as that invisible, yet familiar, pressure stroked her sex. She was going to have to do something about that habit he had of teasing her to the point of distraction with simply his thoughts. Perhaps a dose of his own medicine? Maybe it would reassure him that she could take care of herself better than he thought.

"Hungry?" she murmured as she arched back from him.

"For you, always."

"Then I know a place where I can do all kinds of wicked things to appease your appetite, *amore mio*," she whispered as she grabbed his hand and pulled him toward the stairs.

In less than a minute, they were in their bedroom. As Ares closed the door behind them and turned to face her, she envisioned him pinned to the door. The moment his back pressed into the door, his eyes widened with surprise. She smiled with mischief as she used her mind to slowly slide his T-shirt up over his abdomen then up over his chest.

His surprise gave way to pleasure as her tongue darted out past her lips, and she imagined licking at his nipples. It was easier than she thought to use her mind when it came to pleasing him. And she loved the power and control her ability gave her. Desire etched its way across his face and he sucked in a sharp hiss of air. Just seeing his need for her was exhilarating. Intent on teasing him as much as possible, she released her hold on him. He whipped his shirt over his head to toss it aside. The instant he stepped toward her, she immediately pushed him back against the door. This time he narrowed his eyes at her.

"Are you trying to tell me something, *carissima*?" he asked in a casual manner, but she heard the underlying note of arousal beneath his question.

"Possibly," she said with amusement as she moved toward him. "I seem to recall you saying that I'm a babe in the woods when it comes to my ability."

She visualized the belt he wore coming undone, followed by the snap on his jeans popping open and the zipper sliding ever so slowly downward. As usual, he'd gone commando and a quiet noise of pleasure echoed out of him the minute his erection jutted forth in all its hard, thick maleness. Only a foot away from him, the sight of his aroused state sent her heart racing. The result was a slip in her concentration, and she almost missed his attempt to grab her. She quickly shook her head the minute he made his move and pictured his arms pressed against the door. With a satisfied smile, she met his frustrated gaze, delighted to see the desire and hunger in his stormy blue eyes.

"*Tch, tch, tch.* I told you I was going to do wicked things to you, Ares DeLuca, and you didn't believe me."

"If you're trying to prove you know how to control your ability, *dolce mia*, you've done that," he growled.

"I'm not trying to prove anything, *amore mio*. But I do have to admit that I like being the one in control."

She smiled up at him as she went down on her knees. The excitement and anticipation in his eyes said he was enjoying himself, and she watched him as her thoughts guided his jeans downward and off his body. When she'd finished, he stood naked, his back braced against the door. With only inches between him and her mouth, she blew a gentle breath over his hard erection. He released a soft groan.

"*Christus*," he rasped. "*Inamorato*, I want you."

She had to admit that she was enjoying herself almost as much as he was. Another smile curved her lips and she envisioned her tongue laving up the hard length of him. His entire body went rigid against the door. She blew on him again, before allowing her invisible touch to stroke his staff then circle around the cap of him.

"*Nam amor de Deus*, Emma." His voice was rough and unsteady. "*Carissima*, please."

"Shall I stop?"

The mischief in her voice made him strain at the invisible bonds that held him pressed to the door. He groaned. "No, *Christus*, no."

"I didn't think so."

He stared down at her as she resumed the exquisite torture she'd been inflicting on him for the last few minutes. Eyes closed, her forehead was furrowed in concentration. A fraction of a second later, his sacs drew up tight beneath his rod from the heat sliding over the top of his cock and then downward. It was as if she were really sucking on him. A groan rolled out of him.

It was the most incredible sensation he'd ever experienced. Then he felt the warmth of her physical touch. Her hand enveloped him as she slid her body up against his. The invisible restraints holding his hands immobile slipped slightly, but not enough to capture her in his arms. In reality he knew he could use his ability to manipulate her as well, but he didn't want to. He was enjoying her playful control far more than anything else he'd ever done in his life.

Her thumb stroked the top of him as her fingers tightened around him in a squeeze that was exquisitely pleasurable. She pumped her hand over him while her mouth worshiped his chest and then the base of his throat. *Christus.* He'd married a seductress of the first order. Her teeth nipped at the side of his neck before she suddenly pulled away from him.

What the—if she thought she was going to just walk away without finishing this, she was going to learn a thing or two about Sicari males. With a growl, he broke one arm free of her hold. She'd put about three feet between them and was watching him with surprised amusement.

"Are you sure you want to do that?" Her voice was husky with desire as she met his gaze.

"What I want is *you*."

"And I want you."

The soft murmur promised untold pleasures as it filled his ears. It wasn't just an invitation—it was a proclamation that there was more in store for him. He tried again to free himself from her mental hold, but failed. There were few Sicari women with telekinetic powers, and to have a wife whose abilities almost matched those of a Sicari male was going to prove more provocative than he could ever imagine. Her gaze locking with his, she ran her hands down over her breasts, pausing briefly at her nipples to circle them with her fingertips.

Enraptured, he didn't even try to move again as, one by one, she slowly undid the buttons on her blouse. The material parted slightly and revealed her black silk bra. The one with the lace in all the right spots. *Deus*, he loved seeing her in nothing but that black bra and panties. He swallowed hard. The woman had learned the art of torment well.

The speed at which she undid her jeans and slipped them off her body would have lost a race with a snail. Black lace peeking out from under her shirt hugged her delicious thighs and clung to their apex with aching temptation.

He was ready to explode. He couldn't deny he loved the fact that she was in control. It was the most arousing thing he'd ever experienced, but she'd made him so hot he didn't think he could hold out much longer, and what he wanted most was to be inside her. Joined with her so they were one.

Her fingers drifted along the edges of the blouse and his mouth went dry. That's it, *inamorato*, take the shirt off. Take it off. As if she heard his thoughts, she smiled and shrugged out of the blouse. He barely noticed it fluttering to the floor, because his blood was thundering in his head as he stared at her. The black silk against her peach-colored skin was the most beautiful thing he'd ever seen. *Bella erotica.*

For a moment, he just stood there staring at her, completely oblivious to the fact that she'd freed him of her mental hold. A slow smile of temptation curved her lips as she crooked her finger and beckoned him to her. At the same time, the warmth of her thoughts caressed his cock with loving skill. His body tightened as one sensation after another slammed into him like a sledgehammer.

A raw sound rumbled out of his chest, and in a flash of movement, she was lying on the bed beneath him. His hand slid up a silky thigh to the fragile lace panties. The surge of primitive heat raging through him made him snap the thin lace and tug it from underneath her. Hazel eyes widened with surprise before they narrowed to a sultry, come-hither look.

He dragged in a sharp breath of need as he stared down at her. He'd never thought it possible to love a woman so deeply that giving her up was tantamount to giving up his soul. If she hadn't saved him that night in the Order's Council chambers, he would have never known what it meant to be truly alive.

His palm slid across her thigh and came to rest at her apex, where he slid a finger into her slick folds. He watched her eyes flutter shut as he stroked her. Then, when he found the small nub of flesh hidden in her creamy depths, she arched her back with a soft cry of pleasure. In seconds, she climaxed. *Deus*, it had been good before, but today was something completely different.

There was something unique about this experience. Maybe it was because he knew she'd finally come to accept her Sicari ability or perhaps it was the equal footing they were on now. Whatever it was, it was the best it had ever been between them. He lowered his head and pressed his mouth to the small indentation of her stomach.

With careful deliberation, his mouth worked its way up to her breasts. She quivered against him, and he stared into her eyes as he closed his mouth over one breast and sucked at her nipple through the lace. The pleasure sweeping over her lovely face served only to heighten his enjoyment. *Deus*, she was beautiful.

The fact that she loved him at all amazed him, but she did. She mewled with pleasure as he abraded her nipple with his teeth. His fingers unclasped her bra and it went the way of her panties. The moment there was nothing left between them, he opened the floodgates. A powerful craving filled his limbs as his hands cupped her buttocks and he thrust deep into her. Hot and creamy, her folds contracted around him with a mind-numbing pleasure. He withdrew from her slowly, but her hips bucked in protest. Once more, he pressed deep into her with a leisurely stroke. She cried out her protest.

"Oh God, Ares, please. Now. I need you *now*."

The ragged plea pulled him over the edge into an abyss of pleasure. He answered her cry with one thrust after another, reveling in the sounds of her excited cries of passion. She climaxed first, sending ripple after ripple of sensation across his cock. He hadn't thought it could get better between them, but it had.

"*Deus*, Emma," he rasped. With another shout, he plunged into her one more time and throbbed as her contractions milked him completely. He stayed arched above her for a long moment, enjoying the way her body fit his so seamlessly. His gaze swept over her sated expression, and when her eyes fluttered open, his heartbeat slowed to almost nothing at the love shining in her eyes. It humbled him in a way he'd never experienced before.

"*Ti amo*, Emma. *Ti amo con tutta l'anima*," he said in a hoarse voice. He kissed her gently then shifted his body until he was on his side next to her.

"I love you with all my heart, too."

The quiet response made him trail his fingers across her cheek. He rolled onto his back, and with a happy sigh, Emma snuggled up against him. Her mouth trailed a small path across his side, while his fingers curled through her hair.

He must have dozed a little while because the light outside had changed. The shadows indicated it was late in the afternoon. Nestled against him, Emma's arm lay draped across his chest.

"Ares?"

"Hmmm." He was half-awake, but the sound of her voice made his cock stir.

"Are you awake?"

"It depends on *why* you want me to be awake." Eyes still closed, he smiled at the memory of their last lovemaking session. She playfully slapped him.

"Stop it," she said with a hint of laughter in her voice. "I'm trying to be serious."

"About what?" It sounded like she intended to broach a delicate topic. She hesitated. That sealed it. Whatever she wanted, he was certain the *Tyet of Isis* was involved. He released a patient sigh. "What is it you really want, *carissima*?"

She pushed herself upright, and he opened his eyes to look up at her, unable to help noting how beautiful her rose-tipped breasts were. "I thought we could picnic at the towers tomorrow."

"That's all?" he asked with a skeptical arch of his eyebrows.

"Well, I was going to save it for a surprise, but I guess now's as good a time as any. Atia sent your sword back."

"*What*?" He stared at her as she nodded slightly.

"She said it had been in your family for such a long time, it seemed a shame to let it just rust in her office when you might need it for slaying dragons."

"Praetorians she means." *Deus* help him. He wasn't sure who was going to be the death of him. His godmother or his wife. Still, the thought of having his *Condottiere* back sent a rush of pleasure through him. He couldn't deny having it back made him feel good. He arched his eyebrow at Emma, and she smiled with triumph.

"So, since you have your sword back, I thought we might walk to the towers."

"Okay, we'll walk." Relief swept through him. If all she wanted to do was go to the towers he could live with that. And with his old sword in hand, he felt even more confident in his ability to protect her. He groaned as he saw a mischievous twinkle suddenly sparkle in her beautiful eyes. "Now what?"

"Oh nothing, I just thought that if you didn't want to walk to the towers, we could always explore the caves that run under the house," she said with a grin. "Cook says the caves run from here to the towers. She said the Cathars used them to hide from the Crusaders."

"Caves?" He grimaced. "Emma, I don't—"

"But if you don't want to, we can do something else."

The innocent note in her voice didn't deceive him. She was up to something. His cock stirred at the idea of a picnic in their room. Perhaps some more of that whipped cream and then a leisurely shower.

"Like what?"

"We could go to Rome." Her casual statement made him jerk as he stared into her laughing eyes.

"Rome? *Dulcis Mater Dei*, woman, you're insane," he exclaimed. "Do you really think I'd just carry you into the heart of Praetorian territory like it's little more than a picnic in the woods?"

"Well, you seemed averse to the idea of the caves."

She shrugged, her breasts brushing across his chest in a distracting way as she slid one leg over his. If she thought she was going to seduce him into doing what she wanted, she'd underestimated him.

"I didn't say I wouldn't go to the caves—"

"I know, but then I remembered that dagger I read at White Cloud."

"Dagger? When the hell were you going to tell me you'd touched more just than the Sicari Lord coin at the estate?"

"I was waiting for the right moment," she said with a bewitching smile.

She lowered her head and her mouth caressed his shoulder. A second later, his cock jumped as an unseen hand stroked him. *Deus,* but the woman had a wicked touch. He groaned with pleasure, and soft laughter bubbled out of her.

"You're enjoying yourself, aren't you?" she whispered.

"Yes," he rasped as desire coiled through his limbs.

"Would you change your mind about Rome if I told you I saw Lysander's twin in my vision?"

"No. I wouldn't," he growled.

He barely processed her words as her invisible caress drove everything out of his head but her. The warmth of her unseen hand slid up over his erection then rubbed across the ridge of him. He groaned from the pleasure of it. The pressure on his rod intensified as she slowly straddled him. She stretched her body backward with his hard length brushing up against the seat of her. His gut wrenched as he watched an invisible force guide his cock into her, and then she came forward to sink down on top of him. The sensation pulled a shout from him.

"Do you think I'll be able to change your mind eventually?" she whispered as she bent over him.

"No, but I sure as hell don't want you to stop trying, *carissima*," he rasped.

"I love you, Ares," she whispered. And just before she pushed him over the edge to that place only she could take him, he realized she'd get her way. They'd be going to Rome. It was only a matter of time.